A Bad Bride's Tale

Previously published in hardback as *The Egg Race*

Polly Williams

sphere

SPHERE

First published in Great Britain in 2007 by Sphere
This paperback edition published in 2007 by Sphere
Reprinted 2007 (twice)

A CIP catalogue record for this book
is available from the British Library.

ISBN 978-0-7515-4055-0

Papers used by Sphere are natural, recyclable products made from
wood grown in sustainable forests and certified in accordance
with the rules of the Forest Stewardship Council.

Typeset in Sabon by M Rules
Printed and bound in Great Britain by
Clays Ltd, St Ives plc
Paper supplied by Hellefoss AS, Norway

Sphere
An imprint of
Little, Brown Book Group
Brettenham House
Lancaster Place
London WC2E 7EN

A Member of the Hachette Livre Group of Companies

www.littlebrown.co.uk

Polly Williams is the author of the *Sunday Times* bestseller *The Rise and Fall of a Yummy Mummy*. She lives in London with her husband and two sons.

Also by Polly Williams

The Rise and Fall of a Yummy Mummy

For Ben

Acknowledgements

Special thanks to my agent Lizzy Kremer and the team at Little, Brown, especially Jo Dickinson, Sarah Rustin, Tamsin Kitson, Helen Gibbs, Emma Stonex, Duncan Spilling and Louise Davies. I'm also immeasurably grateful to my husband Ben Chase for keeping me sane and productive while I put life on hold, again. I'm very grateful to you too, Mum. Thanks to Tammy Perry, Sue Peart, Louise Chunn, Wendy Holden and Vanessa Friedman. To my girlfriends – I couldn't do without your hilarious and despairing tales from the thirtysomething dating and mating playground. And Tess McPherson for returning home and making Oxford come alive again. All our walks and talks over the years are embedded somewhere in these pages.

One

Stevie Jonson switched on her laptop. Wobbling on the shelf of her bent knee, its glow washed her round, pale face with green light, leaving the rest of the bedroom in shadow. It was one-twenty-three a.m. She knew what would happen if she shut her eyes. Her wedding – since midnight, only thirteen days, fourteen hours away – had assumed a voice of its own and it was a voice that grew louder as her head sank pillow-wards, whispering questions about monogamy and seating plans or humming an unbearable rotation of late-eighties wedding disco classics. It hung above her head like a cloud made from thousands of tiny black question marks. And she hadn't slept properly for days. Unable to face another insomniac night, Stevie decided to push her tiredness to the limits and stay up as long as possible. This way she would, surely, eventually fall asleep, exhaustion the stones in her pockets that would plunge her into mercifully blank depths.

In the meantime, alcohol would help. She leaned over to the side of the bed, picked up the glass from the side table and took the last gulp of gritty red wine. It mixed not unpleasantly with the aftertaste of toothpaste in her mouth. Feeling fortified, she checked her emails; nothing interesting. She foraged

1

among eBay's handbags; nothing interesting. She mouse-clicked on an intriguing site she'd bookmarked earlier that week, Work Out Your Real Biological Age in Ten Minutes; possibly amusing. The health interrogation took forever. Finally, she ticked the last box. She stabbed the cursor key. The modem whirred. The website did its maths. Her biological age was . . . thirty-*seven*. Oh. Not so amusing. Stevie was thirty-four years old.

She slumped heavily on to the pillows, pushing them down into the dark, draughty gap between bed and wall. Blasted computer. She now felt older than thirty-seven. She felt forty-seven. No, eighty-seven. She was mortal. She was going to die – probably prematurely. She attempted to work out what she'd done so wrong. It was like trying to recall drunken antics at a party the morning after. OK, hands up, she'd been partial to a Marlboro Light in her twenties, but hadn't everyone? Skinny jeans weren't an option but she certainly wasn't obese, a size twelve or fourteen, depending on the shop and the season. She didn't bake – there was little incentive when the sun just dot-to-dotted her freckles – so why did she need a preservation order? Stevie sucked in her breath, locking it in her throat as she read. OK. Aunt Sue's breast cancer; Grandfather's mid-life stroke; caffeine and sugar intake; aversion to gyms; irregular flossing. Oh, and the fact that she hadn't breastfed a baby. Funny that.

Stevie slapped the laptop lid down hard. Biology was blunt, tactless. And it was beginning to seriously piss her off. Only last month her GP, forgetting his bedside manner during a routine contraceptive assessment, drily informed her that at 'her age' (antique, obviously) she should perhaps be more concerned about declining fertility than avoiding conception. As if childlessness was a 'lifestyle choice' as opposed to the way life turned out. In response she'd shrugged like a defiant

2

schoolgirl and, in her eagerness to leave the surgery's steely statistics, snatched her contraceptive prescription renewal out of the doctor's scrubbed-pink hands, their fingers touching fleetingly, somehow inappropriately, before leaping apart. With cruel synchronicity, that night she'd found her first grey hair, pale and curly as an alfalfa sprout.

Two

'Sleep well?' Poppy whooshed back the blue balding velvet curtain, disturbing a ballet of dust particles.

Stevie squinted as daylight flooded the bedroom. 'No.' She smiled sleepily at her younger sister, pregnant and mother of two children under five. 'But I don't expect sympathy.' Yawning, she clambered out of bed, one bare foot, then the other, softly slapping the gnarled pine floorboards. At the basin, she splashed cold water on her face and inspected her reflection in the round toothpaste-speckled mirror: a pillow mark bisected her left cheek like a scar; tired pollen-brown eyes; hair fuzzy with the static of sleep and dreams. In fact she looked as though she had been on some kind of adventure during the night and had just managed to scramble back to bed before dawn. Which in a way she had, she thought, patting her face dry with a towel, wishing she could shake the remnants of last night's dream from her head like water.

It was a recurring, unsettling dream, which had woken her up with a start a few seconds before Poppy had pulled back the curtains and broken its spell. It hadn't involved the wedding, or even the website. It had involved Jez's lip. In

4

particular, the way his upper lip got stuck to his front teeth first thing in the morning. He'd smile and the lip would stretch and pale. It ignited a disproportionate reaction in her, making her flinch away as if assaulted by a particularly fetid blast of breath. And now the lip seemed to have penetrated her subconscious. When had she first started noticing the lip? The last four, or five months, possibly. Had the lip always stuck to the teeth? It seemed rather unlikely that this was a new phenomenon. Relationships are destroyed by details. Could the lip be the tipping point?

'A brew. Sorry, no other drinking vessels available.' Poppy placed a large steaming mug on the pile of yellowing paperbacks next to Stevie's childhood bed. The mug was one of their mother's old favourites, wrapped in a quote by Rebecca West: 'I only know that people call me a feminist whenever I express sentiments that differentiate me from a doormat.' It was a mug that usually made the sisters roll their eyes – they had yet to encounter a woman less like a doormat than their mother – but Stevie was too tired for sisterly collusion today.

'Thanks, Poppy.' Stevie took the mug, aware that her sister was far more deserving of tea in bed. She sat down and sipped the tea, feeling the too-hot sip burn its way down her throat and tunnel deep inside to where anxieties churned. She rubbed her eyes. 'I feel like how I look, Pops.'

'Oh, don't worry. Weddings wreak havoc with one's beauty sleep,' said Poppy breezily, leaning into the radiator, pressing her bottom into its warm ridges. 'I was a right case before mine, remember?'

'Insufferable.' Stevie smiled, pushing the hedge of wavy brown hair away from her face. 'But at least you were organised.'

'Retentive, you mean? Oh, I accept that,' laughed Poppy,

peering out of the sash window into her parents' garden, her belly pressing against the cold glass, a ring of condensation misting its circumference.

Stevie gazed fondly at her sister, who looked more fecund than ever this morning, her cheeks rhubarb-pink, her pregnant belly high and round beneath her crisp white Boden nightie, like a large pudding bowl under the skin. She looked so happy, so light, almost air-filled despite her girth. Poppy was never happier than when she was pregnant. And it suited her. Stevie was certain that when she was eighty she'd be able to remember her sister exactly as she was now, would be able to flip the image up like a favourite old photo and immediately be transported back to this strange heady May morning at her parents' house, the air thick with pre-wedding tension and the smell of burning toast. By the age of eighty she'd know for certain whether, in her own lifetime, she'd managed to capture that same pregnant physicality, the secret galaxy pushing out the belly button, the genetic legacy assured. The thought made her panicky, prickling her mood further.

'Poppy, sorry if I sound a bit neurotic, but does my wedding have the air of disaster to you?' she appealed to her sister for reassurance. 'A fairground crash in slow motion?'

'*No!*' Poppy laughed, twisting her milkmaid-blonde hair over one shoulder. 'Don't worry about all the details. Mum's in control.'

'My point exactly.' But Stevie knew she had to take responsibility. She'd shirked too many of the preparatory nuptial duties and taken up her mother's offers of help fully aware of the risks. For the last six months she'd felt unexpectedly dislocated from the experience. Sometimes it felt like the whole bride thing was happening to someone else.

'You know, what I didn't realise,' said Poppy thoughtfully,

plaiting her hair loosely with slim tanned fingers, the pea-sized diamond on her engagement ring shattering rainbow rhomboids against the white bedroom wall, 'is that the interesting stuff happens *after* the wedding.' She looked up from her plait and grinned. 'Here's to you getting up the duff!'

Stevie raised her mother's mug in a mock cheers. Not for the first time, part of her wished the roles were reversed, as if she'd upset the natural sibling order in some way by not being the first to pop out the first grandchild. It would be nice to be in the position of dispensing sage womanly advice to her younger sister occasionally.

'When are you coming off the pill?' pursued Poppy, circling her belly with a flat palm that didn't indent the flesh in any way, suggesting it was hard as a rock.

'After the vows. Jez is keen to populate the planet as soon as possible.' Fully awake now that the hot dark tea had kicked in, Stevie recalled the website's conclusion about her age. 'Hold off on the Brora cot blanket though. I'm sure it'll take decades to conceive,' she added drily.

'Oh rubbish! Piers barely had to touch me.'

'You were twenty-six.'

In hindsight, although it had seemed a rather dull choice at the time, Stevie mused, Poppy had done the sensible thing. She had eschewed the creative vanities of publishing and PR and gone to work in a male-dominated industry – a city accounting firm, much to her mother's incomprehension – where, at the age of twenty-three, she'd swiftly met the handsome, dependable corporate lawyer, Piers. They'd married two years later, in clouds of white-pleated chiffon, at Piers' small family church outside Winchester. The wedding breakfast, held at Piers' parents' large country house – geographically just outside her mother's influence, thus allowing Poppy to organise *her* day without the intrusion of incense sticks or lentils –

7

involved salmon and a chocolate fondue. Of the two hundred guests, Stevie hadn't managed to snog a single one, because even back then they were all – bar the odd, wet and boring individual – in couples. Poppy's first child, Sophie, darling in every way, was conceived on the Tuscan honeymoon four-poster. Finn came along exactly two years later, as planned. And now there was another Fitzpatrick kicking his heels in Poppy's womb, another perfectly timed sibling.

Stevie tried very hard not to be jealous. She was not always successful. But she consoled herself that fulfilment couldn't have happened to a nicer person. And with the fact that Poppy and Piers were exactly the kind of people – socially responsible, intelligent and solvent – who *should* reproduce. They deserved a government subsidy – their children were hardly destined for Asbos. Well behaved and charming, both had inherited Poppy's benign temperament, the same sane sky-blue eyes, unsullied by any disappoint-ment, so unlike her own odd yellow-brown ones which her father always said were 'far too knowing', and used to get her into trouble at school for 'insolence'. In her dark period – aged thirty to thirty-two – after a particularly long romantic drought when she'd begun to seriously doubt she'd ever marry or have children or, indeed, ever have sex again, it had occurred to her that evolution had cunningly deselected her, satisfied that her sister was doing her bit in continuing the Jonson line.

'I'm afraid the mug of tea came with an ulterior motive, Steve. Would you do me a favour?' Poppy broke her prettiest smile. It made her look about fifteen years old. 'We're attempting a tantrum-free trip to the Natural History Museum. I'd kill for a shower first so I don't get mistaken for a lump of prehistoric taxidermy. Would you mind shepherd-ing Finn for a bit?'

'Seems like a fair exchange for a cup of tea.'

'Thanks, sis.'

Piers poked his head round the door. A tall and tubby thirtysomething in pale Gap jeans, he sported the kind of inoffensive English good looks advertisers used to sell bran-based breakfast cereals. 'Poppy, can we make a move, darling? Please.' He tapped his chunky diver's watch. 'I'll see you downstairs in ten?'

'Sure, sure.' Poppy scanned the room. 'Where the devil is he? *Finn!*' A toddler was on the loose.

'The artist in residence.' Stevie laughed and nodded towards the hall annex, which Finn was creatively redecorating with orange crayon.

'Christ.' Not seeing the funny side, Poppy lurched towards her two year old and scooped him up, Finn's stout fat legs – half baby-half boy – kicked, rigid with defiant energy. She arrested the crayon. 'Go sit with Aunt Stevie, darling.'

'Don't wanna.'

Stevie tried not to feel hurt. He was two, for God's sake. It didn't amount to rejection.

Then Finn spotted his aunt's laptop, wedged between bed and wall where she'd let it slump when she'd fallen asleep. It was blinking irresistibly, a call to mischief. He waddled towards the bed. 'Wanna.'

'Here, Finnballs sweetie.' Stevie pulled back the bed covers, the covers she'd had since she was twelve years old, the colour dragged out of the patchwork by her mother's accidental boil washes. Like a comfort blanket, she slept better under this ratty bit of faded cotton than any of her own crunchy White Company sheets back home at the Bayswater flat she shared with Jez. As the sun beamed dusty rays against her face, she suddenly felt very glad she'd come back to her parents' for the weekend to finalise the wedding plans. It was

9

nicely cyclical somehow. Finn dug under the duvet and reached up to the laptop prize, releasing a condensed-milk smell from the folds of his Power Ranger pyjamas.

'Step away from the technology.' Stevie swiped the computer out of his reach, ruffled his curls. Thwarted, Finn sulkily picked at the bedroom wall, digging his fingernails into buttons of Blu Tak, curly-edged old school photos, a starburst of peeling Wham stickers and a hard ancient pink Hubba Bubba globule that she'd stuck there during a teenage sulk sometime in the late eighties.

'Make sure he doesn't catapult that stair gate, won't you?' Poppy shouted behind her as she clattered downstairs. 'And watch the window that doesn't lock . . .'

Finn listened warily to his mother's retreating footsteps. He stamped a salivary finger on an old dappled school photograph. 'Aunty Stevie.'

'Yes, that's me! About a hundred years ago. Very well spotted.' She kissed his head, staring at the photo. Yes, she was an awkward-looking teenager, with not nearly enough confidence to inhabit that chunky 'big boned' body. Over the years she had pummelled her figure into better shape with gym classes, lifting her flat, rather square bottom half an inch and further cinching in her fifties-housewife waist. But the photo caught her stocky teenage silhouette, the one hard-wired into her self-esteem at the impressionable age of fifteen in chilly school gym changing rooms and verruca-infested municipal pools. In her own mind, no matter how slim she got, she'd always be the girl at school boys teasingly called 'pudding'. And pudding would have been grateful for her fiancé: strawberry blond (verging on ginger), warm-hearted, colourful and handsome, even if he had recently acquired a tummy that shuddered on his middle like an underdone poached egg.

10

'Stevie. Jezzy. Wedding,' said Finn solemnly, as if assimilating the news for the first time.

The word 'wedding' was destabilising. Stevie felt herself tense.

Finn looked up, blue eyes wide and unblinking. 'Want wedding cake.'

She smiled. 'I would feed you creamed meringues for breakfast if I had any in the near vicinity. But I haven't. Cake, later.'

'Later,' parroted Finn, a little sadly, as if later was forever away. 'Wedding, later.'

Stevie bit off a branching split end of hair – recently missed by her hairdresser – and, in a disciplined fashion, tried to conjure up the gooey fondant feelings of the proposal, to compensate for the unsettling and wholly inappropriate feelings of negativity.

She closed her eyes. April. Friday night. Jez had spent the majority of that day with his father playing golf. When she'd met him, at about six p.m., beneath a spectacular gun-metal sky, he'd looked unusually flushed and insisted on taking her to supper at The Wolseley. By that point, she realised now, their relationship had needed good restaurants, theatre, cinema, external drama of some kind, because it had hit a plateau; the initial moving-in-together excitement had faded and the future remained unlabelled and uncertain.

In the restaurant, encased beneath the vaulted ceilings and black columns and shouting above the resulting bad acoustics, they'd discussed Jez's recent promotion at YR-Brand. Jez had told her off for not being more excited for him. He'd paid the bill, which was unusual since he was usually happy to split. After two years they'd got to that stage too. Hand in hand, they'd walked through the West End and over Waterloo Bridge. A gust skimmed across the water from the south, sticking hair to her glossed lips. She remembered cursing for not going to the toilet before they left the restaurant and wondering if she'd be able to endure a Tube journey home when Jez grabbed her suddenly, pincing her elbows tight, pulling her towards him, thrusting his tongue into her surprised mouth. 'Marry me!' he'd said, coming up for air. 'Marry me, pumpkin.' He'd looked as shocked as she, as if the proposal was entirely spontaneous, a bodily function he couldn't control.

Of course Stevie had said, 'Er, yes.' It was the affirmative answer she'd rehearsed as a little girl. Jez had caught her unawares – she had no idea he was close to proposing – and at a vulnerable moment with Perrier Jouet coursing through her veins, the wind rolling over the Thames and tossing her hair from her face like a romantic heroine from a BBC drama. And in that one-syllable puff of air, scented with goat's cheese crostini, both their destinies changed for ever.

Of course, with the benefit of hindsight, she could now see that there was a subtext to her 'Er, yes'. At that point in her life, as she'd crossed that particular bridge into her mid-thirties, Stevie had begun to suspect that she just wasn't marriage material. She'd voiced her concerns to her father. 'I wouldn't worry too much. Marriage is an overrated institution anyway. It suits girls like Poppy,' he'd said distractedly, hole-punching a wad of lecture notes. 'I'm not sure it would suit you.' Her spirits had plummeted. She'd always feared that in love's game of musical chairs she'd be the one left standing. She'd had boyfriends, of course. Not loads of them, just enough to make a regular bikini wax worthwhile. But the relationships hadn't *gone* anywhere. It was hard. But she'd accepted the consoling drinks with girlfriends (which always made her feel more like a victim somehow) and put herself in the ex's Dunlop Green Flash trainers and realised that things

12

were slightly different if you were male, heterosexual, over thirty and living in London.

And then there were the Tube bombs, she reminded herself. The worst could have happened, would have happened, had Jez not lost his striped Paul Smith socks that morning and had his mother not phoned to complain that they weren't visiting his father on his birthday that weekend, had he not been running so late. Had Jez's coordinates matched the bomber's, then all the possibilities of her life would have blown apart too. And that made her love Jez more, need him more, in a visceral sniff-his-neck kind of way. They'd surely been given a second chance, for a reason, she'd rationalised. At that time, that hot, dirty London July, everything felt fragile, vulnerable. The bombs made both of them cling together. It made them want to commit. It had been hard to tell what was love, what was insecurity. Now nearly a year had passed without incident and things felt rather less fragile. Armageddon had been postponed. The future could last for another fifty years quite easily, Stevie thought, burying her nose in the dandelion clock of Finn's hair, a swell of sadness rising in her throat.

Still, facts were facts. She was thirty-four, going on thirty-seven. She was not suited to single life in the twenty-first century, loathing the idea of speed dating, internet dating, plotting her social life around the likelihood of meeting single guys as if she were a dog on heat that needed studding, hanging out in bars, being overlooked by men for her prettier friend, when she'd rather be at home reading or watching her *Lost* box-set. And as for the endless, painful, waiting by the phone, well, she wouldn't do it. She hated that prescribed passivity. So she'd made a habit of phoning men to ask why they hadn't phoned her. Disastrous move, always. So, yes, as her grandmother had declared over a tea-dunked custard cream at the announcement of her engagement, Stevie was lucky. She had managed to get under the wire, *just* in time.

'Cuggle,' demanded Finn, sensing her attention wavering. 'Want cuggle.'

A what? Stevie looked down. A cuddle? How lovely. Of course. Her body ricocheted with endorphins as she pulled her nephew towards her, kissing him behind his ear and inhaling deeply. Only like this, she realised, buried in her nephew's infant deliciousness, could she exist solely in the moment. Only like this did she feel quiet inside, as if suspended in a kind of happy hormone soup. Only like this did she feel that there was a *point* in anything. It was all very weird. Shit. She was broody.

Three

'Kiiiiiiidz, lunch!' yelled Stevie's mother, Patti – abbreviated from Patricia after a drug-enhanced encounter with Patti Smith at a party in Paris, 1969 – her husky voice soaked up by the crowd of coats in the hallway, the unravelling Egyptian tapestries on the wall, the dusty weeping figs and African statues, limbs long since amputated by her son Neil's marble shooter. 'I'm not running a bloody hotel!'

In different corners of the large Victorian house, members of the Jonson family prepared themselves for interaction. Stevie, wondering if her mother would stop referring to her as a kid once she was married, jumped out of the bath, towelled herself down quickly, scrabbled in her old bedroom wardrobe for some clothes that weren't too hideously dated – ancient bootleg jeans, Topshop Charlie's Angel T-shirt – and thundered down the stairs, hand on the once-grand curving wooden banister, skipping the third step where the carpet runner had been shredded by the family's cat in an artfully toe-catching way. Her father had ended up in John Radcliffe's A&E last year. But then he was generally too preoccupied to complete basic physical tasks – walking, eating – without incident.

At this point – her holey socked foot hovering above the second-to-last step – Stevie had no idea that downstairs, beneath a framed poster of a fifties housewife-type in an apron and a Lichtenstein-style speech bubble declaring 'Fuck Hoovering!', sat thirty-five-year-old Sam Flowers, straddling a pine dining chair and picking at pistachios from a mis-shapen hand-thrown earthenware bowl, curling his tongue into the cradles of their shells, sucking off the salt.

Sam's dark eyes flicked from pistachio bowl to Patti, observing her intently as she bustled about the kitchen, long amber beads swinging above the volcanic casserole that spat fatty, rosemary-scented pellets of stew across the kitchen. Obviously once very beautiful – in the hall there was a picture of Patti in a fedora in the seventies looking like Jane Birkin – she was now startlingly handsome, her patent-black hair still thick, long and swishy, framing the kind of cheekbones that defied age, creased only with laughter lines. She had a sur-prising beauty. Just like Stevie's.

'I insist you drink some wine, darling.' Patti filled Sam's green Moroccan tumbler, her widest, most winning smile stretched across her face like a hammock. 'Or *vin*, should I say?'

Sam smiled. 'Twist my arm, Patti.'

'It's so good to see you again.' Patti bent over and kissed Sam lightly on his stubbly cheek. She couldn't help but adore this young man, the one-time schoolboy who'd shot up fast as bamboo and developed this delicious throaty laugh that sounded like it came from a place deep inside, like an earth tremor. There was nothing faux about Sam. No posturing. No brisk masculine ticks like her son Neil seemed to have, revealing what she suspected was insecurity in the company of powerful women. (She feared that inviting her hairiest feminist friends to her son's birthday parties in the eighties might have been counterproductive.) And she couldn't help

16

but be impressed by, and slightly in awe of, Sam's ethnicity, his dark-gold skin and springy curly hair – half afro, half Botticelli angel – which she longed to ping. His father, by all accounts a bit of a scoundrel, was American-Irish and was now settled on Long Island. His mother Pearl, dear Pearl, was part French, part Caribbean (Jamaica? Dominica?). Sam was a walking global melting pot, a Benetton ad made flesh. Much as she adored her own children, they had come out exceptionally Anglo Saxon-looking, like Pears babies, *despite* her ancient American-Indian roots (that's if you believed Grandma Yates' version of familial genealogy, which she most certainly did). 'To think that we haven't seen you for over a year, or is it two now? Goodness, doesn't time just march on heartlessly?'

'Two years, I guess.' Sam was only half listening, focused instead on the postcard-studded kitchen door and the fuzz of long brown hair emerging from behind it.

When Stevie entered the room she visibly started. '*Sam?* What . . .' Her pale, creamy skin flushed. She looked down at the floor, collected herself and smiled shyly. 'Hi.'

'Patti invited me over,' Sam explained apologetically, tucking a pistachio shell discreetly into the corner of his cheek with his tongue and wondering when he'd have a chance to spit it out. 'I've been hanging out at Mum's.'

'Right.' Stevie knotted her hands together. There was a pause. She tried to think of something to say to fill it but couldn't.

'Thank you for the wedding invitation by the way.' Sam rubbed his jaw, in his louche, almost sleepy way.

'You're coming?'

'Of course.'

'*Really?* Oh, wow. I am so pleased. I hadn't heard. I assumed . . .' Stevie flicked an airborne globule of lamb stew

17

off her arm and grinned. The day was improving. 'When do you go back to Paris?'

'*C'est fini.* I've taken my last Eurostar.'

'Really?' Was his French girlfriend here in Oxford? Had they split up? Stevie blushed again, fearing her thoughts transparent. 'How come you've . . .'

'Oh, Paris,' interrupted Patti, voice swooning then rising. 'Paris, Paris. How I love that city. The little macaroon shops. The Left Bank. The riots. It's one of the few places in the world where people are willing to stand up and say, "No more globalisation. *Enough!*"'

Enough indeed! Stevie glared at her mother. When would she stop interrupting? Her mother's habit of inviting her – Stevie's – friends over without warning had always really pissed her off. (All her friends adored Patti, always had. She was one of those mothers – fabulous if they're not yours.) And she really would have appreciated some forewarning this time. In Sam's unexpected presence, she cared that she was wearing a T-shirt with white deodorant stains under the arms, part of her old Oxford wardrobe that was left at her parents' house and consisted of clothes too tattered or unfashionable to wear in London. She did not want Sam to think she was letting herself go just because she was getting married. Like all her male friends, she wanted him to feel at least a pang – preferably a large, painful one – that she was marrying, a sadness not to have snapped her up while available. 'You're staying here? In Oxford?'

Sam raised his eyebrows and laughed. 'No. Next stop, New York.'

'America? Well, well.' Patti frowned and shook her head. 'Still, New York's not like the rest of the country. Greenwich Village. I had a wonderful time there. Have you heard of the Village?'

'*Mum*, of course he has.'

'I'm here for a couple of weeks first.' Sam fisted his hands together at the edge of the table, bent forward and pressed his chest against them, tensing. 'Nana's not well.'

'Oh, I'm sorry.' So was the French girlfriend relocating to New York too? Stevie smoothed down her bed-frizz hair with the palm of her hand and sucked in her tummy.

'It's crap being that old, man.' Sam shook his head. 'You know what my nana's like, teenager trapped in a ninety-four-year-old body. She wants to go back to St Elizabeth, hates being dependent.'

'Run me under the bus when the time comes, Stevie,' said Patti, shutting her eyes for comic import, revealing lids shimmering with leaf-green eye-shadow.

'Will do.'

'And make sure I'm wearing decent underwear.'

'Yes, Mother.' Stevie exchanged a 'nothing changes' look with Sam and sat down next to him. He poured her a glass of water from the chipped blue glass jug. A sense of déjà vu clicked in her head as decisively as a camera-lens shutter. She could be eighteen. Twenty-four. Thirty. It was the same scene: Sam and various family members around her parents' kitchen table, the same conversations, the little-evolved tensions, the same chipped, badly washed-up blue jug. (To her parents, dishwashers amounted to inexcusable consumer decadence.) What was it about being with friends from your home-bound teenage years? They made you feel reassured, that nothing had changed. And Sam, in particular, would always remind her of being the young, free-wheeling teenager who rambled on Oxford's Port Meadow and wove daisies into her hair and screeched with delight when the mud sucked her Wellington boot from her foot and Sam had to pull and pull it out of the mud and they'd fallen back laughing with a muddy squelch and run home to Sam's mum's house like swamp monsters and Sam's mother had fed them hot banana chip-like things and lent her an orange dress to wear that smelled like her own mother's Body Shop coconut body creams. Of course, now things had changed irretrievably. Her life was about to take a sharp left turn.

'Wedding plans going well?' asked Sam, negotiating a gritty lump of organic home-made bread. He winked at Stevie. 'You're all still talking at least.'

'It's going to be wild,' said Patti.

Stevie rolled her eyes. 'I'm not Billy Idol, Mum.'

'Oh, darling. Chill. Have a glass of wine. Now, who's your plus-one, Sam? The lucky lady?' purred Patti, as if barely able to restrain herself from claiming the role.

'Minus-one now, I'm afraid. Camille and me finished last month.'

Stevie felt instantly uplifted by this news, then, a few moments after, disappointed in herself. She wasn't single now. She should be more generous. But the idea of Sam's French girlfriend – surely an Emmanuelle Béart lookalike who lived on steak tartare and Gauloise – had irrationally irked her when news of his Gallic bliss had filtered through the London grapevines last year.

'Oh, I *am* sorry, honey.' Patti put an arm around Sam's broad shoulders, thrusting his curly head against the soft crepe of her décolletage. 'But if it ain't right, it just ain't right. You can't force it.' She looked thoughtful. Then a light-bulb smile. 'But hey, wait a minute! I have an idea. The scrumptious Lara! Lara is a great friend of Stevie's, Sam. A journalist. Terribly glamorous. She's staying for the weekend. You simply *must* meet her. You two will get on famously. Darling, where is she?'

'Meeting whatisname at Balliol or something,' said Stevie. The whatisname in question was Jake, twenty-two, blond, with a rower's shoulders and a devastating knowledge of post-war American poetry, which he quoted like a kind of open sesame to access women's underwear. He was the brother of a friend from London who Lara befriended at a fancy dress party in a Shoreditch loft last month. He was dressed as Simon Cowell, she the fairy queen from *Lord of the Rings*; unlikely bedfellows. 'Should be back later.'

'Yes, of course, of course. Brain like a colander. Now, where are my boys?' Patti flipped the salad with determined flair, lollo rosso leaves flying, silver bracelets crashing. 'Neil. Is that you?'

Accompanied by a loud flush of the toilet and a pungent farmyard stink – like his washing, her brother saved his stools for their parents' house – Neil ambulated in, navigating the flap of his parachute-baggy combats and dragging the smell of stale pot into the kitchen. He collapsed on an old pine chair, as if exhausted from a day of hard physical labour, and poured himself a glass of Merlot. As the last-born in the family by some years (an accident – Patti forgot her pill one month), Neil acted up the part of perennial adolescent, testing Stevie's tolerance. He treated his childhood attic bedroom – all ornamental bongs, posters of Pirelli girls and murdered American rappers – as a pleasant second home, a retreat from his permanent residence, a squat in a large, fully furnished Edwardian house in east Oxford. Stevie had already noted his attic bedroom's distinct soupy sock odour seeping through the floorboards into her room earlier that morning.

'Why don't you ever come when I call? I'm losing my voice, Neil,' said Patti, exasperated.

'I was listening to Cent.' Neil yawned and stretched his arms above his head. 'When are we eating, Ma? I'm marvin.'

'We're waiting for your father. Oh, here comes his lordship . . .'

Chris, a bespectacled, still-handsome, stooped sixtysomething, with a grey-string mop of hair and bushy excitable eyebrows, appeared in the kitchen doorway. He took off his tortoiseshell glasses and rubbed the pinch-pink mark on the bridge of his nose. 'Hello, family.'

Patti moved more quickly around the kitchen now, energised by annoyance at the sight of her husband. She prodded his tummy with a salad server. 'Chris, we need to talk about Jez's mother.'

Chris looked up, aware that this was a siren call to realign his coordinates to the unexpectedly time-consuming 'wedding matters', not the socio-economics of eastern Asia, despite the latter being more interesting and demanding less fiscal resources. 'Yes, Patti,' he said, as he had said trillions of times during the tempestuous course of their twenty-odd-year marriage. 'What is it?'

'The question is . . . *please* do not eat bread like that, Neil, you're not starving . . . is the spare bedroom on the first floor suitable for madam? I don't want to cause friction here.'

'Friction?' Sam smiled.

'It's fine,' said Stevie, stealing a glimpse at Sam, the way his smile curled up at the edges exposing just a slither of pinky brown gum. 'Leave it, Mum.'

Patti didn't leave it. She fluttered her long black lashes. 'The Lewises are just not – how to put this, Sam? – *our* kind of people, that's all. I fear the furniture, what remains of it after your party, Neil, will not be to Rita's fragrant taste.'

Stevie resented her mother hamming up Jez's family for comic effect, showing off in front of Sam. 'They're from Amersham, Mum, not San Francisco. Get over it.'

'Darling, I'm trying here. I'm trying not to be an embarrassment.'

'Yeah right,' mumbled Neil, fork in one hand, new camera-phone in the other, as he thumbed a text message beneath the table. 'That'd be a first.'

'Tolerate your mother, children,' said Chris. 'Lord knows, she is trying.'

Sam put his hand over his mouth, trying to suppress a laugh. He loved this family.

'All Rita and Colin need are clean sheets and a vase of flowers and *no* new-age nonsense, Mum,' instructed Stevie, aware of Sam's amusement and playing up to it herself now. 'Rita won't like the incense. Colin won't like the home-made muesli.'

'Not unless he's got the jaws of a Rottweiler,' muttered her father.

Patti ignored her husband. 'Sam, have you met Jez's folks?'

'No.'

Stevie looked at the table. She'd felt weird introducing Jez to Sam for some reason. She'd sensed they may not end up best friends. She'd sensed right. They'd met two or three times, bristling encounters in which Jez had found opportunity to oafishly boast about something – his job, the excessiveness of the last restaurant bill – in a fit of macho bravado. Sam made him nervous.

'Fucking uptight, the Lewises,' Neil mumbled through a small stoned gap in his mouth, like a ventriloquist. 'Making Jez and Stevie sleep in separate bedrooms.'

'Neil,' Stevie sighed. Was nothing sacred in this household?

'Let's hope he didn't go home after the stag night last weekend. Colin would have loved that. Oh, man . . .' Neil let a chuckle whistle between the gap in his two front teeth.

'What happened?' asked Sam, eyes widening white.

Stevie shook her head, trying not to laugh. 'Shut up, Neil.'

Neil, always keen to impress Sam – a dude in his eyes,

being almost black and having a groovy and vague kind of non-job as a photographer – ignored his sister's pleas for dignity. 'We went out in Brighton, dosed Jez up on Viagra, man. He was walking around with this big . . .'

'That was bang out of order, Neil. Totally tragic,' Stevie said, wondering why being in the company of her younger brother made her regress to her teenage vernacular. 'Let's not relive it.'

'Getting him in training for the honeymoon!' Neil quipped.

Stevie fired a withering look at her brother. 'Oh, please.'

'Don't overreact to, like, everything, Stevie. Aren't you meant to be loved-up or something? I keep forgetting. It's like having a hormonal pit bull in the house.' Neil picked out a cherry tomato from the salad with the yellow tipped index finger and thumb normally reserved for rolling joints. 'Anyhow, I'm sure Rita – monster-in-law – didn't figure it out.'

'*Neil!* Would you stop winding your sister up,' said Patti. 'It's a stressful enough time for Stevie. And let's not be nasty about the Lewis family. It's not . . . not cool.'

Stevie looked at her mother, surprised. Yes, she really was trying. Her mother had obviously got over last Christmas, finally. The Lewises had come to stay and embraced the household like a bout of flu. Rita had complained that the turkey was under-cooked – 'I prefer it dry myself' – and that the music – Sinatra – made her head hurt. While Colin had taken refuge in a bottle of port and an ancient book on Second World War ships, talking only to chastise Jez for his bad language or lack of success in becoming the next Tory prime minister, or at the very least a doctor or lawyer.

'Jez is all right.' Patti put an arm over her daughter's shoulder and squeezed. 'Stevie's chosen well.'

Chris put down his fork, rearing up a little as a mouthful

of over-spiced stew settled in his stomach. 'Jez better be more than all right,' he said, turning to Sam, green eyes twinkling. 'This wedding is taking over our *lives*, Sam. It's like a strange virus has entered the household, turning sensible people into jibbering buffoons and my wallet to mulch.'

Stevie felt a pang of guilt. For all the blustering and joking, she knew her parents were really feeling the pinch of this wedding. ('There goes my Five Rhythms dancing retreat,' she'd heard her mother sigh to Dad shortly after she'd announced their engagement.) She'd wanted to put money in the wedding pot herself as the transaction seemed inappropriate at their age, and with Jez and her combined salary being larger than that of her parents'. But her mother had refused and said she'd just take on more counselling work or add a bit to the mortgage. (Stevie knew that this refusal meant a no-frills wedding.)

Neil blew his fringe off his face. 'It's, like, totally unfair, Dad, being a boy. All Mum's talk about equality, I don't see me getting thrown, like, shitloads of money for basically a *party*.'

Patti looked sympathetic. 'If you like, sweetie, you can invite some of those nice boys from the squat.'

'No he will not!' said Stevie.

'Or a nice girl.'

Neil, who hadn't had a girlfriend since school, glared at his mother.

'All I can say is that it's going to be one fabulously groovy party.' Patti winked, sending an avalanche of green eyeshadow on to her left cheekbone. 'I'll see to that.'

Stevie's heart sank. What was her mother going to do, arrive on a white stallion à la Bianca Jagger?

Chris brushed a stray chunk of over-cooked carrot off his tweed jacket. 'It's perverse that we've spent years conjuring up highly creative excuses to avoid all the relatives and then, suddenly, we've invited them – en masse – to this house. It's going to be . . .'

Stevie deflated. The chipped blue jug swam in front of her eyes. Shit, it felt like there was a flood of tears inside her ready to seep out of the nearest available orifice. Maybe she was premenstrual. Maybe it was hormones. Maybe she was over-emotional at seeing Sam again after all this time.

Sam touched her lightly on her pale freckled forearm. 'Great. It'll be great, Stevie.'

'*Ab-so-lu-ment!*' exclaimed Patti, thick silver Rajasthan bangles clattering like a parade of Hari Krishnas. 'Anyway, folks, *no* going back now!'

Four

A green VW Golf screeched to a halt on the Cowley Road, etching a scar of stinking black rubber across the tarmac. The driver stuck a furious bald pink head out of the car window. 'Fucking look where you're going, woman! You nearly got yourself killed!'

'Sorry, sorry.' Stevie walked shakily over the road, grateful as her foot – still attached – hit the kerb. Since moving to London ten years ago, she treated all provincial roads like rustic bridleways.

'Hey!' someone shouted.

She jumped. What had she done now? But thank God it was Lara, smiling and waving, wearing a fitted black sixties-style dress and red-patent wedges, incongruously glamorous in this part of laidback Oxford student-land.

'Christ, Stevie. I saw that,' Lara said, wide-eyed with concern. 'Are you OK?'

'A bit wobbly, but no radical changes to the wedding dress necessary.'

Lara kissed her on both cheeks. 'You've got to look where you're going, hon.'

'I know, I know. But I was checking out that cloud, the big

grey stormy one up there.' Stevie craned her head back. 'Isn't it spectacular?'

'Fuck, you almost joined it.' Lara shook her head. 'Anyway, forget the damn cloud! This is very, *very* exciting.' She banged out a drum roll with her hands. 'Ta-da! Are you ready for the final dress fitting?'

'As ready as I'll ever be.'

'Let's go then, missus.' Lara slinked her arm through Stevie's and the friends walked along the Cowley Road until they got to James Street.

'Turn left. Dressmaker's this way,' said Stevie, her pace slowing, feeling a growing sense of trepidation. It all felt a bit final. 'That's Gina's house, the one with the green door.'

As they rang the doorbell, Lara squeezed Stevie's arm. 'Don't be nervous. You will look drop-dead gorgeous in that dress, I just know it.'

Gina, a dressmaking member of Patti's book group, had agreed to alter a satin 1930s design that Stevie had unearthed from the dusty basement of a vintage shop on Portobello Road. A neat needle-thin woman in her sixties, she showed them into the studio-cum-living room with long slim hands. 'Girls, I'll leave you to try them on. Lovely, lovely. Call me when you need adjusting.' She closed the door behind her with a smart click.

'You first,' said Stevie. 'I insist, because I'm the bride.'

Lara stripped down to her matching polka-dotted turquoise-and-pink underwear. 'I am so grateful you haven't made me wear a shapeless sheaf of lilac,' she said, stepping into a pale-grey prom-style dress, mid-calf, full fifties-style skirt, its silk layers rustling against each other like summer leaves. 'It's sadistic when brides do that. Zipper me up, love.'

Stevie gave the zip a sharp tug. The dress's bodice hugged

her best friend's petite hourglass figure like a violin case. She stood back, nodded approvingly. 'Knockout.'

'Really?' Lara turned in front of a full-length mirror, twisting to get a glimpse of her backside. 'A get-laid bridesmaid dress?'

Stevie laughed. 'Definitely.'

'I fully expect to be sitting next to someone hot.' Lara camped up a Joan Collins voice. 'I don't do old relatives.'

'Don't worry. You've been strategically placed next to Sam.' Stevie felt a prick of jealousy. She wanted to sit next to Sam, gossip with Lara, drink too much, dance with abandon, be a guest at her own wedding.

'Your old Oxford friend Sam? The photographer guy?' Lara inhaled sharply to decrease her waist measurement. 'And, yes, before you say it I know there are about two single heterosexual men in their thirties left in the whole of London, so I am honoured. There's so much competition for the single men at weddings these days. You need to be like that,' she crossed her fingers, 'with the bride to even stand a remote chance of being seated at a decent table.'

'Oh, I'm good to you, Lara,' laughed Stevie. 'I will inflict freshly divorced Uncle Harry – all inquisitive hands and halitosis – on someone more deserving.'

Lara smiled her slightly over-bitten smile and tugged at the fabric around the waist. 'Gina should nip it in a bit more here, don't you think?' She liked to show her figure off.

Stevie took a pin from between her teeth and pushed it into the seam. 'Sam's moving to New York too, you know.' She adjusted Lara's neckline, pleased about her friend's prettiness in a dress she'd envisioned. 'You'll have stuff to talk about.'

'Is he? Cool.' Lara put one hand on the back of a chair to balance and slid one small tanned foot carefully into a

29

strappy silver heel, then the other, and struck a pose. Content with her reflection, she smiled. 'Your turn.'

Stevie picked up the pile of grey-white satin between forefinger and thumb. It was sheeny and opaque like the skin of a mushroom stalk and seemed strangely insubstantial for its purpose. 'Not much to it, is there? It'll be like getting married in nightwear.'

Lara laughed, nudged her friend. 'It's beautiful. Put it on.'

'I must warn you now. I haven't found the right underwear. It just redistributes my back fat. I've got these, like, bulges.'

'Curves, not bulges.'

'Yeah, yeah.' Stevie stepped out of her print wrap dress and arrowed her arms above her head as Lara lowered the dress over with reverential solemnity. The satin felt heavy against her skin despite its appearance and took a second or two to settle to her contours. She ran her fingers over her collarbone, exposed by the scooped neckline. 'Check out this rash, Lara. I noticed it this morning. It started on my chest and now it's creeping up my neck like rising damp.'

Lara traced the rash gently with her fingers. 'Yeah, I can just feel it. But don't fret. It'll go. Probably stress. Now let me have a good look at you.' She stepped back. 'God, you look . . . absolutely stunning. Check yourself out.' Lara held Stevie's shoulders with cool hands and turned her round to face the mirror. Stevie stared at her reflection. The dress, cut on the bias, swirled around her ample curves and the satin bounced light into her face, which looked, in this bright afternoon light, pale and round as a plate. Yes, it certainly was a flattering dress: simple, nothing too lacy or Oscar dress-like. It now fitted pretty perfectly. Gina had done well.

'Look what you're doing to me. I've come over all queer.' Lara's eyes glittered with tears. She fanned her hands and made a funny noise, a hybrid between a cry and a laugh. 'Sorry, I never thought I'd see you in a wedding dress.'

Stevie snorted. 'Neither did I.'

Lara stood back, putting a hand on one hip. 'It's not that I thought you'd never get married, just that we would always be twenty-two and single.'

Stevie smiled. 'But here I am.' She could hardly believe it herself.

'Here you are.' Lara grinned mischievously. 'Thank God you didn't marry any of Jez's predecessors. Can you *imagine*?'

Stevie raised her eyebrows. 'They didn't ask, actually.'

'Just as well.'

'I hope I would have had the sense to turn them down. But you don't know, do you?'

'I suppose some people just decide to draw a line beneath the search and commit,' shrugged Lara.

'But the problem is that when you *do* finally commit, you never know if you'd have met someone better, like, if you hadn't committed.'

Lara threw her glossy blonde head back and laughed. 'That's why we're all so crap at relationships. Always looking over our shoulders for someone better who might come along.'

Stevie stroked the dress thoughtfully, smoothing out the crease above her belly. 'But then again, you could wait and wait and never meet anyone you loved more than your first teenage crush.'

Lara rolled her eyes. 'Stevie, *stop* it! This is not the time for your morbid introspection. You're going to get married!'

'I know, I know.' Stevie laughed. She needed Lara. Lara lightened things. She stopped her taking herself so seriously.

'Crushes are rubbish indicators of compatibility anyhow. I mean, come on. My most passionate obsessions all had the most hideous traumatic ends.'

Stevie thought of all the men she'd been infatuated with and started to giggle, a nervous giggle rising up from the pit of her churning stomach. 'Remember Luca?'

'Luca? What, the old style editor of *Pop I-Q*? Yes, of course.' Lara smiled, puzzled. 'Why do you mention him?'

'Oh, I don't know. This wedding business makes me weirdly nostalgic.' Memories kept popping into her head, yesterday-fresh, sharp as squirts of lemon juice in the eye. It was as if her imminent wedding had turned the binoculars on her romantic past, enlarging it, bringing it into clearer focus: she'd wasted far too much energy on men who'd turned out to mean too little.

'Ah, Luca. Our gaydars were muted by lust,' sighed Lara. 'But he wore his Evisu so well. Can you believe that was, what, ten? Twelve years ago?'

'Twelve.' In August. She was sure of that. The wedding had given her life new chronological definition, highlighting cause and effect, heartbreak and rebound and the people who linked it all together like a thread of messages in an online chat room. How well she remembered her first sighting of Lara that hot, sweaty August in *Pop I-Q*'s Clerkenwell offices as she peacocked out of the small, dark fashion cupboard, draped in a borrowed gothic black coat by Alexander McQueen, her tiny green court shoes taking fairy steps out of the coat's dark flapping interior. She remembered the voluptuous brightness of Lara's blonde hair. Her glass-blue eyes. The way the air seemed to vibrate around her and how when she laughed the office dynamic changed and everyone found themselves helplessly staring, unable to concentrate, wanting to know what she would do or say next. She and Lara didn't speak for the first three months. She assumed Lara would be insufferably vain. But she found out she was confident and cocky and they'd bonded over their crush for

Luca drunkenly one night, whispering behind their hands during after-work drinks. These days she didn't see Lara as much as she'd like. But whenever she did see her there was still that reassuring emotional shorthand. And she was still one of life's tonics.

Lara looked at Stevie fondly. 'We braved the singles jungle together, girl.'

'Sod that, we survived living together.'

'*Just*. You drove me to distraction.'

'Shit, no wonder we got mice.' Stevie began to shake with laughter. 'Oh God, I haven't changed. I'm going to be the worst wife, ever.'

'A *wife*,' Lara said wistfully. 'Doesn't it sound so unbelievably grown-up?'

'Maybe that's why this feels like dressing up.' Stevie smoothed down the folds of satin, warm now from her skin. Her eyes started to prick. She was all over the place. There was a pause. 'I just wish you weren't going to New York so soon after the wedding.'

'Hey, you'll be a married lady, won't need me no more,' Lara said softly in her best American accent.

'I wouldn't be so sure.' Why did people assume that because she was getting married she'd be able to get all her emotional sustenance from Jez? It hadn't been true in the past and suddenly seemed rather less likely to be true in the future. 'I just wish . . . oh, I don't know. Part of me still feels like I'm not ready to settle, to draw that line. Does that sound ridiculous? I've got grey hairs, for God's sake. If not now, when? Should I wait until I am sixty-five before I shout, "Ready! Any takers?"' Stevie smiled sadly. 'But it's just that when I think about New York . . . Oh hell, why does life have to be so linear? Why can't we do lots of things at once?'

Lara fiddled with her glossed pink lip, rolling it between

33

forefinger and thumb. It was what she did when she was upset about something. 'Couldn't you try to persuade Jez again? You've wanted to move to New York for as long as I've known you.'

Stevie dug her nails into the palm of her hand. Lara had secured a shiny job as senior editor at a new, as yet unpublished, American fashion magazine, currently coded Project J. She'd offered to pull strings and introduce Stevie to the right people, but Jez had objected. Jez's career was here. Jez had some really exciting projects coming up at the marketing company, YR-Brand. 'Anyway, as soon as you sprog, pumpkin,' he'd said, 'you'll be at home with the kid.' The argument had played out in resentful silence. 'I've tried, Lara. He is so against the idea. You know how he hates New York.' She shrugged, trying to justify the decision. 'Besides, slim chance I'd get the job.'

'You always underestimate yourself, Steve. You've got a great reputation.'

'Thanks.'

'Why do you look so sad?' Lara put an arm over Stevie's bare shoulder. 'Smile. You must be a smiley bride, my darling.'

Stevie grinned, perking up again. '"Bride" is rather nice. I like bride. It's kind of pastoral.' She rolled the word around her mouth as if trying to taste it. 'But wife, let's be honest, Lara. Wife sounds frumpy.'

'Could you be over-analysing here, hon?' Lara sat down on a wooden chair and kicked her feet in the air. 'More importantly, did you bring those samples to show me?'

Stevie dug into her bag, smiling at Lara's impetuous enthusiasm. She could never wait for anything. And she was insistent that all the wedding details be viewed together, with dress, to get the overall 'look'. Lara hadn't quite grasped that

Patti – who was in charge of decorating the house for the wedding – was a liability wherever a unified 'look' was concerned. 'Here's the confetti.'

Lara turned the sample confetti box in her hands, watching the little discs of coloured pastel paper toss about like a snowstorm behind the window of clear plastic. She looked up. 'Don't you want rose petals?'

Stevie stared blankly.

'Real flower petals. A bit nicer, I reckon.'

'Shit, you're so right.' Stevie scrunched her hands to her face. Suddenly the fact that the confetti was paper not rose petals mattered more than anything in the entire universe. 'Crisis.'

'Breathe, Stevie. Breathe.' Lara laughed. 'We can get over this.'

Gina knocked on the door, opening it before they'd answered. 'Everything OK, girls?'

'Great, thanks Gina,' said Stevie. 'Just give us two minutes.' But it wasn't all great. There were problems. Endless problems. She picked up her strappy gold wedding shoes. 'See these, Lara. They are too small.' Her voice was getting higher and higher, as if she'd been sucking on a helium balloon. 'Because I *bought* them half a size too small. I'm not sure why. I walked into Jimmy Choo and tried on hundreds of pairs and I got kind of shopped out, you know, all at sixes and sevens in an ecstasy of indecision, and I bought the wrong pair because they were the only ones left in a size that vaguely fitted and I thought I'd wear them in or something. How stupid am I?'

'You haven't worn them?'

'Around the garden.' Stevie cringed. 'Oh, I know. Don't say it.'

'Here, let me.' Lara held one gold heel in her hands, licked her finger and rubbed it on a scuff mark on the leather sole. It didn't budge. 'Never let the wrong size get between you and a fabulous pair of heels. You only have to wear them for a day. Don't be a lightweight.' She put the shoe down on the floor. 'Now, what about flowers?'

'Jez's mum is sorting them out.' Stevie hung the words out for inspection by her friend. 'Don't shoot me that look.'

'Isn't she the mother-in-law that taste forgot?'

'Jez wanted her to "feel involved".' Stevie's anxiety was brushing past her tonsils now, drying her mouth. 'I'm going to end up with yellow carnations, aren't I? Shit. Shit. Shit.'

Lara tried to help. 'Carnations are kind of back, if you keep them bunched all one colour.'

'Well, you'd know.' Stevie was aware that she'd let things slide, not kept on top of the finer details as much as she'd have liked. And there was so little time left to organise anything. Now where was that garter? She rummaged in her rucksack and picked out an elasticky band of blue lace, held it between forefinger and thumb. 'Saucy?'

Lara camped up an eyebrow and grinned. 'I'd say.'

'Do you mind passing those scissors on Gina's work bench? Thanks. See here? Fraying threads. Shoddy workmanship.' She held the scissors up to the garter, pulled the elastic taut and snipped. The garter fell apart like a cut ribbon at the end of a race. Stevie put her hand to her mouth. 'No! What have I done now?'

The two friends stared at the blue garter lying on the cream carpet, its symbolic circle ruptured. Stevie flumped on to a chair, the pale satin dress spilling around her like milk. 'What the hell is wrong with me? Jinxed. I swear I'm jinxed.'

'You're just stressed. It's OK, really.' But Lara looked concerned.

'*Nothing* is going right, Lara. It's spooking me out. To be

36

totally honest with you, I feel like there's something in me, a kind of bridal poltergeist causing havoc.' Stevie felt a tear slide down her face. It landed with a damp staining splodge on her satin dress. 'Shit. You see?'

Lara dabbed carefully and maternally at the splodge with a tissue. 'Oh, love.'

'I'm terrified. I can't sleep. And I've got some kind of smallpox going on.'

'You don't seem quite yourself.' Lara stood up, squatted and bridged her arms on Stevie's bare shoulders, so that they were looking directly into each other's eyes. 'What's really bothering you?'

'Just nothing is . . .' Stevie feared if she voiced her doubts that would give them more substance.

'I promise to be the soul of discretion.'

Stevie searched the stray cotton-threads on the floor for an answer. 'Well . . . I . . . I've been having doubts.' She looked up. 'These funny little doubts, Lara.'

'Wedding nerves? Is there anything I can do?'

'No. Thanks.' She managed a smile. 'They're not huge doubts, you know. Just homeopathic amounts, but enough to colour everything.'

Lara tried hard to understand. But she'd never come close to getting married. She'd had two proposals but turned them both down. She was too good at being single.

'Do I still feel passionate about Jez?' muttered Stevie, partly to herself. 'Is the magic still there? I want to get it *right*, Lara.'

'Of course.' Lara squeezed Stevie's hand. 'But if you think about anything too hard you can talk yourself out of it.'

'The thing is that what I'm feeling is so inextricably muddled with the practicalities, the onward march of the wedding juggernaut: the napkins, the food, the rsvps . . . all this *stuff*.'

37

Stevie held up the offending confetti sample box and waggled it. 'And it shouldn't be about stuff.'

'No, it absolutely shouldn't. It's about what's right for you.'

Stevie decided to test the water. 'And that's Jez, right?'

Lara paused, resisting the urge to break eye contact. 'Only you know that.'

'Oh God.' Stevie dragged the skin on her cheeks with her palms. 'What if I *don't* know, not absolutely, not one hundred per cent.

'It's hard for me to advise you,' interjected Lara softly.

'I know, I know.' Stevie put her head in her hands. 'It's all so fucking confusing.'

'Marriage is a pretty massive step.'

'Till death do us part? Sleeping with one person for the rest of your life? I mean, the mind boggles. What if I stop fancying him?'

'Isn't that what sex shops and handsome gardeners are for?' Lara put her hand over her mouth. 'Not very helpful, sorry.'

'The thing is,' continued Stevie, on a roll now, 'Jez *does* say some pretty foul things sometimes and I wonder if I'm going to be able to stand that for another fifty years. You know, he said I needed to lose half a stone before the wedding?'

'Pretty unforgivable,' said Lara, treading softly. 'But you know what men are like, if you press them about body stuff they'll shoot off the wrong answer.'

Stevie sniffed indignantly. She didn't think she'd ever be able to forgive Jez for that, not properly. 'I wish I hadn't asked.'

'Always a mistake.' Lara pursed her mouth and moved it from side to side, agitated. 'But shit, who am I to advise you, Stevie? I feel so horribly badly qualified. A few hundred years ago I'd be dunked in a pond.'

'It's all right, I'm just thinking aloud really.' Stevie sat up straight, shocked they were having this conversation at all. It wasn't right to talk about Jez like this. Marriage surely demanded a subtle but significant transition of loyalties from friend to husband. She sighed. 'Maybe I'm being even more neurotic than usual.'

'Stevie . . .' Lara paused, solemn-faced. 'You probably are being neurotic. But I'll be there for you whatever.'

There was a silence that went on for just a bit too long. Stevie broke it. 'Do you think my doubts are a deal breaker?' She couldn't meet Lara's eyes, didn't want to influence her answer.

'They must be pretty normal.' Lara sounded hesitant. 'But I don't really know. What do you think?'

Stevie stared at Lara, weighing things up. 'Yes, totally normal.' She pushed the door ajar. 'Gina,' she called out, 'we're ready for the final pinning now.'

Five

Sam padded quietly across the lawn towards Stevie, who was slumped on the cold wrought-iron bench that withstood, year after year, the overgrown ivy and honeysuckle at the bottom of the Jonsons' rambling garden. She wore a Grecian-style jersey dress, a slash of peacock-blue against the green foliage. The sight made him hold his breath. It was something to do with the way the light dappled her hair, outlined her milk-top cheeks with gold. As he came closer, he could see that her eyes were shut, the lashes – straight as a comb's teeth – casting corrugated shadow on her cheekbones. Stevie's creased eyelids pulsed slightly, from right to left, as if following the path of fast-moving clouds across the sky. There was yellow pollen smeared on the hem of her dress. Grass arched between the toes of her bare feet. That made him smile for some reason. Not moving, not wanting her to wake up just yet, he stared some more, unblinking, his six-foot vantage point allowing him a clear view of the triangular planes of her strong nose, the way it counterbalanced her freckled honey-eyed prettiness. In this way her features didn't quite work together, he thought. Stevie was like two different faces merged into one, an echo of someone else, another Stevie, every time the light shifted or her chin tilted its angle. He wished he had his camera. He touched her elbow gently with the pads of his fingers. 'Me again, I'm afraid.'

'Oh!' Stevie's eyes opened quickly but the registering curl of her smile was pleasurably slow. 'You.'

'Didn't mean to disturb.'

'I nodded off. Just trying to escape the family asylum.'

Sam scuffed his trainer into the grass. 'I'm going to stay with some friends in London. I thought I'd pop over before I braved the A40 to give you this.' He held out a package wrapped in leopard-print paper. 'It's not much . . .'

She looked at the package: hard, rectangular. 'You didn't have to . . .' She tore off the paper respectfully, in small crackling strips. 'Oh! What's this?' A pad of top-quality homemade drawing paper, thick and fibrous, and a sheaf of charcoal pencils.

'For the honeymoon . . .' Sam realised this sounded presumptuous, as if she wouldn't have better things to do. 'Well, whenever really. To keep you drawing. Don't worry, it's not your wedding present.'

'That's so sweet.' Stevie blushed. 'Thank you! You are about the only person in the world who rates my drawing . . .'

'Oh, I remember you at life-class in sixth form.'

'Yeah, yeah. My woman with three nipples?'

'She that launched a thousand schoolboy fantasies.'

Stevie laughed. 'I'm very flattered.'

'Use it or lose it,' he said, hating himself at that moment for sprouting a bum-fluff cliché.

To her horror, Stevie felt tears prick and only composed herself by intently studying the paper, its confrontational white blankness.

A pause. Sam shifted from one Nike to the other, his round

bottom elegantly following the shift of his hips, like a ballet dancer's. He dug his hand in his jeans pocket and fixed Stevie with eyes so liquid she could see a reflection of the cumulus clouds drifting behind her. They seemed to be going very fast. She hoped the weather would hold for the wedding. Shit, she was conflicted. On one level she wished something dreadful would happen to disrupt the wedding, put it off. She could break an ankle, get measles or something. On the other hand, she was now starting to succumb to a bride's anxious excitement.

'Guess this is it, isn't it?' Sam said, not consciously intending to ask something that sounded so loaded.

Stevie paused, aware that this was the full stop between them. It was the end of all their possibilities, that collision of opportunity and circumstance that might have led to a relationship. At school Sam had been one of the *it* boys: brainy, sporty and not a little cocky, his darker skin marking him out in a largely white-skinned but liberal school as both exotic and hip. By sixth form, they were in different castes. Stevie was part of the nerdy, slightly gothic, not hugely physically attractive group. Sam was the alpha teenager. Still, after school and at weekends, in pubs in town, Sam and Stevie discovered that they had more in common than their opposing shoes – Sam, Adidas; Stevie, buckled black boots à la Cure's Robert Smith – might suggest. They shared an interest in art. They made each other laugh. Their mothers were good friends. They had a connection of sorts.

But in their twenties they had drifted apart. Sam spent a year in America becoming, in Stevie's eyes, more cosmopolitan and worldly and glamorous than ever. Then he returned to London to study law, before chucking it all in and getting a job as a photographer's assistant at a top London studio. (Like everyone else, Stevie was surprised by this particular career choice.

But Sam kept surprising her.) Meanwhile, in her parallel, rather less eventful life, Stevie inter-railed around Europe, got terribly sick in Prague, fell in love in Berlin and returned, earlier than planned, broken hearted about a man called Hans with a Jon Bon Jovi fixation. She went to a B-list art college up north, before starting on her magazine-designer career in London. When they were both in London she and Sam would still meet up. As friends. Romantically, Sam had always been out of her league. Sam went out with girls, lots of girls, like Katy Norris, all legs and eyelashes. Bloody Katy Norris.

Of course Stevie wondered. She wondered whether her doubts about her own attractiveness had made her colder, more asexual in her behaviour towards Sam than she should have been had she been more secure, more like Poppy. She'd never even flirted with him, never wanting to ruin their friendship by overshadowing it with unrequited lust. But equally, she'd never imagined there would be a finite amount of time. She thought there would always be endless golden midge-clotted summers when they were visiting their respective parents and would bump into each other on Port Meadow, or perhaps meet up for quick snatched drink in Jericho in Oxford, or in London's Soho, that little bar off Romilly Street that did the good house red. It seemed impossible that one of them would ruin the possibility of anything happening by doing something as scarily grown-up and final as *marrying* someone. And now, there remained a niggle, a what-if? Stevie sighed. At least they still had the kind of shorthand that you only ever get with people you've known since school, as if there was a kernel of every person that was only ever visible when young, later masked behind jobs and suits and marriages.

Stevie's fingers explored the paper pad, stroking its pages, testing the ridge of its spine with her thumb. They had spent too long being friends, she thought. It would have felt incestuous.

Besides, here she was about to promise herself to another man, *forever*. Guess this is it? Indeed.

She almost said, 'Don't make it sound so final,' but something stopped her. She suspected, just for a second, what Sam meant. 'I guess this is it.'

'Right.' Sam zipped up his jacket sharply. 'Well, I'll see you in two weeks. On the "big day",' he said, glancing at his watch. 'Is that the time? Better shoot. The nursing home calls. God, I'm glamorous.'

'You are good.'

'I'm not. I hate it really. I mean, I love the old dear, don't get me wrong. But man, that place.' Sam whistled. 'It smells of piss or death or, well, something pretty bad. Last time a lady, ancient old bat, died in her wheelchair. Everyone thought she was sleeping. We got to dessert before the staff realised and wheeled her out.'

'The last supper.'

Sam laughed, bent down and kissed Stevie's soft cheek. 'Good luck with everything.'

'You sound so sombre. You sound like I might need it.'

Sam frowned.

'Don't look like that. What, Sam?'

'Tell me to shut up if . . .'

'I will. Go on.'

'But this wedding, it's what *you* really want, isn't it?'

Stevie jolted, as if kicked on the funny bone. She dropped her eyes to the grass, studied a daisy. 'I think so.'

The muscles in Sam's shoulders constricted. 'Shit, I'm sorry. You're not someone to shriek it from the rooftops . . . not your style, is it?'

'No.'

'I'll shut up then.' Sam scuffed at the grass again with his trainer. 'Better shoot.'

44

'Wait.' Stevie stood up and pulled Sam towards her, his hair springy against her cheek, his skin smelling vaguely of cologne and hot, fried things. She felt it was like hugging part of her twenties goodbye, hugging all the men she'd liked but never explored, all the paths not taken. She watched as he walked – now in his thirties, Sam no longer felt the need for a hip-hop swagger – with the sun saffron on his arched boyish back, up the stony garden path, past the newly tended beds and the apple and pear trees, to the door to the steamy kitchen, where Patti lay in wait with a box of organic medjool dates.

Stevie sat cross-legged on the bench, examining the thick pad of paper. She picked out a pencil, satisfyingly sharp and unused like a new lipstick, and dragged it across the page. Head clearing of thoughts, in a trance-like state, Stevie drew. And she drew Jez. Those pale blue eyes. The bubble curls of strawberry blond hair. The robust nose. The angular fifty-pence-piece cut of his jaw. The mouth . . .

No, she couldn't do it. She couldn't get the mouth right. Every time she sketched it it would be wrong, too cruel, too unforgiving. And then she thought, maybe she couldn't draw his mouth because she didn't like his mouth. Because she no longer liked what came out of it. She put the pencil back in the packet. Or could she no longer draw Jez because Jez would never have bought her those pencils? Jez would have bought her a bottle of perfume that she'd never worn before.

'Is it what *you* really want?' Sam's words looped around her head. A 747 rumbled across the sky. A warm wind rustled the honeysuckle. A wood pigeon cooed. These were the sounds of her Oxford childhood and they were getting louder and louder until the whole garden seemed to vibrate and hum and resonate in her ears with unavoidable truth, like one of her mother's pre-breakfast 'Ommm' exhalations. Stevie gripped the arm of the bench, steadying herself, squeezed her eyes and felt herself whipped and turned around in a dark, emotional vortex, and then, suddenly, peace. She opened her eyes. The wind dropped. The garden was still. The outline of everything – dandelion, apple tree, blade of grass – was as clear and certain as a drawing and she felt the exhilarated release of a decision reached.

Six

Katy Norris reread the pregnancy test instructions. Three minutes? She could wait. Just. Besides, even though she'd missed a pill, it would still be a near miracle if she were up the duff. Since Seb had started the contract with the New York bank they were rarely in the same place long enough to share a meal, let alone bodily fluids. But what if she *were* pregnant? Her augmented lips curled. How would Seb react? Surely with joy, even though he'd always said he wanted to be married before he had children. Not wanting to appear a sperm-hungry psycho thirtysomething, she'd agreed with him and waited for her proposal. And waited and waited.

A couple of months ago, she'd got the courage up to ask the doctor, 'How long have I got left, exactly? The doctor had looked her up and down and told her, yes, fertility falls off the cliff about her age and that, ideally, she should gain a few pounds to enhance her chances of conceiving. Oh yes, and they should be having sex every three days. She'd laughed and explained her situation – the clash between her ovaries and their careers and, well, Seb's rather non-urgent romantic scheduling – and asked if, *in theory*, because they weren't planning anything right now, but just so she knew for the future, was it possible to pencil in a course of IVF sometime later next year, just after her thirty-seventh birthday, just to leave nothing to chance? The doctor thought she was joking.

Katy checked her Hermès watch. Two minutes to go. She wondered what her other half was doing. Seb must be up now, she supposed, stretching his arms, muscles flexing, looking for a tie and shirt. Behind him, midtown Manhattan would be winking awake beyond the vertiginous sheet-glass windows that made her soles tingle and filled her with a strange longing to fling herself out like a rag doll. Did Seb miss her? Did Manhattan compensate for the more homely environment of Notting Hill? She knew it wouldn't work for her. New York was the only place in the world she felt unattractive. The only place in the world she stepped into a party and felt that she could never eat again.

Katy walked across her large open-plan living room, her pedicured toes sinking into the two-inch-thick cream carpet, to a mound of plumped silk cushions, piled extravagantly against an antique Chinese tea chest. She lay down, mentally checked her thigh circumference and, as if Seb were watching, arranged herself in the most photogenic pose, one leg slightly bent leaning across the other straighter one, like a typical Elizabeth Hurley stance but rotated. She lit a Space NK jossstick, breathed deeply, closed her eyes and tried to conjure up some kind of inner Zen. But it didn't work. She didn't feel relaxed. It was hard for a woman of thirty-six to relax when she had been living with a guy for two years and he hadn't mentioned marriage.

Katy's eyes rested on a photograph of them on a windy sand-duned beach in Île de Ré, France's answer to the Hamptons. Exactly three years ago next week. They'd just met. How happy (and thin and young) she looked then, sarong billowing behind her, Seb's tennis-honed arms around

48

her waspish waist, beaming, as if England had just won the rugby. Next to that picture, Katy thought, should be the logical progression, a wedding photograph: ivy-hugged walls, a rose garden perhaps, flower fairies in white tulle, daisies tucked into their curls, little hands clapping. One would just be able to see the lace of her Vera Wang dress, caught on a breeze, her smile, and . . . and, well, probably the carbuncular profile of Seb's father and the upholstered floral-sprigged bosom of his wife swelling with disapproval.

No, Seb's parents had never thought she was good enough for their youngest son. That can't have helped speed things along. She hadn't gone to the right schools. She hadn't come from a particularly wealthy background, but a stolidly aspirational middle-class one – all toilets, serviettes and Rovers – which neither Seb nor his mother made any pretence of being interested in. She also worked as a booker in a make-up artist agency. Even in the twenty-first century a career translated as 'pushiness' to Seb's mother, who'd never had to work. And yes, she was far too old and, with every non-committal month that passed, getting older.

Katy checked her watch again. One minute, thirty-one seconds. One minute, thirty-one seconds before her life could change utterly. She dug around her Gucci handbag for a lipsalve and dragged it slowly across her lips, trying to distract herself from the white stick with its totem-like life-changing powers. She checked her reflection in her hand mirror, gazing back critically at the reflection: the clear honeyed Scandinavian skin (she had a Swedish great-grandmother to thank for that); the slightly slanted Curaçao-blue eyes; the wide, high cheekbones that meant she always looked good in photos.

Katy had been beautiful for as long as she could remember. Her first memories were of people telling her blonde-toddler

49

self that she was the cutest girl in Reading. She'd been christened May queen at school, three years running. While not hugely popular with girls – jealous, her mother had explained – Katy's looks nonetheless inspired a certain reverence in them. For a long time her beauty made her self-conscious – even walking past a building site required nerves of steel – but it protected her from social isolation.

Life improved further when she developed small hard bosoms with upturned nipples, coltish legs and hair that swished and curled into breaking waves like Daryl Hannah's in the mermaid movie. At discos she was first in line for slow-dance requests. The boys had pressed their bony pelvises hard against hers, wispy jaws against her cheek, breathing in jerks. (She'd hummed along to 'True' and pretended she was dancing with Tony Hadley.) By the age of fourteen, Katy realised she'd been dealt a pretty good hand, even if she disliked her nose. She also realised that beauty was a currency. It was a means of transaction, and only the dumbest blondes thought otherwise. All women were born equal but they mostly married and mated according to their waist:hip ratio. Men were biologically driven to select beautiful fecund-looking creatures for their wives, as the mothers of their children. It made evolutionary sense. She'd kept her part of the bargain.

Unfortunately, the horrifying tick of the Heal's clock on the wall was the one thing she couldn't control. The rest of her life she could box up prettily: career – decent job, tick; family – healthy relationship with Dad since Mum's death, tick; health – Pilates, yoga and 'normal' smears, tick; home – great postcode, Matthew Hilton armchair, Arco lamp, tick; and boyfriend – City job, handsome and er . . . 3500 miles away. Needing reassurance, she held up the hand mirror again. No, she no longer looked twenty-five. She'd managed, rather heroically, to hang on to the looks of a twenty-five year old well into her thirties, but this year nature had overridden Crème de la Mer. And as she got older, more lined around the eyes, slacker around the jaw, she was aware that she didn't cause such a devastating impact when she walked into a room (despite the fact that she compensated for the loss of youth's flush with particularly attentive and expensive grooming). This really upset her. Inside, she was the same Katy, right?

Or not? This year, a seedling of a realisation had begun to push up through the city-block creams and anti-ageing peptides on her skin: could it possibly be that the responses she once imagined were responses to the 'inner' Katy – fascinating, charismatic woman about town – were really just responses to her youthful beauty? It was a terrifying prospect.

Thirty seconds to go. Katy took a sip of Fiji water. The timing was unfortunate. If only the whirlwind of her relationship hadn't subsided to a gentle breeze – the shag-fest was now over – at exactly the same time as she'd started to hurtle towards her forties. In her twenties, early thirties even, she'd have blown the closing time whistle by now and moved on to the next handsome, amusing man with a full head of hair and a hard dick. She had been ambivalent about children then. Why sacrifice her lifestyle? Her priorities had only begun to change in her thirties. And, at times, it filled her with a horrible neediness, a vulnerability buoyed up by a sense of entitlement, which turned to resentment when Seb didn't express a desire for the same thing. Their relationship power-balance shifted. He now held all the aces. In her blackest moments, in the early hours of the morning after a few lines of Columbia's finest the night before (it wasn't so pretty doing drugs in your mid-thirties but she carried on anyway as compensation for not being married or having children), she reeled at the unfairness of it all. It was as if the threat of childlessness had somehow jumped species: surely it struck driven careerists surging with testosterone and tracker funds, not moderately successful nine-to-five good-time blondes like herself. She hated the fact that she now needed Seb to secure her future. She hated being the unrequited lover rather than the beloved.

The problem was that Seb was no longer the gawky, slightly square toff who wore embarrassing colourful socks beneath his Savile Row suits. He'd grown into his looks, his job and, yes, quite definitely, his money. If they were to split, or, as was more likely, drift apart on different sides of the Atlantic, Seb would have no difficulty in procuring another woman. A wife. Probably a younger one (Americans loved that posh English thing, didn't they?). As a woman, even a beautiful one, her hand was weaker. She had a finite amount of time left. He didn't. Period. Or until her periods ended. As every month went by without a diamond ring or *even* a nuptial conversation, she felt a little more panicked, a little more needy. And she resented this. Hugely. She had never been needy. She'd always been the one who dumped men. She'd had more admirers than any woman she knew and yet, and yet, here she damn well was . . .

Katy leaned further back on the cushions and admired the triangular gap between her thighs, so sculptural in her skinny dark denim. She pulled a cigarette out of a packet, failed to light it off the joss-stick, lit a match, inhaled and exhaled, holding her arm above her, admiring the sinewy form that was the prize for all that ashtanga. God knows, she tried to preserve herself.

If Katy wanted this relationship to continue – and she couldn't face starting again now – she needed a strategy. She must make Seb desire her again. She must make him jealous. He needed to see that other men desired her. Because wasn't that what desire was about anyhow, for men at any rate? Acquiring something that their peers desired, being on the winning team. Simple souls.

Shit, it was time. With one hand over her mouth, Katy peeped at the test. No line. *No* damn line. She tossed the stick into the silver retro waste bin, clattering against the metal. Shit. Pulling herself out of the valley of cushions, she hunted down her sexiest look-at-me acid-green Miu Miu heels and, rather than mess up the kitchen by tackling the coffee maker, went out of the house to buy a skinny latte to help her strategise.

Seven

Lara froze mid-bite. She put the croissant back on the plate. 'Say it again. I'm confused. You're not sure you want to get married because of some charcoal pencils and, what did you say, a *lip*?'

It sounded so absurd Stevie wanted to smile, but her jaw felt locked – she'd been grinding her teeth in her sleep. Neil's weed hadn't helped either. She'd known it wouldn't help but Lara had insisted and Neil obliged with his best weed because he fancied Lara. A domino of disasters already and it wasn't even twelve p.m. 'Sorry, I know it doesn't make much sense.'

'Not really. But Stevie,' said Lara softly, 'I do know that you must do what *you* feel is right. Hell, it doesn't matter if it makes sense to me or anyone else.'

Stevie put her head in her hands, her chestnut hair falling forward in fuzzy chunks, as if it had been towel-dried after swimming. It struck her as somewhat ironic that here was Lara, radiant and plump-lipped after a sleepless night on a single bed in a wood-panelled room somewhere in Oxford being ravished by a horny twenty-two year old. And here was she, bride-to-be, coiled like a spring, with an unsightly skin disease breaking out over her décolletage and her heart and head locked in mortal combat. 'It's not that I don't love Jez, Lara. I do. But *something* isn't right, something's missing.' A hot tear scraped the side of her nose. 'Maybe I've misled us both. Maybe I so wanted it to be right, so wanted to put myself into a position where . . . where . . . Oh, I don't know. Christ, what a total mess.'

Lara, solemn-faced, spoke slowly. 'Do you think you've confused marriage with the baby stuff?'

'Maybe.' But there was no point in pretending that marriage had nothing to do with having a family. It was the natural progression: boyfriend, girlfriend; co-habitation; marriage; baby; more babies; grandbabies; old age; death. A conventional sequence. She wasn't a freak for wanting all that, was she?

'Don't cry, hon.' Lara stood up from the armchair and sat next to Stevie on the sofa. 'If this doesn't work out, for *whatever* reason, it doesn't mean you won't meet anyone else, or you won't have a baby for that matter. You're hardly over the hill.'

Stevie sniffed. No, she wasn't. If there were no problems, she probably had a good few years left, biologically speaking. Nonetheless, it still felt like a risky age, one which would define the rest of her life in a way that no previous age had done: a window of reproductive opportunity through which she could glimpse children, grandchildren, a life that was bigger and more significant than hers on its own would ever be.

'Please don't buy into that thirties panic thing,' said Lara, as if reading her thoughts. 'It's so not worth it. I could name you literally *hundreds* of women who got up the duff in their forties. Think of my sister's best friend, Lynne. Forty-three. My neighbour was thirty-nine or something. Then there's Liz Armitage. You know, the deputy editor of *Zip*? Forty-bloody-six!'

'Donor egg.'

'OK. Still. And then there's the IVF lot. Christ, you can't move in London parks for women old enough to be my mother pushing Bugaboos stuffed full of IVF triplets.'

Stevie smiled. Lara was right. She was being neurotic again.

'Anyway, babies aren't the be all and end all. Listen, I'm thirty-three years old. I have a better relationship with my newsagent than I did with my last boyfriend. In the last two years, none of my relationships have lasted longer than a few months. And you know what? I'm OK.'

'You get bored, Lara.' Stevie thought of the carousel of attractive young men who entered, then departed from Lara's bedroom. 'And there was Will, wasn't there? That was a proper relationship. You did yoga together for God's sake.'

'OK, thirteen months.' Lara frowned. 'But we wanted different things.'

'He wanted you, Lara,' mumbled Stevie, struggling to pay attention but grateful for a strand of conversation that took her away from the tumult in her own head.

'He wanted children. I didn't.' A flicker of hurt twitched beneath the muscles of Lara's jaw. 'It's not a crime to not want children.'

'It's not.' But she couldn't understand it. Since hitting thirty her urge for children seemed as natural and unavoidable as the urge to breathe.

'In some ways, not having that biological clock thing is an advantage.' Lara pulled her fawn cashmere shrug tight around her shoulders. 'It means I'm not going to compromise. What's the incentive? For me, dating and mating are unrelated. And I'm hardly going to sit around waiting for my prince with my legs crossed.'

A soft breeze blew into the living room through the open

garden doors, shaking the long green curtains, carrying happy spring scents. It made Stevie feel more wretched. This wasn't the time for maudlin introspection. She was upsetting the happy finale of her own story. All the best ones ended in marriage, like a Shakespeare comedy, order restored, a new spring promised. What the hell *was* she doing?

'I'm like one of those *Daily Mail* scare stories about predatory thirtysomething women,' continued Lara, trying to lighten the mood. 'You know, last month I slept with three different men in eight days.' She started a little at how this sounded, spoken out loud. 'Everyone tells me that I'll never meet a man in New York. The singles scene is worse than London. And I probably have a better chance of becoming Anna Wintour than I do of getting married.' Lara looked up and grinned impishly. 'But I wake up in the morning with a smile on my face. I am doing what I want to do. And you must do the same.'

'I know.' Stevie nodded, feeling that the crucial issue – whether to cancel the wedding and lose the only man who'd ever loved her enough to marry her – was getting lost here. She wasn't making a lifestyle choice. This was a matter of love and soul mates . . . or it should be and it wasn't and perhaps that was the problem.

'My mother was stuck in a small terraced house washing out terry nappies from the age of twenty-one. Can you *imagine*? I count myself lucky.'

'Hmmm.' Stevie wasn't so sure. She wasn't so sure that choices made things simpler. 'So what are you saying?'

'Don't get married for the wrong reasons.' Lara squeezed Stevie's hand. 'But then again, if you decide to sashay up the aisle, we'll forget we ever had this conversation. It's your call.' She reached for the plate of pastries on the floor. 'Croissant?'

'No thanks.' Stevie got up from the sofa and paced her parents' living room, stepping over the familiar landscape of her childhood: large African bowls and piles of her father's earmarked books on the floor. 'I feel so guilty, already. Hugely guilty. Apart from wrecking Jez's life, humiliating him so publicly, I'll ruin everything for everyone.' Stevie leaned against the wall, the plaster cold on her back, the weight of the house and the family crushing in.

'Stevie!' hollered her mother from the kitchen. 'Casanova on the phone.'

Stevie and Lara exchanged horrified glances. The normality of Jez being 'on the phone' was like a shot from a stun-gun. It suddenly seemed fantastical that Stevie could *think* of such a thing as cancelling the wedding when the arrangements had been made and her fiancé was on the phone beckoning her back to her safe, mostly happy relationship.

'What the *fuck* do I . . .' hissed Stevie desperately, frozen to the spot.

'Get him down here. Talk things through, hon. Go on . . .' Lara gave Stevie a hug then a little prod and set her in motion towards the kitchen, where Patti was sitting on a kitchen chair, knees drawn to her chest, telephone cradled between ear and shoulder.

'Don't worry, I've organised the music. The band rock!' (Patti had recently borrowed this expression from Neil, thus rendering it unusable overnight.) 'You'll love them . . . here she is.' Patti passed the phone over to her daughter and mouthed, 'In a very funny mood.' She turned Joan Baez down on her ancient cassette recorder and sat down at the table, picking up her Saturday morning task of shelling peas from the garden.

Stevie glared and said, 'Privacy?', but Patti didn't take the hint.

'Stevie, Stevie . . .' Jez sounded distraught.

'What's the matter? You sound terrible.'

Jez was choking on his words, trying to speak. Then he took a deep vibrato breath and composed himself. 'Stevie, Dad's dead.'

'Dead?' Stevie's hands tingled around the telephone receiver. Impossible.

'A heart attack at Sainsbury's, about an hour ago,' he said, as if he scarcely believed it himself. 'The freezer aisle. He died in the freezer aisle. Before the ambulance got there.'

'Oh God. Oh, I am *so* sorry. Oh, Jez . . .' Stevie didn't know what to say. It couldn't be. Not Colin. Not now. 'I can't believe it.'

'It feels like a sick joke.'

'Oh, Jez . . .'

'Come home.' Jez's normally booming voice was barely a whisper.

'I'll leave now. Hang in there.'

'Hurry up, babe.' Jez sniffed loudly. 'I need you. I really need you, right now.'

Eight

Despite being locked into his own bubble of grief, like a hamster in a plastic exercise ball, Jez Lewis couldn't help but notice the tall, lithe blonde scissoring past him on Westbourne Grove, coffee sloshing from a Starbucks cup as her shocking-green heels impacted the pavement. She had a small, hard bottom, perfectly moulded and separated by a pair of skinny dark jeans. Jez Lewis felt his inner caveman stir. The woman – late twenties? – slid her spare hand into her tight flat back pocket suggestively and he was almost overcome by a desire to bury himself in the woman's buttocks. That would take away the hurt, just a little bit. He watched the bottom for two more too-brief seconds as, swinging maddeningly from cheek to cheek, it turned into Chepstow Road. Jez continued his sad amble towards the less fashionable end of Bayswater, near Queensway, to his mansion flat on Moscow Road.

Perfect timing. Outside the flat, turning the key in the lock, was Stevie, tousle-haired, in baggy boyfriend jeans and one of her prissy vintage silk blouses. He wondered why he suddenly noticed her extra weight, today of all days. 'Stevie . . .'

Stevie turned, pulled him towards her. 'Jez, I'm so sorry.'

Jez fell into the reassuring dough of her arms. 'He's gone, Stevie. Dad's fucking well gone.'

'I know.' Stevie held his hand tight, guiding him up the stairs to their spacious two-bedroom flat. They stepped over Jez's twenty-four-pair trainer collection, which had been in the process of being edited when the news broke. Jez kicked a pair of black Pumas against the skirting board before collapsing on to the nubbly grey Conran sofa. Stevie sat next to him, pressing herself against his side, as if she could suck some of the hurt out of his body into hers. Jez slid down the sofa back, ruching his blue-checked short-sleeved shirt, and leaned his head into Stevie's lap, his thinning bald spot a pale pink disc beneath wavy strawberry-blond hair.

Stevie stroked his hair. His head felt unusually heavy on her knee, as if Jez was no longer using any muscles to support himself. His skin was even paler than usual, a Tube map of veins visible on his forehead.

'Why me? Why *my* dad?' mumbled Jez. 'He was only sixty-five.'

'Too young,' said Stevie, suddenly aware that she too could die at sixty-five and that meant she still had thirty-one years left, almost a life again. It seemed quite a long time. 'It's so sad.'

'But he ignored the doctor's advice last year, didn't he? Went on with his morning sherries and smearing butter two inches thick on his toast, like he was the only person in the world who mattered. But he'd never fucking listen to anyone, would he?' Jez dug thumb and index finger into the bridge of his nose and squeezed so hard it left a red welt.

'He had his ideas about how he wanted to live and he lived how he wanted. That's a good thing, I think,' said Stevie quietly, trying to massage some of the grief out of Jez's shoulders. The knots upset her more than his tears. She'd never felt them so tight or seen Jez – loud, laid-back Jez – so defeated and angry.

'Did he? Did he really? I don't think so. Mum and him . . . well, it was pretty fucking joyless.' Jez spat as he spoke.

'Maybe you never know what people get out of a relationship, not even your own parents. Look at mine,' she said, softly. 'You'd have thought they'd have divorced years ago.'

'Dad used to . . . God, I'm already in past tense . . . he used to turn off his hearing aid when she was twittering on. Just turned it off. Click. Silence. She never realised.' Jez shuddered, stuck his fist in his mouth and sobbed loudly, aware that something in him made him want to exaggerate his sobs, play up the drama. He released more of his weight on to Stevie's lap, which was now beginning to ache slightly. She stroked his hair silently. Jez started to cry louder.

It startled Stevie, seeing Jez – so big, so loud – crying like a baby. It wasn't right. She wanted to take away his pain but was unsure how to do it, so she offered him tea instead.

He looked uncertain, shook his head. 'No, I'll have a beer, pumpkin.'

Stevie wished he wouldn't call her pumpkin. But now was not the time to remind him. She started to lever herself up from the sofa to get a beer. Jez pushed her down, gently. He wasn't done.

'Stay with me. Don't leave, babe.' He settled back into her lap. 'You know the worst freaking bit? Dad so wanted to see me married. That's *all* he wanted. "I'm so happy you're finally settling down, son," was the last thing he said to me, like it was the first thing I'd ever done right. That was on Friday night, after . . . after . . .' Jez's throat locked, 'after fucking *Big Brother*, of all things. All he wanted, to see his son, his only son, married,' he repeated solemnly, allowing his father a portentous dignity he had never allowed him in life. Jez had never been entirely sure he liked his father, but it was clear now that he must have loved him. And this was a relief. By dying, his father had improved their relationship immeasurably.

'We should cancel, out of respect,' said Stevie, quietly. There was no way they could marry now. Rita would be in a state. It would be insensitive. Perhaps this was happening for a reason. In a cruel twist, had she shamefully got what she wished for? It made her feel dreadful.

'*Cancel?*' Jez craned his neck off her knee, its veins pulsing violently. 'Don't be ridiculous. I want to do something right. Even if he's gone.' He softened his voice, staring into the mid-distance. 'Mum also wants to bang the funeral out quickly and, you know, proceed as planned.'

Stevie felt her insides sink deeper and deeper until she had nothing left in her chest but an empty cavity and a fluttery feeling, like something was flying about in there, a trapped bird. 'It just . . .' she paused, wondering how hard she should push it, 'feels wrong, Jez.'

Jez brushed Stevie's cheek with his fingers. 'You're so sweet. But really, I want to go through with this. I do.' He clenched his fists with fresh resolve. 'Yes, I do. I think I'd just fucking crumble to pieces right now if I didn't have this wedding to focus on. You are my solace, pumpkin.'

Stevie bit her lip. She looked down at Jez, the man she was to marry, and saw him as he truly was at that moment: needy, grieving and, for what felt like the first time in their relationship, totally in need of her support and love. Did she really have it in her to destroy him completely?

'Hold me tight,' muttered Jez, as he wiped his wet nose on her jeans. 'Hold me while I sleep, that's all I ask.'

Stevie held Jez tight as a baby, as if the tightness of the embrace could arrest the moment somehow, prevent time from careering forward. Jez fell into a troubled doze, tears and snot drying and flaking in his blond moustache stubble. She tenderly stroked his hair away from his sweat-wet temples. The gesture made Jez smile in his sleep. As the smile faded, his lip stuck to his front tooth. Stevie looked away.

Nine

Behind a sheet of shimmering glass, seventy feet above lower Manhattan, Sebastian Compton-Pickett put down his ergonomic phone, relieved. Thank heavens for Absolutely.com. He knew he had to book something as a 'surprise' (as requested by Katy), but the blasted markets had been so unstable in the last two weeks – more terror alerts – and he hadn't been able to leave his desk until nine, let alone research holidays. That he'd become the kind of man who'd use a concierge company to arrange a 'romantic break' gave him a frisson of pleasure. It was a sign he had arrived. He was cash rich, time poor and, for the first time in his life, confident enough with women to secretly insult them.

Seb slid his black Amex back into his wallet with pale, fine-boned fingers. A thumb-sized picture of Katy beamed at him from a small pocket in the leather lip. Katy was a superb-looking woman, no doubt about that. She was clever, funny and hot in the sack. She had her own career, her own friends. But – as Mother had warned him – Katy was becoming neurotic.

Did she look fat? Did she look old? (Yes, sometimes.) It drove him loopy. She needed constant reassurance. Why wasn't she happy? He'd agreed to move in with her. But give an inch . . . She always wanted more. The woman had an agenda. He would marry, *if* and *when* he was ready. And the more she pushed, the bigger the blasted *if* grew. It was now writ across his brain, large as the letters on the Hollywood hills.

Of course, the geographical separation wasn't ideal. He'd allow her that. But New York was a terrific opportunity. He'd have been bonkers not to take a bite. Obviously, the decision had disturbed Katy, switched their roles round, he thought triumphantly, his chest expanding slightly beneath his white Turnbull & Asser shirt. In the past, she was the flighty one with the glamorous career, tales and travels. He was the gawky posh younger guy, twice turned away from the club Boujis for wearing a tie and generally radiating unhipness. As a banker, he was deemed a 'good catch', but one who was still only able to get a woman as good-looking as Katy once she'd hit her thirties. He hadn't realised how much he resented this dynamic until he got the New York contract and felt something within him lift.

Seb took a last bite of his Dean & De Luca brownie – a man needed energy in this city – and gazed out of his sparkling window. To his left was the scar of Ground Zero. It still made him jumpy so he quickly looked away. To the right, was . . . Oh, she was pretty. Nice bottom. And another. Crikey, these New York girls, even this far downtown, the girls were terrific. They were even more Katy-like than Katy. He never encountered the kind of tombstone-toothed country creatures his parents had lined up for him in Surrey. And, more importantly, these women were accessible. His accent opened many doors, his wallet opened the others. But boy did his balls ache. He hadn't had sex for twenty-three days.

Seb slipped on his suit jacket, and took the *elevator* – he loved using that word – dropping down the silvery artery of the building like a bead of mercury, through hundreds of offices where women in tight skirt suits crossed and uncrossed their legs. On the *sidewalk* – so Woody Allen, so cool – he put his arm out assertively to hail a yellow cab. (He'd quickly learned that the wavering apologetic English arm wasn't effective.) As they drove riotously, horn-blasting, up Broadway towards SoHo, he goose-bumped with antici-pation. The city seemed to be waiting for him, hungry to swallow him up. Resisting the urge to redirect the driver up to midtown and pop back quickly to his apartment for a quick self-administered release beneath the sheets, he rolled down the window and, with a sharp inhalation, consumed the American air.

In America – *Ama-ree-ka*, Seb repeated to himself silently – he was free of his past, his parents and his increasingly dull old public-school friends. No one here put him in social boxes. Well, only the English aristocrat box. They all seemed to think that because he'd been to Eton he lived in a stately home with a family crest and hot-and-cold running butlers rather than a six-bedroomed farmhouse in Surrey in need of a new roof. But the Americans' fantasy did no harm.

England felt scary now. Here he felt safe. The underclass were invisible, if they existed at all, and certainly not below 125th Street, his current city limit. (The old man had warned him about Harlem.) There were no hoards of threatening hooded youths blocking pavements. No junkies outside his apartment, as there were in Notting Hill, despite the fact that his mews house cost close to two million squid. But as he had explained to Brad in the adjacent office, money couldn't buy you much in London these days. It was a prerequisite, not a luxury. It was also a liability. It got you mugged. (And all the hoodies carried knives; he'd read about it in the *Evening*

Standard when he was last back.)

Here, Seb was free of Britain's acquisitive and angry society, as well as his increasingly unfathomable girlfriend. Shit, it was almost embarrassing, this urge to be American. Except embarrassment was an English thing, of course. To be stamped out. The taxi juddered to a stop on Prince Street. He tipped far more generously than he ever did in London.

Seb paused on the street, for a moment reverting back to being a hesitant Englishman, feeling slight, pale and vaguely undernourished compared to the beefy, confident Americans. Did it matter that he wasn't actually meeting anyone in SoHo? No, damn it. He'd been out to bars on his own a couple of times since arriving here. Both times he'd collided into women, two human lives randomly enriched, albeit temporarily. And when he told women about his job they laughed more readily and touched their hair a lot. After years of feeling puny and concerned about the girth of his member, here he felt like George Clooney, like he'd had a booster jab of testosterone. Yes, he would go to a bar. He had a strong sense that it was a day when exciting collisions were meant to happen.

As Seb crossed Prince Street, a commotion stopped him in his tracks. There, standing in the middle of the road, dressed like a tatty pastiche of an Upper-East-Side dame – all fur and leopard print and torn fluttering silk neck scarves – was a woman trying to direct traffic, cackling, one arm up, the other hand holding an irate honking cab back, dirty palm exposed. What on earth? It took a second or two for it to sink in. She was cuckoo. Of course. Seb winced, suddenly recalling his mad Aunt Gracie, not a dissimilar physical type who'd lived in a folly of a Scottish castle north of Perth and had descended from eccentricity – female lovers and otter breeding – into obesity and madness – lodgers and anti-hunt

68

campaigning – over a ten-year period. Seb swerved to avoid the mad woman, suddenly afraid of her long, thin painted fingernails, the way they knitted up his English childhood, here on a New York street. It took him a few seconds to feel like his new self again.

Brushing down his olive-green corduroy blazer, fringe flopping to one side of his narrow forehead, he turned into Mercer Street and strode, as manfully as possible, through the curtained doors of a boutique hotel. Inside, a pretty waitress wearing all black, a tray balanced on her upturned palm, smiled, exposing white American teeth. She had one of the neatest hand-span waists Seb had ever seen. From the bar he could peer into the restaurant area, where he was tantalised by identikit groups of attractive blonde women, forking salad, puncturing eggs Benedict, cell phones nestling by their elbows like pampered pets. He sat down on a low-level seat, smoothed his trousers, ordered the most New York drink he could think of – a Manhattan – and decided he would decorate his London home in the muted greys, browns and mushrooms of the sofas and curtains and carpet of the bar. He gulped his cocktail, wiped his mouth with the back of his hand (like De Niro) and waited for the latest instalment of his life to begin.

To his astonishment, it did. Three hours and twenty-five seconds later, his hot heavy balls expelled their salty contents into the open mouth of Charmaine, a twenty-two-year-old waitress/actress from Louisiana under the impression he was twenty-seventh in line to the throne.

Ten

Was sixteen bikinis too many? Could sixteen bikinis fit into a ten-day holiday? Katy perched on her bed's faux-fur throw and pondered. No, sixteen was fine. All eventualities covered.

Her tummy rumbled in a satisfying, reassuring way. It was four p.m. and she'd only eaten porridge for breakfast. If she could just resist the in-flight meals she'd be in fine shape by the time the plane landed. Where it would land, she had no idea. Seb had just told her to pack for 'somewhere sunny, darling'. The surprise element was making her a little anxious, thrillingly anxious, like the night before a big exam you knew you would excel in. Did he have the ring already?

To anaesthetise the butterflies, Katy reminded herself that she'd thought just the same thing a few months ago in Venice. No ring had materialised. Nothing mentioned. Instead they'd argued in St Mark's Square in a heated, public, rather Italian way, about where to eat lunch.

She lit a cigarette, flapped the smoke away so it wouldn't settle in her blow-dry. No, she couldn't help herself. And why should she? Imagining Katy Norris's nuptials – she reverted to the third person whenever she thought about marriage – was too delicious to resist. No rubbish wedding for Katy. No sandwiches curling at the edges and bad table wines and embarrassing relatives wielding video cameras. Oh no. Katy's guests were to be handpicked and would fall into three categories: family (edited, the mad scallies wouldn't be invited), friends (ditto) and contacts (a swell of attractive, well-connected Londoners who would then be beholden to invite her and Seb to their weddings and parties in the future).

The Smythson-printed invitation would be as thick as a small novel, its font – more Harvey Nics than provincial swirls – wittily detailing the wedding cast from flower fairy to matrons of honour (chosen according to bone structure so as not to outshine the bride's). The celebrations would tumble on for two or even three days, with guests (staggered, the best and earliest slots going to the most prized guests) arriving at the castle two days before the wedding for games and shooting and boating on the private lily-padded lake. Everyone would mingle, the hubbub of laughter rising like heat towards the battlements. The sun would shine, threading gold into her highlights (courtesy of Louise Galvin, done the day before). They would conceive a child on honeymoon, move to a large Georgian terrace in Primrose Hill. She'd give birth in a water pool at The Portland. The child would have a very small nose.

The front door slammed. Katy jumped.

'Hi.'

'Seb, sweetheart!' Katy ran towards the front door, freshly-pedicured bare feet slapping the smooth oak stairs. As she got to the bottom step, she felt herself slow down as if resisting the natural arc that would lead a girlfriend into the arms of her boyfriend. This was because Seb was not standing with his arms open. One arm was stiffly locked by his side, the other clawed around a small suitcase. It was a tiny gesture, this absence of open arms, but hurtful. 'Good flight?'

Seb raked his hand through his floppy gravy-brown hair.

'Dreadful. Some actress, can't think of her name, sitting next to me with her screaming baby. They shouldn't allow babies in Business.'

Katy brushed some invisible dust off Seb's angular shoulders, then reached for his hand. 'Hey . . .' She paused and realised she was waiting for a compliment. 'It's nice to have you back.'

'It's nice to be back,' he lied.

Katy kissed him.

Seb squeezed her hand, remembering his role. 'Pretty top. New?'

'Isn't it adorable? Temperley.'

'Right.'

They walked through to the sitting room, where a cathedral's worth of Jo Malone's Lime Basil & Mandarin candles had been burning for hours, scenting the flat in preparation for his arrival. They sat, about a foot apart, on their large cream B&B Italia sofa with its clever reclining back. He picked up a new feather-fringed cushion. 'Shopping again?'

Katy tossed her hair. 'There's this darling little interiors shop opened on All Saints Road.' He didn't reply. She popped a Rioja. 'How's New York?'

'Super. Yeah, super.' Seb's toes tensed in his shoes. He felt bad, but not as bad as he thought he would feel. Nevertheless, his second minor and *meaningless* infidelity (a crucial distinction) did make it difficult for him to meet Katy's eye. He switched on the television. *EastEnders*. He talked evasively through Dot Cotton.

'Are you still in love with New York?' Digging for intimacies, Katy curled forward on the sofa on all fours, her back arched, bottom in the air, trying to nuzzle his neck. 'You seem . . .'

'I *told* you.' Seb bent away from her and picked up a fistful of salted almonds from one of the chic concrete bowls Katy had arranged around the sitting room. 'New York's great.'

'Sorry. I thought . . .' Katy stared at him, expectantly, her all-fours pose crumpling to her knees. She picked up the fringed cushion, hugged it to her chest and sat back cross-legged. 'I've missed you, Seb.'

'Likewise.' Seb's hazel eyes, slightly hooded, inherited from his father's Welsh line, flicked quickly around the room. He nodded to her pile of suitcases. 'So you've managed to pack then?' He grinned, a slightly lopsided grin. 'Do you want me to jump up and down on your suitcase?'

'Later.' Katy laughed appreciatively. This was a popular, long-standing couples joke. Flagging it out now was a sign of solidarity. 'Shall I give you a lovely rub? I've got some essential oils that nail jet lag.'

He crossed one knee over the other, folded his arms. 'Don't fuss so, Katy.'

'Sorry.' Katy hugged the cushion tighter, trying to quell the queasy feeling of rejection. 'So, what do you fancy for supper? What can I get you?' This wasn't really a question. She'd been to the farmer's market especially to buy huge hunks of organic lamb and field-fresh vegetables. She liked to be in control of the household food.

'The Thai place on the Grove. I could eat a bloody horse.'

Katy considered protesting but decided better of it. She wanted to give Seb what he wanted. 'Good idea.'

Later, at The Green Orchid, Katy tried to guess the GI content of the entrées. 'I'm not that hungry, what do you recommend?' she said to make Seb feel manly.

Seb put on his new wire-framed Armani glasses to read the menu, flicking the laminated plastic sheet away from him dismissively, as if used to far more consequential venues in New York. 'You're never hungry.'

Katy looked up. That wasn't the correct response. The

73

evening continued with more incorrect responses, Seb being too fast, too critical. Then, as if catching himself at it, he would overcompensate a few moments later with a squeeze of the hand or an inappropriate clink of glasses. New York has taken it out of him, thought Katy. He needs to recuperate away from there. We need time to get used to being together again. Few couples could go three weeks without seeing each other and just click back into it.

After successfully managing to eat as little as possible of her meal, Katy felt a little happier by the time they got home. Seb, she noted, had a twinkle in his eye. He pressed his pale hand into the small of her back, sliding it down, lingering over the curve that delineated back from bottom. She wiggled into his palm. While she did not feel exactly rampaging herself, she was pleased to have confirmation of her own attractiveness.

Half an hour later, between newly washed Frette sheets Seb entered his girlfriend. He screwed his eyes shut and thought about the waitress in New York.

In her separate world, behind her false-lash extensions, Katy pressed play on a reliable lesbian fantasy. It didn't work. Distracted, she couldn't get into it. So she tried to imagine Seb's sperm swimming, tails wagging like tadpoles, up inside her, to fuse with her round pearl-like egg and . . . Gosh, that *did* work. Baby-making sex was sexy. She decided to push it, test the boundaries. How would he react? Maybe she'd underestimated him.

'Seb, darling . . .'

Seb groaned. 'Yeah?'

'I missed a pill.'

Seb stopped his sawing motion.

Katy felt a deflating feeling inside, a horrible looseness. He hadn't?

He had. Seb had shrunk and slipped out.

Eleven

'I am delighted to be able to declare you man and wife!' announced the registrar with well-practised jollity.

Jez pulled Stevie towards him for the kiss. In the pressure of the moment, his lips collided slightly due east of his intended destination, on the corner of Stevie's mouth, which was tightly shut as if trying to hold something in. A bubble of 'ahhs' erupted from the guests. Then clapping.

Stevie stood very still and smiled back at everyone, glassily. She couldn't quite believe she was here. She couldn't believe she'd gone through with it. Now was when the director walked into the picture and said, 'Cut'.

But it was not a director but Jez's mother Rita who was the first to pull Stevie aside, under the rim of her vast ribbon-bedecked straw hat and splutter a salivary, 'Welcome to the family,' in her ear. Then came her mother, a weeping vision in pleated green silk and enormous lumps of Navajo turquoise jewellery. Then Dad, looking bewildered. Neil. Poppy. Lara. Soon it felt like there were a hundred hands pawing her, dozens of painted lips pursed and poised to attach themselves to her like the suckers of a giant octopus.

But no Sam. Where was Sam? Wasn't he here? Suddenly

feeling unduly anxious – she really needed his seal of approval for some reason – she strained to spot him in the crowd, ducking beneath hats and feather headpieces and silk flowers, all the while thanking people and behaving in a suitable radiant bride-like fashion. Eventually, at the back of the room, standing next to a vase of peonies, she spotted Sam's tall, athletic frame, uneasy and angular in a slim-cut dark suit. His mother, Pearl, had a protective arm around his shoulders. He didn't look too happy. Stevie hoped he wasn't bored. The idea upset her.

Jez squeezed her hand. 'Come on, beautiful. This way.'

Stevie looked up. Oh. Jez was talking to his mother.

They took a few steps out of the registry office before Rita dropped back and Jez and Stevie walked out into the world alone, as man and wife, stopping to wave and smile at the crowd like Royals and shuffling forward hesitantly to the vintage Daimler which was waiting at the back of the Westgate shopping centre.

Patti tossed handfuls of confetti at her daughter trying, rather unsuccessfully, to imagine what her grandchild would look like. She hoped it wouldn't get Jez's pale skin. A liability in this new hot world with its peeling ozone layer.

Rita, taking refuge from Stevie's noisy unfathomable family in a huddle of cousins from Northampton, tossed handfuls of the confetti at her new daughter-in-law and resisted the urge to brush them off Jez's shoulders like dandruff. That was his wife's job now. She was a little doubtful whether Stevie was up to the task.

Lara tossed handfuls of the little paper discs at her best friend and thought Stevie deserved more. More certainty. More love. And, yes, the confetti should definitely have been rose petals, not paper.

Sam watched the confetti embed itself in Stevie's hair like

wind-blown blossom. He leaned back on some iron railings as though punched, letting the railings transmit their coolness through his Paul Smith suit. It occurred to him that this was quite possibly the worst day of his life.

The ancient Daimler, crippled by decades of servicing brides and grooms, had bad suspension. Every time it took a pothole, Stevie bounced up from the seat, her crystal-pinned do crunching against the cream padded-leather ceiling.

Jez laughed and pulled her towards him. He slid an arm up from her waist, below her armpit. 'Uh oh.'

Stevie explored the area with her fingers. Wet. God, deodorant wasn't working. 'I'm sweating like a pig. Nice.'

Jez offered tissues from his suit pocket, which he'd brought in case he cried during the ceremony. He hadn't.

Stevie folded the tissues into pads and wedged them beneath her armpits. It wasn't very romantic but she didn't want to arrive at the reception with blooming yellow stains.

'I'd say that went pretty well, wouldn't you, pumpkin?' asked Jez, sighing and staring intently out of the window as if the familiar sight of the Woodstock road was going to look different somehow, now he was a married man.

'It was lovely.' Stevie interlaced their fingers. Their hands looked different with rings on their wedding fingers. Older somehow. Like the hands of a friend's parents. 'The weather held.' The sun was behind cartoon cumulus clouds, blackening their bulk, outlining them in gold.

'Hmmm. And Neil managed the reading pretty well, *considering*.'

Stevie laughed. The Streets lyrics had been an unusual choice. But Neil meant every word. He had tears in his eyes, bless him. 'And weren't all those flower girls just so adorable?' There was something about toddlers with flowers in their hair that made her stomach lurch happily.

The newly married couple managed to dissect most of the minutiae of the registry service on the ten-minute drive home, from the triumph of Lara in her grey silk maid-of-honour dress to the poor taste of the registrar's brass buttoned *Dynasty*-style jacket, to the moment when Stevie had paused for a hideously long time and then stumbled over the 'I do'.

'You got the nerves bad, baby.' Jez scratched his neck, where his stiff never-worn-before shirt collar dug in and chafed him pink.

Yes, for a micro-second, there in front of all the people who had ever meant anything to her, Stevie had considered apologising and running away. But she hadn't. She had paused, quelled her fears and looked Jez in the eye. She had thought about her barely cold father-in-law, a family, a future. She had stood by her man. She had hoped for the best.

The Daimler slowed down on its approach to the Jonsons' road. Despite the directions from the town centre to north Oxford being what her father Chris called 'Alzheimer-proof', a scurrilous reference to some of the older relatives, many guests had managed to get lost in transit. Nonetheless, there were enough people jostling in the large square driveway to create a welcome. More confetti. More cheers. Stevie quickly removed the tissues from under her armpits and, not knowing where else to leave them, tucked them under the front seat of the car. A large collective whoop speech-bubbled up from the waiting guests as she stepped on to the gravel.

'*Go girl!*' shrieked Lara, arm in arm and can-can kicking with Becca and Louise, sending bits of gravel drive flying up with the confetti. Stevie had asked her to forget what she'd said before. And this was her forgetting.

Neil slapped his bongo, which had been set up near the front door, in a mock march. 'Mr and Mrs . . .' Neil trumpeted laconically and hit his bongo harder, 'Lewis!'

'*Woo-woo-woo!*' An arsenal of confetti again.

She laughed and waved and picked her way carefully to the balloon-strewn front door in her pale-gold Jimmy Choos, wondering if she was convincing anyone.

In the hall her father staggered about beneath a bundle of guests' coats, grinning over the mound of itchy pink bouclé wool. When he saw his daughter he started. How beautiful, how womanly she looked! How surprising it all was. Stevie would forever be ten years old in his eyes. She would always be the little girl who sat quietly in the garden with her sketchbook. The one who drew him pictures of dolphins and teapots. He still had them up in his study. 'Survived the ceremony OK, Stevie?'

'Just about, Dad.' She readjusted her dress, which kept swivelling around to her left side, a biased bias. 'I really need a drink.'

'Very sensible. Where are the waiters?' He glanced anxiously around the now-bustling hallway. 'Goodness, now where was I instructed to dump these, I wonder? Any idea, dear?'

Stevie shrugged. Where *were* the waiters? She looked around. Oh God. Yes, of course. The waiters were Neil's friends Toe and Toe's younger brother, Len, and Cosmic Kevin, stripped of their trainers and baggy skating trousers and trussed up in what looked like borrowed suits. She was oddly touched by the sight of them.

'Stevie!' Patti rushed towards Stevie, weaving between the crowd with her hair and beads and sleeves flapping, like a tropical green bird swerving to avoid hitting something midflight. She kissed her daughter, pulling her into her large bejewelled bosom, where cool outdoor air resided, trapped in the pleats.

'Mum!' said Stevie, as if reprimanding a hyperactive infant bridesmaid. 'Careful. My hair.'

'How I love you!' exuded Patti, loudly so that everyone could hear. She couldn't resist dramatic displays of familial emotion.

'Love you too, Mum.'

'Toe! Get my beautiful daughter a drink!' declared Patti, before launching off to crunch another relative into the cavern of her cleavage.

Stevie took a gulp of champagne and felt the effects straight away, probably because she hadn't eaten and hadn't slept properly the night before. Relatives she hadn't seen for years and others, from Jez's side of the family, who even she didn't know existed popped up on her left, her right, behind her, tapping her shoulder, pulling her elbow, congratulating her, telling her she was radiant, making jokes about the sound of pattering feet which would be heard in the none-too-distant future, no?

'Time to move through. This way!' Her father put on his loudest lecture voice. 'Come on, folks.'

Stevie tottered, almost carried by the swarm of guests like a coiffed actress in an old movie musical, through the large black-and-white tiled hall to the reception room at the back of the house. While small talking and smiling, she could see the work – endless streamers, balloons and banners – that her family had put in and she felt an overwhelming love for everyone. Well, at this precise moment in time, everyone but her new husband. He wasn't around to bestow even the smallest kiss. She hadn't seen him since departing from the Daimler. She looked around the crowded room. Where the hell was Jez?

'You do look very beautiful,' said a voice behind her right shoulder.

'Sam?' Stevie swivelled around, blushed. 'Oh, er, thanks.' He looked even more handsome than usual in a suit. 'You scrub up pretty well yourself.'

80

'Hitched without a hitch then?' he said, his normally loose, motile face clamped shut.

'I wouldn't speak too soon . . .' Stevie intended to refer to her mother's organisational abilities but something stopped her qualifying the sentence.

Sam's hand nervously searched for a jeans pocket that wasn't there. 'You look happy anyway.'

Stevie felt this to be a question, one she couldn't answer. She wouldn't call what she was feeling happiness exactly. It didn't have happiness's pure hum. This was something more mixed. 'Yeah.'

Sam and Stevie stood in silence for a few moments, unsaid conversations and observations surging back and forth between them like water sluicing a glass. Stevie shifted slightly, as much as she was able to within the confines of her tummy-flattening Spanx underwear. 'Well, here I am . . . married!'

Sam's mother Pearl, a well-rounded woman in her late fifties with flecked greenish-brown eyes and the smooth toffee-coloured skin of a thirty-year-old, saved them from awkwardness. '*Congratulations!*' Pearl grabbed her shoulders, kissed her wetly on both cheeks and gave her a little shake. '*Get* you honey! Gorgeous.'

'Get you, Pearl. Love the turban.'

Pearl's head was wrapped in a canary-yellow turban, like an exotic whipped ice-cream. She exuded scent and had the biggest, red lipsticked smile in the room. Pearl was the kind of person who made people feel safe and happy. Exuberant but tactful, she was the perfect wedding guest.

'Hey, I was just chatting to your lovely new mother-in-law, here . . . Where is she?' Pearl stepped aside, exposing a stiff, sober-looking Rita. 'There you are, honey! I apologise. I can hide crowds behind my backside.'

Rita stiffened further. Her frown seemed to be part of the architecture of her face, lines appearing to support whole planes of skin like structural girders. 'I felt someone had to explain to guests about the garden, you see, the way things have been done . . .' she said, eyeing Sam warily and tightening her grip on her handbag.

'The garden?' asked Stevie. 'I'm sorry. Explain. It's all been top secret. I've been exiled from the garden for the last two days.' She exchanged glances with Sam. What had her mother been up to this time?

'Honey, I *love* the garden. Don't apologise,' laughed Pearl.

'Well, it's not the kind of thing one normally finds at weddings,' added Rita. 'And, well, you know, with the weather turning and all that. Patti . . . you know Patti? Of course. Yes, well, she has a few funny—'

'Patti does things her own way,' nodded Pearl approvingly. She adored Patti. When Pearl moved into her Jericho Street home from the grittier confines of Ladbroke Grove that wet grey Christmas of 1985 it had been Patti who'd insisted she come round for mulled wine and rock-hard mince pies, Patti who'd looked after Sam when he had chicken pox and she couldn't take time off at Oxford University Press, Patti who wasn't afraid of affectionately sending her up by calling her 'sister'. This had been in sharp contrast to her other north Oxford neighbours, who'd marched with black women against apartheid but had never dreamed they might actually live near one, and were almost struck dumb by their keenness to say the right thing, terrified they might slip something into the conversation that could possibly be construed as recognition of her colour. Pearl laughed. 'She's one of a kind that woman. You must have been so pleased when you met her.'

Rita smiled stiffly. Was the woman joking?

'I hope when my Sam gets married,' Pearl patted her son's

arm, 'that the lucky lady has nice folks. It's like being blessed with a whole new family, isn't it? Wonderful.'

'Indeed,' managed Rita. 'Now, I don't suppose you've spotted just a plain cucumber sandwich have you? These exotic nibbles are playing havoc with my digestion.'

Pearl looked concerned. 'Oh dear. We can't have that. Let me help you find one.'

Stevie watched the large backsides of Pearl and Rita waddle off into the party, Pearl's high and round, Rita's flat and square in a pink-and-yellow skirt, resembling a slab of Battenberg cake. 'Sam, please tell me my mother is not presiding over a naked sauna in the garden.'

Sam laughed. 'I haven't checked it out yet.' He held out an arm. 'Dare we?'

'Oh, anything to escape Uncle Harry.' She should be looking for Jez again now, but was rather hoping he'd come and find her. Sloshing champagne from its flute – her hands had been trembling since the ceremony – Stevie followed Sam, admiring, once again, the way the planes of suit fabric fell from his strong shoulders. Was he more muscular since returning from Paris or was she more appreciative now that he was totally off-limits?

They walked to the French windows. Stevie pressed her hand to her mouth. 'You look first. I can't bear it.'

Sam pulled aside a wedge of curtain, adorned with ribbons and peacock feathers, raised his eyebrows and stepped back, hamming up mock-shock. 'No, I cannot do it justice.'

Laughing, gripping his arm, Stevie pulled aside the curtain. The large garden had been transformed into an Indian encampment, with six tepees, a clutch of small smoking bonfires and a lawn populated by strange carved wooden, vaguely tribal *objets*, which Stevie recognised from her mother's evening craft classes. Only one tepee was in its proper cone shape, the rest bent to the left or the right like wonky party hats. 'Oh my god, it's the battle of Wounded Knee!'

'Come on, let's check it out.' Sam unthinkingly grabbed Stevie's hand. The skin on skin contact startled both of them. Discreetly, at the right moment, so as to avoid offence and undue attention, their fingers loosened and their hands dropped apart.

Unplugging her heels from the lawn as she walked, trailed by a cone of yellow smoke from the bonfire, Stevie could hear drunken laughter bubbling up through the tepees – familiar hoots and giggles of friends – where the stick frames crossed at their peaks. L.K. Bennetts and cigarettes poked out from under the awnings. Pungent incense hit the nostrils when the wind changed direction. Neil chatted to his cousins around a bonfire, sucking on a roll-up. The cousins swayed slightly, unused to so much champagne so early in the day. Poppy's children ran around, high on cupcakes. Married friends cooed approvingly, as if welcoming her to an exclusive club. Pregnant friends shot her knowing smiles. At first Stevie felt uneasy. Then she had another glass of champagne. That smoothed the edges.

Stevie sighed. Yes, this was a rite of passage. This was her life marching forward. Perhaps all her doubts about Jez really were an immature resistance, a kind of brattish commitment phobia. This was her wedding. How strange. How wonderful. How *almost*-perfect (the groom's presence would help). Then it started to rain. Big, fat splodges of rain, like a power shower at full blast.

'Argh. Sam, save me!' laughed Stevie, bridging her hands over her head. 'My hair!'

'Your hair must be saved.' Sam grabbed Stevie and pulled her towards a tepee slightly apart from the others, to the left of the garden, beneath an apple tree. They ran towards it, rain shaking over Stevie's dress, leaving damp marks on the satin shaped like pressed flowers. Stevie yelped with exhilaration at the rain drops falling into her open, laughing mouth, Sam's hot brown hand guiding her, the strange heady mix of it all.

Sam pushed back a flap of the tepee and stepped aside as Stevie stooped and bent into the little triangular gap, careful not to catch her crystal hair adornments.

'Give me shelter . . .' she sang. Then stopped. 'Oh.'

Jez, crumpled in his dark wedding suit, hair frizzing in the moist air, sat cross-legged at the back of the tepee. Next to him was a pair of long luxurious legs. The legs belonged to Meg, an old university friend of Jez's. At the sight of Stevie, Meg sheepishly folded the legs beneath her.

'Hey, my darling missus,' said Jez, as if it were entirely normal that he should be hiding out during his wedding reception in a tepee with a leggy friend, whom Stevie had never much liked and had wanted to invite for the evening only. 'Sam? That you too, mate? Come in. It's pissing down out there.'

Stevie sat on the cushion, crossed her arms and legs across her satin-skiddy torso. The rain had brought a sudden chill to the ground. She shivered slightly. But Jez didn't put his arms out to her. He seemed jittery, bouncing his knees up and down erratically. The rain drummed hard and bonfire smoke curled beneath the canvas sides. Tension began to saturate the interior of the tepee, like gas leaking slowly and dangerously out of a canister.

'What a day, what a day,' repeated Jez. 'Hey, babe?' He sniffed loudly, rubbed his nose, sniffed again. 'Hey, babe? Good day, yeah?'

'Wonderful,' confirmed Stevie. Out of the corner of her eye she could see Sam's expression hardening, feel his body tense just by the way he wrapped his arms tighter around his bent legs. She followed his sightline.

To the right of Jez, on the floor, partly obscured by his knee, was a little mirror compact, Meg's presumably. The mirror was empty but beside it lay the tell-tale rolled-up twenty-pound note.

Stevie pointed to it. 'Jez, what's that?' But she knew.

Jez sniffed, rubbed his nose. 'Meg had some and, well . . . it's a *celebration*, pumpkin. Don't be uptight.'

Stevie's heart sank. Call her old fashioned, but wasn't there was something sordid and, yes, desperately unromantic about the groom taking cocaine on his wedding day? 'Jez . . . I . . . I don't think . . .'

Jez raked his strawberry-blond waves, exposing the receding hairline, his pale blue eyes unnaturally bright. 'My dad's just *died*. Give me a fucking break.'

Stevie was silent. There was no rebuke, was there?

Meg, also sniffing, nervously clicked open her pink sequinned clutch and drew out a cigarette. The lighter flame flickered up, flashing the inside of the tepee orange. Meg looked at Sam, coiling her hair in her fingers coquettishly. 'Sorry, I don't think we've met. I'm Meg.'

'Sam.'

Meg unleashed her ammunition, a long brown leg. 'Cigarette?'

'No thanks. Don't smoke.' Sam smiled politely and listened out for the rain. 'Congratulations, Jez.'

'Thanks, mate, thanks.' He snorted, laughing at his joke before he'd said it. 'Couldn't turn into a single ageing roué, could I?'

Stevie winced.

'It's great this marriage lark. You should try it sometime.' Jez sniffed.

86

'You're a lucky man,' said Sam, studying the rain through the gap in the tepee.

One drop of cold rain landed in the centre of Stevie's head, trickling down her scalp.

'Thought I'd pick her off the shelf. The world doesn't need another single woman in her thirties.' Jez looked at Stevie affectionately. 'Picked the best one, don't you reckon?'

Stevie felt herself contract. Jez was such an idiot when inebriated, his personality spilled over the edges. He became boorish. But he was rarely *this* bad. What was he thinking snorting marching powder at his *wedding*? Maybe it was his dad's death. Yes, of course. Grief spurted out sideways sometimes. It hurt those closest. Not surprisingly, Jez hadn't been himself since Colin died. And this, well, it was Meg's fault. Stevie shot Meg an acid glance. Not only had Meg been corrupting Jez with drugs, she was flirting with Sam, which annoyed her more than it ought, and exhaling clouds of grey smoke into the confined space which housed her bridal blow-dry.

Meg, catching Stevie's glare, felt she had to say something. 'Jez's been telling me about his . . . his dad,' she stuttered nervously. 'I'm so sorry, Stevie. It must be hard for you too.'

Stevie nodded, tried her best to smile. Perhaps she was being ungracious, paranoid. She had just *married* Jez for God's sake, she need not feel threatened.

Jez sniffed. 'Meg's been so sweet, Stevie. She lost her grandfather last week. She just gets it.'

And I don't? thought Stevie. 'I'm sorry, Meg.'

'It's the hardest fucking thing in the world, it's fucking hard, isn't it Meg?' continued Jez, talking to Meg's slim brown shin. 'If it weren't for Stevie . . .'

Meg made an 'ahh sweet' noise. Sam looked stony faced.

'The best thing, the best fucking thing, is knowing that this is the start of a new life.' He slapped his hand against his leg, the new wedding ring tailing light as it moved. 'A new life. I just can't wait for kids and the country and all that shit. I'm going to call my son Colin. Yeah, Colin.'

Over my dead body, thought Stevie. She felt herself sucked, against her will – she didn't want to feel like this – into one of those crystalline falling-out-of-love moments that everybody dreads. Not least on their wedding day. Could it be possible that the in-love chemicals and hormones that had insulated her from his faults in the past had evaporated and she was seeing him as he really was, *always* was? She swallowed hard and waited for the moment to pass, listening out for the rain. It stopped. Thank God. 'Jez, it's too smoky in here. I'm going to make my escape back to the house. Coming?'

Jez grinned his cheekiest schoolboy grin, brought out to appease annoyed women. 'I'll be with you in five.' He sniffed. 'Five, babe.'

Heart heavy, Stevie bent forward and poked her head out of the wet canvas door flap, water droplets sheering off the canvas and on to her cheeks like tears. 'Catch you in a bit then.'

She walked back to the house alone, flattening the wet green grass, not caring that the mud was spattering the hem of her wedding dress. At the sound of running feet, she turned. Sam. 'Hi there!' she said, as brightly as she could manage.

Sam touched her hand lightly. 'I'm sorry.'

Twelve

Poppy hitched up her dove-grey matron-of-honour dress above her now vast bump and squatted on the toilet. 'There *is* something up between Mum and Dad. You're right. I heard them last night when I went to the loo.'

'What did you hear? I've been dying to interrogate you all day.' Stevie sat on the green Lloyd Loom chair in the downstairs bathroom, opposite her younger sister. 'Tell me.'

'Why don't they ever shut that bedroom door? I mean, *pur-lease*.'

'Anyway?'

'They were arguing.' Poppy's brow furrowed. 'I got the tail-end. Mum said, "I've had enough . . ."'

'. . . Of this bloody marriage?' Stevie rolled her eyes.

'You've got it.'

Stevie fidgeted with her lip between her fingers. 'I suspected something was up. The atmosphere in the house has been deadly recently. Dad has withdrawn further into his shell like a scared mollusc. Mum is . . . well, more childish than ever, let's face it. And rather than talk directly, they speak through a third party – me, Neil or the cat.'

'You don't think it's just another wobble?' Poppy said

hopefully. 'I mean, they haven't had one for about five years. We must be due for a big one . . .'

'It's like living on a fault line.'

'Mum *is* dissatisfied, that much is clear.' Poppy paused thoughtfully. 'I can understand it though.'

'What?'

Poppy shrugged. 'The desire to shake free from the marital shackles.'

'Shackles? That's harsh.' It didn't make sense, thought Stevie. Poppy was not someone who craved freedom. She enjoyed the reassuring limitations of family life. In the highly unlikely scenario that Poppy had remained single she probably still would have adopted a marital domestic routine, all home-cooked dinners and nourishing Sunday walks and monogamy. 'Is everything OK with Piers?'

'Yes. Well, no. Piers is . . .'

'The perfect husband.'

Poppy smiled, tugging at the roll of toilet paper. 'Yeah, he really is.'

'And you have two perfect children, another on the way.'

'I do, I do.' Poppy pulled up her vast flesh-coloured pants, easing them over the bump. 'But I don't know . . . I've been feeling a kind of discontent recently. Oh, it doesn't matter, I shouldn't be bringing these things up on your wedding day . . .'

'What do you mean?' Stevie hated the thought of anything hurting her younger sister who, despite being a mother and living a far more grown-up life than she ever had and probably would, still retained a certain vulnerability.

'It's funny. Ridiculous really.' Poppy sighed, standing up and rearranging her dress. 'But I sometimes wonder what I could have achieved if I hadn't had the kids so early, got married so young. It's all a bit nineteen fifties, isn't it?'

'Don't be silly.'

'I'll never know how far I'd have got in my career. I'll never even know what it's like to go out with more than two men, not that I particularly want to. Silly really.' She laughed, fixing the fall of her vanilla-blonde hair into a silk flower clip. 'But I don't see that many of your friends settling down, Steve. I mean, why would they? What's the big attraction of kids and a mortgage when—'

'Well, muggins here is doing it.' How would Poppy have reacted if she'd confided her pre-wedding jitters about Jez? She normally would have told her but Colin had died so suddenly and there was so much to do and Poppy was in London with the kids . . . And now it was too late. She didn't want to rain on her own parade.

'I know I sound like a tactless beast – blame the pregnancy hormones – but you know me well enough, Steve.'

'But you've got what everyone wants, Poppy. You forget, I think.'

'Have I?' Poppy looked surprised. 'I suppose. But it's not perfect. We row. Quite a lot actually. Piers pisses me off. Yes, he's wonderful but he *really* pisses me off. He never makes the kids' packed lunches. He never gets them ready for bed. I know he works long hours, but just *once* would be nice. And then . . . then, maybe I would feel more romantic towards him. Maybe then I'd choose sex over sleep.'

'Oh, I see.' Stevie tried to imagine how her and Jez's sex life would endure pregnancy, let alone children. 'Listen. As your big sister I feel I should let you in on a secret.'

'What?'

'It's not what it's cracked up to be, you know, on the other side. As a single person I never felt like Carrie Bradshaw. More like one of those plump girls from the Dove ads channelling the spirit of Basil Fawlty. And yes, a career is great, to a point. But it's also a financial necessity for me. And you've brought two perfectly designed prototypes out into the world.' Stevie adjusted her diamante hair pins in the mirror. 'Hey, do you have any powder on you? My nose is taking on traffic-light duties here.'

'In that tote. Yes, the straw one.' Poppy stuck out a foot, swollen and suffering in a strappy kitten heel, and kicked the bag towards her sister. 'But look at someone like Lara. She's had such a rich life. So many . . .' She sighed. 'So many adventures. I'm not sure I've *ever* had an adventure. Not like that.'

'Lara's a romantic. An opportunistic romantic.' Stevie took her turn on the loo, easing down the wide elastic panels of her underwear, sighing with relief as her flesh flopped out of captivity.

'She's promiscuous?' Poppy tried to remove the disapproval from her voice. She was fond of Lara but, as she hadn't been single since she was twenty years old, struggled to understand Lara's world.

'Well, by our age you have to kiss a lot of frogs. She only goes through them because she has such high standards. She doesn't want to compromise.'

'Good luck to her, I suppose.' Poppy stroked her bump, checking her reflection.

'But why all these dark thoughts, Poppy?'

Poppy smiled. 'Oh, nothing really. It's just that life is short, isn't it? I see the kids growing up so fast. They grow out of their shoes every three months. Nothing stands still.'

Stevie held out her hand, a little tipsily, to her sister. 'I think I understand.'

Poppy giggled. 'Hey, don't worry, when you've got your own kids you'll understand.'

Stevie looked at the floor, the bits of broken parquet sticking up like fish scales brushed backwards. She knew this downstairs bathroom floor minutely. Funny that, how we know the floors of our childhood so well. 'Hey, help me up with this dress will you? I'm terrified of it.'

Poppy held up the folds of material as Stevie stood up from the toilet. She helped her readjust the bias. Unexpectedly, she leaned forward and kissed her sister on the cheek. 'I'm so happy for you, Stevie.'

Rat a tat tat.

'Girls? Are you in there?' hissed their mother. 'Let me in.' Stevie opened the door.

Patti parted her shiny raven hair away from the drama of her face like theatre curtains. 'Darlings, there has been a bit of an accident.'

Thirteen

In the taxi Seb sat close to the door, his thigh flat against its padded navy plastic. Katy inched closer and closer towards him, until they were both wedged against the left-hand side of the taxi, causing the cab floor to slope slightly to one side. The further he pulled from her, the greater his magnetism, Seb realised, smoothing down the cream cotton of his pale summer chinos. The myth was that you wooed women with roses and dinners and 'I love yous'. All crock. Women responded to distance. They responded to disinterest. They were like cats.

The worst thing a woman could do was look in need of a lifeboat, Seb mused as he stared out of the cab window. And that was Katy's undoing. He had loved her most when she had seemed to be *his* lifeboat, his ride out of the stifling City and his sexually frustrated twenties. Back then she had compelled and cowed him. And that's all any man wants, he decided, to be forced into submission by a woman, to feel that they are with someone who they don't deserve. He gazed out of the window, wishing that they could be tele-transported to Heathrow so he could skip on the traffic and Katy's endless, questioning chat.

*

A few hours later the plane accelerated down the runway with a loud trolley-rattling screech.

'Oh, is that noise normal?' asked Katy, reaching for Seb's hand and gripping it tightly, her head cocked on to his shoulder in a display of girlish nerves.

'You're not scared of flying,' noted Seb curtly. 'You never used to be.'

'No, I didn't, did I?' Was she that transparent? Yes, part of her wanted to arouse feelings of protectiveness in Seb. She may not have been scared of flying but she was scared of other things and the fears were all getting muddled up, projecting on to each other. 'All that airport security freaks me out.'

Seb massaged his angular shoulders into the seat, sprinkling it lightly with dandruff. 'You're never happy.'

A year ago, Katy would have pulled Seb up on this nasty comment. But her tongue was hiding. Her spirit was hiding. The words never came. Instead she smiled and dug her manicured fingers into her large brown Mulberry Roxy for Seb's favourite confectionery (bought surreptiously from Boots in Terminal Four). Seb took the red wine gum, without thanks, almost resentfully, as if he felt manipulated in some way by the offering of the sweet. Katy always wanted something in return.

Resisting committing to further eye contact, Seb stared at the map on the back of the seat in front of him – highlighting oddly irrelevant places, Banbury, Halifax, Godthab – and the arrow of plane, arching away from England, little England, like a pea from a shooter, out into the big wide world of his boyhood, the world of Willard Price and Phileas Fogg and strong-jawed men of derring-do and cosmopolitan, twenty-first-century global citizens. Like himself. Travelling between London and New York had given him a

95

totally different understanding of time and distance: he could wile away six hours at home with a bad TV programme, supper and a row, yet this was the amount of time it took to jump from one life to another, to hop across the Atlantic into a different self. It was extraordinary. Seb settled back in his seat, enjoying his own lack of fear at the jolting turbulence, his familiarity with the flying experience, pleased that row K was under the hostess duties of a pretty brunette with a bottom fat enough to bite. 37,000 feet now. Climbing, climbing. −44. Altitude 10,972 metres. Ah, it should be a fine flight. If only Katy would stop gabbing on.

Katy watched Seb sleep, his dry aeroplane breath lifting his wispy brown fringe slightly. It annoyed her that he was asleep, rather than excitedly discussing their coming holiday, hinting at the pleasures in store. But men were different, weren't they? There was absolutely no way she could sleep, not when her guts told her she was close, so *very* close, to the inevitable proposal. Would it happen over dinner? By the pool?

She chewed a squeaky unsalted almond, fast and hard, in the corner of her left cheek, avoiding the fillings on her right. Reminding herself that she had to appear in a bikini within hours, she resisted the waxy muffin and the cheese triangle, perfect and plastic in its polythene wrapper. Instead she picked at a bag of nuts, which she'd tucked into her handbag as a gastronomic displacement activity from the real business of lunch, and concentrated on drinking as much water as the beauty editors advised, which meant disturbing the snoring man to her left by venturing to the loo every fifteen minutes.

So, how would she answer him?

a) 'Yes.'

b) 'Can I think about it?'

c) 'You going to make me?'

d) 'Oh God, yes, Sebastian. Yes!'

e) 'I thought you'd never fucking ask.'

On reflection, Katy thought, A would be the chicest reply – less is more. E would be what she was actually thinking.

What would she be wearing?

a) Chloé mocha-brown bikini with shell ties

b) Allegra Hicks kaftan

c) Hotel towelling dressing gown

d) Nothing

Katy crunched into another almond. She would like it to be B, but feared she may have to resort to D.

What would their child look like?

a) Blonde, blue eyed, fine featured like her mother.

b) Cross between Elle Macpherson's adorable brown-eyed/blond boys and Brooklyn Beckham.

c) Like Sebastian but with large nose. Very large nose.

C reared up. At vulnerable moments, the sceptre of genetic inheritance haunted Katy because what she knew, and Seb didn't, was that their child would be extremely likely to inherit her nose, her *real* nose, her large and triangular-as-the-aeroplane-cheese nose, the genetic signature of the Norris family, passed from grandmother to mother to daughter like a monkey's-paw curse. It was a nose that Seb had never seen by virtue of the fact that she'd had it done six months before they'd met. Seb thought she'd escaped the Norris nose. In fact, her barely-bigger-than-a-nipple 'nosette', as he fondly called it, was the most-kissed body extremity in those first few heady weeks. She'd never quite felt brave enough to tell him it was not her nose, not exactly. That little white lie – no worse than knocking a few years off? – had not mattered at all then. But now they were looking at a future together, at marriage and babies, it did. Part of her felt that Seb had a moral right to know. After all, she didn't want him thinking it was another man's child.

Katy tossed three almonds into her mouth as a fresh wave of anxiety and hunger broke. Hell, what was she thinking? She must *stop* this daydreaming now. They were *not* married. Not yet. It could wait. She furrowed around in the seat pocket, picked up a glossy in-flight magazine and started reading an interview about Lindsay Lohan which she knew she'd forget within seconds of finishing the last sentence. The pilot put the seatbelt sign on and the plane began to bronco-buck. Then it dropped. Her hands, slippery with sweat, gripped the arm rests like claws. Gosh, how precarious it all was. Some deranged terrorist two rows behind could be putting a match to his shoe and she'd know nothing about it. This could be the last two minutes, or thirty seconds, of her life. And she wouldn't know.

She'd had these calamity crash thoughts before on previous flights but they hadn't bothered her. She would always reconcile herself with platitudes such as, 'If it's going to happen, it's going to happen . . .' or 'When your number's up . . .' But now she was thirty-six, the pathos of her death hit harder. How tragic to die without ever having had children, or marrying, or making a proper home for your own family. Yoga and good sex and Prada just wasn't enough in the end. Increasingly, Katy felt that everything that her twenties and most of her thirties represented was empty. Even her beauty. Ultimately, it would crack. It was no legacy.

The muffled sounds of Seb talking – at first the dribbly ramblings of a drunkard – rumbled her out of her morbidity. Her heart lightened a little. She missed Seb when he was asleep.

'Seb? You awake?'

Seb's head fell on to her shoulder, hard as a swing punch-bag. But his eyes remained shut and words, largely indecipherable, seemed to escape from his mouth rather than be projected.

'Sweetie, I think you might be talking in your sleep.'

Seb's hand smacked limply against his cheek, as if dozily trying to swat a fly. 'I'll have it on the rocks.'

Katy laughed and gazed at Seb adoringly. He was just like a little boy when he was like this. Just like a little boy.

'Sucked not stirred.'

Katy frowned. What?

'Charmaine, baby.'

The seatbelt around Seb's waist lifted an inch in response to the stiffening beneath the zipper of his trousers. Katy jolted, composed herself, smiled, as if playing to the audience of the seat back. Her tongue agitated in her mouth. No, no, it was nothing. It couldn't be. They'd got this far. The future was plotted out and no airborne hard-on would nudge it from its course.

Fourteen

Stevie noticed just in time. Meg had swapped the place names round on table number eight. The cheek of it! Meg was so *not* going to sit next to Sam. He was reserved for Lara. She swapped the name tags back to their original positions – on such things do destinies rest – and scanned the room for her friend.

Ah, there she was. Leaning against a ribbon-wrapped post, Lara, looking a bit like Scarlett Johansson – all curves and lips – was drinking champagne and eating mini iced cupcakes and giggling, no, flirting with, Toe, of all people. Meanwhile, Mr Eligible, Sam Flowers, was doing his duty chatting to a boring old aunt while check-out-my-shins Meg hovered nearby waiting for a break in the conversation in which to penetrate the group, cheese straw first. Lara! Christ, you can lead a horse to water . . .

'Please take your seats, folks!' shouted her father. 'Food is served.'

The buffet was impressive. Patti had organised a Moroccan-themed feast, provided by Café Maroc near the railway station: tagines of couscous, lamb skewers, humous, salads and spiced stewed beans. Guests queued drunkenly at a long low table – Patti's craft table covered with white cloth and scattered with daisies from the garden – and piled their plates high, laughing and joking. Table number eight was the first to sit down. Sam pulled out Lara's chair for her. Lara looked pleasantly surprised at the gentlemanly gesture, noted Stevie from her vantage point behind Aunty Annabel's large grey-feathered Philip Treacy hat. Yes, yes, she's definitely giving Sam more attention than the other romantic option Stevie had seated strategically on Lara's right, cousin Joseph (a bit tubby, in IT but nonetheless single and sane). Sam and Lara – their names go well together, she thought – were now a fork-width apart. Lara twiddled a blonde curl. Sam laughed, mirrored the hair twiddle. She wondered what was so funny.

Then Aunty Annabel reared up, hooting at a drunken joke. Her hat shivered and moved to obscure the view, leaving Stevie no option but pan in on her own table, the top table, a clash of genes and personalities and agendas sitting in a forced circle and all rather wishing they were sitting with their friends. To her right was her father, bristling at her mother and drinking too much. To her left was Jez, his knee banging against hers when he laughed, frequently and loudly. She noticed he hadn't eaten a thing.

Jez sniffed, leaned his bulk back in his chair, rotating his feet at his ankles, threading his fingers together then jumping forward again, unable to find a permanent position of repose. He pushed his plate away, not wanting to look at it, as if above the need for food right now. Quickened by coke but not overpowered by it, he was charismatic, surprising, tossing sharp controversial opinions into the conversation in between illustrative anecdotes about himself and jokes that popped with perfect pitch and timing. With a growing sense of triumph, Jez witnessed Stevie's family's mouths slacken in admiration at his playful verbosity, their amused silence. He was on fine form. Fuck yes, he thought, the drugs do work.

Jez loved Stevie's family. It was the kind of family, give or take the odd member, like Neil (who made him feel old), that Jez should have been born into, instead of the rather unremarkable tonally grey family life he'd experienced in Amersham. He once told Stevie that it surprised him that she wasn't more bohemian. But maybe that was why they got on so well. He was by nature bohemian, wasn't he? Stevie by nurture. They met in the middle somewhere. He turned to face his new wife. 'You're not still mad at me, pumpkin?'

Stevie was about to say, no. Then she saw that Jez had a rim of white powder on his left nostril. 'Oh my god, Jez. Wipe your nose, *now*.'

Jez attacked his nostrils with a napkin. But the more soothing effects of cocaine protected him from any feelings of embarrassment. 'Gone?' Deciding to combat Stevie's wrath with some good old-fashioned romance, Jez picked up her hand like an eighteenth-century courtier and lifted it delicately to his lips. He kissed it gently, playing to the gazes of the other guests. 'I hope you are having the best day of your life.'

Stevie tried to smile beatifically, aware that they were the day's theatre. 'Hmmm.' Being honest – and it was difficult, almost impossible, to be honest on one's wedding day – the day was panning out even worse than she'd feared. 'Is Rita OK?'

Jez had momentarily forgotten about his mother's accident. In fact he'd forgotten about his mother. He'd mentioned her, well his dad mostly (priority to the sentimental power of the newly dead), in his speech, but what with the cocaine and the exhilaration of the whole thing, it was hard to really focus on anyone but himself. Thank God he now had a wife, to counterbalance and buffer him and make his mother comfortable. 'Ma, how's the ankle holding up?'

Rita forced a tight smile. The painkillers had yet to kick in and her foot was freezing, sitting as it was in a plastic bucket filled with ice and Waitrose frozen organic *petits pois*. 'I fear it is not.'

Stevie looked concerned. 'Oh, Rita. I'm so sorry. You must blame Toe.' She smiled. 'Unfortunately named, considering, I know. Toe and Neil erected the tepees.'

Rita grimaced. 'No one's fault,' she lied. In fact she blamed Patti. 'Just one of those things.'

'You poor thing. Can I get you something more from the buffet?'

'I think I'll resist, dear.'

Suddenly, a commotion of silk, a clatter of metal and ruffle of air, like a parachutist landing. 'Folks!' cried Patti, sweeping her emerald-green embroidered shawl around her extravagantly as she stood up. 'Your attention, *pur-lease*.'

Stevie should have known her mother would have the last word. Dad's speech was ponderous and over-intellectual. He'd said something about how weddings could still be a symbol of light and happiness even in dreadful times of famine and war and terrorism, and quoted Ezra Pound. He hadn't quite struck the right note. But she eyed her mother just as warily. Alcohol and high spirits and the pressure of entertaining and proving herself to the more conservative relatives was a fiery party cocktail where her mother was concerned. (She was a liability at Christmas too.)

'*Folks*,' repeated Patti over the drunken hubbub, breaking wings of black hair from her face and tossing them back. Since her last – fifth – glass of champagne, she had begun to feel extremely nubile. Two of Jez's relatives had made a pass at her. She felt hot, in control, adored. 'As the woman of the

103

house . . .' A round of whoops. 'Thank you, thank you. As the woman of the house . . .'

'The master!' shouted someone from the back.

Chris shrugged in mock defeat.

Patti put her hand on his shoulder. 'Indeed. I'd like to welcome you to my home. And I want to welcome dear Jez and his delightful mother Rita into the family.' She raised a glass to Rita, who returned a constipated smile. 'Rita, it's been a pleasure getting to know you.' At this exact second, with five units of alcohol singing in her veins and an adoring audience, she meant it. 'And Jez . . . Well, Jez. What to say?'

Jez covered his face with his hands. His friends whooped some more.

'Thank you for making an honest woman out of my daughter! As Stevie's negligent mother I *know* that Jez has gone for Stevie for all the right reasons. I never taught her to cook, sew, or clean. She is fabulously domestically incapable!'

Stevie laughed. This was a long-running joke. She turned to exchange glances with Jez and was a little surprised to see a flicker of concern migrate across his forehead.

'She's her mother's daughter. She won't put up with any sloppy behaviour, dirty socks or demands. I fully expect her to be waited upon, adored and pampered!'

High-pitched whoops, cheers, 'Go Patti!' and napkin waving.

'We all know marriage can be trying at times,' a fleeting acid look at her husband felled his smile, 'so it's important to get it right. Stevie could have got married years ago . . .'

Could I? thought Stevie. Who on earth to?

'But no compromises for my Steve. She held out for someone who valued her as a person, as a creative, *sensual* woman . . .'

Oh God. Stevie felt her head incline towards her plate.

'And that's you, Jez.' Patti paused dramatically. 'Well, I hope so! If it's not, you'll have *me* to deal with.'

Jez laughed in short sharp spasms. Chris raised his eyebrows, knowing it wasn't an empty threat. Rita's eyes drilled into her frozen foot. The rest of the guests fell about laughing.

'I'm not going to bang on all night as The Soft Pebbles are ready . . .' Patti beamed and nodded to a group of ponytailed grey-bearded musicians shaped like pints of Guinness, who were tuning their guitars and smoking roll-ups in the corner of the marquee. 'But I'd like you to raise your glasses for one last toast to Jez's late father, Colin, who we all miss *dreadfully*.' Patti smiled at Rita a little apologetically. She could never get the tone quite right. 'And, of course, a toast to my wonderful daughter and her lucky, lucky husband Jez. Here's to their marriage and, of course, the sound of pattering feet!'

The guests stood up, drunken arms extended in public salute. Then a stormy eruption of noise and clapping. As the noise got louder and louder, Stevie slid down her chair, blushing, laughing, embarrassed. Beneath the table she twisted her wedding ring round and round her finger, noticing, for the first time, that it didn't quite fit.

Fifteen

The first dance – Dolly Parton's 'Islands in the Stream', Stevie's choice – went too quickly. The crowd cheered. Her mother sobbed. Lara whooped. Jez, still clumsy with narcotic kinetic energy, stepped on her toes twice. But none of this mattered. All that mattered was that for about three and a half minutes, soaked in the familiar homey smell of Jez's arms, Stevie lost herself. This was what a wedding is all about, she thought. This was a *good* omen.

Then the record jumped, skidded and stopped.

The DJ, a lanky unemployed friend of Neil's, looked up from the decks and fumbled with its buttons as casually as he could while breaking out in an uncool sweat. Balancing a new disc on his shaky finger, he lowered it to the decks. The tempo changed and Dolly Parton and the last dance and that ecstatic bridal moment evaporated into the sweaty pulse of a crowd booty-shaking to Fatboy Slim. The DJ punched the air. Stevie's smile flatlined.

'Relax.' Jez shouted into her ear. 'You're mine now.'

She laughed the comment away, noticing as she did that one of her cushioned plastic in-sole pads – as recommended by Lara to stop 'stiletto-ache' – had shunted out of the sandal and was lapping at the floor like a tongue. She bent down to adjust it. Jez used the opportunity to swivel thirty degrees, away from her, to accommodate Meg, who was shaking the shiny lengths of her otter-like body, spilling champagne from her glass. And as Stevie's spirits had soared a few moments ago, now they hurtled downwards.

'Whoa! Go Stevie!' Her drunken father, all rangy limbs and flapping grey hair, his index fingers cocked like pistols, thrust her back into a bridal this-is-the-best-day-of-my-life mode with a grab and a twirl, pulling her back and forth making her dress fly up. His spectacles clouding like glasses of Pernod, he began to whoop drunkenly as if the song had tossed him back thirty years to the Trinity College ball. (Stevie made a mental note to embarrass her father about it at a later date.) Chris flipped his daughter to Patti, who juddered semi-erotically – the only way she knew how to dance – arms in a sixties weave above her head, bosoms thrusting against the confines of her dress's neckline, while her father clapped along, watching.

It struck Stevie that her parents were not dancing with each other but using her like a morris dancer's baton so they could circle around each other without touching. After a particularly vigorous spin from her father, Stevie was propelled on a north-western trajectory across the skiddy dance floor, bumping past Meg, then Lara, and finally flying into the seeping armpits of Uncle Harry. Engorged with alcohol and wheezing loudly, he appeared to be in danger of expiring any second, and indeed it was the mid-air collapse of Uncle Harry's unexpected Scottish dance move – an extravagant calf flick – and the subsequent flabby load he pressed upon her shoulders as he tried to right himself, that caused one of her Jimmy Choos to curl beneath the other and slip on a puddle of Meg's spilled champagne. Arms outstretched, unable to save herself, Stevie skydived floor-wards and landed in a heap, like a binge drinker on a night out in a provincial town.

Floor, swallow me up, she thought, her knees stinging.

Sam spotted the accident faster than anyone else, rushed over, picked her up gently and brushed down her dress. 'Nothing broken?'

'My shoe! Is my shoe OK?'

Sam squatted down to inspect Stevie's shoe, his hands gently holding the neat turn of her ankle. 'The Choo has survived,' he said solemnly. 'No need for the last rites.'

Stevie smiled, rubbing her leg.

'May I tempt you with a chair?'

'Thanks.' Stevie hooped one arm into the triangular gateway created by Sam's and pretended to laugh uproariously in order to reassure concerned guests and deflect interfering well-wishers. They sat down on two silver opera-style chairs. Her eyes zig-zagged across the dance floor. She wondered where Jez was. She imagined that Sam was thinking the same thing. A bride did not want pity on her wedding day. She broke the spell. 'Lara's great, isn't she?'

One side of Sam's full mouth lifted and parted coyly, exposing white teeth. He fiddled with a cufflink. 'Yeah, yeah. She's cool.'

'You two going to meet up in New York?'

Sam grinned. 'Sure you want us to?'

Stevie blushed slightly, bristling at the possible insinuation. 'Of course. Why wouldn't I?'

Sam picked up a party popper from the table and rotated its barrel over and over as if it were an object of great fascination. 'Lara seems like a great girl.' He coughed, then asked dutifully, 'Has she got a boyfriend?'

'Recently sacked one.'

'I imagine she doesn't suffer fools.'

'Nope.'

He shrugged. 'That counts me out then.'

Stevie nudged him with her right elbow. 'I think you'd be great together.'

Sam looked doubtful. 'Really?'

'Never a dull moment with Lara. If I were a man . . . well, she's clever, funny, feisty . . .' As the adjectives loosened from her tongue, Stevie got one of those insights it is possible to have about other people's relationships (never her own): men do not necessarily want clever, funny and feisty. She tried to feminise the sale. 'She's a lot of fun, big heart.'

Sam bent forward now, elbows on knees, square jaw resting on his hands. He studied Stevie intently. 'Foxy too.'

Stevie felt something drop inside. 'Never short of admirers.'

Sam fixed her with amused eyes, dark irises flashing blue in the disco-box lighting. 'Problem is, you know me, Stevie, I always end up with the most dysfunctional one in the room.'

'Have I introduced you to Meg?'

'Very funny.'

Stevie curled a foot around the chair leg. 'I never met Camille though. Nice?'

'Sweet, really sweet.'

'You make her sound like a *petit four*. Why did you split?'

'Oh, you know, it wasn't right. She wanted to get married, stay in Paris. And, well, I realised that I couldn't offer her that, so we split.' He rolled his eyes. 'If I had to distil the relationship down to two sentences.'

'Oh. Don't you want to get married?' She hadn't yet got Sam worked out. Despite the length of time they'd known each other, parts of him remained a mystery.

'Man,' Sam kicked his legs out in front of him, laughing,

'you sound like Mum. Yes, of course, *one* day. I'd love a big family. But it has to be the right person. Sadly Camille wasn't the right person.'

As a man you'll have more time to find that person too, she almost added, then thought better of it.

'I look around my mates and wonder.' Sam exhaled loudly. 'You know, they reach the age of thirty-three or whatever and start running down the aisle at break-neck speed, forgetting it's about wanting to wake up with that same person forty years down the line.'

'Like Katy, Katy Norris?'

Sam winced and took a sip from an unclaimed glass of champagne. 'What do you think?'

Stevie raised an eyebrow. 'She wanted to "settle" – horrible word – pretty badly, didn't she? I remember you telling me.' She studied Sam for his reaction. Pained. Good.

'I think it was beginning to dawn on her that there was more to life than her career, that she wasn't getting any younger.'

Stevie wondered if, in recent months, she had behaved a little like Katy Norris. The idea horrified her. And yet, and yet . . . Some kind of switch had clicked when she was thirty-two. And yes, she'd definitely tried harder to 'work at her relationship' with Jez. In her mid-twenties she'd probably have just caused a huge scene and got herself chucked, thus shrugging away responsibility for ending it. But with Jez, well, she'd put up with more than she had done when young. 'I'm sure Katy will have frog-marched at least one man up the aisle by now and has a brood of children sired by a captain of industry.'

'Yeah.' Sam casually twiddled a curl with his left hand, leaning back into the chair. 'She likes a few noughts behind a name.' He put on a Jamaican accent. 'Katy Norris didn't want no poor black snapper husband. I got off lightly. Just got to act as thirtysomething counsellor for a couple of months while she planned her next move.'

Was it just sex then? What had he seen in Katy? At least Sam didn't seem at all bothered about being crossed off her list of potential husbands. After a few moments of awkward silence, Sam turned his face away from the dance floor to face her. It was like being followed by a spotlight.

'Stevie . . .' He looked shy, hesitant all of a sudden. 'Do you ever wonder, what would have happened, if Katy . . .'

Stevie started. 'Er, no, not really,' she said quickly.

'Oh,' he mumbled, embarrassed. 'Sorry.'

They simultaneously swung their faces back towards the dance floor, now a little society unto itself, delineated by the speakers at one end and the stationary stand-still-and-wiggle dancers, mostly the older relatives, at the other. The exuberant, young and female were the twirling nodes around which the male guests journeyed, shuffling between swinging hips and long stamping legs in high-heels, while Jez's over-dressed aunts from the Midlands stormed across the floor like vast sequinned galleons. Other members of the happy couple's collective family were locked in stiff mock-polkas, as if to signal to everyone else on the floor (especially the more attractive non-family members) that their choice of dancing partner was purely sealed by familial duty. Susie from number forty was wrestling Stevie's father into her thick hungry arms while her mother glared on, increasingly territorial. And Jez? Where was Jez? Oh, Jez was heading their way, lurching towards them, his hair dishevelled, tie missing, long stubs of ash from his glowing cigarette dropping to the parquet dance floor.

'Guys!' Jez drunkenly boomed, as if competing with a loud speaker. '*Whassup?*'

Stevie's heart sunk. He was pissed. 'I fell over . . .'

'Break a leg.' Jez laughed, pressed his hand to his mouth. His face was covered in red boozy blotches.

Stevie grimaced. Jez was obviously not in a good way. He was not coping with his father's death. If only she could explain this to Sam. 'Sit down. Here . . .' She handed him a glass of water. 'Drink.'

Jez collapsed into the seat next to Stevie, his legs stretched out into a wide V. He glugged down the water, which left him with a crescent of shimmering liquid on his upper lip, like a transfer of a smile. He dropped his head on to Stevie's shoulder. 'I'm exhausted,' he slurred. 'Spent.'

Stevie squeezed his hand. 'I know. It's OK.'

'I miss Dad, Stevie. I want him to be here.' Jez's eyes filled with tears.

Stevie kissed him. Poor Jez. God, she was a cow – not thinking, not being there enough. 'I know, I know.' She kissed his forehead. It was sweaty but strangely cold.

'Dad would be fucking proud, don't you reckon?'

Stevie nodded. 'He would.'

'Right.' Sam, who had been waiting for a break in the conversation in order to make a sharp exit, stood up to leave. 'See you two later.'

Jez's head righted itself vertical. 'Don't feel you have to make an excuse on my account, mate.'

There was a quick, easily missed constriction of muscles in Sam's cheek. But he remained silent, just smiled.

'See you later, Sam,' said Stevie.

'Hey, why don't *I* go? Don't wanna interrupt anything . . .' snorted Jez suddenly, eyes a weak red, like watered wine, the soft vulnerable man of two seconds ago now gone. 'Don't wanna ruin any cosy-cosy chat. But, have to hand it to you, mate, you're doing a better job looking after my missus. Can I take lessons?'

Sam's shoulders squared up. 'That would be preaching to the converted, wouldn't it?'

'Don't be so fucking smarmy.'

'Please!' Stevie, horrified and suddenly very sober, shook Jez's arm. What on earth had got into him? It was the cocaine talking. 'Don't be so bloody embarrassing. I'm sorry, Sam. Jez has had a hard few days, with his dad and everything.'

'And I don't want to make it any harder. I'm really sorry if I've caused a problem.' Sam turned on his heel and walked quickly away, the blue flashing strobe catching the angry muscularity of his back beneath the cloth of his suit.

'Tosser,' said Jez, head falling hard on to Stevie's shoulder.

Sixteen

Jez managed to keep the honeymoon location secret until they arrived at Heathrow and he installed Stevie in a check-in queue beneath the Thai Airways sign, while he stumbled off to find calories and caffeine to lift him from the living death of his hangover.

After a three-hour wait they were both safely planted in their cramped mid-aisle seats. Better tempered now that he had no requirement to hold his skeleton vertical, Jez slumped and exhaled a coffee-scented sigh of relief. He apologised to Stevie for being so crap and told her he'd be better company if he slept. Stevie agreed. Jez held her hand, his grip loosening as he swam into a deep, starless sleep.

Many hours later, Stevie was still watching the sky, charting its impossible change from grey to smeared blood-orange red, thinking about Sam: how Sam had come out to Thailand, then Sri Lanka, as a volunteer that sad, grim January after the tsunami when it had seemed like half the world had been washed away. How long had he stayed? Days? Weeks? She wasn't sure.

Stevie squirted her face with a mist of mineral-water spray. As Jez slept, to kill time, she attempted to sketch the duvet of clouds beneath the plane in the notebook Sam had given her with the smudgy charcoal pencils. But she couldn't do the sky justice. Her mind was elsewhere. Would he be in New York by now? Would Lara? No point in doing her own head in by dwelling on the loss of her two friends to America. Change the record, Stevie. She swigged her bottled water, felt its cool passage slick her hot dry throat, and wondered if they were the only honeymooners on the flight. Unlikely. She wondered whether they were the only honeymooners who hadn't consummated their marriage. Likely. Jez had been too wrecked, the check-in time too early.

'Welcome to Phuket.' A pretty Thai woman in a pale-pink skirt suit and corporate flecked-silk neck scarf bowed quickly, palms together, smile neat and impenetrable. She ushered them through the gleaming airport, with its gunned patrols and, thought Stevie, faint echoes of cautionary drug trafficking films, towards the taxi rank. 'We will take your bags, thank you. Our private bus is this way. It will passage you to the Blue Blossom. Thank you very much, sir.'

Jez glanced at Stevie for approval. She smiled and Jez looked relieved. He was nervous about the honeymoon. He knew she could be over-sensitive and annoyingly right-on about certain things – always quite hard to predict what exactly, until he'd put his foot in it – but felt that a decent enough amount of time had passed since the tsunami to holiday here. Besides, the best way to support a nation in crisis is by spending money there, he'd rationalised to Stevie earlier. What he hadn't mentioned, however, was that he'd got a whopping great discount on the holiday from YR-Brand clients and that it was this, rather than altruism, that had decided the destination. But luxury costs. He wanted her to have the best, just for once. He didn't share her love of authentic accommodation, i.e. cheap and not temperature-controlled. They'd done enough of that. They were married now. Married people did things properly.

'Blimey.' Jez's mouth dropped as he stared out of the minibus window, his hangover pickling in the tropical heat. He'd dozed off again on the car journey but was now awake and excited. He pointed his finger on the glass, leaving a milky smudge. 'Check it out, babe!'

Emerging through perfectly coiffed palm trees and foliage, ablaze with orange flowers, was a square oriental building, all open-air columns and gleaming marble, with a low red roof that turned up at the corners like a handkerchief.

Stevie stepped out of the bus into a wall of wet heat. Goodness. She'd never been anywhere quite so posh before. It was almost overwhelmingly luxurious. Bleary eyed and a little uncertain as to what to do next, she followed Jez as he strode nonchalantly through the lobby, scratching the small of his back above the waistband of his three-quarter-length trousers.

The receptionist was so beautiful Stevie wondered if she were a man. But the hands that offered her a complimentary hibiscus flower, pink and fragrant, its stalk wound with green silk ribbon, were too fine boned. Another Thai woman crept up – silent on her silk flip-flops – offering small bowls of steaming scented jasmine tea and a list of all the spa treatments. She politely gestured for them to take a seat.

'Fabulous,' sighed Stevie, leaning tentatively into the snowy-linen and gold-silk cushions on a lobby sofa, keeping her arms pressed to her sides. She felt like she smelled of plane and wished she hadn't worn her sleeveless black Zara dress as its linen was now crumpled like a newspaper. 'This is amazing, Jez.'

'Celebtastic, isn't it?' Jez grinned, his shoulders dropped

116

and he widened the gap between his sprawled legs. 'Glad it suits.' He squeezed her knee. 'I want you to be happy.'

'I know.' Stevie smiled, touched. Jez would push the boat out for her, she knew that. He excelled at the big romantic gestures. It suited the largesse of his personality. She'd always loved him for that. 'Oh, look, ahh . . .'

Rectangular fish ponds full of tropical fish, long and colourful as ties, were cut into the floor of the lobby with mounds of pale grey pebbles artfully placed around the sides. Palms, perky with care, sat perfectly postured, their trunks in tasteful black pots. Stevie noticed tiny birds, orange and green, dart around the lobby, quick as fireworks. OK. She was seduced.

And the other guests? It seemed that they came two by two. It was a resort of couples: the slim girl in the sarong on the arm of the guy with the huge video camera in chinos, asking about tours of the island at the front desk; the shy Japanese couple sitting a foot apart on the adjacent sofa, reading magazines; the loved-up sunburned British couple, overpoweringly underdressed in their thong swimwear and expensive hippy jewellery.

'I know it's not a typical Stevie kind of place,' Jez burst out, scratching the fuzz of fair hairs on his forearm, 'but I thought we deserved some luxury after the last few fucking nightmare weeks. I know I've been a bit of a bear with a sore head . . . well, a complete fucking pain in the arse, actually. And I'm sorry, Stevie. I'm really sorry.'

Stevie smiled, feeling tender. 'You're forgiven.'

Jez grinned. 'And I thought you'd prefer to relax, you know, rather than go on some mad trip to the Galapagos islands or something.'

Stevie swallowed the undeniable knowledge that she would have *much* preferred a trip to the Galapagos islands. 'Don't worry, it's perfect.'

Jez shrugged a heavy thick arm around her shoulders. 'You see, I already know you better than you know yourself and we've only been married a day. Hey . . .' He looked up. 'Oh right, this is us. Come on, pumpkin.'

They held hands as they walked through the hub of the Blue Blossom, following the exquisite Thai lady along walkways sandwiched between low lily-padded pools, passing three restaurants, all with slightly different functions – as signified by the variation of chairs, from upholstered high-backed to light-cane buckets, and all with varying brochure-worthy views. A few people – all couples – picked at food, slurped chilled French white wine with their Italian salads and spoke sparingly in hushed tones. Bird song was only just audible over the light eastern musak tinkling down from invisible speakers. Stevie felt a strange heaviness in her feet, as if the flight had suddenly caught up with her. Was it meant to be morning or night? The transition, like that of girlfriend to wife, was fundamental but strangely arbitrary.

'Love it!' Jez nudged Stevie. 'Check out that pool.'

The show-piece pool was a huge ring of water, like her blue garter. It was divided into zones: an Eden-styled loop with palms and flowers; a stretch with bridges and tumbling white-peaked waves; a waterfall, a sheet of bubbles; a jacuzzi area of violently spurting jets against which tanned men with white teeth massaged their backs. Slim brown bodies arranged themselves into different stomach-flattering positions on the pool terrace's loungers. Thighs glistened. Cocktails clinked. Suncream lids clicked. All the bodies ignored each other and marked out their space with little cluttered tables and low walls of backs, and yet chose to position their loungers within a towel's throw away from one another, facing the water, as if jostling for space at an outdoor show. Stevie wondered what it was about the sight of these dozens of tanned post-coital couples that made her want to run away to wet, muddy hills, preferably somewhere in North Wales, safely clad in an anorak and walking boots.

'If you would just like to step into the resortmobile, sir, it will take you to your villa,' fluttered the Thai lady, who'd been showing them around. 'Thank you.'

Stevie clambered into a glorified electric golf cart and tried not to feel a little irritated that she'd become invisible in the company of 'sir'. She was in paradise. She must enjoy it.

After a few minutes' buzzing along in the cart it struck her that the resort resembled nothing so much as a vast golf course, all manicured slopes and grass as stiff and green as AstroTurf. Punctuating the luminous lawns were small red modern villas, with eastern detailing like something one might see at the Ideal Home Show: Barratt homes does oriental. It was also eerily empty, apart from the maids and cleaners dressed in traditional black and white but with large paddy field-style straw hats, presumably to give cultural flavour. They stood outside villas, banging down rugs or hauling white sacks of laundry behind them like ants with egg sacs. As the resortmobile lurched past, they'd stop their activity and stand to attention quickly and wave and smile as if their job depended on it, which it probably did. Stevie waved back, apologetically.

The cart stopped with a jolt outside a villa that looked the same as all the other villas. A short man with gleaming petrol-black hair scuttled out: another greeter, with more restricted English. He escorted them into the house, smiling and nodding and offering hard-to-decipher chat about keys and post boxes. He would, they gathered, be their personal 'resort facilitator', should they need any facilitating. The key crunched in the lock as he turned it.

Gosh, it was cold inside. Freezing. The air conditioning

was excessive. Stevie folded her arms tight across her chest and gazed around her. White slithers of sunlight thrummed through the blinds, casting stripes of shadow across the creamy wood floor and the glorious, very low bed, mountainous with taupe silk cushions. The facilitator proudly pointed to the hi-tech details – flat-screen television, stereo, laptop ports – discreetly hidden among the acres of taupe and limestone. Decorative Buddhas were dotted about the room, crosslegged on horizontal surfaces. Two high-backed chairs which looked like they'd never been sat on and a table – thick, dark wood, Thai in style and covered with coffee-table books and Blue Blossom notepaper – fused together to create a neat literary-lite zone opposite the terrace. Stevie struggled to visualise herself sitting at the table.

'Oh, fuck me.' Jez opened the doors on to the terrace at the back of the villa, his wide back silhouetted against the sunshine. 'We can have some fun with this, babe.'

Stevie peeked through the glass doors: a large humming jacuzzi, a deep square trough of a bath scattered with pink petals, set within a small well-tended garden with just enough shrubs to ensure privacy from the neighbours but not enough to scare with its potential for housing exotic wildlife. For a fleeting moment, she had the sense that she shouldn't be here, that Jez should be with the kind of woman who lay around the swimming pool, burnished and lithe, or someone like the women who tripped across the spa treatment brochures in white crochet bikinis. It was a special kind of luxury, this, almost embarrassingly up front about the fact that it was designed for sex and relaxation. This made her feel strangely stressed.

'Cool, don't you think, babe? You've gone all silent on me.' Jez's nose was already pinking in the violent Thai sun, although the skin on the back of his neck, where he'd remembered to put suncream, remained as pale and stodgy as a noodle.

'It's amazing. I'm just a little stunned.'

'And you see those two beds?' Jez pointed to two flat mattresses on the terrace, each annotated with neatly folded taupe towels and a blue-silk pillow. 'His and her's massages . . .' He winked.

Stevie grinned, pleased that Jez's schoolboyish enthusiasm had returned to clear the complex frowns crosshatched by his father's death. Did this mean he'd return more to his former self? Was the oafish cocaine snorter just a symptom of his grief and nothing more? Oh, she hoped so.

'The towels are infused with ginger,' recited the Thai man, beaming blankly. 'And here, sir . . .' a grand pause, 'we have the light-switch dimmer.' Stevie and Jez nodded. Nobody spoke. Guest and host waited for the other to make the next move. It made Stevie feel uncomfortable. Was the facilitator about to leave? Should they tip him?

Jez took the lead. 'Well, thanks very much, er . . .' he leaned towards the man's name badge, 'Lin. Thanks, Lin.' The man smiled expectantly. He didn't move. Jez dug his hand into his tight trouser pocket and squirmed around for some change. 'A fiver any use, mate? Didn't think so. Oh, here we go. Baht.' He handed the man a few dog-eared notes which could have been worth anything, two pence or a hundred pounds. Jez slapped him on the back.

If the note was worthless, the man was gracious about it and exited with a small bow. The atmosphere in the villa immediately relaxed. Privacy at last.

With a large gorilla thump of the chest, Jez squatted down and gripped Stevie around the waist so firmly she could feel each of his fingers. 'You are gorgeous!'

'Jez? What are you doing?'

He scooped her up into his arms, Stevie laughing, screaming, legs kicking out.

'And I'm going to carry you over the threshold if it kills
me,' growled Jez, using all his bulky but not terribly strong
muscles to lift Stevie's nine-and-a half-stone frame over the
terrace, through the glass double door. 'Argh!' he shouted,
staggering. He dropped her onto the bed. 'Me, Tarzan!'

Stevie laughed, head falling into the crunchy fresh linen,
strands of brown hair spilling across the pillow like rays.

Jez threw himself on top, half winding Stevie. 'A fuck in
Phuket, Mrs Lewis?'

It was the third time in a week Jez appeared to forget that
Stevie had decided not to change her name. Well, at least not
for the foreseeable future. But now wasn't the time to mention it. Jez's hands writhed beneath her T-shirt towards her
bra, filling her mouth with his tongue. Stevie fought jet lag's
downward tug. She would feel happier if they made love,
more married somehow. She just wished she'd had a shower
first. Jez's breathing began to slow, each pant as warm and
damp as a slap of a flannel, his jaw pumice against her cheek.
She combed one hand into his hair, avoiding his balding
patch. With the other hand she unbuckled his trousers. This
was more like it. They were behaving like newlyweds at last.

Seventeen

As always, Katy Norris made sure she got up from her siesta before Seb awoke so that he wouldn't see her rapidly maturing face unmade-up, crumpled and swollen with sleep. (Seb had never seen her without make-up.) For some reason, on a foreign bed, on foreign pillows, she could not remain sleeping on her back, as she'd trained herself to do in order to reduce the depressing phenomena of compression wrinkles. Still, Katy supposed, a couple of weeks on her right-hand side wouldn't cause permanent damage, only a little temporary puffiness first thing in the morning. She walked along the beach, which curved yellow into the horizon like a banana, dispassionately wondering when she'd become the kind of woman who worried about whether she slept on her side or back.

Katy tilted her face towards the afternoon sun, soaking up its promise of an even, natural tan. Wrinkles-wise, she knew she should probably cover up, but this final blast of afternoon sun would give her a gentle sun-kissed J-Lo glow this evening. Besides, the air felt heavy, nicely so, full of skin-plumping moisture as it pressed against her exposed body, so sparely packaged in her microscopic bronze bikini.

Katy sighed. Today could be *the* day, she sensed. The day when something might actually happen. Just that morning Seb had mentioned that 'they'd have a good chat at dinner' and she'd felt like cartwheeling along the side of the infinity pool. (She also knew that Seb had no idea who Charmaine was. He was just sleep-talking.) To reassure herself, she'd mentally measured the length of the ring finger on his right hand as he'd slept. The longer it was, the more testosterone, the more chances of being unfaithful, according to a health snippet in her magazine. And Seb's finger was reassuringly on the stout side. Katy licked her lips, tasting sea salt.

As she walked away from the beach, her silver flip-flops hit the yellow paved path – like something out of *The Wizard of Oz*, she thought – with a gritty crunch. And with each impacting step her left big toe throbbed. The throb radiated from a patch of pink flesh she'd accidentally ignored during a lazy application of factor thirty yesterday afternoon. She cursed. Sunburn looked common. The kind of thing sported by overweight British tourists in Magaluf. She bet those Manhattan creatures – unknown rivals so alive in her imagination that she could almost feel her fingers dip as they slid across the taut concavity of their Hampton-tanned tummies – never appeared at dinner, a *proposal* dinner, with a foot like a pig's trotter. Damn it. But there was nothing she could do, not at this moment in time. She had stupidly forgotten to bring any after-sun cream, assuming that she'd buy it at the resort, which of course she could do but it required an annoying detour and a cart ride to the spa shop.

She carried on walking – throb, release, throb – as her foot hit the paving and then arched forward through the air. A tiny electric blue bird, picking at the path a few metres ahead of her, quickly flickered up in the palm above her head, wings fast as a flick-book. A wave of pleasure overrode the throb. In

124

contrast to London, where one never had time to think or notice anything, here she felt more attuned to her surroundings, especially the ground she walked on. Partly because of the necessary vigilance for creepy crawlies, partly because of the painful focus of her toe, but also because she was calmer, thus more observant. She appreciated the care that the managers of the Blue Blossom had evidently taken with this path. On either side of it the grass was as green and neatly trimmed as a Kent lawn, lush with sprinkler use and accessorised by honey-scented pink flowers. Although it could have been, it wasn't designed in a straight line, but meandered subtly on its way, curving carefully up to villa doors but not close enough to infringe upon the occupants' privacy inside. It was well thought out. She liked that. She liked order. It was about time her relationship succumbed to its natural order too.

Katy squinted at a pretty clump of foliage a few feet to the left of the path. Was that aloe? If only there was a facilitator or a guidebook handy. But yes, it sure did look like the image on her deodorant bottle; the same pointed chunky leaves, succulent with something. Feeling emboldened by the lift in her spirits caused by anticipation of The Dinner, Katy decided, rather uncharacteristically, to investigate. Rearranging her rattan beach bag on her right shoulder, she intrepidly stepped off the paved path and walked cautiously across the crunchy lurid-green lawn to the copse of palms and flowers and the aloe lookalikey. She wished that Seb could see her. How intriguing and beguiling she must look, as she tilted her jaw back to smell the huge pink flowers that hung off branches like bowls. Once Katy had finished capturing herself in a shampoo ad, she turned her attention to the stalks of the plant beneath the flowers. This was the aloe, surely? She could anoint her foot, perfectly organically! How Gaia. How eco-chic. What a brilliant idea.

125

Katy snapped the stalk. It required some effort, being trunk-like, about three inches wide, its skin waxy and its edges sharp as a knife. She sniffed it. Hmmm, subtle. Her fingers tentatively touched the transparent goo that oozed from the wound. It was sticky and slid oozily between her fingers like sperm. Giving the grass beneath her feet a quick once-over for killer ants, snakes and scorpions, Katy tugged her sarong out of her bag, spread it on the ground like a picnic rug and sat down, her legs stretched straight out in front of her in a way that only thirty-six year olds who do yoga are capable. She pulled the stalk apart further. The fibres broke with a sound like a splitting apple and it released its succulent milk. Katy dipped her fingers into this sensual substance, bent her left knee and moved her fingers towards her hot throbbing foot.

Jez decided to let Stevie sleep. He wanted to get out of the villa, get some air, clear his head. He couldn't help but feel a little put out that on their first married shag she hadn't come, or even bothered to fake it. It wouldn't have killed her. Still, no point picking things over. He wasn't someone who liked to over-analyse. Jez bent over the dark-wood table and wrote a note on some pleasingly creamy Blue Blossom notepaper – *Gone exploring, back in twenty, love you* – and sauntered out of the villa, his long, crumpled beige shorts exposing Anglo Saxon legs, as grey and freckled as a trout's underbelly.

Jez looked about him, pupils shrinking to pencil points in the sun. The path seemed to lead in one direction towards the restaurants, pool and spa house, the other towards the Blue Blossom's famed private beach. Yes, he'd check out the beach. There must be some decent bars. Jez flip-flopped forward, feeling pale and stocky in the heat and anxious that his white flip-flops were too effeminate. Nearer the beach, the yellow

126

paved path forced him past a selection of prize villas, tantalising as confectionery at a supermarket's exit. These villas were bigger and fancier than his honeymoon villa. This irritated him unduly.

A villa door slammed and a couple ambled out of a large – much larger than his – villa, hushing their voices as they passed but acknowledging him with fleeting eye contact. The woman was something else, all breasts and gleaming brown buttocks. But the man was paunchy, bald, and wearing loud flowery swim shorts. Money. He must have money, thought Jez, feeling an itch of dissatisfaction under his skin, a lust for something better, hard to put his finger on what. He watched the back of the woman's thighs scissor towards the spa house, then quickly re-angled his gaze lest anyone see him and think him a perv. The path lay before him, empty, winding, its yellow surface rising and falling in the shrill afternoon heat as if gently breathing. He continued his heavy flip-flop towards the beach.

Suddenly, breaking the polite accompaniment of birdsong, Jez heard a nasal sound, a sound much like a broken sob, then an inhalation, then a sob again. He looked about him. Nothing. But what *was* that? It did sound very much like the sound of a woman crying. He hoped he wouldn't have to deal with some kind of scene.

'Oh no, oh . . .' could be heard coming from the other side of an exotic tangle of vivid pink flowers and foliage. 'Oh, no.'

A lover's tiff? Too much to drink? Jez wrestled with his conscience. No, better not to interfere. He continued his walk, wishing he could switch off just as his dad used to switch off his hearing aid and absolve himself of responsibility. Then, to his relief, the sobbing stopped. It was only once he was past the copse of trees that Jez dared look to his right – just to check, just to reassure himself that it wasn't a child or someone dying.

Oh.

One impossibly long and shapely leg, the colour of light soy sauce, protruded from the leaves, strangely disembodied from its owner, like an amputated limb of a shop mannequin. He was relieved when he saw it twitch. He walked slower now, mesmerised by the leg, curious about its owner. The leg retracted and he heard the sound of someone standing up and cursing. He looked away quickly, focused on the horizon. And then, sobs, more sobs. Shit.

The vision of leg fuelling his public-spiritedness, Jez strode towards the noise and peeked his head around the palms. Wow. A honey. 'Is everything OK?' he said, feeling a little shy in the presence of this astonishingly beautiful woman, her hair Buddha-gold in the sun, tears streaking beneath her large dark Jackie-O shades.

The siren looked up, quickly wiping the tears from her cheeks. She tried to smile. 'I . . . I . . . Oh God, look. Just *look* at my leg.'

Needing little encouragement, Jez looked at her leg.

'No, this one.'

He switched his gaze to the left leg. Angry livid welts shaped like the cruel smiles of red chillis climbed from her toes up her calf. 'Ouch. Are you OK? What happened?'

The woman sniffed, recalling her stupidity. 'I . . . I . . . I thought this was aloe vera . . .' She pointed at a plant beside her. 'I smeared its goo on my sunburn and . . . and . . .' The sight of her hideously deformed leg brought the tears splashing forth again.

'Ouch.' Jez wondered what constituted appropriate behaviour in such a situation. 'I'm sure it'll clear up.'

This weak reassurance only upset the woman more. 'Today, of all days . . .' she whimpered.

Jez realised a more alpha male approach was needed.

'Listen . . . firstly hi . . . I'm Jez.' He stuck out his hand for a shake.

'Katy,' she mumbled, ignoring the hand.

'Does it hurt?'

'It stings terribly.'

'OK, well the best course of action, I think,' Jez puffed his chest out, feeling like the handsome doctor on *Lost*, 'is to get you home. Well, to a villa, the nearest villa. Mine's not far. Let's get this leg washed. I'll take a sample of the plant to the manager's office, just to check it's not deadly . . .'

Katy let out a yelp of horror.

Jez raised his hands in protest. 'Which I am *sure* it is not. But worth checking in with the natives, isn't it?'

Katy nodded gratefully, part of her beginning to enjoy the rescue.

'Now, er, Kate? Sorry, Katy. Now, can you walk?'

Katy started to hobble forward. 'Bloody painful.'

Thankful he'd put in the work at the gym prior to his wedding, Jez offered a thick, fleshy arm. 'May I help?'

Not taking the arm offered as the linking support Jez intended, Katy, rather forwardly, he thought, extended her slim brown arm over the roof of his shoulders. To counterbalance, he had no option but put his other arm around her waist, which felt shockingly soft and naked, only the ridged hem of her bikini bottoms a reminder that she was wearing anything at all. For a dreadful moment he feared that he might be developing a hard-on.

'Right, onward march, Katy,' he puffed, conjuring up images of his dead dad to keep his cock in line.

Katy turned to face him. She was fine-featured: impossibly teeny nose, a disconcertingly full pink mouth, a clean jaw-line up-lit by the shimmer that bounced off the two glorious orbs barely constrained in a bronze bikini top beneath. Strangely,

129

she seemed familiar. He had a strong sense he'd met her before. But, no, he couldn't have.

'Thanks. You're very kind. I'm sorry about this . . .' Katy managed a weak smile. 'Let's just get somewhere so I can wash this battery acid off.'

Flesh on flesh, linked closer than children in a three-legged race, Jez and Katy staggered slowly back to Jez's villa, which was, it transpired, closer than Katy's.

Inside the villa, Stevie, dressed in nothing but her own insulating layer of soft creamy flesh, was rubbing her eyes, waking up, disorientated and jet-lagged, when the door opened with a soft click.

Eighteen

Sitting outside the spa waiting for her massage, Stevie still felt winded by the sight of Katy Norris. It had brought everything back in a stomach-squirming rush. Closing her eyes, tilting her face into the sunshine, Stevie could see it all happening as if it were yesterday. August, three years ago, Jade's thirtieth birthday party at her parents' Somerset cider farm. A field outside Woodstock. The evening began with two over-excitable girls in red sequinned cocktail dresses, coloured feathers in their hair, directing cars into a field. It ended as a chilly dawn broke over a chaotic rave, with smashed party goers grinding their jaws and couples twisting their bodies together in the long damp grass. Tired and reflective, she and Sam had moved away from the main crowd, sat on a mossy fallen log, shared a spliff and watched the sun drip raspberry pink over the orchards. For a fleeting second, she'd thought that there was no membrane between them. It was a moment of complete intimacy.

Despite the fact that she was knackered, she remembered feeling spectacularly beautiful, aware of the rosy spill of light on her face, the flush on her cheeks from a night spent out-doors. When Sam looked at her she could see *her* beauty in his eyes. And when he cupped her jaw in his soft brown hand, tilted her face up so that her eyes had to shut against the brightening dawn sun, her insides liquefied and a feeling of previously unimaginable happiness spread through her body like a drug. Instinctively, she'd opened her mouth and anticipated the kiss. But the kiss never came. What did come was a mouthful of hair. Spluttering, she pulled the hair out of her mouth, opened her eyes to see a blonde invader sitting on Sam's knee, whipping her head around in the sunlight, folding her tanned limbs into his taut, rangy body, her face flushed, pupils dilated. 'Sorry, but I've been admiring this man *all* night,' she'd whispered breathily, curling her body into Sam's, her mouth close to his ear. The girl was Katy. Sam didn't brush her off straight away. And Stevie wasn't going to wait around to see if he did. She quickly made her excuses and left the party ten minutes later, feeling sad and stupid.

She shook her head, trying to clear the memory. So long ago. Irrelevant now. But it was still fucking annoying. Marriage didn't salve all old romantic wounds. She had to speak to Lara.

'Not Katy there's-less-to-me-than-meets-the-eye Norris?' exclaimed Lara. 'The one who had that thing with Sam?'

'Yes, *that* Katy.' Stevie sighed into her mobile. She couldn't get over the fact that Lara sounded like she was a couple of palm trees away but was actually in another hemisphere, speaking from New York. The call must be costing some-one – caller or receiver, she could never remember which – a fortune.

Lara laughed. 'Oh God, life's too cruel. You go all the way to Thailand . . .'

'I know, *don't*.' Stevie swatted a fruit fly away from her

132

arm. She already had two large angry mosquito bites, rather inexplicably, on her bottom. She wondered whether the divine Miss Norris had spotted them as she had staggered into the villa.

'What about Katy's leg, is it OK?'

Stevie reined in an uncharitable snort. 'Jez said it faded on the way home. But it looked little worse than a nasty heat rash to me. '

'Once a princess.' Lara laughed. 'Now, I want to hear it *all*. Where are you standing? Can you see the sea? Fill me in.'

Stevie looked up. 'Yes, it's turquoise and completely flat. From this particular vantage point I can also admire the state of the art swimming pool, free of stone fish and currents and sand, inconveniences that the typical Blue Blossom guest would rather avoid. I can also see lots of couples. It's like a luxury version of Noah's Ark.'

Lara laughed. 'And why the devil aren't you there sipping a lazy long island iced tea in the poolside bar, may I ask?'

'I'm sitting outside the spa house with a cup of jasmine tea, darling, waiting for my "Blue Blossom relaxing many pressure massage with views of the splendid ocean". Jez booked me in. As a surprise.'

'But you hate massage.'

'Yes. He appears to have forgotten.' Stevie felt disloyal. 'Well, it's not something we've ever really talked about. I just assume he knows everything about me because we're married, which isn't really fair. He means well.' Stevie smiled at a passing spa worker, neatly dressed in a tourist-friendly approximation of Thai national dress and wearing black silk flip-flops. A strong smell of essential oils wafted from the folds of the fabric as she tiptoed past. Stevie checked her watch. 'I'm probably going to have to stop chatting any minute, but, just quickly, tell me about your apartment, your

133

flatmate, *Nu Yoik*. Brilliant that you've sorted yourself out so quickly.'

'I was *hugely* lucky. A girl at the magazine had a friend who was looking for someone to share her apartment, so after a mere two nights of sleeping in a teeny basement in the East Village with banging pipes that sounded like the mad axe-man, I installed myself and my three suitcases in a far nicer place in the West Village yesterday.'

'And, what's she like? Single white female?'

'Casey. Thirty-eight. Single. Works in advertising. Waxes her nostrils.'

'No!' Stevie put her hand to her mouth. 'No!' A woman in a leopard-print bikini striding past to the jangling accompaniment of low-hanging ethnic necklaces gave her a dirty look. It was an unwritten rule of the place that everyone spoke in hushed tones the whole time.

'I am the most hirsute woman in a ten mile radius. But seriously, Casey's cool. Kind of a bit severe and a bit dry but, yeah, I really like her.'

Stevie bit her cuticles. She felt a hollowing emptiness in her chest, like a homesick feeling but it was a homesickness for a city she'd only visited twice, a yearning for a life she could have lived if circumstances had been different. 'It all sounds incredibly exciting,' she said wistfully.

'Well, yeah, it totally is. But what you're doing is exciting too, in a different way . . .'

Stevie smiled. Lara was really trying here. 'I know.'

'Oh God, that reminds me.' Lara suddenly let out a screech. 'Ah, I must tell you . . . wait . . . wait . . . don't go . . . listen up. Casey told me she's checking out sperm donors. I'm so not joking. She said it's like customising a handbag: eye colour, hair, degree . . .'

'God, that's beyond modern.' Stevie checked her watch.

134

'I'm getting beckoned. Time to get pummelled into oblivion. Call me soon. Love you, bye. Oh, wait a minute. You still there? Almost forgot to say, thank you *so* much for the wedding present. Very generous of you.'

'Well, I thought an air ticket was the one guaranteed way of getting you over here. The date is flexible.'

'Ace. I'm in between jobs when I get home, so it couldn't be better timed. Thanks, Lara.'

'Not a problem.'

'And, one other thing, er, just wondering, has Sam phoned?'

'Yeah, he left a message on my mobile last night.'

'Already? Gosh, that's keen.' Stevie's hand clamped her phone so tight its plastic innards creaked. 'But that's great. Gotta rush. Bye.'

Katy pulled the taps on the deep outdoor bath and scattered the water with flower petals, kept nearby in a handy limestone bowl like fresh pot-pourri. 'Bath's ready, darling.'

'You're a pussycat,' mumbled Seb, striding lazily towards the terrace in a Blue Blossom white four-ply-towelling dressing gown. He put one hairy big toe in the water. 'Oh, hot.' He didn't bend down to adjust the taps himself.

She adjusted the cold. 'There . . . that OK?'

'Perfect.' Seb let the dressing gown drop to the ground, pool around his slim ankles.

Katy licked her eyes over his taut torso, the V of his mousy pubic hair, his round, recently worked-out shoulders. He looked better now than when they first met. As age withered women, it improved men, she thought. It caused a strange shift in the gender power base.

'So you were saying, Katy? Sorry I was half asleep. Yes, a bit more cold. Crikey, that's enough! Super. This chap who helped you . . . a husband of a friend or something?'

'Yes!' Katy clapped her hands together in, she half hoped, an endearingly girlish gesture. Charisma was something she felt she had to work at these days. 'The friend is Stevie Jonson. Funny girl. Nice enough, though. We met years ago, when I was going out with Sam Flowers.' She paused. 'Before your time, obviously.'

'Right,' he said stiffly.

'She's on honeymoon.'

'Right-o.' Seb's pale eyes lost their suspicious slant. He periscoped his toes above the water. 'With Sam?'

'No, no, not Sam.' Katy looked thoughtful. 'Jez his name was. Lovely guy, so sweet.' She brushed sand off her knees.

'Terrific. Another couple. It might be fun to hang out tonight,' said Seb, rubbing soap into his neck vigorously. Another couple would provide some light relief. They'd already had five 'fine-dining experiences' at the most expensive terrace restaurant and each one had disturbed him slightly more than the one before. Katy was so silent, as if she were waiting for him to say something, to create drama, conversation. And the more he talked to her the less he felt he had to say.

'Tonight?' Katy tried to hide the needling disappointment in her voice. She was unsuccessful. 'Didn't you say earlier that you wanted to have a chat about something, something kind of important, tonight?'

'Did I?' Seb looked up blankly. 'Oh, wait a minute . . . Yes, that was it.' He soaped behind his ears. 'I wanted to ask you whether you minded terribly if, after the holiday, I went back to New York a bit earlier than planned, rather than hang out in London that weekend. It's work, darling. I want to be there early Monday morning. I really think I need to look totally committed.'

Nineteen

Three-and-a-half hours later, her muscles still feeling bruised by the hands of the tiny but wiry Thai masseuse, Stevie wrapped her warm hands around a glass of icy Chablis and brought it to her mouth, a wide relaxed arch through flesh-warm air. 'The sky, Jez, look at the sky. You can see all the stars. It's like a disco.'

Jez craned his neck back. 'Cool,' he said, eyes quickly returning their focus to his beer glass, then the unmissable cleavage – or was she being paranoid? – of the woman on the next table wearing a fuchsia dress that took no heed of the style rule of only displaying one erogenous zone at a time.

Stevie shuddered, dark thoughts circling. 'To think that this is what those poor people caught in the tsunami must have felt, at peace, on holiday, just like us. And, then, God . . .' She shut her eyes. Yes, it did disturb her. She couldn't pretend otherwise. The sea was dancing with bones.

'Don't be so bloody morbid, Stevie. We're on bleeding *honeymoon.*' Jez stuck a finger in his ear and waggled it to get the pool water out. 'Why all the bloody navel gazing?'

'It's like we have to pretend nothing's happened. And all those poor people . . .'

Jez looked at her sternly. 'Listen, no one's asking you to pretend anything.' He slammed his beer glass down. 'The Thais want to move on. And you know what? I've had enough of death. Can we talk about something else?'

'Sorry.' As always, her father-in-law's subtle spectral appearance, channelled through Jez, chastened her. Colin had become the third party on their honeymoon. She'd learned how he wasn't good in the sun, which would explain Jez's sensitivity; his dislike of Thai food; how he preferred a good old-fashioned deckchair to the vulgar horizontal exposure of a modern sun lounger . . . Yes, it was time to change the subject and quickly, thought Stevie. But to what exactly?

Since arriving in Thailand, conversation seemed to be limited to three subjects: the wedding, Jez's father, the Blue Blossom (the coldness of its beers, the price of a lunch, the confusing labelling of the spa's own-brand suncream). It was not the loved-up soul searching that Stevie had hoped a honeymooning couple might engage in, but the kind of surface chatter she'd dreaded during her pre-wedding wobble. In mitigation, Jez was still grieving. It was she who had to take responsibility, nudge the conversation on to a higher plane. 'Maybe in some ways it's wonderful and appropriate we are here,' she said quietly, fingering the salt cellar. 'It's a place of life and death and new beginnings.'

Jez swallowed a belch and raised his glass with a closed mouth smile. 'And sun, sand and sex.' He took a gulp. 'A gorgeous wife. And bloody good beer.'

No, they were not two people fused into one, she acknowledged. They were two people linked in a neat and arbitrary way, through rings and paper and ceremony and expectations and the presumption of a shared future rather than through messily engorged hearts. But, perhaps this merely meant that theirs was a more mature relationship, planned and measured against their ages and expectations. It was unrealistic to expect the dopamine swell of young love at their age.

'Where the hell's that waiter gone?' Jez looked about him. 'Check out that ocean, pumpkin. Wow, it's, like, glittering.'

It did seem to be lit from within by thousands of LED lights. 'Phosphorous, do you reckon?'

Jez sighed. 'If only Dad were here, he'd know. He had an encyclopaedic mind in some ways. Of course, he'd have gone fishing too. He'd be out there making friends with the fishermen. Good sea legs he had.'

Stevie smiled, trying to visualise Colin, who had only ever eaten fish covered in Bird's Eye breadcrumbs and had been about as intrepid as an old sofa, even getting on a plane. She pressed her hand to her face, supporting her freckled chin on her hand, the skin on skin sweating immediately on contact. Humid gusts of wind filled the palms, making their leaves upturn and rustle like tutus, creating just enough drama to fill in the gaps of their conversation and act as a diverting third party at the table.

Jez suddenly clattered his fork down. 'Hey is . . . that? It is.' He waved and mouthed, 'Whoa! It's that Katy.'

Stevie groaned inwardly. This resort evidently wasn't going to be big enough for the two of them. Spotting Jez's enthusiastic gesticulation, Katy – unmistakable in a floaty rainbow-coloured dress with a large pale-pink bloom tucked behind her ear – got up from her seat with a flirtatious twist of the hips. Shit. She was walking towards them, dress inflating like a sail. Within seconds she was at the table, teeth glowing like white coral in her tanned face.

'Hi guys,' Katy chirped. 'Isn't this just, like, dreamy, no?'

'Stunning.' Stevie smiled and nodded, noting the humiliating way that Jez was gazing at Katy. He might as well dribble.

'How's the leg?' asked Jez, his eyes inevitably homing in on her long brown limb.

Katy giggled and stuck her left leg forward rather unnecessarily, thought Stevie, like a model on the catwalk. 'All better. Thanks to you.' His jaw twitched with pleasure. 'I must congratulate you on your brilliant choice of husband, Stevie. Quite the saviour.'

'Glad he was of service.' Stevie nodded towards a handsome bored-looking man sat a few tables back. 'Is that your husband?' When her gaze returned to Katy's face, she suspected she'd asked the wrong question.

Katy looked quickly down at her feet with a pained expression, her hands twisting over and over each other like tussling judo players. 'No, not husband. Not yet.'

As was common in the second after an awkward moment, when the moment could either be extended or erased, Jez felt the wrong thing perch precariously at the end of his tongue, like a diver at the end of a quivering board. 'Oh, you should get married. Everyone's doing it.'

Stevie kicked Jez under the table.

'Yes, yes, quite. One day, hopefully, er . . .' Katy fiddled with a ribbon that circled her waist. 'I'd better go . . .'

Not wanting to lose Katy's company, Jez tried an alternative tack. 'Have you two finished eating? Fancy joining us for a nightcap? Welcome, aren't they, Stevie?'

Stevie forced a smile. 'Sure.' Oh God. Welcome to Thailand.

Katy looked from Stevie to Jez and back again, seeking reassurance. 'Yeah, Seb and I have finished up.' Not even a hint of a proposal had been forthcoming. She couldn't sit there opposite him any longer without wanting to dive over the white linen and slap him around the face. And Jez was already giving her puppy stares. It wasn't going to hurt Seb to

140

realise that other men looked twice. 'That's a sweet offer, thanks. I'll go get him.'

Jez watched the alternate mango cheeks of Katy's backside swell then empty the fabric of her dress as she walked. 'She's a great lass, isn't she?'

Stevie had never been able to drink in the heat. And the service was so prompt and smiley and it was all on a tab so there was complete disassociation between consumption and purse. No wonder she was drunk.

Katy slapped her hand on the wooden table. 'Wake up, girl! No rest for the wicked. It's only midnight.'

Stevie protested about jet lag and the others snorted and ordered another round of shorts, the glasses' clink just audible against the slap of sea and a low vibrating hum which probably came from a generator or insects but seemed to Stevie to be the sound of stars burning white holes in the vault of sky. How she wished she were alone under this sky, staring up until her focus went funny and it felt as if she were hurtling into space.

'So yeah, it's through Sam that we know each other, isn't it, Stevie?' asked Katy, directing the question with an olive.

'Yup.' Stevie resented the 'we', the assumption of collusion, that they agreed on the same friendship history, the same version of events.

'Dear old Sam. Do you ever still see him? How is he?'

Thinking of Sam, Stevie smiled. 'Really well.'

'Married or still breaking hearts?'

'Single.'

'Breaking hearts then.' Katy turned to the waiter, her voice becoming colder and posher as it always did when addressing staff. 'More water, no, *still* water. Thank you.'

Stevie bent her head back, felt the weight of her chestnut

hair swinging beneath her shoulders. How she used to love that just-cut-hair feeling when she was a little girl, the immediate release of that downward pull. 'I don't know if he's breaking hearts. To be fair, he's changed a bit since you knew him. Well, he's grown up, I suppose. It actually happens to some men.'

'About time,' Katy snorted. 'Sam was always one of those men who seemed . . . well-intentioned. Not an arse, but distracted. Do you know what I mean? Forgive the cliché, but you know, a bit of a commitment phobe? He couldn't even stick to one career.'

'He's doing what he really wants to do now. Some people take longer to find their thing.' And some men take a while to refine their taste in girlfriends, she wanted to add, but didn't.

'Yeah, yeah. Photography.' Katy laughed. 'God, I know the photography business. I know how hard it is, babe. He wouldn't accept help off me, you know. I tried not to take it personally.'

'I wouldn't.' Obviously it was personal, thought Stevie, unable not to feel a jolt of triumph.

'I offered to introduce him to a few people, but no, didn't need me, did he? High-tailed off to Paris to manage that studio. Great. He did well to get that. But you need all the friends you can get in this industry, babe,' Katy added, as if Stevie was a fourteen-year-old asking for career advice. 'Still, he'll find out how hard it is soon enough. Is he still taking his own pictures too?'

'Yeah, I think so. He's got various personal projects on the go. I haven't seen his stuff. He hasn't been around.'

'Projects. Ah,' said Katy with a knowing nod. 'The world is filled with young photographers working on "projects". I feel sorry for them. It's so hard to earn a living. And if he ever wants a wife . . .' She blew some air out of her pout

142

dismissively, as if the idea was slightly absurd. 'Well, he'd better get back to law school.'

Jez lumbered into the conversation, beer bottle first, waving it for emphasis. 'I like you, Katy. You have common sense. All the other girls fawn over Sam. They get sucked in by that "I'm a creative sensitive type" thing. It takes a guy to see through it.'

Katy grinned at Jez, recognising an ally. 'Sam always thought about stuff far too much. It used to drive me bonkers. You'd never know to look at him, would you? Most photographer types are either rather short or rather ugly. They become photographers so that they can get laid. But Sam is . . .' coy grin, 'damn athletic.' She nudged Stevie and whispered, 'Did you hold a torch for him? You did, didn't you?'

Stevie shook her head furiously and checked Jez's expression. No, he hadn't heard or was too drunk to listen. '*No!* I'm actually trying to fix him up with my friend Lara. They've both just moved to New York.'

Seb, busy squashing an explorative ant on the table with the back of a matchbox, perked up. 'New York? Crikey, I should hook up with these friends of yours. They sound kind of cool. Could you fix that?'

Stevie nodded. 'No problem.'

'That's what I love about Manhattan. You can phone up any old chap for a drink. Nothing embarrassing about it. It's like if you're the type of person who has gone to New York, there's immediate common ground.'

Katy looked irritated. 'Yes, darling.'

'And, my father would shoot me down for saying this, but it's better than ol' Blighty,' continued Seb. 'Safer. Easier to get around. The people are up, take it on the chin, you know. There's none of that defeatist English negativity. That whole Vicky Pollard thing? Forget it.'

143

'Man,' Jez snorted, leaning back in his chair and kicking his legs out. 'I *hate* New York. Hectic, overrated place full of jumped-up wankers who think they're the last word in urban sophistication. Why is it that all Brits who move to New York become evangelical about it?' He noosed the nose of his beer bottle with his fingers, leaned back in his chair and swung the bottle casually by his side. 'It's just fucking embarrassing, especially when the Americans are so dismissive of London. Why don't you all just wrap yourself in their flag and be done with it?'

'Wow.' Katy turned to look at him, hand across her mouth. 'You stole the words right from my mouth.'

'All this "ultimate city" stuff? Let them keep it.' He looked at Stevie and sighed, shaking his head. 'The missus loves cities, don't you? But city living doesn't suit when you get older, I don't think. The country is the place for families. We'll probably move to Norfolk or somewhere in the next five years.'

'Excuse me?' Stevie bristled, unwilling to have a row in front of Katy and Seb but annoyed all the same. Since when had they *ever* agreed to move to the country? Norfolk? Over her dead body.

'New York's been a revelation to me, old chap,' Seb interjected earnestly.

Jez shrugged, not in the mood to invest time listening to the revelations of some guy he'd just met. 'How can you bear to be parted from your beautiful lady?'

Katy beamed. She couldn't have put it better herself.

'It's tough,' replied Seb, distractedly. 'Toss over the insect repellent, Katy.'

The edges of Katy's glossed mouth tightened. She grabbed a spray out of her handbag and slid it across the table towards Seb.

Seb rolled up his sleeves and sprayed his pale forearms. 'It's hard being on different sides of the Atlantic. But it kind of works, doesn't it, Katy? It means we both have our own space.'

An awkward silence changed the atmosphere suddenly, like a drop in cabin pressure. Only the exhalation of cigarette smoke and the sound of Stevie slapping a persistent mosquito on her ankle provided relief.

Katy broke the silence, slamming her wine glass on the table as a prelude. 'You know what, Seb? I don't want my own space. I'd rather share yours.'

Eight feet shuffled under the table. Oh dear, they were hanging out with a couple even less suited to a honeymoon environment than themselves, thought Stevie. Time for bed.

'Easy, girl. It's not forever.' Seb patted Katy's hand but his body recoiled away from her, back pressing into the linen-backed seat.

'Man, plenty of time for forever.' Jez pulled lazily on a Marlboro. 'Once you two are married and have a load of screaming toddlers tumbling around your feet you'll look back on these days as your last days of bleeding freedom, mate. Enjoy it while you can.'

'Don't sound quite so wistful, please,' clipped Stevie. But she smiled. This was like the old Jez talking. The Jez she'd fallen in love with once. The one who enjoyed life, who was reluctant to grow up, irreverent and irrepressible. 'I can always release you from your burden.'

'Don't bother.' Jez put a heavy arm around her shoulders and planted a sloppy kiss on her cheek. 'Love you, missus.' He gestured drunkenly at Seb. 'OK, I . . . I take it all back. Marriage rocks.'

Seb snatched Jez's cigarette packet and knocked the soft carton hard against the table. 'Who said anything about *marriage*?' The words, loosened by alcohol and the oddly

145

liberating combination of sun and strangers, dropped from head to tongue easily.

A terrible silence. No part of Katy moved, not a blink. She didn't speak. Eight eyes tracked the waiter. The wind stopped. It was like the retreat of the sea before a big wave, thought Stevie.

Jez looked at his Rolex. 'Hey, what about turning in soon? Don't know about you but I am knackered.'

'Good idea,' said Stevie quickly, feeling a surge of gratitude towards Katy and Seb. They were the first couple she'd met in a long time who made her feel better about her own relationship. Maybe it wasn't so bad being married after all. At least they'd dealt with the commitment issue. 'Let's just sign off the bill.'

'No, *wait*,' implored Katy. 'Don't go.'

'Honestly, I'm fried . . .' attempted Stevie.

Seb put a hand on Katy's back, which she shrugged off. 'Come on, Katy, the guys have just stepped off the plane . . .'

Katy ignored him. 'Jez? You fancy one more? You're no lightweight.' Her eyes filled with either candlelight or tears. 'Please.'

Jez stood up, brushed down his cream linen trousers, looked at Stevie for guidance. 'Well . . . I . . .'

'Right. That's it then,' announced Katy. 'You're staying. If you don't want to stay out, can I steal your husband – my rescuer – for another drink? Would you mind horribly, Stevie?'

It all happened so quickly. The consent. The departure. The kiss on Jez's lips. It was only when Stevie got back to the villa in the unfamiliar darkness, the sky squid-ink black, shrieking with insects, that she realised that she was returning from the first dinner on their honeymoon alone. And she didn't mind as much as perhaps she should.

Twenty

Stevie unscrewed the lid of the brown glass bottle and tipped a folic acid pill into the creased palm of her hand. It was quite reassuring to swallow a pill again. Since finishing her contraceptive before the wedding, her mornings had lost their drill. No longer did she have pills to announce the days of the week, cycle after cycle, her life broken down to a succession of shiny foil packets, each new packet satisfyingly full, signalling a new month of inconsequential sex. She wondered whether her body would suffer withdrawal symptoms. She'd been on the pill for more years than she cared to remember, feeding her body oestrogen or progesterone, she forgot which, swapping between brands, excluding the ones that made her fat, psychotic or libido-less through a messy process of trial and error. Although mostly she'd been happy to lose the damn things and yield, finally, to her biological imperative, she was surprised to find that she also missed her contraceptive routine, missed the sense of control and predictability it brought. It was as if by stopping it, she was actually handing over control to a man and this made her uneasy.

'Nice one.' Jez, sitting on the edge of the terrace, watched her take the pill with an approving smile. 'We'd better get practising.'

'Aren't you meant to leave it a couple of months, use condoms to give the body time to adjust?'

'Bollocks to that,' snorted Jez, stretching out a leg. 'Your body will make a baby if it's ready, not if it's not.' He looked up, denim eyes bleaching in the sun, as if hardly able to withstand the tropical light. 'I don't want to wait anyway.'

'We only got married last weekend,' she laughed, flattered by Jez's eagerness.

Jez sat back on his heels, agitated, his body weight turning his toes white. 'Hurry? You've changed your tune. And in case you're forgotten, babe, I'm . . . thirty-six. You're no spring chicken either.'

'Thanks.' Stevie stood up, irritated now. She pulled a sarong from the floor, where it had slipped off a chair, and tried to work out the best way to wrap it so that it didn't fall down at an inappropriate moment, as it did yesterday at breakfast when she'd gone to get seconds of mango and papaya slices.

'Sorry. It's just, well, with Dad dying and everything. It's like I kind of want to replace him . . .'

Stevie froze.

'No, no, that's the wrong word, sorry,' said Jez quickly. 'But you know what I mean . . .'

'"Thou meetest with things dying . . ."' Giving up on the sarong, she screwed it into a ball and tossed it at her beach bag and reached for a blue jersey sundress. '"I with things newborn."'

Jez frowned, walking into the villa. 'What you on about?'

'*The Winter's Tale.* Shakespeare. Oh, it doesn't matter.' She pulled on the dress. 'I'm going to the beach. Coming?'

Jez kicked his legs into his shorts. 'Are you pissed off

148

about last night? Is that why you've got a face like a wet towel?'

Stevie scooped up her beach bag roughly. 'What time did you get in?'

Jez fisted his hands in his pockets. 'Not late. Probably half an hour after you left.'

'Right.' She didn't believe him. She was sure she heard someone padding in drunkenly in the early hours.

'We had a good chat actually. You know, Katy lost her mum two years ago. Ovarian cancer.'

'Really?' Wait for it, thought Stevie. She really understands.

'It's all so random, just meeting someone, a stranger more or less, someone, who, well, just really gets it.' He twisted in front of the mirror. 'Hey, where's that suncream? My neck's barbecuing here.'

'Sounds very cosy,' Stevie said, sliding her feet into polka-dot espadrille wedges. 'You and Katy.'

Jez grabbed her arm gently, on the fleshy bit above her elbow. 'Pumpkin, you're being uncharitable. She was in a real state last night after that Seb guy said that marriage thing . . . What was I meant to do? I mean, seriously.'

'Er, go to bed with your new wife?'

Jez harrumphed. 'Sorry, I find it hard to say no. You know what I'm like.'

'I do.' Jez liked women with problems, thought Stevie. When she'd first met him that was one of the things she'd loved about him. His clumsy big heart. Now, she wondered whether he just liked to step in, to rescue. And having done the ultimate rescue – marrying her – did he need to move on to other distressed damsels? Still, she supposed he was trying to do the right thing. 'Katy shouldn't have asked you.'

Jez considered this for a moment, found the argument

149

suited him well. 'You're quite right,' he said emphatically, tearing open one of the gourmet ginger chocolates, routinely left on their pillows by maids. 'She really shouldn't have put me in that position, babe.'

Stevie successfully managed to avoid Katy for the next four days, at one point hiding inside the beach-bar loos while Katy sauntered past in a barely there marshmallow-pink bikini and 1970s aviator shades. Another time Stevie was forced to swim underwater for almost the length of the pool – certain her lungs would burst – while Katy cautiously dipped a temperature-testing toe in the water. Jez, however, seemed to bump into Katy, but rarely Seb (who she suspected was also in hiding), with regularity and would return to the villa with frequent and exhaustive updates on Katy's leg condition – the rash had apparently gone on to scab prettily – and her sweet 'uncannily perceptive' words about the grieving process.

Soon Stevie began to expand her avoidance strategies to her husband: the intensity of twenty-four-hour couple time in this living holiday brochure, unbroken as it was by any other commitments, was becoming surprisingly testing. Their relationship was evidently one of those relationships that worked better with a few distractions, she thought. Such as a ten-hour working day.

Appealing to Jez's sportsman ego, particularly encouraging him in the direction of water sports, proved successful. The 'Aqua Zone' headquarters was helpfully set at least a mile from the villa and staffed by more than two knock-out blonde Australians. Under these women's long salty lashed eyes, Jez showed off, tackling the windsailing and surfing with an air of competitive machismo, as if the flat Andaman sea was a furious ocean straight out of *The Perfect Storm*. And he would return from these adventures – muscles pumped, sun-bleached hair splattered flat across his bald patch, nose burned – like a conquering hero, bellowing about his needs for massage, cold beer and, if she really loved him, a blow job. And if Jez couldn't be shifted from the villa or the poolside, where he liked to hunker down with a beer, nuts and a memoir of a great sporting hero, Stevie found other ways of ensuring her own privacy. Half a metre below the surface of the sea, where her breath sounded heavy and coital as it rushed up and down the snorkel tube, her thoughts flowed free and her only companions were shoals of fish in eye-shadow shades and occasional backwash from the high-performance flippers of a German tourist.

'More coffee please,' grunted Jez at a waiter. It was ten-thirty a.m. They were not supposed to be at the Blue Blossom breakfast buffet at ten-thirty a.m. They were supposed to be exploring the island, noted Stevie. She was desperate to leave the resort for a few hours. But Jez had a hangover and a dodgy tummy, which he blamed on the previous night's sea-food tempura. He groaned at the sight of the food, contemplated ordering a beer for a bit of hair-of-dog action.

Stevie made him eat some fruit. But she had to look away while he ate it. There was something about the way he ground the bits of banana with his molars, the way tiny beads of pul-verised fruit clung to the corners of his mouth like sleep scurf. She'd never even noticed his eating habits before, so why now? This question whirled in Stevie's head as she crunched down on her muesli. She realised that ever since the wedding she'd been struggling *not* to notice some of his personal habits, such as the way he napalmed the toilet every day at precisely nine-seventeen a.m. (Thai time), blew his nose in the shower, stuck out his tongue as he yawned so it emerged from his mouth like the meat in a mussel, a fleshy animate pink. These things had begun to turn her stomach, ever so slightly. Is this what happens when you fall out of love, wondered Stevie with a growing sense of dread. Or is this just marriage? Or was she just a bad wife?

Jez leaned over and kissed her on the cheek.

'What's that for?'

'Being my gorgeous Stevie.' Jez grinned, scratched his stubble sleepily. 'Hey, pumpkin. A surprise. I've booked us in for a couple's Thai massage tomorrow.'

'Oh.' She looked at Jez's expectantly happy face . . . and relented. 'Lovely.'

Jez paused. 'With Katy and Seb.'

Stevie spluttered on her freshly squeezed orange juice. 'No way!'

Jez put his hand up. 'Don't look at me like that! Listen, I was going to tell you earlier—'

'No.' Stevie had an urge to jump, to douse herself in the swimming pool, as though running from a stinging cloud of bees. 'Absolutely no way.'

'Well, Katy offered. As a wedding present. A thank you for helping with her leg. Listen, they've got this amazing villa, the des res. This fucking huge, A-one, top-of-the-range villa with its own private infinity pool and spa house and butler. The dog's bollocks. Makes our place look like a YOtel. Apparently Doherty and Kate Moss stayed there . . .'

Stevie stood up, brushed the creases from her green floral fifties-style sundress. 'You go. I'd rather explore the island.'

The sharp, sudden movement and pitch of her voice alerted fellow dining couples to the possibility of a scene and the terrace restaurant tuned into table number five. This filled Stevie with a disproportionate toddler-like rage, an urge to stampede over the buffet table, crush the fruit salads beneath her toes, toss croissants and pastries and soaked prunes at the smug couples who were staring at her

152

through their enormous designer sunglasses like dumbstruck ants.

Jez put his hand over his eyes, as if sheltering from bright light. 'Stevie, please ... What's got into you?' he hissed. 'We're on fucking *honeymoon*.'

Stevie, chastened by the incomprehension on Jez's fleshy sunburned face, sat down, turning to face off the other guests as she did so. 'Nothing. It's just ...' That she wanted more time alone with Jez? Well, actually, at this exact moment that wasn't true. A gecko darted across the floor.

'I want you to be happy, pumpkin.' Jez rearranged his features into those of a suffering misunderstood lover. 'But I'm doing it all wrong, aren't I?'

Twenty-one

The palms seemed fuller, greener here, like groomed heads of hair. The proportions of the villa – the bricks a hot chilli red in the searing heat – were more or less the same as their dwelling, but the scale was super-sized. There were also architectural additions that advertised the higher tariff: a suburban-style porch over the front door edged with a high trellis; their own stretch of yellow paved path, branching from the main tributary. Another key difference, also relating to the sliding scale of Blue Blossom price points, was that this villa was nearer the beach – not the main one but a small private sister cove. Here, Stevie could actually smell the sea. It smelled different to English sea, she thought, salty but without that wind-lashed fish-and-chip heaviness, more a hot scent that hit the lungs like a powerful exotic bloom. And its colour was the luminescent green of children's jelly. As she inhaled the smell, sucked in the view, she had a small holiday epiphany: no longer could she remember the air smelling any different or the sky being anything other than these miles and miles of endless cloudless blue. Yes, she had finally arrived in Thailand.

Thump thump thump.

Both Jez and Stevie started. What the hell was that? Bass.

Loud dance music pounded over the high wall that surrounded Katy and Seb's villa. It was the kind of tune, unnameable but familiar, that she felt she should know but didn't. Not for the first time she wondered how on earth she'd let herself be persuaded to embark on such an afternoon. Then she remembered. Jez had effectively brought up his father, once again. He needed some 'healing touch' to help with the bereavement process. What on earth was she thinking, planning on going off on her own like that? Leaving him! On their honeymoon!

Jez tugged at the tight waistband of his knee-length Ted Baker shorts. 'Ready, babe?'

Stevie nodded as graciously as she could. She must take responsibility for agreeing to come. For all of this.

Seb answered the door, beer in hand, wearing a Thai sarong around his waist. Jez noticed, with irritation, Seb's gym-pumped biceps, the lack of dough around his waist.

'Hey, guys,' said Seb, allowing himself to sound a little American. 'Come in. Madam's by the pool. Beer? Champas?' He turned around and shouted, 'Turn the music down, Katy!'

Stevie noted that Katy had done what all the magazines suggest you do when you go to a hotel: 'make it a home'. Brightly coloured silk scarves hung over sidelights, Diptyque candles burned on the table. There was even a photograph of Seb and Katy on the mantelpiece. She thought about her and Jez's own smaller villa, already accessorised by dirty underwear and lidless tubes of Boots own-brand suncream. She peered out of the identikit patio doors. Oh. Wow. Rather than just a jacuzzi, there was a glittering trench of an infinity pool, the water spilling over the sides, its blue surface bleeding into the ocean's green horizon like tie-dyed colours on a sarong. On either side of the pool was a jacuzzi and plunge pool, each intricately tiled, with gold-bellied cushions

155

plumped around their perimeters. At the end of the pool, breaking the vista, was a square glass atrium housing daybeds and a vast flat-screen television flickering with Sky Sports. Stevie plucked her bikini bottoms out of her bottom and readjusted the top that kept riding up, her breasts not being firm enough obstacles to hold it in place.

'Just ditch the damn thing, hon.'

What? Stevie looked up to see Katy, now the colour of tropical hardwood, sprawled on a sunlounger, wearing nothing but the tiniest of black bikini bottoms. Her stomach was so flat that there were gappy bits on either side that gave Stevie a sideways shot of her waxed pudendum. And resting on top of her ribcage were two impossibly spherical breasts.

'Just ditch it,' Katy repeated. 'Don't you just loathe bikini tops?' Katy craned up from her lounger on her forearms, eyes squinting in the afternoon's white glare. 'Plonk yourself here, sweetie.' She pointed to the adjacent lounger.

Stevie froze. No, no, no. This was so wrong. She was not going to spread her pale sloppy body next to Miss Perfect's. And she was not about to show off her lopsided breasts which, unlike Katy's, had a tendency to droop into her armpits like icing bags the moment she was horizontal.

'Don't be shy.'

God, she hated it when people said that. It was like saying, cheer up, it may never happen. Well, fucker, she'd always want to yell back. It already has.

'Here, Stevie.' Relief came in the form of Seb's hand, offering a glass of champagne. So early in the day? Oh, to hell with it. Stevie took a grateful swig. She lay on the free lounger next to Katy's, neatly securing her sarong, legs clamped together. She didn't last long. 'It's like a furnace. I'm not sure I can bathe out here. Jez? Can you toss over my hat? Yeah, yeah, it's in that beach bag.'

Jez frisbeed over a large straw hat and sat down on the poolside next to Seb. After a few moments of blokey awkwardness, they alighted upon discussion of the villa's sound system, kicking their feet in the water.

'Look at our boys. Sweet.' Katy's face was on one side, one cheek pressed against the lounger, facing Stevie. 'So, how *is* it?' she whispered conspiratorially.

'What? Sorry, not with you.'

'The honeymoon sex, of course. I bet it's awesome, no?'

Stevie's flush lit up the rim of her hat. The question took her unawares. 'Oh, er, great.' Why did she feel that she had to give her honeymoon good press?

Katy leaned her chin on to her arm. 'Like that, eh? I always imagined—'

'Yeah, well, we all come to marriage with such expectations, I suppose,' said Stevie, quietly. She could feel sweat pooling at the back of her knees.

'Oh, that's a very sensible attitude,' Katy laughed. 'But I always think that if we girls can't expect romance and knee-trembling sex on honeymoon, when the hell can we?'

Stevie shrugged. Inside she felt something plummet. No, she wouldn't let Katy, of all people, tell her what was and what wasn't normal. 'I think when you've been with someone for a couple of years and, well, you know, you've moved on to that more stable stage in your relationship . . . it's not always . . .' Stevie stopped. She despised herself for justifying her relationship to Katy. She despised herself for not being a loved-up endorphin-soaked honeymooner. Perhaps Katy was right.

'I suppose.' Katy looked thoughtful, dabbed at the beads of her sweat on her forehead with a towel. 'Maybe that's where I've been going wrong . . . you know . . . expecting too much, putting too much pressure on Seb.'

Stevie looked up from the brim of her hat, surprised at this

157

cliff-fall descent into intimacy. 'He hasn't proposed. You want him to, right?'

Katy looked down at the chewed-up airport bonkbuster that she'd been using as a pillow. 'I'm thirty-six. I want to move this relationship on. I want a family.' She sighed and turned over on to her front, suddenly resenting the way Stevie had got her to spill her insecurities while she sat there so smugly, safely married.

'Yes, I understand,' said Stevie quietly, staring at Katy's buttocks, the way one crease so clearly marked the transition from thigh to bottom, unlike her own which were largely indistinguishable from each other.

'Masseuses are here!' thundered Seb, standing up on the poolside. 'Come through to the atrium.'

The Thai masseuses were not young spa girls but tiny bird-like Thai women with grey-streaked black hair, gnarled hands and limited English. Katy dropped her arm over one of the women's shoulders, hinting at familiarity. But she did not bother with the courtesy of putting her bikini top back on before the massage, noted Stevie, who over-compensated for Katy's insensitivity by chattering nervously.

She was soon silenced, lost for both words and air. This was not a soft Swedish massage. This was more like common assault. Her Thai masseuse sat on her back, yanked her limbs, pushed her legs into her chest, pulled them apart, kneed her spine. It was like being run over, drawn and quartered. Stevie gasped with surprise and pain, unnerved by the unexpected skin-on-skin contact with a stranger, and no, so *not* relaxed. But the others seemed to be enjoying it. Seb grunted noisily. Katy released small mews of pleasure. While Jez – unbe-knownst to anyone else – was desperately trying to conjure up a vision of a half-finished plate of phad thai or his mother-in-law's crepey cleavage, anything, in fact, to stop him getting a boner.

'She has no mercy. Is it over? Tell me it's over,' joked Seb an hour later while the rest of them lay still, collapsed like jellyfish out of water. He got up and pressed a fistful of baht into the hands of the masseuses.

Stevie, relaxed now that the torture had ended, heard the soft shuffle of the women's barefoot steps and the swoosh of the sliding door as they left. She opened one eye.

'Wow . . . man.' Jez stretched out. 'That was quite something. You all in one piece, Stevie?'

'Survived, just.'

Seb and Katy laughed, slow, conspiratorial laughs.

'Yup, it's pretty hardcore. I asked them not to give us the toned-down tourist version,' said Seb. 'Hope you don't mind.'

Bastard, thought Stevie.

'It was delicious,' cooed Katy. 'Right. Pool, drinks . . .'

Stevie opened one eye and watched Katy step delicately down from her massage bed, brown feet on the limestone tiles. Seb followed her. She and Jez were alone at last.

Jez reached a hand across. She took it. He squeezed her hand. 'You OK?'

'There is something I need to tell you, Jez.'

He frowned. 'What, pumpkin?'

'I hate massage. I've always hated massage. Please do not book me another massage. *Ever*.'

Jez's face fell. 'But . . . why didn't you say?'

'Because you'd booked a honeymoon at a spa resort?'

Jez put his hands to his face and groaned. 'Shit. Sorry, babe. I can't believe . . .'

They both looked at each other and burst into laughter. Stevie wondered whether the massage hadn't done some good after all.

A few minutes later in the pool, the water cool against her hot flesh, the sky and sea azure, her head a little pickled by champagne, Stevie's spirits soared as she dived beneath the surface. Gosh, it was beautiful here. And Katy and Seb were tolerable enough, generous to share this extraordinary villa. Her body was alert, alive and tingled every time somebody inadvertently brushed against her underwater. In fact the massage seemed to have pummelled down the physical barriers between all of them, lubricating previous awkwardness. Katy dunked Jez. Seb grabbed Stevie's ankles. They laughed and splashed and screamed. And when her bikini top continued to ride up her torso in the water, Stevie felt it preposterous to persevere. She whipped off her green Topshop bikini top, allowing her white breasts to flop out to the glare of sunshine as the others cheered her on. Free and streamlined, she dived underwater, enjoying the tug of water against her nipples, its unimpeded rush across her body. This is more like it, she thought, blowing out a cloud of bubbles that jumped above her head like boiling peas. She stood up, shook the water from her hair, rubbed it from her eyes. She looked up. Oh no.

Katy was standing on the side of the pool, kicking off her handkerchief-sized bikini bottoms. Then, she was nude! Just unsisterly hardened nipples and a narrow pubic landing strip. Stevie looked away. Seb clapped. Jez stared in rapture. 'Come on guys!' Katy giggled, tossing her hair back. 'Who's for a skinny dip?'

Seb, needing no further encouragement, squirmed out of his shorts underwater. (He couldn't wait to see Stevie's body, so different from his girlfriend's, more robust, more honest somehow. He could imagine giving a girl like that a good . . .) 'Come on, guys.'

Stevie looked at Seb. Her field of vision couldn't help but narrow and become entirely filled with the spectre of his penis, which tubed long, thin and scallop-white out of a frizz of wispy brown hair. She looked away quickly.

'Stevie?' Jez looked at Stevie for a smile of permission. He didn't get it.

There was a loud slap as Jez's trunks hit the poolside by her feet, spraying her calves with water. 'Jez!'

'Come on, pumpkin,' laughed Jez, kicking up the water. 'It's a private villa. No one can see your bits.'

'Yeah, kit off, Stevie!' yelled Seb insistently. 'Kit off, girl!'

Stevie resented being made to feel like the repressed party pooper. She'd spent years witnessing her mother's skinny dips, hiding in the dunes while her parents paraded like characters from a 1970s sex book on nudist beaches. She hated all the skinny dipping then. She hated it now. Her body was private. She'd like other people's bodies to remain private too, unless she was sleeping with them. And if she were being strictly honest, she didn't want her body compared to Katy's, not right now, not without a tan.

'Didn't think you were the prudish type,' roared Seb insistently.

Stevie resisted the urge to shout back, 'Didn't think you were the small dicked type either.' Instead she hauled herself out of the water and sat on the poolside, legs clamped closely together, feet trailing in the water.

'Leave the girl alone,' said Katy as she stood up on the poolside and prepared to dive in, arms arrowed above her seal-wet head, stretched tummy concave. 'Not all women feel comfortable nude.'

What? Stevie's defences prickled. Oh, damn it, she wasn't going to be patronised by Katy Norris. She stood up and drew one foot up out of her green bikini bottoms. The manner of her strip was less elegant than she'd have liked, as the lining of the panties flopped inside out and the gusset stuck on her left knee. But after a little damp tussle, there she was, all startlingly white bottom (which hadn't seen the sun since Paxos, 1991), hips and pubic triangle. She resisted the urge to fold her arms across her freckled chest and covered up by belly-flopping straight into the pool, where she avoided all eye contact with everyone, bar Jez to whom she delivered her sharpest you're-a-dead-man stare.

'I'd suggest we all play strip poker but it would be a bit pointless,' purred Katy, fully aware that she was in danger of doing a Sharon Stone as she re-crossed her legs beneath her blue batik sarong. 'Another beer, Jez?'

Jez sank further into his lounger, his eyes trailing Katy as she sashayed across the terrace in the dipping afternoon sun, the palms dappling the golden flesh of her smooth back, before disappearing into the villa's cool dark interior.

'Gosh, is that the time? We better make a move. It's been lovely, thanks Seb,' said Stevie, glancing at Jez for back-up. She got none. No, of course Jez didn't want to move.

'Hey, you two aren't going anywhere,' muttered Seb sleepily. He was enjoying the company, dreading the intensity of being alone again with Katy. 'Hang out here. Please stay, guys.'

'No, really . . . we must be getting on,' said Stevie, putting suncream back in her raffia bag and smearing white gunk on to her sunglasses case in the process.

Jez shrugged, defeated. 'I'll just finish my beer then.'

'I hope you realise you've totally incapacitated my husband, Seb.' Stevie smiled, zipped up her iPod and whispered, 'Bad daytime drunk.'

'Ignore the missus, mate,' muttered Jez, swigging from his beer bottle.

'Hey, let's order supper in,' said Seb. 'Lobster, anyone?'

'Man . . .' Jez rubbed his stomach. 'Now you're talking. That sounds damn good.'

Stevie bristled. She wanted her own space now. She would

happily just have a bowl of plain noodles by the beach, any-thing for a bit of privacy.

'Come on, pumpkin. We're on honeymoon,' Jez pointed out unnecessarily. 'It's been such a tough few weeks . . .'

'I know that, it's just . . .' Stevie gave him a look which had the riot act written across the retinas. 'Listen,' she lowered her voice to a hiss, 'don't put me in this position. Do I really have to spell it out?'

'Guys . . .' Katy was back, three beer bottles held between her fingers. Oh God, thought Stevie, she's done it again. Katy had shed the encumbrance of her batik sarong and was wear-ing nothing but a large red bloom behind her ear, like a beautiful Hawaiian dancer.

'You got your suncream on, Katy?' asked Seb, sounding a little bored. His girlfriend's nakedness irritated him. Oldest trick in the book, he thought. She's trying to make me possessive.

'Yes, baby-block.' Katy didn't look at Seb but handed a beer to Jez, flirtatiously, back arched, bum tilted skywards, a burlesque silhouette. If romantic meals under tropical sunset skies wouldn't make Seb propose maybe a bit of jealousy would jolt him into action.

'Wow . . .' said Jez, open mouthed. 'Thanks for the beer.'

'No problem. I suggest we all move to this table, no?' Katy arranged some chunky teak chairs around the table, so that they were looking out at the pool and sea. 'It's in the shade, Stevie,' she added, as if Stevie were particularly oversensitive.

'Don't worry about me. I'm off.' Stevie folded her towel, a little pedantically because she was trying to control her anger, and placed it in her bag.

Jez, sensing immediate departure, put one hand firmly on her reddening freckled arm. 'A little bit of lobster isn't going to hurt anyone now, is it, babe?'

*

It is nine p.m. I cannot believe it is nine p.m., Stevie thought, an afternoon of beers and food slurring her thoughts as it did her speech. Within a few hours it will be dark. The day will just close down suddenly, as it always does here, within seconds of the last flare of sunset, like a light switched off. And I will still be here in the star-lit dark, sitting in a jacuzzi – hot, soupy, naff things – drunk, sunburned and not having a good time, a naked Katy Norris on one side, my Katy-enraptured new husband on the other.

'Don't you think all those other couples,' Katy nudged her beneath the hot foam, 'you know the ones you see at the beach, not talking to each other at breakfast. Don't you think they must *hate* each other? It's like they've given up, on communication . . .' she raised an eyebrow, 'on sex.'

'Er, yes.' Stevie wondered if Katy was inferring about her and Jez. So did Jez.

Katy sighed and looked at her boyfriend with puppy-dog eyes. 'I'm so pleased we're not like that, Seb.'

Seb looked away. 'Hmmm.'

Katy bent one knee up, hugged her arms around it, her two forearms squished tight to the skin of her knee, cocooning herself from Seb's evasion.

Jez stared at Katy's knee, mesmerised. Framed by the white-green jacuzzi foam, it looked shinier and browner than any knee he'd ever seen. He wanted to cup it with his palm.

'You know what?' Katy said in a squeakier kind of voice, as if she had to force the words out, 'I feel hornier than I've ever felt.' She leaned her head back, her wet hair whipped like rope by the jacuzzi jets. 'A woman's thirties are her sexual peak, you know. Wouldn't you agree, Stevie?'

Stevie had heard that factoid of course. But her marriage certainly wasn't testament to it. She brushed Katy off. 'Oh, old hat, Katy. Sixties is the sex decade now. OAPs are swinging from their zimmers.'

Katy laughed. 'Well, thank goodness for that. Another twenty fi—' She stopped, jiggled the maths. 'Thirty years to go then.'

'The problem with peaks is that they come with troughs,' added Stevie, thoughtfully. 'It's like you know good sex by our age. You know bad sex too.'

Jez shuffled on his seat, remembering that Stevie hadn't come the other night. He pushed his bottom against a particularly powerful jet then jumped back sharply as it spurted a prickly fume of water against his buttocks. He forced a laugh. 'Easy, easy, pumpkin . . .'

Seb grinned at Stevie. He liked this girl. So dry, so damn unshowy next to Katy. He liked her pale freckly fleshiness. Those soft but stern yellow-brown eyes, like Nanny Nairn's. She looked like the kind of girl who would give as good as she took in bed. No pretence. No feminine Katy-mewing. That put him right off. He liked her ankles, in particular, neatly turned like fine antique table legs. Seb leaned back into the seat. Beneath the foam his toes touched Stevie's. She flicked hers away sharply. Pretending to ignore him, was she? Seb shot her a knowing smile. He found the rejection sexy. It was like the playful ritual of a geisha, or, perhaps, a Manhattan thirtysomething.

'Well, for guys, it's like, how to put this delicately in the company of ladies? We need to sew our oats *before* we get hitched,' declared Jez confidently, unaware of the psycho toe drama acting out beneath the frothing water. 'You've got to be ready to settle. Can't do it if you're restless . . . I mean, man, I knew, didn't I, Stevie? Stevie? Hey, back me up here. Well, I knew I'd done all that other shit. The time was right to bed down with one good woman. Listen here, men get the settle-down urge too, you know. It's just that we get it later. Don't you reckon, mate?'

Katy fumbled with the jacuzzi controls, turning the jets up, super-power, the wilder and noisier the better to distract Seb. She didn't want him getting ideas.

But Seb had heard. He held his beer bottle above the furious bubbles, tilted it in salute. 'Hell, yes. *A lot* later.' Alcohol gave him the confidence to try on a more swaggering vernacular. 'You've got to get it out of your system first, mate. Hey, one night stands . . .' He thought about the waitress in New York and smiled. 'Older women . . .'

Katy glared at Seb.

Stevie sensed a scene brewing.

'Threesomes.' Seb took a sip of beer, looking pleased with himself for going so far.

Katy glared harder, then changed her strategy. Could she? Would she? 'Or, like, swinging.'

'Swinging?' asked Stevie, hand over mouth, repressing giggles. It was the kind of thing her mother might have done in the mid-seventies. Jez would be terrified.

'Have you ever,' Katy fellated her beer bottle and looked up at Jez coquettishly, head on one side, 'swung?'

If Jez were a dog he'd be wagging his tail, Stevie thought. She spoke for him. 'Oh, all the time. We used to pop down to Primrose Hill, didn't we, darling? Took off the Myla lingerie with the best of them.'

Seb stared intently at Stevie. Was she joking? God-damn this broad *was* sexy.

Stevie, partially reading his thoughts, kicked his leg gently. 'Yes, *joking*.'

'Are you now?' purred Katy. 'How do we know you're not double bluffing? Just pretending to be prudes.'

Jez's mouth opened and closed, as he fought to contain the

riot of images – Katy's pink nipple in Stevie's mouth – that invaded his head space. It was his turn to feel like the repressed one, cornered. 'And you, you two make a habit of it, right?'

Seb, amused to see Jez rise so easily, thought he'd spare him Katy's goading. 'Katy's teasing I think, old chap.'

'Am I? Who's teasing?' A smile played with the corners of Katy's pout. 'Besides, there's always a first, no?'

Something changed then. The air hung stiller, the sun pumped heat harder on their heads. In seconds the sea shaded from blue-green to aubergine purple, as if a coloured green lens had been pulled from beneath its surface. Everyone wondered if anyone else was thinking what they were thinking. No one dared speak.

'Hey, did I say something wrong?' Katy put her arms above her head and flipped her wet curtain of hair up from her back, lifting her breasts two inches out of the water as she did so, exposing cones of nipples, hard and pink as shells. 'Jez, talk to me.'

Jez's cheeks were now not dissimilar in colour and texture to the lobster flesh he'd devoured at lunch. He squatted further down on his seat with a wolfish grin, praying that Stevie wouldn't spot the erection stirring beneath the waters. He cupped his hands in his lap and laughed too loudly.

'What's so funny?' Katy purred. 'Let's not be bourgeois. I think there's probably a consensus in here somewhere, if anyone just dared . . .'

Stevie fought the urge to run from the tub screaming. Calm, she told herself. Calm. It was just Katy, drunk. It was such a ridiculous situation, sitting in a jacuzzi next to a naked woman, Katy Norris of all people. It should, perhaps, have been more ridiculous and more strange, but foreign places normalised things. She turned to look at Seb, a silent plea for him to rein Katy in.

The sight of Seb did nothing to reassure. He wasn't looking at his beautiful girlfriend. No. He was staring at her very own breasts, intently, joyfully even, as if watching stocks rise on his computer. 'It's time to shoot, I think, Jez.'

'One down!' giggled Katy. 'Jez?'

Jez looked from Katy to Stevie back to Katy again. He knew what he *should* do. It was his honeymoon. But his whole body was aching, pining, like it hadn't in years and years to do something else. At this very second in time, he decided he was madly, deeply in love with Katy Norris. He had to come all over her breasts or he would die.

'Jez?' repeated Stevie. Despite the heat, goosebumps rose up her arms, clustered on her exposed mosquito-savaged knees. 'I'm tired. Can we go *please*?'

'I . . . I . . . let's stay a bit longer,' mumbled Jez, not daring to meet her eye.

The rest of the group exchanged looks. They nodded at one another, gentle, slightly bewildered, but acquiescent nods. And as the nod travelled from Seb to Jez to Katy, like a Mexican wave, a line was drawn excluding Stevie from the decision process, from Jez, her marriage. With the final nod from Jez to Katy, Katy slid further into the jacuzzi and brushed her fingers against Stevie's cheek.

'What are you doing?' asked Stevie, barely able to breathe.

'Shuussh . . .' said Katy and tilted her head towards Stevie's, breath hot on her cheek, lips pursed.

'Fuck this.' Stevie stood up quickly, water dripping off her in sheets, splashing Katy's surprised upturned face. She whipped a towel around her body, speared her flip-flops between her toes and left.

Twenty-two

'Yes Mum, honestly, I'm having an amazing time,' Stevie managed to muster. Despite the warm evening air she was shivering, standing on the beach in a towel still damp with jacuzzi water. She'd fled to the beach to think, to watch the wind crabs scuttling sideways across the sand and the scuffed blue fishing boats, to not have to speak to anyone. Trust Mother to phone now.

'Well, I'm glad to hear it, darling. It's probably just the line, making you sound faint.'

Stevie put on her upbeat voice and spoke louder. 'How's everything at home? How's the old man?'

Patti laughed uneasily. 'Oh your father's fine. You know, we just about manage to put up with each other, all these years . . .'

'Everything's OK, isn't it?'

'Well, actually, no.' A long pause as Patti took a deep breath. 'I didn't want to worry you on your honeymoon, Stevie. But I know that you'd want to know . . .'

Oh God. Stevie sat down on a rock, dug one foot into the warm sand beneath a fallen coconut, where it felt safe. Please don't say you're splitting up, she thought. Not now. I'm not sure I could cope right now. 'It's about you and Dad, isn't it?'

'Your father?' Patti sounded surprised. 'No, no. It's Poppy, darling. She's had the baby.'

'Oh. Oh, wow.' Stevie's heart began to thump. 'But she wasn't due for another seven weeks.'

'Her waters broke two days ago, while they were all here for lunch, and she had to be rushed into the John Radcliffe for an emergency caesarean. He's a little boy, a dear little thing. Weighs three-and-a-half pounds.' Her mother's voice was high, tinny and cheery – her sugar-the-pill voice.

'Three-and-a-half pounds?' Stevie burrowed her feet further into the warm sand, agitating the toes beneath the surface. Even with her sketchy knowledge of birthing matters, she suspected this wasn't good news. 'Isn't that tiny? I mean, isn't that a bag of sugar weight?'

'Yes, he's tiny. It's been a terrible shock, as you can imagine. Poor old Poppy's still in hospital, on a different floor to the baby can you believe? Not that we should be surprised these days, what with the state of the health service. Piers and the kids have moved in here. He can't manage on his own right now, poor lamb. He has to commute to London. But they can't all go back to Queen's Park while the baby is in the JR, can they? Logistically it's a bit of a nightmare.'

'Is the baby going to be OK?' Stevie spoke with her hands over her mouth, as if this would somehow delay getting an answer. She heard her mother stifle a sniffle.

'He's *very* little, Stevie.' Patti sniffed again. 'He's had difficulty breathing. But medicine has improved so much for these prem babies, the prognosis improves all the time. If he can just get through the next few days . . .'

'I'm coming home.'

'No,' said her mother insistently. 'Poppy feared you'd say that. She didn't want me to tell you. She wants you to stay in Thailand. It's your honeymoon. You've only been gone a week.'

170

'Fuck the honeymoon . . .'

'Poppy doesn't want to be responsible for ruining your honeymoon. I understand that.'

If only she knew, snorted Stevie, eyes swimmy with tears. 'Mum, Poppy needs me.'

'She will need you, but not right now. Listen, darling, the baby could be in hospital for weeks, you won't be able to do anything for the moment . . .'

'I could look after the kids, while I'm off work. Or at the weekends?'

'You know Poppy, she's got everything organised, as well as she can in the circumstances. I think you should respect her wishes.'

Stevie looked out at the sea, the palm trees and long white beach, and longed to leave it. 'Can I speak to her?'

'Soon. It's a bit difficult at the moment. She's all wired up to catheters and such. No mobiles in hospital and the hospital phones are temperamental to say the least. But I'll phone you. I'll keep you informed, I promise, darling.'

Stevie scooped up a handful of sand and let it pour through her fingers, gritty particles catching beneath her wedding ring. 'I just don't think I can stay here, knowing that all that is going on . . .'

'Please try and enjoy your honeymoon. Everything will be fine, I'm sure. The Jonson genes are made of sturdy stuff, aren't they? You should see some of these other babies in the ward, far tinier than Poppy's, make him look like a toddler.'

'No name yet?'

'Tom, they're thinking. Like Tom Thumb, as suggested by Sophie. Although her first choice was Maisy Mouse.'

Stevie smiled. 'Tell Poppy I'm thinking of her, won't you, Mum? And if she needs me . . .'

'Of course.' Her mother paused. 'Oh, I almost forgot to

171

say. Sam popped round yesterday. He's back and staying with Pearl.' Patti sounded more upbeat. 'He's a sweetheart that boy, I tell you. He looked after Sophie and Finn while we all went down to the hospital. He's so good with those kids. They worship him. Anyway, he told me to say hi.'

'Right.' Stevie felt a sharp pain kick in her chest, something akin to homesickness.

'I should get on. God knows how much this call is costing me. But I am so happy you're having such a nice time. Phone soon. Remember to drink lots of water in the heat. And say hello to Buddha for me. I love you, darling.'

'Love you too, Mum.' Stevie flipped her phone shut, her throat locked. What the hell to do now? She could hardly hunker down on a sun lounger after that news. Nor did she have any desire to share her worries with Jez, who for all she knew was still steaming up the jacuzzi. Crumpling on to a rock, head resting on her knees, she looked across the darkening sea. Was that . . .? Yes, it was. It was an extraordinary sight. A butterfly, large as a pancake, fluttering over the waves, its vulnerable powdery wings just inches above the spray. Entranced, she watched it for a couple of moments, lifted by its brave beauty. A sequence of small waves rolled towards the shore. The butterfly disappeared behind the last largest wave as it crested. When the wave broke, foamed and flattened, the butterfly had gone.

Twenty-three

Seb rolled off Katy, slipping out of her with a squelch. 'Wow.' He was still thinking about the erotic frisson with Stevie and Jez in the jacuzzi. It turned him on. 'That *was* good, Katy.'

Katy turned her head towards him, her hair static on the silk-polyester-mix barrel pillow. She needed eye contact, but even now, even after the most passionate sex they'd had in months, Seb killed her with his distance by looking away at the exact moment her eyes pleaded for connection with his. She kissed his elbow. It pulsed sunburn heat against her lips. 'Very good,' she echoed, leaning her forehead against his. Her orgasm had left her feeling vulnerable and a little needy.

'Hmmm.' Seb pulled his head away, looking thoughtful.

At last, he's musing about our future, Katy thought. Maybe this will be the moment. How stupid I've been. Of course, the way to the aisle is through his loins. She studied his face intently, waiting for him to speak.

'Damn it.' The clamp of concentration released from Seb's features.

'What, darling?'

'I'm going to have a blasted cigarette. Won't smoke when I get back to New York.' Seb tapped a packet against the bed-side table, lit a cigarette and watched the white smoke ringlet against the green lotus-flower wallpaper, mingling with the yeasty smell of sex.

Katy tightened one shoulder, raised it against him like a shield and turned away from him.

Seb picked up on the body language. 'Baby, baby . . .' He put his hand on her hip and tilted her to face him again. 'You've never expressed a preference for, well, sex in the plural before.'

Katy blushed. The exhibitionist effects of last night's alco-hol had waned, leaving her with an achy drum behind her eyebrows, a gnawing self-consciousness. Did she really insti-gate . . . Oh God. She squeezed her eyes shut as if closing them was an editing process. But when she opened them nothing had changed.

'I like Stevie, though.' Seb winked. 'Shame she stropped off, eh? Kind of ruined the mood.'

Katy frowned. Seb was talking to her like she was a mate on the pull. This was not how it was supposed to be at all. Not at all. He was supposed to get jealous . . . or fall in love with her louche bohemianism or *something*, not start fancying Stevie. She'd never considered that as a possibility. She'd imagined that Seb would have got his kicks watching her doing some-thing vaguely vanilla. No, she hadn't thought it through at all. And now she felt dirty, soiled rather than titillated. And she also hated the idea of Jez – her new friend – thinking she was a harlot, that she was like some plastic desperate wannabe on a reality game show. She respected Jez. She wanted him to respect her back. Some chance. What a horrible mess. 'I . . . I don't really know what came over me.'

Seb snorted. 'Well, whatever.' He swatted a black fly that

was attempting to gorge on his sticky thigh. 'Don't stop it in a hurry.'

Katy, trying to reclaim some romance, pushed his fringe off his forehead tenderly. 'It's not . . . well, it doesn't reflect how I feel about you.' She swallowed, her taste buds revisited by the taste of Seb's sperm, making her shudder slightly. She hated the taste of it afterwards, like eating a meal gone cold. 'I don't want you to think that's what I want.'

Seb hunched up on his elbows, smoking, exhaling. He kissed her lightly on the nose and laughed. 'Don't apologise! I mean, crikey, that was terrific. Next time, eh?'

Katy sat up on the day bed, rubbing her knees. He'd got her on all fours again (what was that, a New York thing?) and she had begun to ache. 'Next time? I don't think so. Seb . . .' She turned to face him, widening her eyes. 'Earlier, it was a mistake. I don't want to sleep with Stevie . . .'

Seb's face fell.

'Or Jez. Or anyone. I want to sleep with *you*. I love you. I really love you, Sebastian.'

Seb crunched out his cigarette and lay on his back, staring up at the vaulted silk ceiling. 'Just when I thought things were about to get interesting.'

Katy deflated. It had all back-fired horribly. Should she try the direct approach now? Why not? Nothing else seemed to have worked. She took a deep breath. 'Seb, darling, I think we need to move things along.'

Seb, looking less distracted, bridged his head on one arm. 'What? Our sex life? I'm open to ideas.'

'No, no.' She put her hand to her mouth, losing her nerve, suddenly terrified that by putting him in a corner she might get the answer she didn't want. 'Shall I order some drinks in?'

Seb raked his hair off his face. 'Move what along?'

'It's . . . oh please, don't make me say it.'

Seb sat up quickly. 'Say what?'

'I want to know where I stand, Seb.' The words no woman ever wants to utter, she thought resentfully. She may as well scribble her name on the relationship's death warrant.

Seb groaned, covered his face melodramatically with one palm. 'Is this about babies?'

'Well, yes and no.' She tried her best to sound breezy. 'It's about the future. We've been together for two years. I am thirty-six years old. Or, put it another way, in four years I will be celebrating my fortieth birthday.'

'You look about twenty-three. I wouldn't worry if I were you.'

'My eggs are *still* thirty-six years old. If we want to have kids we need to get on with it.'

'Whoa! Kids? Slow down, Katy.' A muscle twitched in Seb's fine-boned jaw.

'*Slow down?* We couldn't get any fucking slower!' Something snapped. Katy jumped off the bed, a hot angry flush spreading across her naked breasts. 'You're treating me like a teenager trying to pin you down to a date. What is your fucking problem?'

Seb coughed, biding his time, scrabbling for retorts. 'I am sorry you feel like that, Katy. I hope I haven't misled you in any way.' As he spoke he was aware how much he'd hate that line if someone pulled it on him. He reached out and placed a hand on her silky shoulder, experiencing a pang of shame. 'I know it's been difficult with me in New York and everything. And . . .'

Katy sniffed, trying to stifle the humiliation of tears. 'In the early days, you said to me many times that you wanted marriage, kids . . . God, I hate sounding so pathetic. But nothing ever bloody well *happens*, Seb.'

Seb rearranged his features into something reassuring. 'Katy, sweetheart, I *am* sorry. It's just that my career is taking off, finally, and I adore you, you know that, but I'm not in a position to . . .' He looked at Katy's face – streaming with tears now, snot bubbling in her perfect tiny nostrils – and felt anger, anger that she could make him so guilty. He hadn't *promised* anything, had he? 'Katy, it's OK for you. You've had your fun, your career. That's all we ever talked about when we first met. The make-up artists, the magazines, your glamorous life in your twenties. But now it's *my* turn. I'm younger than you. I am a man. And I don't want domesticity right now. I want New York. Possibilities, promotions, travel! I wouldn't be around enough for kids. You *know* that. I know you do. Just because you've suddenly decided to unwed yourself to your career for babies, you can't expect me to do the same. It's not fair.'

'But I don't have endless time.' Her eyes glinted desperately. 'I'll sign a pre-nup. Would that change things? I'm not after your money, you know that. I hope you know that.'

'I know.'

'Let's just forget the marriage thing, Seb. I can live without a wedding, really I can. But if we want children . . .'

Seb's shoulders sank a little. He softened. 'I don't know. I just don't know if I *do* any more. Not yet.'

Katy's legs lost all their strength. She sank back to the bed, defeated, and suddenly feeling exposed and selfconscious she crossed her arms over her naked breasts. 'I'll look after it and everything . . .'

'I'm sorry, Katy. One day maybe, just not now . . .'

Katy stood up and reached for her sarong, wrapping herself up carefully, concentrating on not howling or hitting him. 'Right,' she said, wondering what to do now. 'Right.'

Seb reached for her shoulder. 'Let's reassess the situation in a year, yeah?'

Katy bit too hard on her lip, tasting blood.

Twenty-four

The following day Stevie finally managed to prize her repent-ant (always repentant after the event) husband off the Blue Blossom sun lounger to visit the rest of the island. He agreed, of course. Out of guilt. Even though he had been sheepishly waiting at their villa for her when she returned from the beach yesterday, full of apologies and mitigating excuses of drunkenness and high spirits, something had palpably changed between them. His desire for Katy – even if it had been fleeting and unconsummated – was an ugly and treach-erous thing that had put a metre-wide stretch of sheet between their bodies in bed last night and had made her guard her nakedness when she dressed in the morning.

Stevie stepped back off the road as a moped spluttered past, narrowly missing shaving off her toes. She wasn't used to the bustle and traffic after the luxurious sterility of the Blue Blossom. But it felt surprisingly good to be back in some form of urbanity. She was grateful for the distractions: the jugglers; the hippies; the middle-aged western sex tourists; the were-they-were-they-not lady boys – Lara would love them, she thought; the chopped pineapple wedges which stung the corners of her mouth; the charred corns smoking on roadside stoves, sweeter than anything she'd had in London; the fast *ack ack* of Thais speaking, laughing; the seedy hassle. Stevie realised how much the Blue Blossom, in all its facilitating luxury, had been sucking her inwards. But here, so viscerally distracted, she could almost enjoy herself.

But, as had become apparent, what she enjoyed and what Jez enjoyed did not always dovetail. His quest for repentance soon forgotten in the afternoon heat, Jez began to moan. About being tired. The hassle. The noise. The sun. To placate him, she agreed to pick up a taxi and venture out on tarmac roads, then a dusty track, past huts with tin roofs and children scratching sticks in the dust and gnarled old men smoking and staring at the passing traffic, away from the town, to a small cove that the taxi driver recommended, and a reggae bar, owned by the driver's uncle, that sold pancakes and seafood. Rather than discuss jacuzzi-gate, they small-talked about the scenery, like polite strangers thrown together in a group package holiday. Whether out of guilt or embarrassment, Jez seemed distracted now, dreamy even, a little lost to her. Stevie made her escape, leaving Jez nursing a Tiger beer while she walked down to the ocean's edge, the water frilling around her feet, the wet sand squidging between her toes like potter's clay. A teenage jewellery seller approached, offering beads and hair braids and Buddha necklaces. Stevie smiled but turned down his invitation to bargain for a fake Prada purse. No, she didn't know his friend George Armstrong in Hemel Hempstead. England was pretty big but, sure, she'd look out for him.

Keeping her eye on Jez, a pink figure pulling down his sunhat, nodding his head in time to Bob Marley's 'No Woman No Cry', Stevie walked further along the beach, studying the surrounding landscape: a steep cliff, then a gentler slope upholstered with the roofs of palm trees like a button-back chair. She wondered about the tsunami's legacy. The Blue Blossom had hardly been touched. But a few miles down the coast, lives had been flooded and smashed, she knew that. Was this one of those places? Were the boats mashed here? Had those buildings been recently rebuilt? It was hard to believe anything had happened here alongside the calm sea.

As she stared at the beach, eyes half shut against the glare of the sun, the clearer she could see Sam, his muscular frame bending over a shovel, silhouetted against the bleached-blue sky. She took off her sunglasses, rubbed her eyes. Get a grip, girl. The figure in the distance was a Thai fisherman. And Sam had volunteered to help in Khao Lak, not here. Still, how much she'd give to be with him right now. As this thought hit her, she clamped her hand across her mouth, shocked at the inappropriateness of her own imaginings.

Stevie sat down, arranging her skirt to protect her bare legs from the blind heat of the sand. How did she get here? How did Jez? It seemed suddenly preposterous that they were together, married, on honeymoon. If he wanted to sleep with other women, why did he marry her? Why did the thought of children make her increasingly anxious when she'd spent the last two years yearning for them? None of it made any sense at all. All she knew was that this exotic paradise only served to highlight the failures of a marriage that had barely begun.

She could see that Jez was chatting to the bar owner now, slumping back in the chair, laughing. He made friends easily. She'd always loved him for his readiness to accept people, from whatever walk of life, a certain generosity of spirit. Perhaps the jacuzzi incident, however cruel it seemed to her at the time, actually came from the same guileless place. You couldn't edit your lover and marry only the good bits, could you? Wasn't that what marriage was about, compromise, acceptance? Stevie gazed across the ocean. As she watched, it darkened and roughened, consecutive lines of peaked waves moving across its surface like a rough weave.

Was Jez waving? Feeling the temperature of the air drop, Stevie got up quickly, her heels creating two little potholes in the sand, and walked towards him across the beach. Each drag of her feet took her away from the image of Sam digging and closer and closer to her husband, who was waving a beer bottle in greeting with one hand and scratching his armpit with the other.

After lunch the next day, a cool, polite lunch – things felt even more awkward now – Jez dropped off to sleep in the villa, mouth agape, lip stuck on tooth. Stevie pottered, pleased to have space to think and do all those necessary little tasks such as washing out her bikini bottoms and emptying the sand from the bottom of her handbag and trying not to think too hard about her marriage. Her mother phoned to tell her that Poppy's little boy had stopped breathing again, been resuscitated. It really wasn't good news, she said. Little Tommy's survival hung in the balance. Stevie clicked the phone shut and before she could react to the news was startled by a loud groan coming from the bedroom. She walked through, bare feet slapping the air-con-cold tiles, to find Jez sobbing into his pillow. 'Jez? What's the matter?' Cradling him in her arms, she felt her anger dissipate and the sad tenderness she felt towards Poppy's baby projected on to him. She suggested that they walk down to the beach, but Jez preferred the idea of a stiff drink in the pool bar.

'I can't see his face when I shut my eyes,' Jez explained quietly, twizzling two pink plastic straws in his cocktail. He

181

splashed his feet, which dangled from the pool-submerged bar stools. 'I can't remember my poor dad's fucking face.'

'Did you bring a photo?'

'I didn't think of it.' Jez gulped his cocktail, the more fibrous parts wedged within the pink straw, demanding a noisier suck. 'I can't believe I've forgotten what he looks like already. It's shit. It really is fucking shit.' Jez gave his balls, which were being nipped at by the trunk elastic, a nudge with his glass. They sat in silence for a few moments. Someone was waving from the poolside.

Stevie looked up. Christ. Katy. She waved, hoping she wouldn't come over. Jez just stared, struck motionless. Katy waved more furiously, mostly at Jez. And Jez broke into the biggest smile Stevie had ever seen and started waving back furiously. Katy walked past the poolside back into the main atrium, disappearing from view. Jez, as if buoyed and healed by the Katy sighting, smiled and turned to Stevie.

'You're still angry, aren't you, babe?'

'Yes.' Why lie? Stevie ran her hands over her neck, noticing that the pre-wedding rash was still there, faint pink bumps under the skin. 'It doesn't bode well.'

He shrugged and raised his glass. 'Nor does the sky.'

Stevie looked up. The rain hit simultaneously, huge fat droplets, a shower of water bombs. The pool area erupted with activity as sunbathers grabbed their towels and dived for cover, neat Thai staff running after them, picking up the lounger cushions, the trays of cocktails, spraying water as they opened parasols. Jez and Stevie shuffled further towards the bar on their stools, away from the water's splash-back. They sat in silence for a while, awed by the thundering rain, relishing the rare cold.

'How many times do I have to say sorry?' asked Jez quietly.

'It's not what you say, is it?'

'Really, pumpkin, I am sorry.' Jez, moved by the sincerity of his own apology, felt his eyes water. 'I'll make it up to you.'

'Another drink, madam?' The waiter smiled at Stevie.

Stevie shook her head.

'Why you sad?' the barman asked kindly, as if he knew the answer.

Because this is not how I wanted my life to turn out, Stevie shrieked silently inside. Because I am on a paradise island wishing I were somewhere else, with someone else. Because I always imagined that one day I'd get married and it would complete me, make life more meaningful. And it hasn't. Because I want babies but the thought of an endless future with this man, the father, really seems inconceivable right now. She smiled at the barman and sipped her beer.

'Don't worry, mate. The missus is prone to moods,' said Jez, trying to keep up his bar banter so that everything would return to normal and they could get on with the tricky business of having a romantic honeymoon, like normal couples. He leaned into his wife, shrugged an arm around her shoulders.

'Jez,' she said, quietly. 'I'm going home.'

Twenty-five

Stevie stared, transfixed by the veins in Tommy's hand. His skin was as translucent and delicate as the membrane that separates the shell from the white of an egg. She put her arms into the gloved hole in the incubator and reached out to her new nephew with giant rubbered hands. Tommy's fingers, his impossibly tiny fingers, closed around her thumb, covering her one thumbnail. Despite appearing as fragile as a featherless newly born bird fallen from its nest, he had notable grip, an instinct for contact. His chest – covered with round suckers and plasters, like the medals of a war veteran – inflated and deflated quickly. Oh God. Poor thing, little creature. She wiped a tear from the side of her nose before Poppy or her mother could see it. She'd never really imagined anything could go wrong with baby making before, not to her, not to anyone she knew. She'd only ever worried about finding the father of a potential child. That something could go wrong after this enormous accomplishment was too cruel for words. 'He's beautiful.'

Poppy smiled, exhausted but proud. 'I know.'

Patti interrupted her Tommy-directed Reiki transmission. 'He looks like a little Red Indian, darling. Look at that olive skin, what a throw-back!'

'Grandma Yates' Apache genes at last,' said Stevie drily. 'He's got the prettiest nose I've ever seen too.'

'Not his granny's hooter that's for sure,' said Patti, trying to bring a little laughter into this beeping ward where the battle for life or death was played out in rows of clear plastic incubators that resembled fish tanks. 'Is he smiling?'

Poppy shook her head. 'Wind.'

'No, no, look! He *is* smiling. Oh, Poppy. He's such a gentle, happy soul, you can always tell, even at this age. He's your own little Buddha,' said Patti wistfully.

Poppy nodded blankly, her sky-blue eyes someplace else.

'He's been OK today?' asked Stevie, trying to engage her sister.

Poppy nodded. 'Yes. Touch wood.' She reached for the wooden legs of a medicine cabinet and tapped them. She was now familiar with those wooden legs. 'The doctors say he's stable. The milk is doing its job.' Poppy spent half her time in the hospital 'milk bar', expressing breast milk via an industrial milking machine, then feeding it through a tube into the pinprick of Tommy's nostril. 'He's going to be fine. I just know it.'

Stevie exchanged a fleeting glance with Patti. They desperately wanted to share Poppy's faith. But it was hard to believe anything this small could survive. Tommy turned slightly, his skinny limbs shifting awkwardly from one side to the other, as if backing off from the invasion of the giant gloved hand. Stevie withdrew from the incubator carefully.

'Stevie, darling, why don't you pick something up from the café for your sister?' Patti squeezed Poppy's knee. 'You must drink lots of fluids if you're feeding. You need to keep that dairy well stocked.'

'Tea? Coffee?' asked Stevie.

'Tea. Builder's. I'd like that.'

185

'Mum?'

'Oh, chamomile, something mainstream.'

'You'll be lucky to get Earl Grey.' Poppy sat back in her chair, watching the incubator intently. 'When is Jez back?'

'Tomorrow afternoon.'

Poppy acknowledged the information with a nod but didn't look like she'd processed it. Stevie was grateful that she and her mother were too preoccupied to probe any further right now. She'd only been back four days and was already sick of having to explain the situation to friends, all the embellishment, the spin. Her story went like this: her sister's baby was dangerously ill so she'd decided to cut short the honeymoon, wonderful as it was, to support her sister. They'd agreed that Jez – who'd obviously booked time off work and didn't want to waste it – should stay in Thailand for the remaining five days. Hell, what was the point of *both* of them losing the luxury holiday?

But as Stevie's plane had plunged through cotton clouds into the tarmac-grey skies of Heathrow, the salty smell of the Andaman sea still hovering incongruously in her hair, Stevie was less convinced about this solo return. It made rational rather than emotional sense. It felt as if she and Jez were running away from each other. Consequently, she hadn't been able to face going back to their flat – even if it was only a fifteen-minute hop on the Heathrow Express – to drop off her luggage as planned and instead had got straight on a train to Oxford, to her parents' house, where she'd found a stoic but exhausted Poppy and her family huddled around the kitchen table discussing steroid jabs and her mother reluctantly accepting that her grandson's predicament was beyond the help of Arnica and positive thinking.

'You must miss Jez,' said Poppy quietly, caressing Tommy's bony spine with the tips of her fingers.

'Oh, I'm surviving.' Stevie stood up, tugging her T-shirt down over her barely tanned tummy. 'Right, now for that tea.'

A nurse buzzed Stevie out of the ward where security was reassuringly tight. She picked up her handbag from the coat hook outside – bags were not allowed into the ward for fear of transporting nasty microbes – and followed the signs to the café through endless pale-green unsettling corridors. What shall we paint the corridors in a place for sick people? Pale green. And if the paintwork didn't make you sick, the smell – bleach, cheap municipal disinfectants, dressings and toilets – would do the job nicely, she thought, the smell hitting the back of her throat with a sharp snap like an elastic band. She slowed her march. Oh. Oh. She really didn't feel too good. What the hell . . . Right. A toilet. Yes, a disabled one will do. Mouth salivating, stomach churning, she ran, hand over mouth, to the bathroom and vomited into the sink. What had come over her? Must have been that dicky tuna mayo sandwich she'd bought in town. But then she remembered that she'd been feeling below par for a while, since the wedding. And the rash hadn't gone. After washing her mouth out and smoothing her hair she felt infinitely better. Back on the café trail, walking through the corridors past rushing nurses, patients in dressing gowns, stretchers and wheelchairs, she had a strong sense that someone was staring at her, boring holes in the back of her Earl Jean jacket. She turned.

'No way. Stevie? Is that you?'

A familiar voice. Her cheeks flushed, her body recognising his voice before her brain confirmed his identity.

'It *is* you!' Sam grinned, all curly ended smile and pinky-brown slithers of gum.

'What the hell are you doing here? Aren't you meant to be

187

in New York?' Stevie, mortified that she might smell of sick, air kissed him – *mwah mwah* – careful not to get too close.

'Aren't you meant to be lolling on a beach somewhere exotic?'

Stevie blushed again. 'Thailand. But you've heard about Poppy's little baby? I . . . I came back early.'

'Little man.' Sam's face fell. 'I've been trying to navigate the ward for about half an hour. Thought I'd check up on him. I saw him the other day.' He felt he needed to qualify, fearful of intruding into Stevie's family business. 'I was in the hospital . . .'

'Oh?' It was always really awkward bumping into people you knew in medical establishments, and not the done thing to ask why they were there in case it was for something embarrassing.

'Nana.' Sam shook his head, a shadow of his springy hair like a puppet show on the glossy green corridor wall. 'She's been ill. She died. So I'm over from New York for a few days to be with Mum.' He looked at the floor. 'To sort things out . . .'

Stevie put her hand to her mouth. 'I am so sorry.' She knew how close Sam had been to his grandmother.

'She was ninety-four.' Sam smiled weakly and shrugged. 'And she'd prepared herself. And, well, I suppose as far as deaths go, it was a good one. She was high as a kite at the end.' He nodded at the two closed doors she was about to pass through. 'You're after that elusive café? That's the laundry room, dear. This way. Come on.'

Stevie and Sam escorted each other to the café, hands brushing as they walked. Stevie pressed the button on the drinks machine and a gush of treacle-dark tea splattered over the rim of her cup. They sat at one of the laminate tables and talked about Thailand, Sam eagerly demanding to know

188

details. Was the debris all gone? Was the seafront rebuilt? Stevie was ashamed to be able to give only perfunctory answers, explaining that she'd spent most of the time incarcerated in a five-star spa avoiding Katy Norris, yes *that* Katy Norris. 'The husband's flying back tomorrow.'

'Oh, right.' Sam looked puzzled, put his coffee cup down gently. 'He's still in Thailand?'

'Yeah, well, no point in completely wasting the holiday, is there?'

Sam shrugged, looking unconvinced. 'Suppose.'

'So, how's New York?' she asked brightly, swiftly changing the subject. 'Lara mentioned you'd met up.'

'She did?' Sam drained the cup in one quick gulp. He spread his hands on the table top, as if to lever himself up. 'Shall we head back? Fancy an escort to the ward?' He stood up, hitched the waistband of his jeans. 'You'll end up in Birmingham otherwise.'

'Lara?' Stevie tried to assume a cheeky casual look. 'You were saying . . .'

He grinned resignedly. 'She's a lot of fun.'

So that's the only information I'm going to get out of you? I'll just have to interrogate Lara later, thought Stevie. 'I miss her.'

Sam held open the café door for her. 'But you're coming over soon, aren't you? Hasn't she bought you a ticket or something?'

She nodded. He looked relieved.

Carrying the drinks, they walked back to the premature-baby ward, Stevie eyeing his left hand, strangely entranced as it swung by his side, warm and brown and so much bulkier than hers. She found herself so magnetised by Sam on this grim afternoon in the green corridors, drawn to his personal space, that she had to stop herself from walking into him. At times their chat would fall silent. They'd continue walking, soft footed, hands swinging, brushing each other when Stevie got too close, and would occasionally glance up and grin stupidly, happy to find each other accidentally in one another's orbit.

Inside the ward, Poppy and Patti were as Stevie had left them, staring at the incubator, Patti trying to persuade a nurse to play her 'Sound of The Womb' tape, the nurse saying it wasn't hospital procedure. When she saw Sam, Patti stopped mid-sentence, mouth dropping open.

'Sam, *darrrrrrling*!' The other incubator-watchers in the ward looked up sharply. Patti reached for Sam's hands and held them. 'Come here. Give us a snog. Oh, watch the tea!'

Sam grinned bashfully, kissed Patti and Poppy and cooed at Tommy, trying to entertain him with goonish faces at the side of the incubator. Every so often, his eyes would flick back to Stevie – her round pale face lighting as she caught his eye – then he would concentrate on the little bundle in the vast oversized Babygro again. 'You've grown, haven't you, bro? Easy on the milk, now.'

Poppy smiled at Sam appreciatively. He was the only person who didn't look at her tiny son and wince.

Tommy turned in the cot, setting off a loud beep. Poppy jumped up, paling. The nurse rushed over. 'Don't worry, Mum. False alarm.' She fiddled with the settings. The beeping stopped. The nurse looked at her watch. 'Visiting time over. It's quiet time for the babies now. Just mums I'm afraid.'

'Oh, yes, of course,' said Sam, leaping up. 'Sorry.'

Patti stood up and rattled the keys to her old VW. 'Poppy, come home for a bit? Have a long bath and a stiff drink. You look deadbeat.'

Poppy shook her head, stifling a yawn.

'Come on, Poppy,' said Stevie, holding her sister's hand. 'I can look after the kids if you want to come back later.'

Poppy hesitated and looked at the incubator. 'Oh, OK. Otherwise my other kids will forget they have a mother.'

'Lift?' asked Patti, looking hopefully at Sam.

Sam shook his head. 'No, no, sadly not. There's paper-work . . .'

'Of course.' Stevie's spirits dropped. 'How long are you around?'

'Just until Monday. We've got this big project going on at the studio . . .'

'Oh.' Stevie felt irrationally hurt. 'I'm going back to London tomorrow.'

There was an awkward pause, broken by Patti lurching forward to embrace Sam again. 'Goodbye, Mr Flowers.' Patti put a hand on Stevie's elbow. 'Come on, girls. Let's hit the road.'

Stevie didn't want to move, but the group around her dis-assembled. Sam leaned forward to kiss her lightly. He smelled of cooking and vanilla and human things, in complete con-trast to the sharp clinical tang of the hospital. He smelled just right. For a second or two she was entirely lost in an invisible fug of pheromones, eyes closed, before forcing herself to pull back.

She watched him walk down the corridor, pushing open the double doors with two fingers, like a cowboy walking out of a saloon, his figure retreating in the rectangular frame of the door's window, until his foot, leg, back, head, last jaunty spring of black hair, disappeared from view. She wondered how long it would be before Sam was in Lara's bed.

Twenty-six

'You hitting the sack already, Dad?' asked Stevie. 'I'm going home tomorrow. Don't you want some,' she assumed an ironic American accent to undercut the sentimentality that had no place in his liberal north Oxford household, 'like, quality family time?'

Chris pushed his glasses further up his nose. 'I will pass. Your mother has other ideas anyway.'

'*Jesus*, Chris!' snapped Patti, kohled eyes ablaze. 'I'm not suggesting we watch reruns of *Big Brother*. It's Scorsese's biopic of Dylan. Don't be so bloody highbrow. Oh, damn it, why don't you just go upstairs and throw yourself into a good book?'

Stevie's father drained his whiskey and clinked his glass back on to the dull unpolished silver drinks tray. 'I might just do that.'

'*Plus ça change.*'

'Let's talk in the morning, Stevie.' He kissed her drily on the cheek.

Stevie felt a sharp prick of sadness that her father didn't kiss Mum on the cheek too. What was wrong with the pair of them? What was the point of all those years of marriage –

what her mother had once unforgettably described as 'decades of compromise, peace negotiation and exhaustive invention in the bedroom' – if you got to your mid-sixties and started to loathe the sight of each other. Shouldn't they be enjoying the fruits of their old age, the free bus pass and Viagra or *something*?

'I'm off out,' Neil grunted, sliding off the sofa. 'Hooking up with Toe.'

'But it's *Dylan*,' pleaded his mother. 'The main man. Come on, sweetie. Hang out with me and your big sis for a bit.'

'Some whiny OAP? Let me think about that for one second.' Neil dug his hands into low-slung trouser pockets. 'Er, no thanks! Nice to catch up with you, Stevie. I'm sorry about your tan. Better luck next time.'

'Very funny.' Stevie smiled. 'Have a bath one day soon, won't you?'

'Later.' Neil departed with a whiff of socks and slammed the front door in a manner designed to make his mother click her tongue with annoyance.

'That boy . . .' clicked Patti, carefully rolling up the sleeves of her taupe Betty Jackson tunic shirt to show off her bangles. 'I'm worried about him, Stevie. He says he's going out with Toe, but . . .' She frowned. 'Oh, I don't know. Last week he told me he'd spent the weekend camping with Toe near Wytham woods, but I'd seen Toe in Cornmarket on the Saturday.' She bit her lip. 'He's lying to me, I'm sure of that. Why, I don't know.'

'Mum, he's twenty-two. He's not going to tell you where he is all the time. Why the hell should he?'

Patti looked hurt. 'He used to.'

'Maybe he's growing up? Like, finally.'

'Possible.' Patti shrugged, defeated. 'Now, how about a glass of something nice? Your father was given a bottle of

193

bubbly at college, some keeno student or other, shall we be naughty and open it?'

'I should say so.'

'Shall I get Poppy and Piers from upstairs? Or just leave them to chill on their own for a bit?'

'Leave them, Mum. They'll come down if they want to.'

'Oh, OK. One sec.' Patti disappeared into the kitchen.

Stevie heard the familiar sounds of the ancient family fridge suck open and then shut, the creak of a kitchen drawer, the pop of a champagne cork. They were the sounds of her childhood, layered with the laughter of her parents' drunk friends, the spicy pipe and cigarette smoke that used to thread its way up through the gaps in the old floorboards into their bedrooms, a happy, reassuring adult smell, before it was labelled passive smoking.

Patti re-emerged with two glasses of champagne and a bowl of greasy Bombay Mix. She sat down on a low-lying leather cushion, a torn relic from the seventies that had weathered being the height of unfashionability throughout Stevie's childhood only to emerge decades later, unbeknownst to her parents, the paragon of vintage hip. Patti sat cross-legged, bare toes curling and stretching. Stevie noticed that her mother sported blue nail varnish. 'What's eating Dad?' she asked, trying to forgive the varnish.

Patti glanced at her oversized watch. 'We've got a few minutes before it starts.' She sat up straighter. 'Your father? Usual grouchy self.'

Stevie trod carefully. 'Things seem, well, a bit strained. A little less like *The Waltons* than usual.'

'Nothing gets past you does it, darling? Incense, hmmm, shall I light incense?'

'*Mum.*' God, she was annoying.

'Oh, OK.' Patti drew her knees to her chest, resting her

chin on the hammock of linen, the flickering blue light of the telly revealing the age of her face but not diminishing its dramatic black-eyed beauty. 'Well, we've been married a long time, Stevie. You've all left home. I mean, obviously right now we've got a full house, what with Poppy and the kids, and it's wonderful, it really is, to have laughter in the house again, a queue for the bathroom, I can't tell you. But most of the time it's just me and Chris, this big rattling empty house, that damn cat.'

'And that makes you hate each other?' Try a honeymoon in Thailand.

'We don't hate each other, silly.' Patti paused, chose her words carefully. 'It's just that successful marriages need distractions. They need the dilution of kids or . . .' Reluctant to break the marital pact of privacy, she covered her mouth with the giant silver and stone rings on her left hand.

Stevie hoped her mother wouldn't cry. She hated it, shamefully resented it, when her mother cried. She never felt grown up enough to deal with the role reversal, even though it was something her mother had demanded since she was about ten years old and the marriage had developed its 'rough patches', as Mum had called them, as if referring to dry elbows. To Stevie, these rough patches had been barely endurable cataclysmic events when one parent would disappear for a few days – it felt like years – and her entire universe collapsed and she felt that somehow it were her fault. Weeping into Judy Blume at night, she'd told herself then that one day she'd have a 'proper marriage'. A marriage like her school friends' parents' marriages. Huh.

'As time goes on, couples need a reason to be together. There has to be an objective that binds you together, something bigger than yourselves. Poetry, politics, children, *something*.'

'If that's what you advise your warring-couple clients, they might start asking for their money back.'

Patti laughed, shaking her head. 'Don't be silly, Stevie.'

'You've got your friends, your work. Dad has the university, his books. Can't you professionally counsel your own marriage, for God's sake? I don't understand.'

Patti smiled gently at her daughter. 'And nor should you.'

'But everything's going to be OK, isn't it?' she persevered, disliking the childish whine in her own voice.

Patti massaged her left ankle's pressure points with her knuckles. 'In the end, whatever happens happens for the best. Life's natural rhythm must take its course.'

'Translate.' Stevie felt a familiar feeling of rising exasperation. Why was her mother so infuriating?

'Oh, Stevie, oh darling, I shouldn't be telling you this. It's not fair burdening your children. It's me. I *want* . . .'

'What? What do *you* want, Mum?' It was always about what her mother wanted, wasn't it? Or was she being too harsh?

'Well . . .' Patti didn't pick up on Stevie's sardonic 'you'. 'Me, me and your father, we're so . . . so different now. I want to explore, darling. India, Marrakesh, Berlin . . . Myself! All those secret places. Is that really so dreadful? Chris wants to hide himself away in the Bodleian Library.' She looked down, the day's remnants of turquoise eye-shadow now just a colour wash on her crinkly lids. 'Our stories are beginning to diverge.' Confiding in her daughter seemed to verify Patti's feeling of estrangement, reinforce its credibility. 'It's a transitional time. I'm trying to be philosophical.'

Stevie rolled her eyes, wishing she'd never probed into her parents' marriage. Her parents had their own dynamic and their own dramas that had to play out. Nothing she said would make any difference, she should know that by now.

They were not one of those couples who'd put their children at the centre of their worlds. She would always be slightly peripheral. 'But Mum, you are quite capable of dragging Dad to a souk. Drug or bribe him or something.'

'I *could*.' Patti laughed. 'But force him to be something else? No, no, that goes against everything I hold dear. You can't force things . . .' Patti looked at her daughter, alarmed. 'Oh, baby. You're crying. Baby.' Patti engulfed her daughter in a hug. 'Oh, darling. I've upset you, I'm sorry . . .'

Stevie took a guttural unladylike sniff of snot and tears, cross with herself for allowing things to get to her. She'd tried to hold it all in and failed. 'I just hate the thought of it . . . childish I know . . . you and Dad.' She looked up at her mother's face, realised that it was more familiar than her own. 'What hope for my marriage if you and Dad can't make it?'

'Your marriage?'

'How can I believe mine will work if yours can't?'

'Faith, darling.' Patti looked sad. 'Faith.'

'But . . . but . . .' Stevie sucked back her tears, tried to grapple hold of herself again. 'It's awful.'

'My marriage? Or your marriage?' Patti smiled. 'Yours? Don't be silly. It hasn't had time to get awful. If you think it's bad now! Goodness me, you've only been married a couple of weeks.'

'I know.' Stevie sat up, pulled hair out of her mouth, the irritation she had felt towards her mother now replaced by an overwhelming feeling of love and childlike neediness. 'It's . . . it's . . . oh God, I think there's a chance I've made a mistake, a big mistake.' She extricated herself from her mother's hug. 'There, it's out.'

'You're probably just being over-emotional after seeing Tommy.' Patti's face seemed to fold in on itself, losing the bright-eyed enthusiasm that so often got mistaken for youth.

197

Stevie wiped her face and took a deep breath. She felt a huge load lighter for her honesty. The panic subsided. 'The honeymoon it . . . well, it wasn't great, Mum.'

Patti smiled gently. 'Oh, that's a shame, a big shame, but *darling*, it can take a bit of adjustment. The romantic thing – all hearts and flowers – it's a myth, cooked up by courtly male poets in the Middle Ages.'

'You always said you *know* when you know.'

'Yes, I did. I believed in love at first sight. But I *thought* I knew about me and your father, didn't I? And now . . . well now I suppose I don't. And lots of my friends are in the same boat, or worse. Pam Hamilton's Michael has become emotionally incontinent and agoraphobic since he retired. What life is that for her? Sue's Jesse has had an affair with his secretary. I mean, the horrific cliché of it. Anyway, I'm digressing. What I mean to say is that maybe I was wrong. Maybe the human heart is more complicated than I gave it credit for.' She held Stevie's hand and stroked it lightly. 'And let's not forget, Stevie, I was twenty-one when I met your father. It was all quite different.'

'You were young and naive enough to believe in true love?'

Patti smiled. 'No, mostly relieved to leave my parents' house, relieved to be an adult, relieved to be having sex. You girls, well, you've had so much experience already. You've lived full independent lives. And what with the divorce statistics it must be harder to see any reason to get married at all. But you have to work at it. And it will be worth it. I *know* you, darling. You're the loyal type. You need stability.'

'A nineteen-fifties housewife trapped in a noughties thirty-something body?'

'Not exactly.' Patti smiled and picked a strand of dark brown hair from her daughter's sleeve. 'Jez is a good man. A little loud and insensitive at times, but colourful, which is good.' Patti lowered her voice for import. 'And, let's not forget, you want a family.'

The euphoria of confession evaporated. Stevie hunched over and sighed. 'There is that.'

'But, darling. Stevie, look at me . . . *look* at me.' Patti pressed her daughter's hand into hers and searched her face quizzically. 'That absolutely doesn't mean you should do something that makes you unhappy. If you are unhappy, truly unhappy, you must tell me.'

'Am I telling you? I'm not sure.' It was impossible to tell where one feeling ended and the other began; she was a conflicted mess.

'Nothing that's done can't be undone . . . Stevie? What's the matter? You've gone white as a sheet. Are you OK?'

Stevie stood up quickly, hands over her mouth. 'Oh God, sorry . . . I think I'm going to be . . .'

Plugged into her dad's broadband, Stevie checked her emails, keeping an eye on the time so she wouldn't miss the next London-bound train. New work interest. Great. That would supplement her New York spending. Becca having a party. Dom Roberts getting married, telling her to save the date. Yes, he came to her wedding, she'd have to make the effort for his, even though it was in Edinburgh. And a flurry of emails from Lara: Lara's date with the almost-famous illustrator she met at Bungalow 8; Lara's escape from almost-famous almost-mad illustrator via bathroom after one martini; Lara's heroic line-up of three dates ('romantic multi-tasking') in one night, none of whom was second-date worthy and one of whom told her he was grossed out by his earlier evening date because 'the woman ordered this obscene obese-making dessert. No one orders dessert'; Lara missing British men's way of doing things – getting her drunk, lunging – and wondering when American women actually get to have sex ('at engagement party?'); Lara's forwarded e-invitation – 'the answer to earlier sex conundrum' – from hot divorcee TV producer for casual hook-up weekend at The Breakers, Palm Beach. What was this? Lara turning down a swanky hotel in Palm Beach? Surely not. That didn't sound like Lara. She read Lara's final email more carefully.

> Have decided Palm Beach is too far to go for shag with man with receding hairline, even if otherwise hot and stinking rich. Also, Steve, I find that my head is turning towards Sam, you'll be pleased to know. Think you may be right – shit, aren't you always right? About time I went for a decent guy. Not hopping into sack too soon either. Almost playing Rules, i.e. not behaving like English girl at all. Crossing off days on BlackBerry until you arrive. ☺ L

Stevie swallowed, responded.

> Great! Am SO pleased about Sam. To add to your social menagerie, have passed your number on to Katy Norris's boyfriend, Seb. Hope you don't mind. He's a banker recently relocated to NY – wants to make new friends. He's less annoying than Katy (not hard, I know) but don't feel you have to hook up on my account. Just the messenger. And keep those legs crossed, girl. See u soon! S x

'Steeeeeeeevie!' Patti hollered up the stairs. 'Chris? Have you seen our daughter?'

Then the sound of her mother's feet on the stairs. The office door flew open. 'Stevie,' she hissed, bright eyed and animated. 'Got *it*.'

'It? What's it?'

'A test, darling. A pregnancy test.' Patti drew the test out of a paper chemist's bag. 'You don't mind, do you?'

'Mother!' Stevie put her head in her hands. 'Yes, I do mind. I'm only a couple of days late. I've got some kind of weird bug.'

'Perhaps. But you say you were sick at the hospital too.'

'Please don't look at me like that, like you're about to unwrap a Christmas present or something.'

'What's the harm? I'm sure these tests can tell seconds after conception these days. Now, can you manage a pee?'

Outside the toilet, Patti hopped from one bare foot to another nervously, like a father-to-be outside a labour ward. She pushed the door slightly ajar. 'All OK in there? Have you done it yet?'

'Yes, yes. Give me a second, for God's sake, Mother. I'm doing my trousers up.' Stevie opened the bathroom door, holding the white stick as far from her body as possible, as if this might somehow influence the outcome, her heart pounding. Yes, things had been tricky with Jez, but he'd been grieving. A baby would be a new start, wouldn't it? 'I can't believe you're making me do this. There's absolutely no way I'd start being sick so quickly.'

'I started throwing up a few days after bonking. Here, let *me* look at it.' Patti took the pregnancy test from her daughter and studied the two boxes. 'One line . . .'

'What does that mean?'

Patti re-read the instructions on the side of the box. 'Oh.' Patti pointed the stick at her daughter. 'No. How strange. This suggests . . .' She studied the instructions again. 'You appear not to be pregnant.'

'I knew it,' said Stevie quietly.

Sensing her daughter's deflation, Patti put an arm around Stevie and kissed her hair. 'But it's very early to test. It says

201

here to do another test in a week if your period still hasn't come.' She put her hands on her hips. 'You know my intuition is never wrong.'

'That's a slight exaggeration.' Stevie stared at the white stick again. 'Anyway, it's probably just as well I'm not pregnant. All things considered.'

Patti looked upset. 'Darling, if you were, it wouldn't be a disaster. I think you're just having early marriage wobbles. And I'm sure a baby would make Jez grow up a bit. It would be something—'

'Bigger than ourselves that glued us together?' interjected Stevie.

'*Exactement.*'

Twenty-seven

Did love in your thirties mean wanting the same things at the same time? Because without a consensus, love faltered. And at thirty-six she was no longer interested in the journey, she wanted the god-damn destination. Katy sighed, scanned through her camera phone for pictures of Seb in an attempt to feel closer now he'd gone, hotfooting back to New York at the first available opportunity. Ha. There he was standing stiffly on a beach wearing his navy Armani trunks, frowning after an argument about who forgot the factor twenty. There he was again, caught just as he turned his back. And there? Oh, bless. That was Jez, a halo of strawberry-blond hair ablaze in the sun, smiling a little forlornly: Stevie had left the day before. Seb had gone diving, so she and Jez had gone for a long walk along a beach to cheer him up. He had discovered a cute little off-the-track reggae café hidden in a delightful cove. And there they'd sunk too many Tiger beers and chatted and chatted, about everything really. She'd been nervous at first. After the jacuzzi incident. She'd feared that he'd crack jokes about it, as Seb had, or, worse, avoid the subject altogether as if it were something unspeakable. Instead he'd laughed and brushed the debacle off as 'too

203

much booze in the sun', as if she'd done little more than dance on a table in high spirits. And because he saw it like this she did too.

There was an easy simplicity to Jez, he didn't over-analyse. She liked this. And she also liked his crackly cough of a laugh, his straightforward sense of humour, his loud maleness, the kind of loud maleness that took up its own space and made her feel comparatively small and delicate and feminine. Because they were new friends – yes, they really had developed a genuine friendship in those few days after Stevie left, she thought – there was no history of disappointments, no agenda, just a delight in discovering common ground and the joy of male company without the complications of sex.

She remembered his last day in Thailand all too clearly. They'd sunbathed on the beach while Seb windsurfed. Between slurps of his melting pineapple ice-cream, he told her about his wedding, just a silly anecdote about his mother and a tepee and frozen peas, but an anecdote so sweet and familial that, to her horror, she'd burst into tears and, red-faced, tried to explain that she feared she'd never have a wedding anecdote, good or bad. And when she'd cried, snuffling her tears and snot on to the sleeve of her kaftan, Jez hadn't been embarrassed, he'd just wrapped her in his arms and said it was OK. And in his arms, for a few magical seconds, she felt as if she were suspended in warm salty sea water, supported, cleansed and weightless.

Katy checked her watch and sighed. There were so many things she should do this Saturday. And she'd done none of them. She'd only been in the office for two days since getting back to London on Tuesday, as she'd taken the Friday off sick. She'd tried to cheer herself up, filled her day with shopping, manic shopping in Selfridges for shoes, lingerie, a new dress, more treats, a facial – all the things that magazines advised as pick-me-ups. None of it had worked. Which was why she was sitting on the limestone floor of her bathroom in her pyjamas at twelve o'clock in the afternoon, nursing her third glass of wine, black salty rivers of MAC mascara streaming down her face, pooling in her new nose-to-mouth lines.

Damn it. What she'd give to be back on that warm Thai sand now. London had reinforced a sense of unease and help-lessness. Right now, she had never felt less in control of her life. She'd worked hard, so bloody hard -- she'd never expected a man to keep her – throughout her twenties and thirties to get to a position, career-wise, where she was able to step back, have a family, settle down and step off that tread-mill. And now that she could take her Marni heel off the accelerator? *Rien!* She couldn't make Seb propose. Or want babies. Want her, even. In fact the more she strove towards her goal, the further it slipped from her reach, as if the mere act of reaching out repelled it further, like swimming towards a beach ball in the sea.

Perching on the edge of her oval pod bath, Katy put down her phone and picked up the fertility home kit she'd bought from Boots, marvelling at how her life was beginning to be dictated to by these shrink-wrapped boxes of thirtysomething-friendly science, always packaged with a picture of a woman wearing a pink jersey holding the indicator stick, smiling dreamily – as opposed to peeping at the results through gaps in her crossed fingers – and pastel, always pastel lettering. She read the instructions. She had to come off the pill first? That would go down well. She could see Seb's face now. Well, she thought, a little more defiantly, Seb will just have to cope with it. He will have to use condoms. *She* wanted to know how long she had left, even if he didn't. And this little box of tricks would do just that, by measuring something called FSH – sounded like a face cream ingredient – in her urine.

Hopefully it would tell her that everything was working normally – 'normal ovarian activity' – and that she wasn't about to evaporate into a flaming vortex of flushes like a menopausal Wicked Witch of the West.

Katy tossed her contraceptive pills into the bin. As she did so, her answermachine clicked on. She stood up, not intending to get the phone – she couldn't face speaking to anyone, not unless it was Seb. It wasn't.

'Hi, hon, it's Louise. Hope you had a fab holiday. I have to tell you . . . this is so exciting . . .' Laughter in the background. 'Me and Hugh are getting married! I can't believe it! We're having an engagement party at the Lonsdale next month. Invite to follow shortly. Lotta love.'

Katy walked over and stared at the machine, its red blinking devil eyes, and, for one second, hated it as much as she'd ever hated anything. Nonetheless, it was harbouring another message – surely, Seb – so she depressed its button again.

'Hi gorg. Tom here. As honorary gay godfather-to-be, I am inviting you to Liz's baby shower. Thursday the twenty-third. Liz's house, Belsize Park. Bring lots of heinously expensive presents, obviously. Ciao.'

Oh God. Was there some kind of fucking conspiracy going on? Couldn't one of her friends just get divorced or something? Katy picked up her fertility indicator and threw it across the room where it slammed against the flat-screen television. 'Bollocks!' she shouted. '*Bollocks*!'

She slurped back the dregs in her wine glass, swimmingly realising as she did so that she was already drunk and could hear the hissing rush of her own misery which, up to this point, she'd managed to contain like bubbles in an unopened bottle of champagne. After all the preening and scheming and cajoling in Thailand, here, alone in her Notting Hill flat, unwitnessed, she could finally sink to the dark flagellating depths of a French film noir heroine, hair ratty, make-up rubbed wild, long legs starved heron-thin. Yes, she was fucking miserable. And unseemly drunk. Because what was the point? What was the point in anything? She pulled her fingers through her hair manically and stumbled towards the bathroom cabinet. Rifling through the aspirins and Nurofens, Katy suddenly got a very dark thought indeed, a blacker than black thought. For one crucial minute it made perfect sense.

Some time later – Katy had no idea how long she'd lain on those cool hard tiles – she awoke on the bathroom floor. And she awoke to a foul smell. Bleary eyed, she looked around her. Yuk. A lake of acidic liquid vomit was splattered across the tiles. Revolted, she pulled herself up on the cistern. What was that thing rolling around by her feet? She kicked it. Oh. No. Pill bottle. Empty bottle. Only then did she remember.

Katy managed to drag herself to the phone. She didn't phone Seb. He couldn't hear her like this. So she phoned the only person in the world she wouldn't mind hearing her like this, praying he wouldn't go to voicemail.

'Jez? Is that you?' she slurred, the words thick and hairy in her mouth.

'Who's this?'

'It's me. Katy.'

'Oh. Oh Katy. I've been thinking about you. You got back OK?'

'Jez . . .' Katy started to whimper. 'You've got to help me. I've done something very silly.'

'Huh?'

'I've overdosed.'

'What? Where are you? Katy? Katy? Are you there?'

'I'm at home.' She sniffed back tears. 'Alone.'

'Right,' said Jez, his voice becoming officious. 'I know your address. You're just down the road. Now, what did you take? Think carefully, sweetheart.'

'Wait a minute.' Katy scrabbled around on the floor for an empty pill bottle. How long did she have left? Was this how it was all going to end, in a vomity heap on her limestone bathroom floor?

'Katy? Katy?' Jez sounded desperate. 'Please talk to me. Are you still there?'

'Hang on. Found the bottle.' She read the label with rheumy eyes.

'What is it, Katy. Tell me.'

'St John's Wort.'

Twenty-eight

Rita lay on the sofa, her furry slipper-shod feet on the sofa arm, Typhoo in hand, cucumber slice on each eye, a fuzz of hair as white and wiry as a thistle poking through her hair net, a rerun of *A Place In The Sun* blaring. Still here! Stevie couldn't quite believe it. Rita had kept her word and stayed in their London flat while she and Jez were away. OK, fine. Rita, understandably, could not face being in the old marital home right now. And, as Jez had pointed out, they had house-plants that needed watering. But they'd both been back a week and Rita was yet to make any leaving-soon sounds. Every day Stevie came back from work – late all this week because they were putting the magazine to bed – with the intention of chilling out in front of the Channel Four news with a glass of icy Pinot Grigio and a bowl of Twiglets, only to find her space squatted by a bovine woman in beige slacks and faux-fur sheepskin slippers, smelling of talcum powder. The front door banged.

'Hi girls!' shouted Jez.

'Jez,' Stevie said, relieved to have Rita's company diluted. 'You're back from hospital. How is Katy?'

'Being very brave,' he said solemnly.

'On a twelve-step programme yet?'

'That's very mean spirited of you.'

Yes, it was. But at this moment she didn't want to work at her marriage, as her mother had advised, she wanted to fire it. She was seriously pissed off that while Jez had not yet found time to accompany her on a visit to the hospital to see Tommy, he'd been to St Mary's to hold Katy's manicured hand, who, while scarcely ill, had been kept in for observation after her comedy suicide attempt. No, Jez hadn't done much to salve her post-honeymoon doubts. Buoying up her belief in the marriage was increasingly difficult.

Rita removed the cucumber cuts from her eyes. It did not improve her appearance. 'Stevie, I'd kill for a refill. And would you be a dear and pass over the *Daily Mail*?'

Stevie rummaged through Rita's pile of newspapers and cheap papery weeklies. She handed her the paper and hoped it might absorb her for a few minutes.

Jez walked over to the fridge, drew out a packet of thick sliced ham and dropped each slice into his mouth, loudly grinding his teeth, like a rubbish truck pulverising discarded bits of plywood.

'What's for dinner tonight, dear?' asked Rita, not looking up from her newspaper.

Knowing the question to be directed at her, Stevie turned to Jez and looked at him quizzically. 'Jez?'

Rita stabbed violently at the *Daily Mail*. 'It says here, I quote,' she assumed her posh Radio Four, reading-aloud voice, 'goodness me, that "only a shocking three per cent of today's working women below the age of forty know how to cook quiche". Can you imagine?' She shook her head and tutted. 'Goodness me.'

Stevie howled a silent Munch-style scream behind Rita's back.

Jez noticed. 'Shall we pick up a takeaway or something?'

'A lot of saturated fat in those you know.' Rita looked disapprovingly at Stevie. 'Home cooking is best.'

'Quite. Feel welcome to use the kitchen whenever you like,' replied Stevie, as politely as she could manage.

Rita ignored her, rubbed her left foot vigorously. 'This foot is still not better from the wedding. I'm just not sure I'll be able to manage on my own at home you know, Jez.'

'You take as long as you need to recuperate here, Mum.'

As long as you *need*? That could be decades! Stevie didn't think she could stand it any longer. 'Actually, Jez, I might have something to celebrate. VIP Group Magazines have been in touch wondering whether I would meet the art director of this new magazine project, you know the new launch scheduled for next year I mentioned? No. Of course not. Oh, it doesn't matter.' After the extravagances of the honeymoon, especially Jez's spending after she'd gone, they could do with a good cash injection. He should be pleased, especially since he lost out on the last round of promotions at YR-Brand. Jez didn't look pleased.

'But at what cost?' interrupted Rita. 'Working so hard doesn't suit women. Stress eats away at fertility. Goodness me, look at these statistics!' She shook the paper.

Stevie tensed, sensing something was coming. A tightness in the head, like the minutes before an electrical storm.

'You poor modern girls,' Rita continued. 'It's no wonder you've still got that rash on your neck. And it's no wonder you haven't conceived yet, dear, really it isn't.'

How the hell would you know? Stevie felt a surge of love for her own mother, a gratitude that she'd been harvested in such a different womb. At least she could talk to her. She didn't understand lots of things, but she understood the need to escape from Rita. Stevie turned to glare at Jez. 'I thought we could go out for a meal, to celebrate?'

211

'I don't think living in a fumy city like London helps either,' Rita added.

'Fancy eating out, Mum?' Jez looked at his mother for acquiescence.

'Just the two of us,' Stevie hissed, behind Rita's back.

'Oh.' Rita sniffed loudly. 'Don't worry about me, Stevie. I'll just have some cheese on toast or something light. My bowels have been giving me no end of trouble since I've been eating the fancy organic food in this household.'

Stevie absentmindedly snapped off another shard of poppadom, even though she was already stuffed. 'Since I haven't got any work lined up for next week, in between shifts, I should go to New York then, you know, while I can. Don't you think?' The question was academic. She was going, whatever he said. 'It would give you and your mum some quality time alone together.'

Jez masticated his chicken tikka grumpily. 'Suppose. But what about your cycle?'

'I'm planning to take the plane.'

'Ha bloody ha. I mean fertile days.' Jez wiped his mouth on the back of his hand. 'Don't want you to be away when we should be at it like rabbits.'

Stevie coughed. 'I'm still waiting for my period to come actually. It's a bit late.'

'A bit late?' Jez dropped his fork with a clatter. '*Yes!*' he exclaimed, like he'd scored a goal, leaning back in the chair, raising a fist. Diners stared. 'Turbo sperm! Babe, that is so fucking *fantastic*!'

'Shhh. It doesn't mean anything. I did a test and everything.'

Jez looked hurt. 'When? You didn't tell me.'

'No. Sorry. You were still in Thailand. It was negative.' She shrugged apologetically. 'I didn't want to disappoint you.'

Jez looked at Stevie hopefully. 'But your period's late?'

Stevie nodded. She wondered how he'd react if she couldn't have kids. He'd never even considered that as a possibility. Nor had she.

Jez picked at an in-growing hair on his neck. 'I tell you, it won't be long. Not with my equipment.'

They left the restaurant, habitually hand in hand. The night was clear and cool, the smell of summer lemon-sharp. At that moment it couldn't be any other month but June, she thought. Other couples passed by them on Westbourne Grove, leaving trails of expensive perfumes and titbits of conversations. All were good-looking, as if they'd stepped out of the pages of a glossy magazine. It was as if attractiveness was a requisite of the W2 postcode, thought Stevie. Like a kind of geographical dating agency.

One year into the relationship, Jez had saved her from a rented one-bedroom flat – she'd never got round to buying – in Shepherd's Bush, where she was regularly woken by the shift worker and his girlfriend having sex on the floor above in the early hours of the morning. And once by a mouse in her underwear drawer. When Jez had asked her to move in with him it was a no-brainer.

7 January last year. The day she moved into her new life. Jez had hauled all her stuff out, incredulous at the amount of clothes and shoes and 'crap' she'd managed to squeeze into such a small space. Without her things, the flat had looked dusty, as empty and soulless as a vacant cargo box, nothing to do with her. She'd felt little sentimentality as they'd driven away from her single life in that rented van, just relief that her life was moving on, finally. When she arrived at his flat on Moscow Road it was baking, hot as a holiday. She'd opened the door to his – *their*! – bedroom and found it full of red roses, long stalked, many still

213

budded, which was why he'd turned the heating up to max, to make them bloom. She imagined then that this was a taste of things to come, a pay-off for her more miserable single-girl-dwelling moments. It hadn't been quite like that.

'Hey, dreamer, sure you don't want a nightcap?' asked Jez, just before they turned into Moscow Road.

Stevie shook her head.

'I shouldn't be encouraging you anyway. Don't they say you shouldn't drink even if you're *trying* to get pregnant?'

'Obviously the fun starts here then.' Stevie hadn't realised they were trying as such, more just not trying not to get pregnant, which after decades on the pill still felt pretty revolutionary.

When they got back to the flat, Rita was standing in the kitchen holding a steaming cup of hot chocolate, her vast bulk swaddled in a pale-pink towelling dressing gown, hair net on, like a witty wax-work installation you might find in an East End art gallery. 'Choci, Stevie?'

'No thanks, I'm going to crash.'

'Good night then.' A neck flush betrayed Rita's pleasure at her daughter-in-law's departure.

Stevie was still awake twenty minutes later, wondering why she couldn't sleep. It bothered her that she and her husband seemed to be experiencing the marriage in two entirely different ways. While the honeymoon appeared to have cemented Jez's certainty about their future – he certainly didn't want to waste any time getting her up the duff – it had made her uneasy about their marital compatibility to say the least. In fact her doubts were smashing into one another like cars in a nasty pile-up on the M25. The very things that she used to love about him – his loud enthusiasm and bombastic boyishness – were the very things that now irritated the hell out of her. She sighed, dug her hands beneath the pillow. Perhaps, she thought, a little more kindly, the groan of these thoughts were merely the sounds of a relationship shifting on to more mature ground, like the creak of wood expanding to fit. Perhaps all good relationships changed as they developed and trying to hold on to the relationship's past reality was as futile as trying to stay forever a teenager. Yes, perhaps that was it. She must ask Poppy. She knew about such things.

Damn it, she wanted to sleep. She had that meeting at VIP Group Magazines tomorrow. She needed to pack for New York. Her brain was like Oxford Circus, a constant crowd of thoughts, barging past one another, popping out of tunnels underground. Or perhaps she just needed to pee. Yes, she needed to pee.

Stevie reached out for her dressing gown. As she opened the door her dressing-gown belt tangled around her waist. She stopped and fumbled with it. She was dozier than she'd thought. And then she heard Jez's voice.

'Yes, Mum. Will you stop going on? I *know* that the money will come in handy. It's only been a few weeks. Do you not think we're trying?'

Stevie stood still, her curiosity aroused.

'I tried to discourage your father,' said Rita. 'What if you didn't want children? I said to him. What if your wife, what if she couldn't have them? I said to him. It puts a horrible pressure on a couple. But you know your father, bloody minded to the end.'

What on earth were they talking about? She couldn't join the dots on this one.

'Yeah, bleeding bloody minded,' agreed Jez quietly. 'Sorry, excuse my French.'

'Still, I can't see a girl like Stevie complaining.'

'She doesn't know, Mum.'

'She doesn't *know*? Goodness me, Jez, I think the girl has a right to know.'

It was at this point that Stevie, full of the rage of exclusion, stepped out of the shadows and into the halogen-lit kitchen like an understudy claiming the stage for the first time.

Twenty-nine

Jez hauled Stevie's sole piece of luggage, a nondescript black brick attached to two wobbly wheels, off the Heathrow Express rack on to the concourse. 'Hey, come on, babe. Overreacting isn't going to help, is it?'

Stevie snorted and pulled out the handle from her black wheelie suitcase. It clicked tartly. She started walking, the suitcase wheels rattling on the tiled floors and jamming in the ridiculously narrow metal gateways which some idiot had obviously designed with the sole intention of pissing her off. Stevie walked just slightly too fast so that Jez had to trot a little to keep up. He was out of his comfort zone, she thought. And so he damn well should be.

'Can we talk about it again? There's time to kill.' Jez put his hand on hers, locked in a white-knuckle grip around the suitcase handle. '*Please*.'

Stevie slowed down. Unlike Jez, she was not breathless. Rather, it was as if she'd been turbo-charged by quiet rage. 'OK, let's grab a coffee.' Her voice was quick, restrained.

They sat on two high uncomfortable bar stools at a small round table with a view of the concourse. The coffee was thin, the wrong shade of brown, and tasted of the plastic cup

217

that contained it. Stevie bit unenthusiastically into a stiff croissant. 'You really want to go through it all again, Jez? OK. Let's do it.' She cleared her throat, paused. 'You've kept secrets.'

'Secrets?' Jez raked his hair, in a show of exasperation. 'No, that's not exactly fair. But I realise now that I *should* have told you. I'm sorry.'

'Your father reveals that you will inherit a decent trust fund on the birth of your first child,' she repeated, still disbelieving, 'as long as you're married.' She shrugged. 'A few hours later you propose?'

'That doesn't mean *shit*.' Jez pressed his thumbs into his temples, dragging his skin in small circular movements. 'What the fuck are you suggesting?'

'Why did you never tell me? *Why?*'

Jez hung his head in his hands. 'Here we go again. For the hundredth time, I didn't tell you because I . . . I . . . I wanted it to be a surprise! I thought you'd be *thrilled*.'

A waitress scooped up the plastic packaging from their table with a claw-like apparatus and dumped it in a bin. Stevie wished the woman would scoop up her husband too. She shook her head. 'I don't buy it.'

Jez's eyes began to water. 'Oh please, Stevie. Don't go off like this. Let's just plan what we're going to spend the money on. Look on the bright side!'

'I don't want to think about the money. There's something ugly about it.'

Jez looked crestfallen, colour draining beneath his fast-fading tan. 'Don't say that. That's not fair.'

Stevie softened. Was she being too hard? No, damn it, she wasn't. His secret inevitably cast a bad light on his subsequent enthusing for a baby, over their whole marriage. 'Listen, I'm going to check-in now.'

Jez rubbed the small of her back, round and round, harder and harder, as if this might massage evidence of his devotion into her soft tissues. 'I'm sorry, really I am,' he said gently. 'I feel so bad. You should be going off on a high, what with your new contract and everything.'

Stevie nodded. Yes, VIP Group Magazines had offered her a job. A six-month contract. This, despite the fact that her mind was whirring with the recent revelations during the interview. Somehow she'd managed to string a sentence or two together, made a couple of wildcard suggestions. Luckily the art director had loved her ideas. But celebrating? No, she didn't feel like celebrating. It was like trying to sunbathe beneath a parasol.

'Didn't I say going freelance was the best thing you could have done?' said Jez, happy to change the subject.

No, actually, Stevie thought. If anything you seem slightly peeved that I am doing well.

'You'll soon be working with all those style-obsessed wankers.' Jez gazed up to the cathedral-height ceiling, the intersection of metal rafters, plastics and glass. 'This will all seem very humdrum, I'm sure.' He pressed his fingers to his temples and balled his face into a frown. 'And where's that period, eh?'

Stevie shrugged, the same mix of excitement and fear curdling in her stomach when she thought about how the absence of her period could mean the presence of something else. She should have done another test. It made sense. She just couldn't face it. She would wait until she got back from New York by which time her period would almost certainly have come and if it hadn't, then she'd do the test.

'Bang bang.' Jez cocked his fingers in the air. 'Super sperm!'

Stevie glowered. There was a time and a place. Neither was

219

now. She looked up at the board. She really had to go. 'Will you call Poppy for me? Just check in with her, won't you?' She hadn't been to Oxford for a week. Perhaps she shouldn't be going to New York at all. But there was something pulling her, tugging her across the Atlantic and now an even stronger force pushing her away.

'I'll visit them in Oxford, if that would make you happy.'

'I'd like that. Thanks.'

'I'll take Mum.'

Stevie frowned. That's all Poppy needs. Stevie stood up, brushed croissant crumbs off her jeans, delaying saying goodbye to Jez. A few months ago she'd have kissed him softly on the lips. Today, she could hardly bear to skim his cheek.

'Take care, pumpkin.'

Stevie pulled up her bag handle and wheeled it sharply towards the check-in signs, a lump rising in her throat as she walked away, her shadow a smudge on the glossy lino floor. They were diverging. She was off on a journey without him. The opposite of the honeymoon.

'Stevie!' Jez bellowed. 'Wait up! Stevie!'

She twisted around, stopped and stared at the thick-set man – her husband, God, her *husband* – waving a large pink hand.

'We could use the money for a bigger flat or something?' he shouted. 'We could have some fun with it, couldn't we?'

A group of travellers, all sucking coffee through lidded cups like infants, swivelled on their high stools and stared expectantly, waiting for a marriage proposal or tears, as if this was the last scene of a rom com.

Thirty

On the bumpy taxi ride from JFK, Stevie gazed out of the cloudy window, taking in the huge green road signs and their foreign fonts, the super-sized vehicles, the bridge and then, she gasped, Manhattan! It rose before her, almost exactly as she'd remembered, reminding her of the sparkling crystal towers she used to grow in chemistry classes at school. Heart drumming, she leaned back into the vinyl-covered seat to get a better view as the driver rattled an Arabic-sounding language into his mobile phone. As they drove through Queens into the city, its streets heating up with the afternoon sun, the air surged gritty and warm through a dollar-wide gap in the window and Jez began to almost drop away from her, like recollection of an inconsequential actor a few hours after the film has finished. The persistent feelings of exhaustion and queasiness that had been nagging at her for the last two days also seemed to dissipate.

'This good?' grunted the cabbie half an hour later.

Stevie flicked open her small red address book and squinted at the sign. This must be it. 'Great, thanks.'

The cabbie flung her suitcase on to the pavement. It wobbled on its two wheels, penguin-like, then tipped over. She pressed a clutch of crisp dollars into the driver's hand and stared up at the building, eyes wide, mouth agape, wondering if she vaguely recognised the street from an old episode of *Sex and the City*. Trying and failing to curb her provincial awe, she noted the New York details: the air conditioning boxes stuck to the brickwork like old cardboard boxes, the helter-skelter fire escapes, the model-type walking past with her two black poodles, cell phone glued somewhere beneath a sheaf of gleaming copper-red hair, the endless stream of skinny supermodel-alikey moms wheeling brightly coloured Bugaboo Frogs and sipping giant lattes. With a physical jolt she realised, for the first time, that Lara really was living an entirely different life to her own. She hadn't just transplanted herself to new geographical coordinates with a better wardrobe. It wasn't just a new job. It was a new life.

Apartment five? 'It's me,' she shouted into the grates of the intercom.

'*Stevie!* Ohmygod! Come up.'

The door clunked open. Stairs. Lots of dark wooden stairs. Stevie hauled her bag up, listening to a clatter of footsteps coming downwards, matching hers going up. Their footsteps met. Lara threw her arms around Stevie. She smelled of rose perfume and hot toast. Wearing black wide-legged trousers, a white vest and bare feet, she looked slimmer, blonder, more glossy than she did in London, like something from a Donna Karan ad. Lara took her bag and, careless in her excitement, lumped it up the stairs by the handle – *bang, bang, bang* – which looked like it might snap. Stevie held the hand rail, wobbly and unfamiliar in her grip, aware that as she walked up into Lara's life and this startling vertical city she was walking into the life she turned away from for Jez, for a more prosaic dream of a marriage and children.

'Great for the butt,' laughed Lara. 'This is it. This is home.'

The apartment's forest-green door was ajar, teasing the dark stairwell with a segment of sunlight. The toast smell increased in intensity. Lara threw the bag at the door and it flew straight into a living room and landed with a thud, banging the door wide open. Stevie stepped through into a pale airy room with large windows that faced the street. It was sparsely decorated with a few pieces of worn-in but chic furniture, a white linen sofa, a battered leather chair, an old utilitarian 1930s angle-poise lamp, lots of books.

'It's like a sitcom set,' Stevie said.

'Yeah, we get all the best lines here.' Lara peered around a door. 'Guys, the lady has arrived.'

Oh, they had company? A good-looking, pencil-slender woman in her thirties appeared, dark-brown hair cut in a short boyish crop framing sooty eyes and the kind of flawless complexion that either sported a brilliant foundation or didn't need make-up at all. 'Hi,' she said, American accent. 'Casey.' She had a strong handshake.

'Nice to meet you, Casey.' Stevie grinned. Then she looked across. Someone else. Tall, dark, feet big as loaves. She knew those feet.

Sam and Stevie hugged, giving Stevie pause for thought. His presence was a clear indicator that he and Lara were together, wasn't it? He'd probably spent the night. Head nestled on Sam's shoulder, she was able to lock looks with Lara and raise her eyebrows. Lara acknowledged her friend's quizzical appeal for romantic information with a shy smile and dug her eyes into the floor. Confirmed then.

Sam held her arms tight just below the shoulders and stepped back, as if to get a good look at her. 'Managed to rip yourself away from wedded bliss?'

Stevie laughed tightly. 'Just.'

223

'Tea?' asked Casey, sauntering nonchalantly into the kitchen, as if she were used to British guests descending upon her apartment on a regular basis and had learned not to spend too much time fussing over each one.

'I'd kill for one, thanks.'

'Grab a pew,' said Lara, pointing at the sofa.

Stevie hesitated, quickly checking out the seating arrangements. One sofa. One chair. Was she imagining it or was there a second of awkwardness, an indecisive hovering as she, Lara and Sam rearranged themselves in this new alignment of relationships? She sat down on the leather armchair, leaving the sofa to the lovers.

'How's my man Tommy?' asked Sam, leaning forward, elbows on his knees. His brown skin gleamed, burnished with the rays of the American summer sun. He was wearing cords, not his usual dark jeans, a white shirt, artfully untucked, chunky boho-scuffed brown brogues, an older, sharper, hipper look. Of course, he was a different person in this new context, not a neighbour or an old friend. Not even the person who gave her the pencils in the garden of her parents' house. All those past Sams now seemed strangely nostalgic. He was an English guy living in New York with a life she knew little about. It was a reminder, she thought sadly, that familiarity is not the same as knowing someone.

'Breathing is a bit better.' She gulped. Talking about Tommy steamed her up. 'But he's not out of the woods yet.'

Lara put her hand to her mouth. 'Poor mite. I'm so sorry.'

'Is your apartment nearby, Sam?' asked Stevie, switching subjects, not wanting to be the needy visitor who arrived on the doorstep leaking problems. She wanted to forget all the bad stuff, just for a weekend.

'No, I'm in Brooklyn. Ben, my cousin – did you ever meet Ben? No? – well he's in LA for a year. It's a sweet deal.' He

224

smiled, rubbed his cheek lazily. 'I'm looking after his rent-controlled apartment.'

'And cat,' added Lara. 'A neurotic, homosexual cat.'

So she's been there, thought Stevie. OK. She wished Lara had forewarned her quite how close she and Sam had become. It affected the group's dynamic. There was a pause. Stevie wished she could think of something interesting to say.

Sam broke the silence. 'I'm flying out Monday night too.'

'Not the nine-twenty per chance?' Her heart thumped inappropriately.

'The very same.'

'I thought New Yorkers weren't allowed holidays.'

Sam shrugged. 'Watton has given me the week off while he's vacationing at his pleasure palace in New Mexico . . .'

Casey came back into the room carrying a pot of tea on a Chinese lacquered tray and a plate of pastries. 'Fresh from Claude's. Dig in.' She kneeled down, curling her pink painted toenails beneath her and poured tea, glancing up at Stevie. 'Fleeing London?'

Stevie laughed. 'Kind of.'

'A great city.'

Stevie and Lara snorted at the same time. Like most Londoners, patriotism was not in their repertoire.

'The weather sucks. But cute men,' Casey said. 'I mean, look at Lara. Comes four thousand miles across the Atlantic to make out with an Englishman! It's the same with all my Brit friends over here.' She put her hands up in mock defence. 'No, no, I don't blame you.'

'Take no notice,' said Lara with raised brows. 'She had a bad date last night. Still smarting.'

Casey sipped her tea. 'He was the human equivalent of mid-town.' She glanced at Stevie's finger. 'You're married then?' She smiled. 'Quaint.'

'Just married.'

Sam looked down at his shoes, tightened his grip on his tea cup.

'Oh, you're still in the blissed-up stage. Lara, you should have warned me.'

Stevie smiled, engulfed by a sudden wave of exhaustion. If only they knew. She yawned.

'No yawning!' Lara tapped her foot against hers. 'Don't crash yet. You've got to stay up to get in the right zone. Now, what do you fancy? Shower? Bath?'

'Bath? Are you kidding me?' said Casey. 'Typical journalist. Bucket would be a better description I'm afraid.'

'A shower would be great, thanks.'

Lara stood up, then quickly sat down again on the arm of the sofa, agitated. 'Now, I've got to talk to you, Steve. I've got some bad news. You are, in fact, going to kill me. And you have every right to.'

'Hit me with it.'

'I know I said I had Monday off, but I've now got an interview in LA so I'll have to fly out Sunday night. I'm so sorry. I know. I know. But I've only just found out. Little Hollywood princess keeps changing the dates.' She looked at Stevie appealingly. 'There's nothing I can do apart from not go and get fired.'

'Oh,' said Stevie, disappointed. 'Don't worry.'

Lara scrunched up her face apologetically. 'Sorry, Steve.' 'But we've got the weekend. And the man's around all Monday, if that's any consolation.' She looked at Sam and smiled gently.

Sam cupped his chin in his hand, studying them all with an air of laid-back amusement. 'I fall short on many levels. I don't do Bloomingdale's, Barneys . . . But I wondered if you'd be interested in seeing the studio and just knocking about a bit afterwards.'

'Absolutely.' Stevie waved their concern away. 'But I don't expect your lives to stop just because I've arrived. Honestly, I can easily spend a day at the Met or whatever. Don't worry.'

Lara looked relieved. 'Well, now that's all sorted I'll show you the shower.'

The shower was coffin sized but accessorised with more designer toiletries than Stevie had ever seen in a domestic bathroom. She rubbed herself down with something foamy and spicy by Hermès and studied her body in the mirror. Yes, fat. She'd put on weight, definitely. Her boobs looked far larger than normal and ached. Was that a sign of pregnancy? And was it her imagination or were her nipples darker than normal, browny coloured rather than the normal pale pink? The more she looked at her body the more it seemed to conform to the pregnancy 'signs and symptoms' list that she'd found on a pregnancy website. But she still wanted to hold out for a conclusive pregnancy test, to be done at home with Jez. Perhaps there was also a part of her that wanted to delay the test because she didn't want it to contradict her positive diagnosis.

'Come on. Put your glad rags on. We're off out,' shouted Lara, just as Stevie's lids began to shut in accordance with the British time zone.

The cab blasted towards the meatpacking district. Stevie jolted awake when they entered Soho House, taking the padded lift up to the cavernous bar area where the carousel of faces seemed strangely familiar, like she might have seen them in a TV show sometime long ago, beautiful faces all flatteringly lit by low drum lights, the hum of collusive whispery gossip hanging over them like smoke. But after a while the jet lag began to pull her down once more. She huddled into the button-back sofa, seeking sensual reassurance in its

227

olive-coloured velvet, half-listening to Lara and Casey analysing the case of a magazine editor who'd started leaving a tell-tale smell of vomit in the staff loos and whether she'd do the same thing next weekend when they all went to stay at her place on Shelter Island.

Sam put his hand on her elbow. 'Man, look at you. Can I carry you home?'

'Sorry for being such a lightweight.' Stevie tried not to yawn in his face. When she stretched her arms it felt like they were cracking. 'I'm fried, Sam. Fried.'

'You do look like you belong in bed.' He grinned sheepishly at his verbal slip. 'But I imagine it's been pretty tough since you got back, what with Poppy and everything.'

'Yeah.' She had the sense that he was digging for something and instinctively counter-responded by closing up, betrayed only by the fact that her eyes had begun to water. Get a grip, girl. She'd feel so deeply humiliated if he ever, *ever* found out about Jez's baby money. Then it occurred to her, perhaps she couldn't tell Lara about that either, now that they were together. Lara would tell Sam: her best friend's loyalties were now divided. It gave her a sudden unexpected kick of isolation.

'I'll get this.' Sam settled the bill, refusing all offers of contributions.

Ten minutes later they stood outside on the street, the streams of car lights reinterpreted by Stevie's tired eyes as streaks of yellow powder paint. It was a relief when Sam did not get into their cab but kissed them all good night before striding off towards the Brooklyn-bound subway. It would have felt a bit weird if he'd spent the night.

Stevie settled into the sofa bed, trying to ignore the spring that thrust into her left buttock, safe in the knowledge that there would be no post-coital awkwardness in the morning.

A few minutes later, Lara padded into the room, barefoot, wrapped in a Chinese silk gown. She perched on the end of her bed, cradling a cup of chamomile tea, her hair hanging in a gleaming plait across one shoulder. 'Having you around reminds me just how much I've missed you,' she said softly, the city lights escaping through the gaps in the blind and painting the soft planes beneath her cheekbones pewter.

'Me too. But you've got a good thing here.'

'I know.' Lara sighed. 'You like Casey?'

Stevie nodded. 'Very much so.'

Lara beamed, as if it were important to have her new life witnessed and approved by an old friend.

'You like Sam?' Stevie retorted.

Lara blushed, one finger tracing the rim of her cup distractedly. 'Yeah, I like Sam,' she said slowly. 'He's a good guy.'

'He is.'

'Proof that I'm not a *total* calamity zone when it comes to relationships, Steve.'

Stevie pulled the duvet tighter under her armpits and smiled sleepily. She was dying to go to sleep. 'Don't be ridiculous. You're not a calamity zone. There's nothing dysfunctional about being choosy.'

Lara rolled her eyes. 'Come on, Steve, we both know that unsuitable men exert some kind of weird lunar pull over me.'

'Well, hoorah for breaking the pattern.'

'Hoorah,' whispered Lara, bending over to kiss Stevie good night. 'Thanks for being so understanding about LA and . . .' Stevie dropped her eyes. Lara picked up the evasive signal and lost her nerve, '. . . *everything*.'

Thirty-one

Every time Stevie felt a kick of dark nuptial introspection, New York City kicked back. The distractions began with an egg-heavy late brunch on McDougal Street, a scoot around Mulberry Street flea market where she bought some old amber beads that smelled of someone else's Chanel N° 5, then a long walk downtown towards Century 21, the city's warm winds blowing down Broadway like breath through a giant straw. Lara kept her moving, kept her stopping, shopping, until there was no point of repose, no point at which there was not something or someone who invited comment, no point at which Stevie could stop and crumple into Lara's arms.

Of course she couldn't resist telling Lara about the cash-for-baby issue. But it didn't get the outraged attention Stevie felt it deserved (suggesting Lara wouldn't mention it to Sam anyway). Lara, seeming a little preoccupied, dismissed it as 'typical Jez', a buffoonish but benign mishandling of events. And then they'd spotted some superb wedges in the Marc Jacobs shop window and laid the conversation to rest prematurely. They circumvented the Sam issue too, for different reasons. Stevie had been unsure how to play it: it felt disrespectful to Sam to treat the affair with the usual interrogative hilarity. She was more comfortable waiting for information volunteered rather than poaching it herself. But the volunteering never came. Lara was discreet to the point of oddness, Stevie thought. Was Lara in love?

After a final Sunday afternoon shop they got back to the apartment, exhilarated and exhausted and their numerous shopping-bag handles burning their palms, and burst noisily through the front door. In the living room Casey sat very still at a table facing a laptop, her yoga-honed neck and shoulders outlined fuzzily against the back-drop of a green screen. Ella Fitzgerald's voice spiralled up and down, filling the room. Casey didn't turn around, but greeted them with a 'Hey' and continued to stare at the laptop and pick at an outsize carton of blueberries.

'How's it going?' Lara asked.

'I'm good,' Casey said distractedly, not turning around, beckoning them over with one hand. 'Look, look at this, Lara. He might actually be perfect. I'm feeling a connection with him . . . he could be *the one*.'

Stevie craned her neck forward to see. Internet dating?

'Sperm hunting,' Lara informed her drily.

Stevie's mouth dropped open. Was she joking?

'Listen up,' said Casey, starting to read from the screen. 'Jens. Six foot four. Medical student. Blond. No, wait a minute, the writer, yes, he's a contender too. Although it would help if they elaborated a bit. There's me thinking, we've got a young Ibsen here but he could be scribing labels for tins of sardines.' She put her hand to her face and groaned. 'Check out this one. Two hundred and forty pounds! A genetic predisposition to obesity anyone?' She tapped a key and laughed. 'I don't think so.'

'You're hooked,' laughed Lara, dropping her bags to the

floor in a heap. 'I bet there are chat rooms full of recovering addicts.'

Casey swivelled round on the chair, smiling impishly. 'You call me when you've got your white picket fence all sorted. Until then,' she swivelled back sharply to the laptop, 'hold your tongue.'

'But Scandinavian?' asked Lara. 'Why Scandi?'

'Oh, OK, I guess I'd probably check the Jewish sperm, if I could find a vial without a diabetic grandmother.' She sighed. 'But it's nice to dream of blond babies.'

Stevie collapsed into the sofa, her feet as heavy as bricks. 'Isn't this a bit extreme? You're bound to meet someone.'

Casey shook her head kindly, as if humouring a naïf. 'Honey, even my mom has given up on that one.' She flipped her mouse to another donor, talking slowly as she read his details. 'I don't want to be waiting around for the right man, who may or may not deign to make an appearance in my life. I want to be proactive about this while I still can. Hell, I'm proactive about everything else in my god-damn life.' She sat back in her chair, stretching, like she'd finished a long work assignment. 'Juice?'

As Casey sauntered through to the kitchen in her skinny jeans, Stevie whispered to Lara, 'She's serious?'

'Kind of.'

'I can hear you! Don't project your English romanticism onto me,' shouted Casey from the kitchen, rustling through the cupboards. 'This is New York. Now, where's the ginger?' The whirr of a juicer followed. 'I'm thirty-seven years old,' Casey shouted over her shoulder. 'I haven't been in love since I was twenty-six. The last time I got to third date stage was when I was thirty-five, and that was because I lied about my age.' She walked back into the room, smiling broadly, with a tray of murky looking brown juice in a jug and three glasses.

232

'Can't you have a one-night stand or something?' joked Stevie.

'Totally. It'd be a lot cheaper.' Casey grinned. 'And you get a good look at the prototype. But it's not as easy as you might imagine. Men have got wise to it. My friend Anna is having an impossible time getting any one-night stand to mate *au naturel*. They're not stupid. Well, not the ones you'd want to father your child at any rate.' She kicked out her lean legs. 'Still, it doesn't seem like fair play to me. I'd rather pay for a neat sperm-washed sample.'

Washed? She wouldn't go there. Stevie marvelled at the way Casey seemed so matter-of-fact in her appraisal of the situation, so lacking in self-pity, so unlike the neurosis-in-Prada she'd half expected. It was liberating meeting someone who so clearly refused to become hostage to her dating history, as she always feared she would if it hadn't been for Jez. Yes, perhaps there was, in theory at least, a way of reconciling maternal urges with partnerless independence. Stevie nodded, feeling, for no particular reason, a flush of gratitude. 'Yeah, I get it.'

'Well, I don't, I'm afraid,' said Lara quickly, sipping juice, leaving burrs of pulverised ginger stuck to the glass. 'Human beings are a plague enough as it is. The whole planet will soon have the same person-to-square-foot ratio as Manhattan.'

'Argument sucks I'm afraid.' Casey raked through her choppy crop with her fingers, leaving the hair spikier and more boyish than before. 'The West's birth rates are declining. And this is evolution: high-earning intelligent single women – the kind of women who *should* procreate, let's face it – adapting to a changing sexual habitat, assuring the continuation of the species.'

Stevie grinned. Hard not to agree with that.

'The other not-so-minor point is that I'm perfectly happy to adopt. I may yet have my Angelina Jolie moment.

'I just don't understand. You've got this great independent life . . .' Lara paused and shrugged. 'Well, I suppose I'm just not made that way. Not like you two.' She looked at her watch. 'Shit. Six-thirty already. I'm going to have to shoot.' She winced at Stevie apologetically. 'This is crap, isn't it? I feel like I've hardly seen you.'

'Don't worry.' This was Lara's life. Not her holiday. She'd just parachuted into it for a few days. And actually she was much more comfortable with this situation than she would be playing the role of fussed-over visitor.

'And I'll see you the evening you fly out. We'll get you nice and comatose for the flight.' She stood up. 'Right, shower.'

Casey came back from the kitchen with some pretzels in a small gold china bowl. She offered the bowl and Stevie noticed how each of her shell-pink nails was subtly manicured, not chipped at all. Despite the magazines and growth of salon-culture at home, British girls, like her, were still no good at nails. Not on a Sunday at any rate, a day when her fingers were usually stained with newspaper-print ink and there were croissant crumbs beneath her nails. Their grooming default setting was far lower on the scale.

Casey's dark eyes scanned Stevie's face intently as if noticing her for the first time. 'So, you going to have kids soon?'

Stevie swallowed a too-big chunk of pretzel. 'That's the plan.' She wondered, once again, where her period was. She planned to do a test as soon as she got home. It struck her how very much simpler it would be to get pregnant by Jez than have to buy in sperm from Scandinavia.

'You don't sound too enthusiastic about it.' Casey rummaged around in a bag, pulled out a small ball of dark-grey wool, streaked with silver. She yanked the yarn and started pulling at the corners of a half-knitted square.

'I don't?' Stevie asked. 'Shit, I totally *am*. I'm so broody it's

234

embarrassing. But, oh, it's just . . . Oh, I don't know.' She stumbled, unable to articulate something she hadn't yet fully assimilated. 'I'm feeling quite a lot of pressure to start . . .'

'Oh, husband's going totally tribal, is he? Wants you to populate his cave?'

'Yeah, a little bit.'

'I love the sound of him already.' Casey laughed, bent one leg up, her toes curled over the side of the chair. 'Broody men are kind of endearing. There's something so old fashioned and feudal about them.'

Was that it? Could the explanation be so simple? Had she misjudged Jez completely? For a moment she considered blurting it all out to Casey, just to see her situation refracted through the sharp prism of a New Yorker, someone, perhaps, with a harder, more pragmatic view of hitching and hatching. But then her nerve failed. What was there to say really? It was all in her head. There was no *evidence* that she was not in love with her husband. There was no evidence it was the wrong relationship. There wasn't even any evidence that Jez had seriously set out to get his hands on a trust fund by marrying. He didn't have to marry *her*. He could have married a million other far prettier girls. And he chose her. So yes, she was married, imperfectly, but weren't all relationships imperfect? How to explain to Casey that she had all this and still yearned for something more: something more passionate, more meaningful and more consuming. Was this a yearning for a child or was it a yearning for something else? And could the yearnings be reconciled? And was it possible to sometimes feel like she was imploding, while the exterior of her shopped and smiled and exchanged information about the best muesli brands with her mother-in-law.

'Are you OK, honey?' Casey asked, one eyebrow raised, the expanding knitted square gobbling the thread of silver wool as her needles clicked.

Stevie shook her head free of thoughts like a dog shaking water from its coat. 'Fine, fine. Jet-lagged, miles away. Sorry.'

'Right! I'm off.' Lara bounced into the room, wearing a Pucci print dress that succeeded in making her look sophisticated but also five years younger. She tugged at a small cargo-friendly wheelie suitcase. 'Sam just phoned. He's coming to pick you up first thing tomorrow morning.' She winked. 'At your service.'

Thirty-two

Snip, snip. The scissors' stainless-steel blades sliced through finely woven pale-blue wool and Seb's Pringle jumper fell to the floor in a shredded heap. She hated that jumper, horrible banker-boy preppy gear. Snip, snip. Down went two Thomas Pink shirts. Snip, snip. The navy Burberry V-neck she'd bought him in the January sales. Guillotined: a knitted Prada tie. Seb hadn't returned her calls for over a week. He had slunk out of the relationship, without even turning out the lights.

Katy bundled the strips of cloth and wool into an old Tesco Metro bag and carefully placed it at the base of the wardrobe, near the door, so he would find it when he came back, as inevitably he must. She was not crying now, but fuelled by a new unexpected energy, a precarious joyful exhilaration that came from certainty in her own mind that things were finally over, that he had no intention of ever marrying her or settling with her or fathering her children. She didn't know what to do with the hurt, so let it conduct itself through the stainless-steel scissor blades. Snip, snip. Katy Scissorhands.

She stopped. Enough already. Damn it. Damn it. Katy's

rage suddenly exploded, once again, into a furious sobbing sadness. She would never wear her late mother's wedding veil. Her DNA would never spiral helix-like with Seb's. She was never going to see whether her nose would pass to the next generation. Her life, as she'd planned it, was over. Katy's phone rang. She delved into her large Chloé handbag, rummaged for the phone. Tara? She put it to voicemail. After a few moments it rang again. Emma? She put it to voicemail. She noticed that her rings swivelled on her fingers. She'd lost weight. For once, this gave her no pleasure at all. Shutting the door of the flat, she headed out into the rain along Westbourne Grove. She pressed the last dialled number on her phone. There was only one person she could face seeing right now. 'I'm here. I'm walking towards the market,' she said, breathlessly.

Jez ducked into the sitting room. '*Mum*,' he shouted above the *Antiques Roadshow*. 'I'm off out.'

Rita turned the volume down on the remote. 'Oxford?' she asked wearily, her wan tone carefully selected to arouse sympathy.

'Er, no. Just popping down to Portobello.' Jez had not been to see Poppy yet. He felt bad about this. But not bad enough to spring into action. Moreover, Katy needed him, in a way that someone like Poppy, surrounded by that big family and all her friends, never would. And it was nice being needed after his own spell of grieving neediness. It reassured him that he wasn't a victim, shored up his masculinity in an indefinable way. Not that it was a great sacrifice to help Katy, of course. He felt privileged just to look at her, aware it was a fleeting pleasure, like when you visit an art gallery and manage a few minutes in front of a famous portrait before the crowds of Japanese tourists jostle in and ruin your view.

'I thought we were going to Oxford together? I thought it was going to be a nice daytrip.' Rita turned the volume down.

'My friend, she's in a state, Mum.' He was answering the call of gallantry. He was rising to an occasion. He didn't rise to many. 'I have no choice.'

'Maybe I'll go on my own.' Rita looked thoughtful. 'I could visit Margaret – remember Margaret Dawson, who slipped her disc in Whitstable last year? – she lives in Banbury, a very smart bungalow apparently. I've been meaning to visit her for years. It's only a short bus ride from Oxford she assures me.'

'Really? But your foot . . .'

'Oh, I fancy a change of scenery. I'm going a bit stir crazy here. You know Patricia and I don't see eye to eye exactly. But she's got a lot on her plate with this early new grandchild, hasn't she? She could probably do with some company. Yes, I'm sure she could. And Chris is nice. I like Chris. A decent chap. And I think my ankle will hold out, if I'm terribly careful.'

'Well, that would be great. It would spare me . . .' Jez checked his reflection in the hall mirror. 'The coach goes from Notting Hill Gate, a ten-minute walk. Remember? I showed you the other day. Or the train from Paddington.' Jez ran his fingers over his jawline. Bit of stubble. Good. Kind of Daniel Craigish. He patted his stomach. If he could just motivate himself to do a few early morning Hyde Park jogs then the phad-thai tummy would be annihilated. Marriage wasn't a great motivator. But Katy, he was discovering, was. Jez cupped his breath, sniffed it, then set off, trying to break in his stiff denim jacket – annoyingly, his mother had ironed and starched it – by flexing his arms at the elbow, like a power walker. Using a mobile phone tracking system ('Opposite the bank.'), he located Katy gazing into the highly polished windows of an interiors shop on Westbourne Grove, focused on a modern ketchup-red sofa. His mouth dried as he got closer to her. 'Babe, are you OK?'

Katy pushed a tangled clump of blonde hair away from her eyes. Strands stuck to her tear-streaked face. Her cheeks were unusually convex, puffy and shiny, like tinned button mushrooms. Her eyes were about half their normal size and red rimmed, making them more electric blue than ever. Even her tiny nose had swollen to vegetal proportions. Jez thought he'd never seen her look quite so lovely, so vulnerable.

'I cut up his clothes,' she said, matter of factly.

'O-*K*.' Jez rubbed his chin and smiled. 'That's pretty radical.' He hoped she'd got Seb's suits. Smarmy bugger. 'Did it feel good?'

'Yeah. It was a rush, kind of like chocolate. But now I've slumped.' Katy allowed herself to wilt fragrantly into Jez's arms, pointing at the shop window. 'He loved this sofa.' The tears started again. 'People are staring,' she sniffed. 'I can't deal with Notting Hill fuckers staring right now.'

'Shall we go to the park, my sweet?' Jez had never called a woman 'my sweet' before. He wondered where the poncy words had come from. They weren't in his vocabulary. But, oddly, a woman like Katy seemed to require a whole new language. With an arm around her shoulder, he supported her frail weight, surprised he was so moved by her sadness and vulnerability, in a way that he never was by Stevie's tears, certainly not Stevie's righteous anger. 'This way, Katy.'

Jez directed her to the café by Princess Diana's playground in Kensington Gardens. They sat at a slatted wooden table and nursed over-frothed cappuccinos. Katy sniffed and moaned about Seb. Jez listened carefully and crunched a Kit Kat, admiring the rise and fall of Katy's décolletage as she sniffed.

'You are such a good man, Jez,' Katy said, wiping her nose with a Kleenex, wondering if Jez found her too ugly to look at. He could hardly meet her eye. She felt snotty, unkempt. Repulsive. 'Listening to me whinge on like this.'

'I try.' Fucking good to hear these words after the criticism, the constant criticism, from Stevie, he thought. Nothing was ever good enough for her. Fuck it, not even unexpected windfalls of money. Some people were never happy. 'Seb is certifiably insane.'

Katy sniffed appreciatively. 'You think so?'

'Damn right.'

A rabble of noisy toddlers jostled past, chattering like monkeys. Mothers and nannies carrying discarded coats and trikes and half-drunk cartons of juice tailed them into the fenced-off playground area. The playground gate clicked open and the toddlers screamed at the sight of the sand and swings, lurching forwards. Katy stared at them, her eyes swimming with tears. 'I have a dream . . .'

'A dream, Katy?' Weirdly, he couldn't help thinking that coming from Katy's mouth the words seemed to regain some of their original dignity and import.

'Yeah.' She pulled her hair back into a ponytail, twisting it to stay in place, her face exposed now, in all its cheekboned glory. 'The funny thing is, I always thought I was allergic to the country, but recently I've been dreaming,' she wiped her eyes, sniffed, 'that I'd get married, have children, lots of children with ringletty blond hair, and we'd move to the country, Devon or Sussex, a big house with old fireplaces and nurseries and utility rooms, somewhere I could give up work, pad barefoot around the Aga, grow organic vegetables . . .' A teary laugh. 'Oh, I know it sounds completely ludicrous.'

Jez was silent for a moment. 'It doesn't.' He cleared his

throat, paused. 'I'm with you on that one, babe. You know something? I'd love all that stuff too.'

'*Really?*' Katy smiled. A flicker of recognition lit up her face. 'You and me are quite alike, aren't we?'

Jez tried to hide the blush by scratching the stubble on his chin. Blushes weren't normally in his repertoire. Alien emotions were breaking out in him. It was like being in a girlie movie. This woman was getting to him. But stop it. Stop it. They were friends. Just good friends.

Katy didn't notice the blush, too absorbed by the challenges of her central role in the drama. 'I'm tired of working, Jez. I'm tired of the fashion business. I'm ready to downshift. I'm sure I could think of a small cottage industry, set up an agency promoting local crafts, something like that. But now . . .' she started sobbing again. 'Now there's no point. I'll be turfed out of the fashion industry sooner or later, you know, the moment middle-age hits. I'll have cats rather than children. I'll live alone in a Marylebone mansion block.'

Jez leaned across the wooden table, placed his hand on hers. '*Never.*' As he patted her hand, he suddenly became horrifyingly aware that what he really wanted to do was push aside the cappuccinos and the last half-eaten finger of Kit Kat and spread-eagle Katy across the wooden table. Like a Paris Hilton video. He felt himself stiffen. Shit, what had come over him? Get a grip, man. Get a grip. He paused, collected himself.

'You OK, Jez? You've gone all silent on me.' Katy studied him quizzically. 'Am I boring you?'

'Boring me? Never, never.' He held her hand, his surging desire to be noble, only complicated by an equally surging desire to fuck her. 'I would do anything, Katy. *Anything*, to make you feel better.'

Katy smiled sadly. What would she do to hear Seb say

242

those words, just once. 'Only Seb can sort this mess out, I'm afraid.'

'Of course.' Jez felt stupid. It started to drizzle. Time to leave. He took Katy's arm and they walked along the wide gravel-strewn path towards the ornate iron gateway where the park met the Bayswater Road. Katy refused his offer to escort her all the way home and, feeling reassured by the male attention – Jez always made her feel better – and able to face the world again, she took a bus towards Holland Park to see a single girlfriend, smiling as she waved from the top deck, face dry now, features shrunk back to their normal pretty delicacy.

Jez gripped one of the cool iron railings to steady himself as he watched the bus speed down the road. He felt dizzy. His heart drummed erratically. Something had happened. A switch had flipped, inside where he couldn't control it. Although he walked slowly, not wanting to get to any destination too quickly, inside he was careering out of control, like a Porsche 911 with a broken brake belt. He felt unable to return to the flat, the marital home, so he turned back to the park, crunching up the gravel once again towards Kensington, past skaters, roller bladers, pushchairs, joggers, dogs and flocks of tourists. He walked and walked. Then something caught his eye. At first he thought it was a pile of clothes on the gravel, beside a bench. Then the clothes belched. It was a human being: a man, young but prematurely aged, green eyes bright against his exhaust fume-coated skin. Jez's instinct was to walk faster. The man stretched out an arm, cupped dirty palm upturned. Usually at this point Jez would break into a quick trot and once out of earshot mutter, 'Get a job.' Today something made him stop. The beggar stared at him reproachfully, preparing himself for a Jesus-can-save-you speech or an offer of half a Pret A Manger sandwich. Jez dug into his wallet, pulled out a tenner. Then another. The two notes fluttered in his fingers. The heap-of-clothes man snatched at the money before Jez had a chance to change his mind. 'Thanks, mate.'

Jez walked on, heart full, singing and swelling beneath his Ted Baker shirt, reliving the moment of his generosity. The rain quit. The sun burst out from the clouds, wrapping everything in glorious custard-yellow light. And as Jez walked he felt almost overcome by an unprecedented desire to be a better person: to throw away the porn mags he stashed in his desk at work; to fire crap hirelings more nicely; to stop moaning about immigration; to live a good life.

Fuck me, thought Jez, something freaky is going on.

Thirty-three

The New York City air was scorching hot. Foreheads glistened. Wet patches bloomed beneath city shirts. Duane Reade had a rush on deodorant. Stevie wore the simple white Gap vest she'd planned to wear beneath a light jersey top, but without the top. The vest clung to her boobs, which had grown to such Jordan-like proportions in the last few days that they made her stoop self-consciously. She kicked her legs into a pair of baggy linen trousers, slipped on her favourite pair of shoes, turquoise low-heeled Prada sandals, and tied her hair back into a ponytail, enjoying its shoulder-to-shoulder swish as she walked along Twelfth in Chelsea, sandwiched between choking traffic on one side and the grey moving mass of the Hudson, glimpsed between buildings, on the other. Now that Lara had gone she felt strangely alone, small in the city. She looked up at a forbiddingly large concrete warehouse. Was this it? Above the entrance – huge panelled sheet-metal doors – in industrial grey lettering it read TW Studio. OK. She'd arrived. She felt uneasy, nervous even. Perhaps she really should have gone to MOMA on her own, licked her wounds in front of abstracts that she'd never understand, rather than hang out with Sam. How would she keep up the act? The chit-chat? How could she do that when she could almost feel Jez's breath on her shoulder and hear the tick-tock of the clock as the hour of her flight home raced closer and closer? This was all just a distraction from her real life, a reminder of what she would never have. She rang the bell.

After a lift journey in something akin to an old crate, she creaked open a prison-heavy door, rang more bells. Ah, a human being. The receptionist was all elbows and huge green eyes, dressed in black. She didn't smile. 'Can I help you?'

'Hi. I'm meeting Sam Flowers?'

The girl's face immediately softened into a white-toothed smile. 'Sam? Sure. Sit down, I'll buzz him.'

Stevie looked around. The waiting area of the studio was homage to the studio's owner, the photographer Ted Watton, who was now in his late seventies but, unlike most of the subjects he'd photographed over the years, had never gone out of fashion. His black-and-white pictures lined the walls: a gun; a boned corset; an assortment of movie stars and sinewy fashion models wearing nothing but Watton's trademark molten lighting. Stevie sat down on a low battered brown-leather sofa the size of Lara's living room, entranced and subdued by the spectacular images on the walls.

'Stevie?' Sam appeared wearing black-framed glasses, his curls messed up, rubbing something wet off on to his jeans, something of the mad professor about him.

'Not one red eye.' Stevie pointed to the walls. 'Awesome.'

'Aha, we edit the red eyes out.'

'Don't. I want to believe they all come out perfect.'

'I've just finished up some of my own stuff. Do you want a quick look around?' he beamed, full of boyish enthusiasm.

'Love to.' Stevie followed Sam down a dark corridor, noticing how he walked with a bounce, his body graceful, purposeful, all parts of him – bottom, thighs, arms – moving separately, like the joints of an artist's wooden model. 'So you manage all this?'

Sam shook his head. 'A lot of it. But Watton's moved me from an organisational role to more hands-on stuff, which is great. I'm learning so much. He's kind of taken me under his wing.'

'Clever you.'

Sam smiled. 'Well, it's not law, as Mum keeps pointing out.' He put on his mother's accent. '"Not a job for life, honey. You make sure that old man treats you right . . ." Yes, you can imagine.' He stopped by a large door. 'One sec, just need to check it's empty . . .' He poked his head around the door. 'Yeah, yeah, it's free. Come in. This is my favourite studio. It's a monster.'

The room was dark, cavernous, of airport proportions. Sam pressed a button. The far wall, which appeared to be a vast window covered by one black shutter, began to slide and click as the shutter came up, exposing New York City in sun-shiny slices. There was the usual paraphernalia of a photographer's studio – white light boxes, foil metal umbrellas, industrial spotlights with bulbs the size of human heads – but on a spectacular scale. Stevie had never seen anything like it.

'We had Nicole Kidman here last week,' grinned Sam, unable to contain himself. 'Condoleezza the week before.' He laughed. 'Sorry, I'm insufferable. Come on, through here.' He touched her hand lightly.

Stevie jolted at the touch, a charge of energy shooting up her wrist, almost like a sharp pain. Their hands leaped apart. Where the hell did that come from? Shy of meeting his eye, she concentrated on the studios, the dark chemical-smelling rooms, the closets with clothes racks as long as runways, the light-bulb-studded make-up areas, where mirrored walls reflected beautiful faces to infinity, more printing rooms. Sam carefully explained the processes and chemical alchemy that took place in each white space. Stevie listened, fascinated. She'd never seen him in a professional environment, infused in the things he loved. At that exact moment Stevie felt she got her first real glimpse of Sam who, like a photographic image dunked in the developing fluid tray, was beginning to fill out and take form in front of her very eyes. And his enthusiasm was catching. As a designer, she shifted things around on the computer screen, enlarged, shrank and rotated them, but here was the physical industrial process behind the very best of those images, where the alchemy from spotty to supermodel took place. It was strangely humbling.

In the last dark-room, lit by a soft-pink light, Sam pointed to some prints, dark, shadowy images, some still wet, pegged up on wires along one wall. 'Mine,' he said quietly, unable to keep the pride from his voice.

'You did these?' Stevie looked at Sam, wondering why she hadn't seen his work before. 'They're great.' There were moody cloudscapes, abstracts. One print, small, with mottled edges, caught her eye. She leaned towards it. 'That is very beautiful. Although, if I may be so crude as to assume it's meant to represent something, I have no idea what that is.'

'A dandelion clock. Very close up. Hand tinted.' Sam effected an exaggerated expression of sheepishness. 'Originally from your parents' garden.' He unpegged the print, blew on it. 'Hope you don't mind. It was so perfect . . . Do you remember the day I gave you those pencils? I picked it then and shoved it in my back pocket in a Morrissey-like fashion. When I got home I found the dandelion had survived the encounter with my Levi's, more or less. It was still this defiant round ball. I thought that was kind of cool. I liked its spirit.'

She hesitated. Sam Flowers picking dandelions? It all just seemed too unlikely for words. And yet it also made a kind of perfect sense. 'Where is this denim-defying dandelion now?'

'Oh, in the ether somewhere. Seeding some front garden in Jericho probably.' He offered the photo in his upturned palm. 'Would you like it?'

Stevie nodded hesitantly. She didn't want to betray the fact that her mouth was dry, her heart thumping.

Sam stared at the floor, embarrassed. 'I know it's not exactly Irving Penn. I won't be offended . . .'

'No, no. I love it.'

'Then you must have it.'

As he handed her the photo she took hold of one of its corners. For a strange intense moment both their hands were attached and connected by the same square of photographic paper, neither of them wanting to let go. She laughed. He smiled and finally dropped his hand away, relinquishing the image. Stevie stared at the picture, wondering why it felt inappropriate, this bit of home, picked and trapped so beautifully and returned to her in this small room suffused by blossom-pink light. Her heart began to pound. 'Thanks, Sam,' she managed.

Sam shuffled his feet, coughed. 'Let's shoot,' he said quickly, as if eager to escape the intimacy of the room.

The door opened. An old man, sporting a beanie hat, architectural glasses and a crumpled black linen jacket, stood in the doorway, his small wiry frame silhouetted by the corridor's bluish light. He didn't smile. 'So you're here, Flowers.'

Sam stood up straighter. 'Ted, this is my old friend Stevie, from London. Stevie, Ted Watton.'

'You've not come to take him away, have you?' asked Watton gruffly, looking Stevie up and down with unmasked irritation.

Stevie shook her head, in awe of the great man with his famous piercing eyes embedded like blueberries in folds of crinkly suntanned skin.

Sam smiled, unfazed. 'I've just finished up. About to head off, if that's OK?'

Watton whacked him across the back. 'Say hello to foul old London for me. See you . . .?'

'Week on Tuesday.'

'Early. It all kicks off again early.' Watton turned to Stevie, smiling for the first time, exposing small, bone-white teeth set with precise regularity in exposed gums. 'He's a good one, this one. And he belongs here, you know,' he said matter-of-factly and left the room.

'I didn't think you'd want to go to New York – the movie places,' Sam said, leading her into a small Cuban café at the end of Prince Street for faultless corn on the cob and hot chocolate, then up to the new MOMA for a whirlwind tour and then back towards the West Village to one of his favourite coffee shops. Hidden behind faded dark-blue velvet curtains, the café was small and dark and hissed with coffee machines. The walls were lined with shelves of books, rows of apothecary-coloured liqueurs. Louche thirtysomethings hammered away on iMac laptops, solitary on small tables, nursing pint-sized coffees. Stevie and Sam instinctively sat at the bar, as if recognising that they needed the interruption of the barman to dilute the strange intensity that had begun to clot between them. They chatted about photography, good art and the bad, Thailand and the tsunami and his cousin's homosexual cat. They gossiped about Oxford, Toe, the failing marriage of her parents, all the people who'd populated their past, dated them, humiliated them, made them who they were, Stevie suddenly wondering whether one day Jez would be consigned to this ex waste-bin, a person who'd helped her evolve, passed through her life, but left no permanently damaging footprint. Two hours passed. It felt like five minutes. Sam told her that no one believed his accent here in New York because few imagined black, even pale-black, people lived in England. He was ashamed to tell her that when a black guy had asked him, 'Where you from, brother?' he'd said Brixton, even though he'd been living in Borough and grew up in Oxford. How tragic was that? He told her that people stared at him and Lara on the subway. There weren't nearly as many mixed-race couples here.

Stevie jolted. Lara. The first mention of Lara. She reached for an appropriate response. 'Everything seems to be going swimmingly there.' It sounded trite.

Sam shifted on his stool. 'Well, yes, early days. But it's nice. Civilised.'

'Civilised! You two?'

Sam laughed and kicked his large feet against the bar at the bottom of his stool. 'Relatively speaking.'

'Oh.' Stevie felt disloyally – shamefully – deflated that Sam hadn't confided some dissatisfaction in the relationship. But it seemed that he and Lara were far better suited than even she'd imagined. Her matchmaking skills had surpassed her. She sipped her beer, wishing she hadn't chosen such a gassy drink, wishing the subject of Lara hadn't come up and ruined the mood and brought her back down with a bump.

'And you?' Sam's intense dark eyes scanned her face. 'You are happy?'

'Oh, yeah. Things have really picked up. Work . . .'

'I mean happy married.'

Stevie paused, prepared to lie. 'Of course . . .' Then something flipped. It was impossible to be anything but herself with this man, familiar as her own brother in some ways, thrillingly alien in others, with his ready smile and the passion for pictures and the wiry hair he twiddled around his little left finger when he was thinking. She wished that they were cocooned in the soft-pink developing room together again. 'Not terribly happy right now. No. Since you asked.' The confidence felt like a betrayal.

'Man, I hate to think of you . . .' He put his hand on hers. It felt solid and hot. She didn't want him to remove it.

'Shit.' He lifted his hand off hers. Stevie breathed again. 'Sorry. It's none of my business.'

'Oh, it's probably teething trouble, isn't it?' she said flippantly, unnerved by the hand-on-hand gesture, beginning to jibber nervously. 'Marriages are notoriously difficult in the first year.' She laughed, too high, faux-breezily. 'You know us thirtysomethings. We get used to our individualistic noncommittal ways. Marriage is an adjustment.'

'But you'd lived together for a year beforehand.'

'I know. I know.' In Sam's presence her defences melted. 'OK, it's not working.'

'Not working?'

'No. Hell. God. What am I saying?' Stevie felt her emotions threaten to overwhelm her. Quashing thoughts about the cash-for-baby secret, she swallowed hard, shifted on her stool, pulled herself together. How could she be so disloyal? Even if he was a lying shit. He was her husband. 'Oh, you know Jez. You know what he can be like. He's had a tough time recently.'

Sam bent towards the zinc bar top, the metal reflecting a silvery gleam to the underside of his jaw. Stevie looked down and noticed how wide and square his knees were beneath his jeans, straining against the denim. She wanted to place her palms flat against their width. She leaned towards him slightly, encroaching the warm fuzz of his personal space.

252

'Yeah, I know what he *can* be like.' Sam grinned, opened his mouth, as if about to speak. Then seemed to think better of it. 'Stevie . . .'

'And he's still grieving for his dad. Even though he doesn't talk about it as much . . .' she justified. 'Poor thing has had a horrid time.'

'Stevie . . .' repeated Sam quietly, bending forward on his arms, ridges of veins just visible beneath his skin, veins that began to pulse faster.

'And there's Rita, of course. She really doesn't help. Who wouldn't have problems with having their mother-in-law in the house? Watching *Antiques Roadshow* re-runs? Drives me totally insane.'

Sam was sweating now, tiny beads forming on his wide nose and his broad high forehead. 'There's something I need to tell you . . .'

'And, despite the fact that I've got antique ovaries, I think I might be *pregnant*! Which means it's probably *all* my hormones . . .' As if to back her up, Stevie's breasts throbbed beneath her bra.

All of Sam's features crumpled inwards at once. 'Oh.'

Stevie put her face in her hands, unburdened by her outburst. 'Forgive me rabbiting on like some deranged Desperate Housewife. What did you want to tell me?'

'Nothing.' Sam shook his head, two fingers pulling down on his bottom lip. 'It was nothing, really.'

Back in Lara's apartment, waiting for Lara, Stevie shuffled on the sofa, uneasy at how close she felt to Sam after just a day alone with him. She wondered what would happen if she'd spent two, three days alone in his company. She mustn't think about it. Did he feel it too? Or was her excitement about New York City – surely the best city ever – projecting itself on to the nearest handsome human form? Pull yourself together, girl. You are *married*. You are thirty-four, going on thirty-seven. You can't succumb to a crush like a teenager. She brushed invisible crumbs off her jeans, as if this might tidy her head too, and looked at Sam, who had his back to her and was peering out of the window. Was he searching for Lara, even Casey, someone to intervene and normalise things again?

Casey rushed in first, tired, suited and heeled, with only a manic spare half-hour in which to get some fuel and fluid before her appointment with her therapist.

A few moments later Lara followed, bright eyed, pulling a windswept strand of hair from her mouth and wearing a sun-yellow fifties-style dress which made her resemble a young Marilyn. 'Hi guys! I'm back!' Wafting scent, she wrapped herself around Stevie, then kissed Sam neatly on both cheeks. 'You taken care of my girl?'

Stevie laughed abruptly, overcome by a peculiar guilt. 'He didn't budge on Bloomingdale's.'

'Oh, next time. I'll work on him.' Laughing, Lara flung herself at the sofa, collapsing on to it with a puff of air, kicking off her Marc Jacobs ballet flats, stretching out her shapely sun-kissed legs. She looked flushed, sexily mussed-up. Stevie felt a pang of jealousy.

'Steve, I can't believe you're going. Sure you don't want to pack in the whole marriage caboodle and come and work in New York?' Lara rubbed her neck. 'Marriage is bound to be overrated.'

'Don't tempt me.'

'My art director just called to say he's fired a senior designer. There's a great job going. Shall I fix you an interview? They'd love you.'

Sam cocked his head on one side, smiled cheekily. 'Go on. Do it.'

For a fleeting moment, the word 'OK' wobbled precariously at the end of her tongue, ready to unleash its chaos. To disappear to another continent just after your new husband's father had died? And what about Poppy? Tommy? What about her parents' marriage which was crumbling into the ground like an old north-Oxford house with subsidence? All these people needed her. And what if they didn't? Would she go then? No. She wouldn't. She *couldn't*. She was thirty-four years old. There wasn't time to be reckless. There wasn't time. No. She had made her choice. She had made her choice that summer's evening on Waterloo Bridge. But had she known then what she knew now, would she have said, 'Er, yes'? Could she ever really forgive him for hiding his father's cash-for-baby promise? Did their relationship stand the remotest chance?

Casey reappeared from the kitchen and interrupted her thoughts. 'Don't listen to those guys.' She buttoned a cropped black jacket, ruffled her hair in the hall mirror. 'You stick with your cute hubby. They're jealous.'

Stevie twisted out a smile and went to hide in the bathroom. Enthroned on the loo seat, knickers around her ankles, she put a palm across her belly, wondering whether she had a secret in there, precious and tiny and revolving in its own space like a lone prawn in a vast ink-black sea.

It felt strange leaving New York prematurely. Stevie had just adjusted to its time zones and now she had to leave. Saying goodbye, Lara threatened to kidnap her and hide her in the apartment closet and said she was sorry that she'd been a bit distracted, what with work and everything and she loved her very much.

'I love you too,' said Stevie, pressed against Lara's perfumed neck.

'Girls, keep it together.' Sam rolled his eyes. 'We're going to miss the plane.' He loaded the bags into the back of a cab and kissed Lara lightly on the cheek. 'See you next week.' Lara squeezed his fingers.

As they stood on the street, Casey waved from the apartment window, leaning out over an air-conditioning unit. Passing strangers glancing up at Casey collided, entangled by their dogs' leads. Stevie bent down and stepped into the cab, so small after London's roomy black beasts. She looked up at the apartment block, the toy-tiny Stars-and-Stripes flag someone had stuck out of a neighbouring apartment window, the restless shadows of inhabitants moving behind the fume-greyed glass. How she wished that she could be one of those anonymous New York City shadows, just once. But her chance had gone. It was time to be philosophical.

As soon as the captain had turned off the seatbelt signs, Sam moved from row 16A to 33B, the empty seat next to her. They drank wine – she kept her intake to a few sips, in case she was pregnant – and ate over-salted pretzels that shattered crumbs in their laps and between the seats. They didn't watch any movies. They talked. They giggled. When everyone else on board blinded themselves with the eye patches and reclined to slumber they stared in comfortable silence into the oval of pitch-black window – sugared with ice crystals – waiting for the sky to bleed into dawn. Stevie was still awake when Sam finally fell asleep, his head slumping on to her shoulder, sleepily nestling into her neck like an animal burrowing home.

There was nothing inappropriate about a head on her shoulder, was there? He was Lara's boyfriend, yes, but he was also her old friend. And she was married, possibly pregnant. They hardly required chaperones. As Sam slept he snuffled slightly, the dry recycled air audibly catching in the back of his throat. Stevie found the sound oddly reassuring.

When her shoulder eventually began to ache, she held Sam's head gently between her hands, propped it back up, carefully wedging a blanket against his left cheek and the seat back. She studied him as he slept, examining the traces of Jamaica detectable in the soft curves of his nose and mouth, the wide cheekbones, the fusion of genes that had created that milky olive skin and the ribbon-shiny curls of black hair. She couldn't remember ever finding a man quite so gloriously beautiful, so edible. With a jerk of pain, she wondered what would have happened if Katy Norris hadn't barged between them – all lashes and cleavage and dilated MDMA pupils – with such alacrity at that particular moment at that particular party all those years ago. She wondered what her children would look like if Sam fathered them.

Then she must have fallen asleep, because she awoke a few hours later, snuggled into Sam's shoulder. Something had woken her. Turbulence? Breakfast? It took a few seconds to connect with the sensation of warmth and wetness between her legs. She looked down. Oh *no*! Oh shit. A crease of rust-red blood in the gusset of her jeans. Barging past the breakfast trolley, Stevie rushed to the toilet, tears in her eyes, dreams dropping off her like pretzel crumbs.

257

Thirty-four

Initially Katy thought it was Seb's chest, rising and falling gently beneath her cheek. Then she remembered. She eased her head off Jez's tangle of fine copper chest hair, the skin on her cheek sucking to his chest, as if reluctant to let go. She looked at the digital clock on her bedside table. Not even six a.m.? No wonder it was dark outside.

The details of the day initially felt sketchy. But, as she rubbed the sleep from her eyes, they punched with more clarity. Seb had emailed – a terse, matter-of-fact email explaining away his previous non-contact with 'manic busyness, a weekend away in LA' – and said he'd phone at eight, her time, raising her hopes of a reconciliation of sorts. He hadn't phoned. And Katy had waited and waited, feeling like a bad pastiche of Bridget Jones, until her willpower broke and she phoned him. Voicemail. Again. Voicemail. Absence was the message then. So she'd swished the silk curtains angrily shut, creating privacy in which to dissolve. She'd opened one bottle of strong Chilean red, then another, before calling Jez. After that? It was all rather smudged. She vaguely remembered answering the door in silk cami-knickers and vest. She vaguely remembered weeping. She vaguely remembered

258

falling into bed. Shit, had they slept together? Katy looked down. No, she was still wrapped in a silk dressing gown, knickers and vest in tact.

Katy stared at Jez, out for the count and snoring like a baby, his crumpled shirt ruched up, exposing a beer belly, soft, inviting and squishy, so unlike Seb's newly acquired confrontational six pack. Wedges of fair hair stuck up from his head like fins, pink scalp visible in places. She smiled. There was something of the dishevelled faithful Labrador about him, she thought. And it was so cute the way his lip gripped his front tooth as he slept. Just like her daddy's did.

She lifted Jez's arm – circled heavily around her shoulders like an engorged just-fed snake – edged herself up gently, careful not to wake him. He continued to snore. Padding into the kitchen, she grabbed a bottle of mineral water from the new American-style fridge Seb had insisted upon – ridiculously large for two, let alone one – and poked around, suddenly starving hungry, as if she hadn't eaten for weeks, which she hadn't, not properly. There was nothing bar goat's cheese and champagne. She had a sudden, inexplicable urge for a fry-up.

Clarin's Beauty Flash. Touche Éclat beneath the eyes, in the nostril creases. Laura Mercier concealer. Chanel gloss blusher. Katy hadn't allowed any man to see her without make-up since she was twenty-five years old and wasn't about to start now. She patted the products in.

'Katy, are you there?' Jez shouted throatily from the bedroom.

'One sec.' Katy walked back to the bedroom, bottle of water tucked beneath her arm.

Jez was sitting up in bed, crumpled shirt smoothed down, stripy green-socked feet rotating at the ankle. 'How are you feeling?'

'Much better.' Katy sat down neatly on the edge of the bed. 'Thanks to you.'

Jez cleared his throat, scratched his head. 'I hope you don't think . . . Er, nothing happened. I'm sorry I'm still here. I was holding you. We both must have fallen asleep. But you mustn't think . . .'

'It's OK. I wasn't that far gone.' Katy smiled gently, picked up one of Jez's large white hands, turned it over so that the palm faced the ceiling and traced a finger along it. 'You've got a nice long life line.'

Jez raised his eyebrows. 'Better live it right then.'

They exchanged a glance. It was clearly a meaningful glance. But Katy was unsure as to what it actually meant, only that it was the opposite of the way Seb looked at her. She let his hand drop.

Jez stood up slowly, reluctantly searching out his discarded shoes. 'Well, um, suppose I better hit the road.' He looked at his watch. 'My old ma will be wondering where the hell I am.'

'Of course, she's staying at your flat, isn't she?' Katy thought it was the cutest thing ever that Jez had his mum staying at his flat. She missed her mother so much. How lucky he was. 'Don't rush away. Stay for breakfast. A fry-up?'

'I shouldn't really . . .' Jez looked at his feet, wished he'd worn better socks. 'Oh, OK. Why not?'

'Tom's won't be open yet. But there's this little cafe off Westbourne Park Road.' She'd never eaten there before. It looked far too cheap and didn't serve egg-white omelettes. But today, for some reason, it would be perfect.

Katy ordered the full English. Builder's tea. Orange juice (undiluted). The mound of food was garishly coloured and oozed greasiness: it was probably the biggest calorie order she'd ever made in one sitting.

'So you've decided not to kill yourself and donate your reproductive organs to fertility research then?'

'I said *that*?' Katy covered her face with her hands. 'I'm such a drama queen. God, I'm sorry.'

'You? Drama queen? No!' mocked Jez gently. 'Pass the ketchup.'

Katy didn't pass the ketchup. She squeezed some on to his plate, unthinkingly, as a mother would a child. Jez didn't baulk. It was so easy between them, she thought, so unbelievably natural, like they'd been married for years. 'Stevie's back from New York today?'

Jez stopped chewing his mouthful of fatty bacon. 'Yup.'

Of course, Jez would go back to being a married man. He'd have children. Stevie wouldn't put up with their friendship. Why should she? *She* wouldn't. She sensed Stevie didn't much like her anyway. Their introduction on Sam's lap that cold sexy dawn all those years ago would never have got their acquaintance off to a good start. So yes, everything would return to normal for Jez, while she'd just join the amorphous, rather hopeless mass of London's single thirty-six-year-old women. 'You must miss her.'

Jez stared at Katy, unnervingly intently. Did she have hash brown stuck on her face or something? She dabbed at her mouth with a thin, shiny paper napkin. But she couldn't drag her eyes away from Jez's. The longer the silence went on, the less Katy could think of what to say.

'Are we going to talk about this or not?' Jez said eventually.

'Huh? Not sure I know what you mean.' Katy fiddled with a corner of gingham tablecloth.

Jez inhaled deeply, reared up, filling his shoulders and chest with air, as if preparing himself for the punch of rejection. Dare he? 'This . . . this . . . connection.'

'Connection?'

Jez banged a frustrated palm against his forehead. 'Katy, am I going bonkers or has something happened? I feel ... like ... like ... Oh God, I don't know how to put it into words.'

'You seem upset. I don't understand. Have I done something? I never meant to do anything.'

Jez reached out for Katy's hand, now wrapped in a rigor-mortis embrace around the ketchup bottle. She wondered if he'd completely got the wrong idea. Or had she? Jez had meant to be just a goading tool to entice Seb into proposing, but somewhere along the line he'd become more than that. He'd become strangely essential. But he wasn't hers. And she wasn't worth it. 'You're a good friend, Jez. A really good friend.'

'Am I?' Jez craned over the table, bending over the ketchup-bloodied bacon, blocking out the cabbie drivers sat eating at other tables and obviously listening in. 'Katy, I don't *want* to feel like this. I mean ... God, this is so confusing. I love Stevie. I really do.'

There. You see. Katy relaxed back into a reliable state of sadness. What was she thinking? Jez wasn't an alley cat like Seb. How could she entertain even the *possibility* that he'd be attracted to such a moaning ageing neurotic. No, she was under no illusions. At the present moment she was the kind of needy thirtysomething woman men run away from screaming. The kind of past-her-sell-by-date woman who kept plastic surgeons in business. Seb had made that perfectly clear. 'Of course you do.'

Jez stared at her, eyes zig-zagging as he searched her face, then sighed, as if in resignation. 'Yeah, Stevie's great.'

Thirty-five

A soggy flannel of cloud insulated London from summer. Malodorous damp conducted itself through the soles of Stevie's shoes. The short walk to the Tube rimmed the legs of her black trousers with salivary wetness. The weather was fitting: inside, aching behind her pubic line, was a little void. She felt mocked by her non-pregnancy. There was no reason to stay with Jez now. She could accept she'd failed and try to move on. But something in her wasn't ready to accept failure. Something in her said that she had to 'work' at things even when her gut was telling her it was hopeless. She was also too dispirited, too lacking in energy to actually take on such a life-changing decision with any confidence. Mostly, she doubted herself. If her judgement was so bad that she'd married Jez in the first place, could it be trusted to call time on the marriage? So on returning from New York, she'd done the easy thing and thrown herself into work, starting her contract at VIP Group Magazines the day after she got back. In the offices behind Regent Street, she focused hard, overriding the free-floating distracted feeling that swam inside her, smiling, heels on, head down.

Career-wise, things had taken a better turn. She was

working on a higher class of magazine now. The artwork was better. The staff were thinner than those at any other publishing house and they wore better shoes. There was a pride about the place, a smug satisfaction at the prospect of one's name on such a prestigious masthead. And, of course, she got first dibs on sample sales. But still, it was a case of same shit, different shovel, thought Stevie, because when she walked out of the office into the heaving mass of Oxford Street, everything was the same as it always was: buses bumper to bumper like a line of red bricks; seething aggressive crowds wielding endless plastic shopping bags; fights over clothes at Topshop; cheap bad sandwiches. She wondered when exactly she'd fallen out of love with London. Since the bombs? The wedding? New York? Whatever, the city no longer enchanted her as it had in her twenties. It pulled her down, made her feel tired and cynical. Moreover, London now symbolised the life she'd chosen, the whole package. Stevie kept reminding herself that she'd chosen it, as if the notion of choice might empower her in some way. It didn't.

Stevie worked late all that week, later than was necessary, not to impress the boss, although she did, but because she didn't want to return home. Then Friday came. She *had* to go home.

Since returning from the States the atmosphere in the Moscow Road marital flat was arctic. She and Jez now bit at each other over the smallest of things – leaving the fridge door open accidentally, breathing too loudly – as if there was an accumulation of angriness that needed lancing. Jez was also strangely distant. She'd walk into a room and find him staring out of the window. He'd barely look up to acknowledge her. When she'd told him her period had finally arrived she'd expected something more than a shrug in response. But he had looked almost relieved and certainly didn't want to discuss it. At night Jez snored, his back turned away from her, feet dangling out of the bed as if he couldn't quite bear to share the same musty space beneath the duvet.

For the last three days they'd successfully managed to avoid each other, one entering a room, the other leaving it, one watching the telly as the other tore through the pages of last Sunday's newspapers. They hadn't made love. This was a relief on one level but vaguely disappointing on another, not because she actually felt any great desire for him but because a small, irrational part of her wanted to make sense of their union. Yesterday morning she'd even walked in on Jez in the shower, naked, planning to join him, soap him up. But she'd started at the freckled slab of Jez's torso, the mossy mound of red pubic hair, as if seeing him naked for the first time. Disturbingly, Sam's contrasting creamy cappuccino skin immediately came to mind. She'd shut the door and left quietly, leaving Jez to wiggle his fingers in his ears, snort the content of his nose into his hands, blissfully unaware that she had ever been there.

The phone rang. She threw herself at it.

'Hello?'

'Darling, it's Mama.'

Stevie smiled. 'I heard the news about Rita. I know, I know. I couldn't believe she'd actually visit you without Jez. She's been with you three days already, hasn't she? You must be making her feel *extremely* welcome. Is it all OK?'

'Hmmm.' Her mother put on her shrill can't-talk-now code of voice. 'She's just about to have a little doze, aren't you Rita?'

'Oh, she's right there?'

'*Very* much so.' Patti cleared her throat. 'But Rita doesn't feel up to going back home yet, do you, darling? No, no. The memories are "too strong" and the ankle's been playing up

265

again, which makes it – *ahem* – difficult for her to get on the train today.'

'Oh dear.'

'But she's planning to return to Bayswater on Wednesday.'

'Back here *again*? You are joking.' Rita would be the final straw.

Patti coughed. 'Darling, I've got some bad news.'

'That wasn't it?' Stevie felt herself anticipate the news greedily, part of her wanting some justification for her sodden spirits. 'What?'

'Tommy. He's had a turn for the worse, darling. He stopped breathing again.'

'Oh shit. He's OK?'

'*Just*. I think you should come down, if you can.'

'Oh, Mum. I thought he was out of the woods . . .'

'I know. We all did.'

'I'll jump on a train tonight. Tell Poppy I'm coming tonight.'

Stevie hooked the phone back and slid down the wall, head in hands. She didn't cry. Instead, she was filled with a viscous cold feeling. Keys rattled in the lock. Jez! Anger prickled. It pissed her off that he hadn't gone to see Poppy last weekend while she was away, as he'd promised. She slid back up the wall and walked to the living room, sat down on the sofa and waited, anger stirring inside her like eddies in a pan of almost-boiling water.

When Jez walked into the flat he looked strange, his pale-blue eyes ringed by a bruise-like shadow, his usual bulky swagger now unsure, apologetic. He tried to smile, but didn't seem to have enough energy or conviction. 'I need to talk to you, pumpkin.'

'Yes?' She hated the way her voice sounded so clipped, the way she was no longer a person she liked in his company.

'Aren't you going to ask me where I've been?'

'Work, I presume.'

'No, I haven't. I took the day off.'

'Where have you been then?'

'Katy's.'

Again? Typical Katy forging friendships with married men. It pissed her off. But it got Jez out of the house. And, in theory, she approved of platonic friendships. She had Sam after all. 'Overdosed on echinacea this time, has she?'

Jez sat down on the sofa, at the far end. Their bodies didn't touch. He slumped his head to his hands. 'Pumpkin, I've done a terrible thing.'

Something in his voice alarmed her. It wasn't like Jez to accept blame for anything. 'What's so terrible?'

'*Shit*.' He exhaled loudly, dragged his fingers down his face, pulling down his eyes, ploughing vertical wrinkles. 'I don't know how to say this.'

Stevie started to feel scared. Maybe something had happened. Was Katy OK? She didn't want the woman to die or anything.

'It's a fucking mess.' He swallowed.

For a fleeting moment Stevie could almost feel the words hanging icily in the air. Then he spoke them.

'I . . . I . . . I've fallen for Katy.'

Stevie swivelled on the sofa to examine him face on. Jez's eyes were screwed shut. A purple vein throbbed in his forehead. Her brain went blank, unable to process the information. This couldn't be happening. She squeezed her eyes tight. It was happening.

'I'm sorry. I'm *so* sorry,' he muttered.

She'd been so deeply stupid. She felt sick. 'Are . . . are . . . you telling me you're having an affair?' she stuttered.

'No. I mean nothing's *happened*.' Jez spoke through his fingers.

267

Oh. Stevie felt a strange mix of relief and disappointment. What was he talking about then?

'I . . . I . . . I don't even know how she feels. But I can't pretend. I can't do *this*.'

This? The marriage. The sham. Jez was leaving *her*? The irony broke over her head like an icy wave. She clamped her hand over her mouth, pinching her lips white and rolling them with her fingers. 'You're serious?'

'I don't expect you to forgive me,' he said quietly.

An image of Katy, nude, standing at the side of the pool, arms arrowed above her seal-wet head. Her air strip of pubic hair. It all fell into horrible focus. A hurt, rejected feeling hollowed out her chest. She had to pant to breathe. Dumped. She was being *dumped*. For Katy Norris. It was like leaving that party on her own on that cool summer dawn all over again. Except this time she was a whole lot older. This time it was her marriage.

'Please *say* something,' he pleaded.

'How long . . . when?' She sounded like she had laryngitis. But speaking was pointless. She could read the future by looking at Jez's flat blue eyes. The softness they used to have when they looked at her had gone. A distance yawned between them, as if in one moment they'd gone from spouses to strangers. Had their marriage been a case of mistaken identity?

Jez started to cry. 'I think it . . . it . . . started when I first saw her.'

'It?' Her voice cracked.

Jez squirmed on the sofa. 'The attraction. This weird connection . . .'

'*Please*.' Stevie stood up and walked to the window, back turned to Jez, not wanting to give him the satisfaction of seeing her cry. 'I don't believe it. I can't believe this . . .' But she knew she should believe it. It was happening. Jez had escaped first. He'd left her.

'No.' Jez leaped up, attempted to put an arm around her. She shrugged it off. 'No. We've just been friends. I swear. Nothing has happened, not sexually. Pumpkin, I know this is so fucked up.'

'Don't call me pumpkin.' Stevie put one hand to her cheek, as if she could shield herself somehow. Would it stop if she walked away? Would she wake up? The whole marriage, its existence, its unravelling, felt beyond her. She pulled up a chair and collapsed on to it.

'It is wrong. Because we're married,' he said, as if reminding himself of the facts, digging his hands in his pockets, unable to meet her eye. 'But I can't help how I feel, I just can't. The feelings won't go away. I've tried to make them go away. I can't.'

'Oh.' Why wasn't she screaming? That was what women were supposed to do. Scream and throw pans across the room. Instead she just felt overcome by an almost anaesthetic exhaustion. Of course. It all made gruesome sense. How stupid of her to think that she was the only one with doubts, the only one unfulfilled by the relationship. She flattered herself. Darker thoughts nagged. What the hell would happen to her future? She was almost thirty-five. This shouldn't be the way her life turned out . . . The tears started streaming again. She wiped them away, angry at her own self-pity.

'And I feel terrible because I don't want to hurt you . . .'

'*Don't.*'

'But *this* has never happened before.' Jez looked up at her and tried to smile, as if attempting to appeal to her better nature. 'I had no idea. I thought I was dead inside and I'm not.'

'Don't dress it up,' she managed, wishing there was a deep

black hole she could throw herself into at this moment. All those precious years wasted. She should never have married him. She should have had the courage to follow her instinct and pull out all those months ago. Oh, the fucking sad irony of it all.

He knelt down, earnest face centimetres from hers. 'It's not a crush, Stevie.'

'Love, is it?' She didn't like the scorn in her voice. She didn't even want to be here, staring at this man who'd opted out of her future so easily. This conversation was almost irrelevant.

Jez paused, weighed up his answer and for the first time in his life didn't take the path of least resistance. 'Yes, I love her.'

Whoomp! Winded. Yes, that hurt. She didn't love him. Not enough. Maybe she couldn't ever love him enough. But it still hurt that he loved someone else. It hurt a lot. She looked at Jez, the way his eyes seemed lit from within like a born-again Christian's, the bloody flush beneath his pale skin, even his hair seemed to be newly charged with some kind of emotional static. Jez had never spoken like this before, about her or anyone else. To her shock, Stevie started to cry, shuddery spasms of tears. She wanted to retain some dignity but it was impossible. '*Love*, Katy Norris?' That woman. Of all women. 'What the fuck has this marriage been about? A few days ago you were trying to get me to have babies so you could get your grubby hands on your dad's money . . .'

'No!' shouted Jez, leaping to his own defence. 'That's not true.'

'Explain.' Her voice fell to a whisper. For the first time in months she realised she was actually interested in what Jez had to say, what he was feeling. The first time in months she'd properly listened to him. 'Just explain.'

'I loved you.'

270

'Past tense,' she scoffed, pride dented. 'Nice.'

'No, I still love you. In a . . . a . . . different way. When I proposed, it was for the right reasons. I meant it.' Jez wiped away a tear. 'Fuck, this is *hard*.'

'Stop blubbing.' Despite everything, she believed Jez had loved her in his own limited way. But she was still angry. Why should he cry? Who was the victim here?

'I wanted to settle down,' Jez sniffed. 'I wanted to have a family.'

'And I seemed like a nice girl? Gullible?' Part of Stevie knew this was unfair. She knew that theirs had been a mutual deception. Still.

'No. Please don't be like this, Stevie. It's difficult enough as it is . . .'

'What do you expect?' she screamed now. It felt better to scream. She needed to blame someone for this mess. She was sick of blaming herself.

'You . . . *are* . . . amazing, Stevie. You're an incredible person. One in a million. When we get on, we get on brilliantly. We used to have such a laugh. And we thought we wanted the same things. And yes, don't look at me like that, yes, Dad's offer, it was kind of enticing. It might have speeded the process up. But I was at that stage of my life anyway. Kids, family . . .'

Cheap shot. Stevie wiped away an angry tear. What if she *had* been pregnant, what then?

'How was I to know that I was capable of feeling *this*.' Jez slammed his fist against his heart, like a Shakespearian actor rising to a soliloquy.

'Good timing.' The ground seemed to fall away from her feet, her soles tingling vertiginously. She steadied herself on the sofa, quietening. 'Did you have doubts before we got married?'

Jez shuffled from one foot to the other. 'Doubts?' He paused. 'OK, yes. If you really want to push me, if you want to make this really ugly, *yes* I did, kind of. But I thought, well, you know, that things would work themselves out, as they do. But, to be honest, it was hard to tell what the fuck I felt after my dad died . . . it was all such a blur of freaking emotions and shit.'

Stevie snorted, inhaling snot and tears down her throat, trying to regain some composure. All that time. All that agonising. It was so grossly unfair. 'Right.'

Jez stood up and walked towards the window, arms flapping loosely at his sides, as if his new emotional state hadn't yet found its physical expression. 'But I am *trying* to do the right thing here, can't you see that? I could have an affair. I could lie to you. But she's changed me. She's made me a better person, Stevie. I can't pretend now.' He turned to face her, his raw pink face streaked with tears. 'All my life I've fucking pretended . . . done things because I thought that was what Dad wanted me to do. Gone through the fucking motions. With my career and everything. Did I want to marry? I think so. But I don't know if I ever wanted to work in marketing. It seemed like the right thing to do at the time because Dad approved, the next best thing to going into the City, he said.' Jez wiped a tear that bulged in the corner of his inner eye. 'And since he's died, it's like I've been cut free. It's like I can feel something, like, *real*, for the first time ever. I feel like I can do what I want.'

Stevie shook her head, disbelieving. Her marriage had come to this. It was like witnessing a house partly demolished, the flank wall removed, its wallpapered rooms ripped open, any sense of secure permanent structure that its inhabitant once felt exposed as a fragile illusion. It felt like she'd been kicked in the teeth.

'I never thought I'd say this, but you know what? I admire

your mate Sam. I do. I admire him for walking away from the corporate bollocks, for sticking to his guns.' He snorted derisively. 'It's no wonder your face lights up whenever he walks into the room.'

'What do you mean?' But she knew. She stared at the floor.

'You haven't looked at me like that, ever.'

Stevie dug her nails into her palms. 'And Katy does?'

He paused. 'She does. And it's my turn to do *my* thing now. Maybe I want to be an organic farmer. Maybe I want to bring up pot-bellied pigs, like that guy on telly. Maybe I want to move to the country. Who knows?'

Pot-bellied pigs? Stevie almost laughed. 'What the hell are you talking about, Jez? Have you had a personality transplant or something?'

'Listen,' he said quietly. 'I feel connected to the real me, for the first time in my life. Katy's changed me. She's woken something up in me. I don't know how or why. But I do know that I can't walk away and ignore it.' He looked at her, his eyes bright. 'Tell me you understand.'

Yes, she understood. She almost wished she didn't. It would be easier if Jez had behaved like a total arsehole. Her bottom lip quivered. 'What about me?' How pathetic she sounded.

Jez walked over, knelt by her knees. 'You?' he said, gently, lovingly even. '*You* don't want *me*, not really. I can't make you happy.'

'I married you.' That meant something, didn't it? It had to mean *something*.

'You don't need me.'

She couldn't argue with him. 'And Katy does?'

'Yes. And I need to be needed.' Jez studied the maple laminate flooring. 'I know that sounds wanky.'

In any other circumstances Stevie would have scoffed.

Instead she squeezed her eyes shut tight. Had she emasculated her alpha-male husband? Impossible. The truth, she realised, was that he never was that alpha. He needed weakness to feel strength.

'Stevie, pumpkin, don't you understand?' he whispered, eyes bright and trying to appeal. 'There is no baby. It's like we've been given another chance. *Both* of us. You might feel like this about someone one day too.'

She suddenly thought of Sam and Lara. A strangulated howl tore silently through her throat. But nothing came out.

Thirty-six

Patti wedged a tray on her hip and knocked on her daughter's childhood bedroom door. 'Darling, I've brought you some tea and some flapjacks. Can I come in?'

Stevie put on a weak smile, in an attempt to minimise the emotional impact she might have on her already over-emotional mother. 'Is it safe? Has Rita gone? I couldn't bear to see her told-you-so face.'

'Yes, she left last night after Jez phoned. But she was genuinely sad, you know. I think she'd just come to the conclusion we weren't all such a bad bunch after all.' Patti, wearing a voluminous craft overall stiff with splattered paint and clay, placed the tray on the floor and sat down, cleaving to the side of the bed. She wore turquoise chandelier earrings and had her hair tied back, secured with a wide printed head-band. She smelled of mother smells: lentil soup, incense and Body Shop glycerine soap. 'Oh, my honey-bun, my baby,' Patti muttered, stroking Stevie's cheek.

Stevie tolerated it for a few seconds then brushed her off.

'It's not the end of the world. I *know* it feels like it. But it's not,' Patti tried to reassure her.

'I know.'

'You're a young woman. You've got your whole life in front of you.'

Stevie hugged her knees tight. 'I'm five months, six days from my thirty-fifth birthday.'

Patti smiled tenderly. 'That's a seedling.'

'It's kind of not, actually.'

Patti bent towards her daughter. 'Are you thinking babies?'

'In the abstract.' Who was she kidding? 'I've just got to adjust to a new . . . a new way of thinking, that's all. I'll be fine, Mum.'

'Cherie Blair had a baby at forty-five. Madonna . . .'

'*Don't*.' Stevie pulled the duvet up around her neck. Despite the blazing sunshine outside, she couldn't warm up. 'I . . . I've only been married a few weeks.' Her voice cracked. She inhaled, reclaimed it. 'It's so humiliating, Mum. So fucking *Trisha*.'

As if reading the voice crack as repressed emotion and thus an invitation to get up close and personal, Patti enveloped Stevie in a swathe of crusty craft overall. 'Who's Trisha?'

'Doesn't matter.'

'It's a scandal,' muttered Patti, her breath tickling her daughter's neck. 'A scandal. Women are criticised for "leaving it too late", but it seems to me that in your generation it's the men who don't want to settle. Why would they? They have it too good.' She sighed. 'Or they're scared off by the financial burden of having a family in this ridiculously expensive country. They're a scared generation.'

'Mum, you're sounding more and more like a back-bench Tory.'

'I fear I may be getting more conventional in my dotage, darling.'

'Let's hope so.'

They sat in silence for a few moments. Patti coughed. 'Perhaps this is my fault.'

'How do you figure that?' Many things were her mother's fault but she reserved the right to claim full responsibility for cocking up her life this time.

'Seeing you like this . . .' Patti's eyes filled. She batted them, absorbing the tears in her mascara. 'All through your childhood I was saying to you and Poppy, "Girls, get a career, secure your financial independence. Don't be like poor old Aunty Janet." Do you remember?'

'Yes.' Stevie smiled. 'It was good advice, Mum.'

'Was it?' Patti looked unconvinced. 'Recently, oh, I never thought I'd say this, but recently I've been thinking that I should have given you the confidence to choose a family first, if that's what you wanted. You know, have kids early, go back to work later.'

Come again. Did her mother just say that?

'Like Poppy,' Patti continued. 'She ignored me, didn't she? And part of me has always thought it was a shame, that she hasn't fulfilled her potential in that way, but . . .'

'She's OK, Mum.'

'She *is*. And she's a brilliant mother. Most importantly, she is happy being a full-time mother, in a way that I never was. And she's filled her potential in her way, I can see that now. I think what you have to deal with is worse, fearing time is running out. It's a horrendous pressure.' She sighed. 'You know, it never occurred to my generation, all this biological stuff, it really didn't. Our main concern was *not* getting pregnant.'

Stevie's eyes watered now. Her mother's misgivings were genuine, even if they came rather too late. And, really, would she relive her life any differently? No. She wouldn't. If she had reproduced at her prime age she'd be tied for life to Aaron, the canker of the rose of her early twenties who'd once shouted 'goal' during sex. She'd never have travelled to India or New York. She'd never have met Lara and all those colourful, bitchy but life-affirming characters who made office hours go faster. In fact, she'd never have found a job she loved . . . most of the time. Because you can't start work experience at thirty, can you? And yet. Would she encourage her own daughter to do the same as her? Tough one.

'Are you OK, Stevie? I didn't mean to upset you.'

'Don't worry, just thinking. I feel a . . . a failure. I suppose that's it.' She gulped, allowing herself to plunge into self-pity in the way she only could with her mother. 'It's hard to believe I'll get another chance.'

'Life has a funny way about it. In my experience, when you think things can't get worse, they flip. Let me tell you something.' Patti whispered to her daughter's ear, assuming a soft book-at-bedtime voice. 'Before I met your father I was with a guy called Jean. As in French,' she pursed her lips, '*Jean*.'

'The one in advertising? Yeah, you've mentioned him.' She really wasn't in the mood for nostalgic repeats from the late sixties.

'Well, I loved him. Goodness, *how* I loved him.' Patti sighed wistfully. 'I thought we were going to be together *forever*. We'd be old hippies, living in a large house in Provence, surrounded by babies and chickens and big bushes of lavender.'

Stevie had to restrain herself from an insolent 'Whatever'.

'Then a year into the relationship he ran off with my best friend.'

Stevie sat up a bit. She hadn't heard this one. 'Who? Not Sandy?'

'No, of course not! Agnes. You've never met her. She wasn't . . .' Patti's face clouded, 'sisterly. I could forgive Jean, but not her.'

278

'Hmmm.' Perhaps female betrayal would always be worse. But it was on a sliding scale, Katy Norris at one end, her attraction to Sam on the other.

'I thought I'd simply die of a broken heart,' continued Patti, eyes shutting dramatically as she recalled her *grand* Gallic betrayal. 'And I do know what you're saying about the humiliation. But you must remember that people are just feeling sorry for you, that's all.'

'I don't want to be an object of pity.'

'I thought I'd just fade away.' Patti pressed on, caught up in the slipstream of her story now. 'I stopped going to parties, readings, all the things I'd loved. That we'd done together. Just to avoid gossips or bumping into him and Agnes. I hid away, couldn't be bothered to do anything. So,' she pulled aside curtains of glossy black hair, her face lined by the harsh sunlight beating through the window, 'I decided to become a lesbian.'

If Stevie had been a child she'd have clamped her hands over her ears at this point and squeezed her eyes shut. She'd heard rumours – from a school friend, mortifyingly enough – about her mother's Sapphic experiments. 'O-K.'

'Lynne was a nice enough girl . . .'

'Too much information.'

'Oh, I didn't get very far. Because out of the blue,' Patti clapped her hands together, her silver bracelets chiming, 'I met your father! There he was at Hilary's lunch, nerdy, tall and skinny in those days, with this fifties-style short-back-and-sides. He wasn't at all who I thought I wanted, quite the opposite of Jean. I only agreed to go out with him as a dis-traction. But I fell in love with him, on the third date in a little Greek restaurant off the King's Road. Head over heels in love.'

'Right.'

Patti grabbed her hands urgently. 'And life started *again*.

And I had you three. And I may not have been the best mother but you've been the best kids.'

Stevie rolled her eyes but she was oddly touched.

'Don't you see? You never know what's around the corner, darling. *Never*. Now, have a flapjack, all lovely and gooey from the oven.'

Stevie bit into the block of flapjack, realising it was the first thing that had passed her lips in hours. 'But, let's face it, even your tale hasn't quite the Mills & Boon ending, has it?'

Patti shut her eyes for a second, revealing lids quivering with petrol-blue eye-shadow. 'Things have been better between me and your father. I admit that. I'm not going to attempt to pull the wool over your eyes.'

'I wouldn't bother. You're a terrible liar.' Stevie frowned and spoke quietly. 'You're going to split this time, aren't you?'

Patti stroked the peak of her daughter's bent knee beneath the duvet. 'We want different things, darling. You know your father. He's *so* stuck in his ways. He wants to spend the rest of his life in the library. You've all left home . . . we've got a few savings . . . there's no need! I'm desperate to go away, to travel, to see the world. There's no need to start living like a pair of bloody OAPs! I still feel about fifteen years old. Honestly, I really think he'd be happier with someone like Rita Lewis.'

'Dad was never going to be Jean, Mum.'

Patti looked up a little startled, as if the idea had never occurred to her before, her eyes darkening as they crowded with a million thoughts. 'No, I suppose not.'

There was a knock on the bedroom door. 'It's me.'

Poppy leaned wearily against the doorframe, blonde and fragile in a blue-and-white striped Toast shirtdress. 'The doctors have sent me home. Said I needed to rest.'

'The most sensible thing that consultant's ever said,'

remarked Patti, who was yet to lose her suspicion of the medical establishment. She stood up, rearranging her overall. 'I'll leave you girls to it then. My famous Spanish stew for supper!'

Poppy and Stevie exchanged glances.

'Good nutritious stuff is what you both need right now.'

'A burger and chips is what I need right now,' said Stevie.

'I've got Sophie's tube of Smarties in my handbag. Fancy taking them for a turn around the garden?' asked Poppy. 'I'm craving sugar and fresh air.'

The garden was fully awake to the late English summer now. Flower heads drooped under the weight of their pollen. A column of midges buzzed a couple of inches above lush clumps of lawn. Daisies, buttercups and the traditional semi-weed flowers that many households plucked out but which the Jonsons loved, punctuated the garden with dashes of yellow. Clumps of clematis, wisteria and honeysuckle grew out of control, unpruned bulks slumping haphazardly off the lattice fencing, their blooms and vines tangling. Small blue flowers curled up the crumbly old stone Venus statue on the front lawn. It seemed incongruous that the garden could look quite so luscious while so much shit was going down with the inhabitants of the house.

'Ah, oxygen.' Poppy waved the midges away and spread out a moth-eaten tartan picnic rug on the grass. They both took off their shoes, wiggling their toes in the sunshine. Poppy popped the lid off the Smarties tube with her teeth and scattered the multicoloured sweets on the rug. 'Here. Eat.' She lay on her tummy, crunching a sweet between her teeth. 'I'm so tired, but I shut my eyes and all I see is the hospital lighting. You know, those fluorescent sticks. There are always dead flies stuck to them. And the light they give out is just horrible. Makes everyone look like the living dead.'

Stevie lay back on the lawn too, feeling the grass damp beneath the rug. A breeze filled the trees, shaking the leaves with a soft dry rustle, one of those quintessential summery sounds that would normally make Stevie want to inhale and say, 'Ahhh'. But it didn't seem appropriate today. 'If anyone deserves to sunbathe it's you.'

Poppy sighed, her breath coming out like a long whistle. She rolled her hips into the rug, unable to get comfortable. 'I feel guilty. I feel there's something more I should be doing, not lying here while Tommy languishes in some godforsaken MRSA-infected ward.'

'The doctor sent you home, Poppy.'

'I know, I know. But I should be with Finn and Sophie. Piers insisted on taking them out but I feel like I'm neglecting them.' She sighed, rolling over on to her back. 'I'm always neglecting someone.'

Stevie searched her sister's sky-turned face tenderly. Poppy looked tired but more beautiful than ever, gravity pulling her skin tight over her round, high cheekbones, her uncharacteristically unbrushed hair a fuzzy gold halo. 'Do you remember what we talked about at my wedding?' She spoke softly, not wanting to over-step the mark. 'You know, about you and Piers. Has that sorted itself out?'

Poppy smiled. 'I haven't really thought about it, to be honest. My head's been full of Tommy. But now I think about it,' she rolled her eyes, 'I didn't know I had it so good, did I?'

Stevie shrugged. 'Life wasn't so bad.'

'But, you know, I expected everything to be perfect,' Poppy continued, gazing up to the apple tree's rustling crown. 'But why should it be perfect? It's not a right. I realise that now. So, yes, the short answer is that I *do* feel better about me and Piers.' She turned to face Stevie. 'You know what? I think perhaps I've just lowered my expectations. You should try it sometime.'

'I think mine are quite low enough already, thanks.' Thirtysomething panic had arguably already lowered the bar.

Poppy laughed. 'Maybe.'

Stevie stared at her sister, wondering about her new stoicism. 'Do you ever think, why me? About Tommy, I mean. It seems so unfair.'

Poppy turned on her side. The sisters' noses were so close they almost touched, the slightly upturned tips mirroring each other. 'No. I think, why not me?'

'Oh, OK.' Stevie struggled to get her head around her sister's absolute lack of self-pity. She'd always wondered how Poppy would behave in a real crisis, whether she'd be unable to cope. She felt bad for doubting her. Stevie squinted against the brightness of the summer sky. 'No mother should have to go through what you're going through. It's bad luck.'

'I am lucky!' Poppy sat up suddenly, her face flushing with anger. 'Tommy could be dead, Stevie. But he's not, he's going to pull through. The doctors see him as a cot-blocker, using up resources, hardly a human being.' Poppy never shouted. She was almost shouting now. 'But he's a baby, Stevie. He's *my* baby! He deserves a chance. And I know he'll pull through. But no one believes me. They're all waiting for him to die.'

Stevie touched her hand lightly. 'I believe you.'

Calm again, frustration vented, Poppy crumpled back down on the rug. 'Thank you.'

They stared at the sky for a few minutes in silence, gazing at the clouds – puffy white domes like giant meringues – which migrated from east to west, disappearing into the leafy bulk of a towering pear tree.

'Do you want to talk about it?' asked Poppy tentatively.

It. That was what her marriage had become, an almost unmentionable it. 'Not really.'

'Would an orange Smartie help?'

Stevie received a Smartie in her cupped palm. 'What's to say? It's crap. But it's not as crap as what you're dealing with.'

'You can't compare the two. I'm worried about you, Steve. Seriously. I mean, what are you going to do?' Poppy's smooth brow furrowed. 'Where will you live?'

'It's OK. Honestly. Lara says I can stay in her flat for the time being. She hasn't got a tenant for it yet. So that tenant will be me. Don't look so anxious, please.' Stevie folded her cardigan tighter across her chest. She wasn't sure other people's concern helped, even her sister's. The whole disaster still felt unbearably private, if only because talking about it made her feel worse not better. 'Shit happens, right? Ice blocks fall on to one's head from a great height. Bombs go off. Marriages break down.'

'Not . . .' Poppy stopped.

'Not before the wedding-list company delivers, no.' Stevie winced and bit her lip. The task of writing to all the wedding guests awaited her: a grim reversal of the wedding planning.

'I hope you don't think this is out of turn . . .'

'Go on,' said Stevie, turning her face towards her, intrigued. Poppy rarely spoke out of turn.

'If it's any consolation, well, I don't think Jez would have coped if you'd had a Tommy. I'm not sure he was strong enough for you. Too much of a big baby. Or is that harsh?'

'No,' Stevie replied after a pause. 'He should be in nappies.'

Poppy picked a daisy, held it up above her, rotating the frill of its petals against the glassy blue sky. 'You evidently weren't meant to be together.'

'I guess not.'

Poppy shot her sister a fast glance. 'You're holding it together very well. Many women would be in pieces.'

284

Stevie bristled. 'I apologise if I'm not fulfilling everyone's preconceptions of how a cuckolded wife should behave.'

'You know I don't mean it like that.' Poppy rubbed the daisy stalk between her fingers until it released green juice on to her skin. 'But you're allowed to be sad.'

Stevie stared moodily in the direction of the vegetable patch. Her grief was onion shaped, layer upon layer could be peeled back, emoted, shared. But ultimately she knew that Jez wasn't in the centre of that onion. And this made her sadness feel almost fraudulent. What or who was she grieving for exactly? For a few moments neither of them spoke. A warm breeze whipped through the trees and across the lawn. Stevie swallowed. 'I thought I was pregnant you know.'

'Mum said. You should have told me.'

'Well, you had your hands full. And anyway, I'm not pregnant.'

Poppy thought about this for a second. 'A lucky escape.'

Was it? Or would they have just got on with it if she had been pregnant, made the relationship work because they had to? Or would she have been a happy single mother? 'Yeah.'

'There will be other chances, Stevie.' Poppy spoke softly, carefully, as if aware of the dangers of usurping the role of older sister.

Stevie chewed a stem of grass thoughtfully. 'Lara has this flatmate in New York, Casey. American, in her late thirties, totally given up on dating. But she's planning to adopt a kid or use a sperm bank or something.' She turned to face Poppy to gauge her reaction. No big reaction. Just a troubled convergence of eyebrows.

'Sperm bank?' Poppy looked at her sister, puzzled at first. 'You wouldn't. God, things aren't that desperate, sis.'

Stevie was silent, eyes tracking a bumblebee drunkenly helicoptering above her left ankle. Maybe she would. Who wrote

285

the rules? Ultimately, biology, albeit stretched by science. And if biology allowed it, why not? Would that child be worse off than one with parents trapped in the wrong marriage? No, she didn't think so. 'I have decades to find another relationship, Poppy. My reproductive window is a tad smaller.'

Poppy nudged her. 'You know you could win him back if you wanted to, don't you? His behaviour has thirtysomething life-crisis written all over it.'

'*No!*' Stevie said, without hesitation. 'No. We could never get back together. You know the weirdest thing about this?' She articulated her thoughts as she spoke. 'The thing that gives me a sense of closure? I really believe Jez thinks he loves Katy, that he's being genuine, possibly for the first time in his life.' She sighed. 'It's a fait accompli.'

'Hmmm.' Poppy sat up, pulled her creamy blonde hair away from her face and fixed her sister with a penetrating stare. 'What about Sam?'

Sam? Stevie froze. Even his name spoken out loud by someone else felt like an intimate thing aired. The bee landed on her leg. 'What about him?' She half hoped the bee would sting her. A sharp needle of pain might help release something.

Poppy shrugged. 'Come on, Steve. It's perfectly obvious to everybody. Sam is besotted with you. I may not be the sharpest tack in the box but I know that those visits to the hospital when you were in Thailand weren't *entirely* for Tommy's sake. He wanted to talk about you. Stevie this, Stevie that. Besotted. He has been for years, I reckon. Me and Mum were discussing it only the other day.'

'Oh right.' Stevie's stomach fisted. 'No one thought of telling me?'

Poppy turned to her side, rested her chin on her hand and bit into the crunchy shell of a chocolate. 'But it's not reciprocal is it? You married Jez.'

286

The words hit with the force of a punch. Stevie felt sick. Her shoulders began to shake. Her throat contracted. All the tears she'd contained so well beneath the thick reptilian skin erupted in spasmodic sobs. The bee made a sharp exit.

'Gosh. I'm sorry.' Poppy sat up and cradled her sobbing older sister in her arms. 'I didn't mean to upset you.'

Stevie couldn't speak.

'Hang on a minute.' Poppy braked suddenly from the embrace, leaned backwards to get a good glimpse of her sister's face. 'You? Sam?' She smiled. 'Tell me. *Now.*'

'Nothing. Nothing to tell. I'm so sorry for blubbing, you're the one who should be blubbing.'

'You have feelings for him? You *do*, don't you?' Poppy grinned.

'It's a bit strange. I'm not sure . . .'

'You do!' Poppy clapped her hands together. 'Gosh.'

No, they were friends. That was the fact of the matter, the prosaic architecture of their relationship. But the thought of him liking her? The very thought released a cage of beating butterflies inside her stomach. She smeared away the tears from her cheeks, regaining composure. 'Some things *don't* happen for a reason. Even if we don't know exactly what that reason is.'

'Well, marrying someone else is a pretty good one.'

'But . . . but . . . we've known each other for years. Nothing's ever happened. Seriously, he was never interested in me.'

Poppy rubbed her jaw, assessing the evidence. 'Sam's led a pretty peripatetic existence in the last few years. Maybe you've just not been around at the right time. *You're* the one who always bangs on about timing being everything.'

But she'd always been referring to her and Jez, realising, perhaps only now, that theirs was a union soldered together by timing and incident, rather than intimacy. No wonder the whole fucking thing unravelled. What did she think would happen? That she and Jez would last happily ever after? She sniffed. How stupid could one woman be?

'If you like Sam, you must fight for him,' said Poppy solemnly.

'*Jesus!* Poppy, my husband only left five minutes ago! Give me a break. I'm not—'

'Oh, OK.' Poppy smiled coyly. 'But I've got a feeling. You may think I'm your dippy younger sister. Don't look like that! Yes you do . . .'

'Poppy, even if you *were* right . . .'

'Yes?'

'Sam is going out with Lara.'

'Oh.' Poppy looked crestfallen.

'I fixed them up.'

'Oh.'

Stevie covered her eyes with one hand, pressing at the temples, trying not to cry; her chestnut hair tumbled over her face like a veil.

Poppy nudged her. 'One good thing?'

'Huh?' Stevie looked up. What good thing could there possibly be right now?

'Look, your rash. It's completely gone.' Poppy touched her sister's neck. 'And you look far less tired. You know what? I think you had a husband allergy.'

Thirty-seven

The back door slammed. Stevie looked around to see her father urgently crashing through the grass in his tweed suit, tufts of grey hair lifted by the wind like a crown of feathers. 'May I interrupt your artistic reverie?'

'Sure.'

Chris peered over his daughter's shoulder. She was sketching, quick hard strokes, whorls and slurs of lead grey. He pointed to one of the faces in the chaotic doodle with a finger. 'A good likeness.'

'Likeness?'

'Sam isn't it?'

'Huh?' Stevie stared back at the sketch, squinted to get a better view.

Chris leaned forward and turned the sketchpad a hundred and eighty degrees so that she stared at him upside down. 'Sometimes things make more sense inverted.'

'Oh, OK. Yes, I see it.' Gosh, it *was* like Sam. No wonder. She couldn't get him out of her head, even though she knew she should be mourning Jez. But grief at the marriage's collapse was already beginning to be replaced by a more dominant and unexpected feeling, one of overwhelming relief. 'Not intentional.'

'Everything's intentional on some level, dear.' Chris smiled.

'Hmmm.' Stevie put the paper pad down, hugged her cardigan tight. It was cold, the weekend's sun long gone. Poppy was back at the hospital and the weather had turned. The summer skies were now a strange yellowy grey, the colour of bonfire smoke. She'd been sitting here on this garden bench for what felt like an age, unable to motivate herself for the journey back to London and the various unpleasant tasks that awaited her there: acquiring the keys to Lara's flat, talking practical logistics with Jez, moving her clothes, facing Rita. 'What are you up to, Dad?'

Chris's eyebrows deepened. 'Looking for Neil, dear. Your mother wants him. He was last seen lurking around the rockery, high as a kite, apparently.'

'Oh, I saw him briefly this morning, seemed his usual non-communicative stoned self.'

Chris rubbed his beard. 'This, I fear – your mother fears – is the concern. Patti believes Neil might have developed a drug habit, a hard-drug habit to be precise. He scribbled down the lyrical ramblings of Pete . . . is it Dogerty or some such? . . . on the telephone pad. Don't ask me, dear. And he has been behaving, I quote, "irregularly".'

'He was born irregular.'

'This is possible.' Chris tried not to smile. 'But the suspicious trail does not stop there, I'm afraid. I've also been informed that Neil's been washing his clothes rather a lot and bathing – can you imagine! – and generally being overly furtive, jumpy and non-communicative with his mother,' he added archly. 'Patti has deduced that he's trying to wash away the odour of crack cocaine. There's a plague of it in Oxford, she tells me. She made me sniff his jacket.'

'What does crack cocaine smell like, Dad?'

'I have no idea. But something smelled bad.' Her father sat

down, pulling up his corduroy trouser legs as he did so, exposing navy socks and a straggle of thinning leg hairs. 'But I won't let anything burst my bubble this week.'

'You do seem buoyant.'

'Rita Lewis no longer haunts my house. The troops have withdrawn.' He sighed. 'Oh, you have no idea.'

'I do, actually.'

'Myopic, invasive and . . . so . . . so . . . *old* somehow.' He rubbed his beard. 'She's done more than any marriage counsellor, I can tell you that. She's made me appreciate your mother more than I can say.'

'Something needed to.' Stevie sounded sharper than she intended.

'What do you mean?'

'Dad, come on. Can't you and Mum just sort it out?'

'Well, dear, I'm sure things will sort themselves out. They always do, eventually.'

Her father's passivity enraged her, just as it enraged her mother. Why couldn't he work at something other than his books? 'It won't! Mum is seriously pissed off, Dad. You've got to *do* something.'

'Flowers? Chocolates?' He looked baffled. 'Should I pop to Thorntons? What then? What do you women want?'

It struck her that that was exactly the kind of thing Jez might have once said. Even though one was diffident, the other loudly bombastic, there were similarities. They shared their least-good qualities. Had that been the attraction? Stevie pulled her legs up to her chest, hugging her knees protectively. What could he get Mum? The only thoughtful presents she'd received in recent years had been from Sam: the sketch pad, the photo. 'Get her something she subliminally desires. Nothing too intentional.'

Chris laughed. 'Goodness, now that could be dangerous.

291

What on earth scurries around the boggy depths of your mother's consciousness?'

They laughed, falling into easy silence. Stevie felt close to her father. She wished he'd put his arm around her, do something paternal. She guessed he wouldn't. Their relationship wasn't really like that.

'I *am* sorry, very sorry, about Jez, dear,' Chris said finally with a relieved huff, as if he'd been building up to the comment all day and could relax now he'd aired it.

'You never liked him.'

'Hmmm . . .' He dislodged his glasses and wiped the bridge of his nose, which had a little pink ridge on either side from decades of not-quite-fitting NHS glasses. 'Jez was unfinished, that's what I always thought. An unfinished man. He wasn't grown-up enough for you. I should have said so at the time.'

Her father acknowledging responsibility? This was a first. Stevie realised this was her father's hug, the arm around her shoulder. 'No, *I* should have known better.'

'Well, perhaps you were unfinished too. You both rushed in. Your respective mothers didn't help, ploughing ahead with that wedding at any cost, digging up this garden with those ridiculous igloos . . .'

'Tepees. Dad, it wasn't shotgun. We'd been together for two years. I'm thirty-four years old.'

'Don't get distracted by the maths. Abstract numbers, that's all they are.' He cleared his throat. 'If something's right, a perfect fusion, as it was between your mother and me when, er, when we first met, then after only a few hours together you'll be closer to them than to someone else with whom you've spent a lifetime. It's all relative. Love shrinks time.'

'Nice theory.'

'Just a bit of advice. A bit late in the day, granted. I've not been the best father, in many ways,' Chris said slowly, as if reading her frown. 'Poppy had enough sense to marry Piers, no credit to me. She's always been sensible. But you and Neil? You could have done with a bit more guidance.'

Stevie felt herself welling up. They didn't really do intimacy very often. It made her slightly uncomfortable. 'What's wrong with me?"

Startled by the force of the enquiry, Chris' caterpillar brows shot up. 'Wrong with you? Nothing's wrong with you, dear.'

'I wish I were more like Poppy.'

'Life might be easier.' Chris smiled gently. 'But we all start out at different angles from the universe. Poppy is, let me think, nine degrees out. You're, say, twenty-five.'

Stevie felt old childhood anxieties resurface. 'And as we grow, upward on that trajectory, the angle becomes more and more exaggerated?'

'*Exactly!*' Her father beamed with pleasure. 'Clever girl.' He put his arm around Stevie's shoulders and squeezed. 'I wouldn't have you any other way. Twenty-five degrees to the universe is perfect, just perfect.'

Stevie's phone vibrated. A text. Sam.

Fancy wlk befr I go bk to NY?

Stevie stared at the screen, trying to decode the subtext like a girl on a second date. Or maybe there wasn't a subtext. Maybe he just wanted to go for a walk. She hastily texted back an affirmative and was rushing up to her bedroom to apply make-up and dig out a half-decent dress when the doorbell went.

'I'll get it,' shouted Stevie, clattering back down the stairs, crossing the black-and-white-tiled hall floor, pushing aside a mound of post and opening the front door. 'That was quick.'

Sam smiled, shoulders hunched, hands dug in pockets. He was wearing old torn jeans and a faded red hooded sweat-shirt which Stevie remembered from years back. It displayed the wide contours of his shoulders, the boyish arch of his lower back. 'Port Meadow? Old times' sake. Er, if you're feeling up to it, of course.'

OK, he knew about her and Jez. Well, of *course* he did. Lara, his *girlfriend* would have told him.

'Darling!' Patti thundered down the stairs, blue kaftan bil-lowing out behind like a sail. 'Lovely to see you!' She kissed Sam energetically, leaving his cheeks marked with opalescent prints of Body Shop 'Nude' lip-gloss. 'Gosh, you're scrump-tious. Isn't he scrumptious, Stevie?'

Stevie ignored her mother. 'I'll get my trainers.' Damn it. She was wearing old bootleg jeans and one of her dad's Jurassic white shirts. At least it didn't look like she was dress-ing up for him.

'There they are, Stevie.' Sam pointed to an old pair of Adidas trainers by the door. His wide white smile curled upwards, exposing that seductive slither of pinky-brown gum.

Stevie liked the sound of her name on his lips. It struck her that though she'd always felt uncomfortable taking Jez's sur-name, she would have relished taking the name Flowers. What the hell was that about? She tugged on her old trainers, amazed that Sam had identified the dirty-laced Adidas shell-toes as her own.

They walked down the Woodstock Road, turned right into Leckford Road, which led towards the bijou terraces of Jericho, then over the oily khaki-green canal to Port Meadow. Sam pointed to the new identikit Berkeley homes that had sprung up by the canal-side, neat and bright as children's plastic toy houses, in place of the grubby old ironworks, Lucy's. 'I can't

believe they knocked Lucy's down. I really dug that building.'
He sighed. 'I mean, come on, they could have redeveloped the
old structure or commissioned exciting new architecture.'
Sam shook his head. 'It pisses me off.'

'I liked that scruffy old factory too. But Oxford's changed.
It's prime real estate now.' Stevie peered down at the canal
towpath. A powerful déjà vu, clear as a film sequence, froze
her to the spot: early evening, the darkness creeping up the
muddy canal banks, she and Sam walking home from a pub
in town along the narrow path, slightly drunk on snakebite
and black. Sam had stopped and looked up, then when she
couldn't see what he could see he had held her by each elbow,
swivelled her around until she was facing the cauldron of molten
flames framed in the ironworks' metal-paned windows, the
flames repeated again in the black slick of water. The memory
still hovered just beneath her skin: the secret excitement of
being close to Sam on that narrow towpath; the electric current
that ran up her arms at his touch; the sparks in the window
mirroring what was going on between her legs. She'd known
what it meant to be desired from a very young age, most
girls did. But that moment was the first time she'd felt desire
for someone, that cannibalistic hunger. She must have been
what, seventeen? 'It's a shame,' she said, looking up at the
sharp new-build bricks. 'Wasted opportunity.'

They continued to walk, over the railway bridge, through
a swing gate and into the expanse of Port Meadow, which
rolled out like an old bumpy green carpet from Jericho to the
village of Wolvercote. A natural ancient floodplain, Stevie
loved Port Meadow for its rough charm: its thistled grass;
its spray of buttercups; its wide stony path that damaged
shoe soles; the winter floods that turned it into one vast
sky-reflecting mirror and protected it from development; the
horses and cattle that grazed free and fenceless. She'd taken

Jez here a couple of times but he hadn't really liked it – 'Don't get all sentimental on me, babe. It's a field.' – and they'd ended up in the local riverside pub, queuing for an over-cooked lunch and bickering.

'The mother of all meadows.' Sam shaded his eyes with his hands. 'I forget sometimes.'

Stevie smiled. It was part of their connective tissue, this landscape, its big skies, its shared history. Whenever they came here together it felt like a consummation of sorts.

'Shall we park ourselves here?' Sam squatted down at the side of the river where it frothed shallowly over stones beneath a flat bridge, its planks rattling loudly every time a cyclist whizzed over it. Stevie sat next to him on a wall of solidified sandbags, which lay hard and long as a French pillow. Neither of them spoke for a few moments. Unusually for them, it wasn't an easy silence.

'I'm sorry about you and Jez,' said Sam eventually. 'Are you OK?'

Stevie smiled shyly, looking him directly in the eyes, their blackness unlocked by the sunshine, exposing flecks of chocolate and his warm intelligence. 'Actually, you know what? I think I am.'

Sam frowned. 'You're not pregnant? I thought . . .'

'No. I'm not pregnant.' She shrugged. 'False alarm.'

'Oh, OK.' Sam's shoulders dropped. 'Life starts again, right?' He put his head in his hands and groaned. 'Corny. Sorry.'

'Well, it's hard to know what to say.'

'I'd say Jez is a wanker.'

'He says he's fallen in love.'

'He's a wanker.' Sam shook his head. 'Katy Norris, of all people.'

'One woman's wanker . . .' She sighed, watched two ducks

do-se-doing around each other in a mating ritual. 'He didn't love me. Maybe I can't blame him.'

Sam looked at her sternly. 'Don't go there, Stevie.'

'Well . . .' She stretched out a leg, quickly retracting it when she spotted a sprout of hairs in the gap between sock and jeans hem.

'It's not your fault.'

Stevie snorted. 'Tempting though it is to absolve myself—'

'Why do women always blame themselves? What are the odds that Jez is flagellating himself right now?'

Stevie laughed. 'I should never have married him, Sam. That's all I mean. It was a short-cut but it turned out to be the long way round.'

There was a silence. Sam broke it. 'Why did you then?' He leaned away from her slightly, as if wary of the answer.

Stevie sighed, resignedly. 'Well, I almost cancelled the whole thing, you know. A few days before the wedding . . .'

'You did? Shit. Why?'

'All the right reasons.' She broke off a tuft of grass, rolled it in her fingers. 'We weren't suited. We'd fallen out of love. Maybe we were never in love, really. He doesn't seem to think so now.' A shaft of sunlight, momentarily absorbed by cloud and then released again, lit up Sam's face. For the first time, she noticed a similarity between their features – a similar curve to the lip, the arched eyebrows, the breadth of their faces – a similarity that created a strange chemistry.

'Easy to be harsh in hindsight.'

'I loved him. But not like . . .' She blushed. Not like what? Not like how she felt for Sam. He caught her hesitation: his face twitched with recognition so fleetingly that if she hadn't known him for years she would have missed it. 'When Colin – Jez's dad – died,' facts: she was on firmer turf now, 'well, I couldn't cancel. Not then. I wanted to stick by him.'

297

'You didn't just lose your nerve?'

Stevie looked at Sam sharply, almost angry. 'Lost my nerve?' She blew air out of her mouth. 'Oh, shit, maybe.'

'It feels easier to stick with what you know sometimes.'

'Hmmm.'

'Real intimacy is scarier, isn't it?' Sam grinned, stretching his legs out towards the river's edge, scattering the ducks. 'Man, scares the shit out of me.'

She stole a sharp glance at him. 'You're presuming quite a lot.'

He shrugged. 'Just a hunch.'

'It was more than that . . .' her voice trailed off.

'Babies?'

'Kind of, I suppose. Well, the bigger picture. Aren't you the perceptive one?' A fish plugged its silver nose above the bubbles, turned to its side, its fins visible. Stevie pointed. 'You see that?'

Sam ignored the fish, not so easily distracted. 'You're hardly in line to become the world's oldest mother.'

To Stevie's mortification, her eyes filled. She didn't want pity. 'I have to accept the possibility that I won't do the whole marriage and babies thing, that that won't be my way. I think acceptance is healthier ultimately.'

'You're right.'

'You're agreeing with me?' She whacked him playfully on the knee. 'You're not meant to agree with me.'

'I think you should take the pressure off, Stevie, that's all. You can't plan everything.' He rocked back and spread his hands out preacher-style. '"Plans are there to make the Lord laugh." I quote my dear departed grandmother.'

She laughed. 'I could show you countless women who didn't plan and ended up aged forty-five throwing money at dodgy IVF doctors.'

'And I could show you countless women who scare men off with their baby hunger. We're not sperm wands.'

Stevie wanted to grab his face in her hands and say, 'You would never be a sperm wand. You would just be you, more than enough.' Instead she threw a pebble into the river. It sank rather than skimmed. She thought of Jez and his father's financial incentive. It had made her feel just a little bit how a man with a baby-hungry partner might feel, perhaps. A little used. 'And I'm not an omelette.'

'Huh?'

'Oh, it doesn't matter.' Stevie gazed at the river wistfully as the faint rhythmic shout of a rower's captain made its way upstream. 'Well, I'm sure Katy won't waste any time getting knocked up.'

'Katy Norris!' Sam shook his head. 'What an exchange. I will never *ever* understand, man.'

'Can't you?' Stevie said quickly, sharply, probably revealing too much. 'I thought you'd understand perfectly.'

'It wasn't like that, Stevie.'

Stevie winced, sucked her cheeks in. They'd never spoken about the incident in that party field before. She'd never flattered herself that their near miss was part of Sam's romantic narrative, however large it loomed in hers.

'There hasn't been one day . . .' Sam stared at the river, at the fat speckled fish rolling beneath the green churned water. His words started to choke. '. . . that I haven't wondered . . .'

A mobile rang. Damnit. Stevie and Sam glared at her handbag, its leather vibrating. The phone stopped after five rings. They continued to stare at the bag, its focus offering momentary respite from the conversation.

Sam coughed, looked up. 'I was really into you, you know.'

'You were?' Stevie smiled, tears pricking the backs of her

eyes, the rejection wound-fresh again. 'But you went off with Katy. We were sitting on that log, remember, and Katy kind of attacked, but you didn't brush her off. Then you went out with her.' No excuse there.

'It happened so quickly, Steve. I know that sounds weak. But it did. Suddenly this hot blonde girl was on my knee and you'd disappeared and I succumbed. I was a stupid idiot.' Sam picked up a round pebble and dropped it from palm to palm like a ball. 'After that? It was just sex, really. Casual. Nothing.'

Stevie was silent. Sex? It hurt to think of them having sex. She felt like jealousy was forking off her body in jagged bolts of green lightning.

'Did you like me?'

'*What?*' She couldn't possibly answer that!

'Did you like me?' He bent his head to one side flirtatiously. 'Come on, I have an ego to massage here.'

Stevie paused, took a deep breath. Dare she be honest? What was there to lose, really? She stared ahead steely eyed, daring not to look at him. 'I did.'

Sam sighed, tossed the stone into the water. 'I really fucked up, didn't I?'

'Yup.'

He stared at her for what felt like an eternity then leaned his face closer to hers. She felt like she was shaking. As if equally disturbed, the ducks on the river started quacking, paddling in a circular flurry of sudden movement. Sam's long curled lashes gave his eyes the unflinching wide-eyed stare of a child's. He moved closer. Oh God. Oh God. If he touches me I will surely explode, she thought, unsure whether the river was rushing faster now – an insistent curdling whoosh – or the sound came from somewhere inside her head. The breeze strengthened, changed direction, carried Sam's scent – a light spicy musk, easily distinguishable from Jez's fleshy pink smell.

She wondered what Sam would taste like and her mouth salivated, her breath came short and shallow. Then she thought of Lara. No, nothing could happen. *Nothing.* Sam was Lara's first decent boyfriend. What kind of friend was she?

Sam reached his hand out to her face, pausing torturously a few millimetres above the surface of her skin. She thought she might just faint there and then. His palm, dry and electric hot, closed in, cupping her cheek. She leaned into it.

'Why didn't we get together then?' he said.

'I never thought . . . I just never thought you'd be into me.' Something compelled her to be honest. 'I settled for Jez. I thought I had to settle.'

'Idiot.' Sam put an arm around her. They sat silently like that for what felt like an eternity, in an arm-over-shoulder friends hug. 'You know what? I was scared of you,' he said eventually.

She laughed and fell towards his chest, which seemed to catch her and envelope her body perfectly. 'Don't be ridiculous.'

'I was. I was scared of . . . well, I knew if we got together, it would be full-on. I wasn't ready. I didn't have the guts.' He winced. 'Or does that sound like bollocks?'

She smiled at him gratefully, enjoying the warm bulk of his body next to hers. 'It sounds like a good excuse.'

'When I finally realised, that I had to act, that I couldn't live my life running away, well, it was too late.'

A smile played at the edge of her mouth. She couldn't quash it, this rebellious uprising of joy. 'Why didn't . . . why didn't you ever *say* anything?'

'You were with Jez.' Sam sniffed her neck, she could feel him nuzzling around the back of her ear, sucking her up. 'Besides, I couldn't offer anyone much. No steady job . . . hardly a catch. I thought that's what women like you wanted. Something stable.'

'Now *you* sound like an idiot.'

'I know. And I still could have given you lots of cute babies,' he whispered against her neck.

Stevie squeezed her eyes shut. Oh God, I can't listen to this.

'Your wedding was the worst day of my life, Stevie.'

That was enough. A huge well of emotion bubbled over her. Her throat closed. Tears dropped in big splodges. How could something so horribly wrong feel so delicious?

'Don't cry.' He wiped away a tear from her face with the pad of this thumb. 'Please don't cry.'

'It's just . . . oh God, I'm sorry.' She unpeeled herself from his chest, fanned her face with her hand. 'What a mess.'

'It's not a mess.' He looked joyful. 'It's beautiful. It feels beautiful to me.' Then he came close again, his breath hot and sweet against her cheek, his hand in her hair, cradling the back of her skull. As he bent to kiss her, she pulled away, flinching at the hurt on his face as she did so. 'I can't do this.'

Sam's face balled. 'Lara?'

She nodded, a hollow feeling of disloyalty already gnawing in the pit of her stomach.

'But I can't come back from this . . . from you now,' pleaded Sam. 'Can't you see that? Me and Lara, we're already over.'

She shook her head, tears rolling down her cheeks, trying to stop them with sharp intakes of breath that shook her shoulders.

'Don't shake your head.' He grabbed her hand. '*Please*, don't. I've waited so long. I never thought. Fuck, Stevie . . .' He was shouting now. 'I'm so in love with you. Can't you tell?' There was a long uncomfortable pause. He sat back, subdued, astonished at his candour. 'There, I've said it.'

Stevie wouldn't, couldn't say it back. She had no idea how

302

to reconcile how she felt about Sam with Lara, all the futures that would unravel. It was too much to take in. Her phone rang. And rang.

'You want to get it this time?'

Thinking it might be Poppy, Stevie nodded, wiped her face and dug into her handbag with trembling hands. By the time she'd adventured past the disintegrating Tampax, receipts and Tube tickets and located the phone it had rung off. She held it in her hand, switched on voicemail and pushed the silver flip phone against her ear, grateful for this pause in which to pull herself together.

'It's Lara. Where the hell are you? I'm trying to track you down. Stevie, you're not going to believe this . . . *I* don't believe this . . . and don't tell anyone, not Sam yet, I need to explain . . . Ohmygod, I'm pregnant! Call me. Call me. *Call* me.'

Stevie felt faint. This could not be. It just couldn't. She flipped the phone shut and held it tight.

'Stevie, are you OK? You've gone pale.' Sam bent his head down and looked up at her face through a nest of lashes. 'Is it Tommy?'

She shook her head, trying to take it in. Of course Lara hadn't had a chance to tell Sam yet – he was here. With *her*, a hateful, disloyal friend. Irrespective of what had just happened – what had just happened? – Sam would do the right thing by Lara, she knew that. It was all over before it had even begun. She stood up stiffly. 'No, it's something else. I'm going to head off, Sam.'

Sam leaped up. 'What's happened?'

'It's nothing. Look, I need to go, OK?' She turned her face away from his, refusing to connect. 'This . . . it isn't going to work. Really, it's not. Never.'

'We can sort this out with Lara, I'm sure. We're all adults.'

'No, it's not going to happen. Let's forget we had this conversation.'

Sam grabbed her hand. 'How the fuck do you expect me to do that? No, no way, man. What the hell's going on? Who was that?'

Stevie pulled her hand away and started walking off, feeling dream-like, unsure of what was powering her feet because it felt like they were walking in the wrong direction.

'Stevie?' He stopped her, held her wrists. His grip hurt. 'Please don't walk away like this.'

'Just let me go,' she said, flicking him off, with as much conviction as she could muster. She needed to be cruel to be kind, cut it all dead now. 'I'm not into you. I won't ever be.' She continued treading up the stony path for five minutes and only looked back once. Sam had gone.

Thirty-eight

Katy tipped the taxi driver three dollars and got out on Canal Street – catching a wolf whistle as her bare leg protruded out of the cab – because the traffic was honking, not moving, and the longer she sat in the cab the twitchier she got. New York stressed her out. Part of this stress was due to her *trying* to like the city – it was one of the hippest in the world, what was wrong with her? – and failing. The tall buildings all seemed to be closing in on her, their long phallic shadows predatory. The people made her feel provincial. And downtown spooked her. It wasn't like Katy to be affected by world events – she avoided listening to news, too depressing – but not even she had been able to ignore 9/11. While the London bomb carnage had happened mostly underground and thus created little memorable iconography, when she closed her eyes she could still see that photo of the falling man. And today the sky was the same Sky News-blue of that day. It made her uneasy. She folded out the stiff Manhattan map she'd bought at JFK. Finding the grid system baffling in its simplicity, she walked up the few blocks to the offices, double-checking she was walking south not north. Her acid green Miu Miu shoes bit into her big toes, swollen in the heat. But her buffed legs were shiny and skinny as knives. Her hair was big. She had demons to slay and had groomed accordingly.

Katy looked up. Seb's building, constructed almost entirely from glass, reflected a relentlessly moving city in its panes. The doors whooshed open automatically. Men and women in dark suits, mobile phones glued to their ears, neat shiny brief-cases swinging purposefully, strode through the foyer, heels clicking on the marble floor. The reception desk was large, black and intimidating in scale, but the man sitting behind it, in contrast, was small, in his fifties, jowly and humourless. The sun bounced off the gleaming windows, creating a disc of light on his bald forehead.

'He's in a meeting,' said the man at reception with finality, when she'd asked to see Sebastian Compton-Pickett.

Katy batted her new eyelash extensions. 'May I wait in his office?'

'Not possible, ma'am.'

The tears came to order easily enough. 'Sir, please have pity. I've flown all the way from London – London, England – to surprise my fiancé.' She slid a photo from her purse showing a picture of her and Seb on holiday, arm in arm in Thailand. 'Recognise him? It's his birthday. He does-n't know I'm here . . .'

'Sorry.'

'It would make one man very happy.' She carried on star-ing at him, knowing eye contact was the way in, catching the quick flicker of the man's eyes as he took in her cleavage, then a bird-quick lick up her legs. '*Please?*'

'I'm obviously as stupid as I look,' he said wearily. 'Name?'

'Katy Norris.'

The man wrote her a name card, inserted it into a pinned plastic badge that read 'Visitor' in red. 'Take one of the ele-vators on the left. Fourteenth floor.'

She walked quickly, in case the man changed his mind, catching the double-takes from the suits as she moved. There were ten rows of gleaming polished chrome lifts. She stood by the third one on her left. Three was her lucky number.

At the second interrogative base she smiled at the receptionist – another older man, thankfully – and flashed her pass. 'Third door on your left,' he said, staring at her legs.

It took her about five seconds to get to Seb's office, the longest five seconds ever. Upper thighs sweating where they (just) touched, she paused at the perspex name on the door. It looked like a stranger's name. Not for the first time on this impetuous fury-fuelled trip across the Atlantic, she wished Jez was with her. Then she reminded herself – the final part of the sequence of this particular recurring emotional tick – that Jez *wasn't* hers. Jez was on loan only. Right now, she had two choices: resign herself to becoming a dried-up old husk, snivelling at home, or confront and get some closure. She knocked. No reply.

Turning the brushed-chrome doorknob, edging the door open, she stepped in. Whoa! Directly in front of her, behind a large dark desk, was a vast window, a seamless sheet of glass framing lower Manhattan. She walked towards it and lay her palm across its cool smooth surface, not wanting to lean too much of her weight against the glass in case it suddenly gave way. One hand still on the window, reassuringly connected in some way to the world outside, she studied the office. It was smart, obviously, but impersonal, with few signs of Seb or indeed any human being's existence within its polished planes of stainless steel and dark wood. Only Seb's light tailored coat, slung on a peg on the back of the office door, provided any clue he inhabited the space. She picked up the coat. It was new, black, with a Dandyish fuchsia-pink satin lining, quite unlike the conservative coats he usually wore.

307

She sniffed it. Scalpy smell mixed with the Czech and Speake Cuba cologne she bought him every Christmas. That was Seb's all right. It didn't make her miss him though. She carefully put the coat back on the peg and scanned his desk. No photo of her. Well, she supposed there wouldn't be. Not now. She sat down in the large chair and swivelled around once, heels up, like a child. Unable to resist, she opened the top drawer of his desk. It rolled out soundlessly. But she didn't have a chance to rummage. The door opened.

'Crikey!' Seb stood in the doorway, pulling at his tie, mouth gaping open, frozen at the point of impact. 'You made me jump out of my skin!'

'I wanted to surprise you.'

Seb rubbed his draining face. 'Mission accomplished.'

There was an uncomfortable silence. The sweep-up into the arms wasn't going to happen, that was clear. Seb's arms hung awkwardly by his side, his feet shuffled, as if twitching to walk back to wherever he'd come from.

'Do sit down,' she said mock officiously, gesturing to a smaller chair on the other side of his desk.

Seb didn't smile, nor did he sit down. He walked over to the window, gazed out, without seeing anything. 'I guess I should know why you're here.'

Katy swivelled on her chair. 'Not sightseeing.'

'No.' Seb shrugged off his suit jacket and hung it on a hook next to a filing cabinet. He'd put on a bit of weight. And he looked anxious and sweaty and not particularly happy, she observed with a frisson of satisfaction. 'I've got some apologising to do. But . . .' He gestured around the office. 'Heavens, Katy, you do pick your moments don't you?'

Katy leaned back into the office chair, crossing her bare tanned legs with a sharp professional flourish. The more she played a role, the less she revealed, the less vulnerable she felt.

'There's never a good time to dump your long-term girlfriend, no?'

Seb pressed into his temple pressure points – as Katy had taught him many years ago – with his thumb and index fingers. 'Katy, please . . .'

'Or should I consider myself already dumped?' She bent forward on the desk with a brittle smile, enjoying the feeling of superiority the large desk fostered, as if acting out scenes from *The Apprentice*. 'The thing is, I don't recall having, like, *the* conversation in question.' She wondered where the hell the strength to speak so curtly had come from. But she was on a roll, enjoying Seb squirming. 'I just recall that you haven't phoned me at all, and when I do finally get through to you, you speak to me as though I'm wasting your precious New York minutes. And I want some closure.'

'I haven't behaved like a gentleman.' Seb slumped against the wall. 'I'm sorry.'

'A gentleman?' Katy scoffed. 'A *gentleman*? Pur-lease.'

'I know, I know.' Seb shook his head from side to side. 'The thing is . . . it's been tough . . . I didn't know what to tell you . . .'

Rage bloomed inside Katy, flushing the skin of her décolletage. The rage was empowering. 'That you wanted to be single? That you never had any intention to properly commit to me? That you wasted some of the most important years of my life when I could have met someone who wanted what I wanted. And why should I be ashamed? Yes, I wanted to settle with someone who loved me. Is that so fucking freakish?'

Seb groaned and covered his face with his hands. 'But I couldn't give you that. Not then . . .'

'Not then.' Katy switched over her crossed legs. 'Not ever.'

Seb walked over to the desk and for the first time since

arriving in New York sat down in the smaller chair, facing Katy. 'Ironically—'

'I don't smell any irony here.'

'Well, it's just that I *have* been doing a lot of thinking . . .'

'And fucking?'

Seb's face fell.

Katy waved her hand, as if dismissing a bad sales pitch. 'Let's save that for later, shall we?' She couldn't go there, not now. She knew that if, as was likely, Seb had met someone else, she wouldn't be able to hold it together. And she wouldn't give him the satisfaction of seeing her cry. It struck her that normally she'd have demanded to know and picked apart the gory details. But a new sense of preservation prevailed. She wouldn't do it to herself, not this time.

'Gosh, I am sorry,' said Seb, hand over his mouth, staring at Katy. 'I didn't realise you were so upset. I thought you realised it was kind of over . . . or ending, somehow in the process of self-destructing. But you always left such cheery messages.'

'I do good phone.' Hell. Why should she apologise for being in her mid-thirties and wanting a relationship that was deeper than phone sex? Jez had reinforced a little of her old self-confidence. He'd affirmed her moral rightness. 'But I *was* hurting.'

'Of course. Crikey. What can I say?' Seb, looking devastated, picked up a pen, nudging its retractable nib nervously along the edge of the desk. 'But the rotten thing is . . . shit . . . how do I say this.' He inhaled, sat up straighter and pushed his fringe out of his eyes. 'OK, being straight with you, Katy. I thought we were over. That my life was here. And then, well, recently, I began to miss England, the whole English summer thing, the boat race, hanging out at my folks . . .'

One thing I won't miss, thought Katy.

'Tuscany. Remember we talked about going to Tuscany? Down to Widgi's villa?'

'Did we?' Oh God. Why did she have to listen to this? She should leave now. It was O-V-E-R. The gravitational pull had gone. She must accept, no embrace, singledom and move on. She had her closure. Perhaps that was all she needed – just to see him, one more time.

'I'm rambling. Sorry, you know I'm an imbecile when it comes to expressing my feelings.' He smiled. 'The point is, I started to miss *you*.'

'*What?*' Katy's heart thudded faster.

Seb's eyes pinked. 'But I've cocked everything up . . .' He sniffed, desperately trying to keep a stiff upper lip. 'There is a tiny problem.' He gulped. 'The thing is . . .'

There was a knock on the door. Seb froze, terrified a colleague was about to discover him in a compromising moment of abject weakness. It would be all over the office in minutes. He stood up, brushed himself down, tightened his tie. 'Yes?'

'The documents you sent for.'

Seb opened the door. As he did so, Katy's eye was drawn to the open drawer on her left hand side. What the hell was that? She picked it up. Oh God, it couldn't be. It was a sick joke? 'Seb?' she said weakly, all bravado gone. 'Seb?'

A bundle of documents in his arms, Seb turned around. When he saw what Katy held in her shaking hand, he sank into the chair, eyes shut, head in his hands. The game was up.

Thirty-nine

Beneath grey skies – densely matted like damp cotton wool – and with a heavy heart, Stevie walked up Walton Street, past the steamed-up windows of the Jericho Café, Le Petit Blanc restaurant, the deli and florist, the bloom of possibility that she'd felt that afternoon on Port Meadow shrinking shut again. Without Sam to bring it alive, Oxford seemed just part of her past again, disconnected to her, like an old book she'd reread once or twice as a teenager, it's relevance to her thirty-something self now gone. The street was eerily quiet today. There were no cars. No noise. It all felt horribly empty.

A familiar figure cycled towards her, swerving his bike in exuberant and dangerous figures of eights. Could it be? Neil? She squinted again. Yes, it was her brother, standing above the pedals, grinning, his hair shorter and neater than last time she'd seen him, blown stiffly back by the wind like tufts of meadow grass. Sitting on the saddle, hands clinging around his waist, was a girl, a petite twentysomething, laughing, dark wavy hair streaming back off her pretty heart-shaped face. Neil screeched to a stop. 'Sis? What are you doing in the manor? Shouldn't you be at work?'

'Oh, just . . . oh, it doesn't matter.'

'You don't look too chipper, whassup?'

'Nothing. I needed a break from London.'

'You're pulling a sickie?'

'Not exactly.' Stevie looked at the girl, then Neil. 'Introduce us then.'

Neil's hand instinctively reached out for a rope of dreaded hair to twiddle but found none. 'Er, this is Claire. Claire, my sister, Stevie.'

Claire smiled eagerly. 'I've heard so much about you.'

Stevie looked from Neil to Claire and back again. Something about these two made her wonder. She'd never seen him in such close physical contact with a girl before. Could this be – gasp – Neil's first girlfriend? 'Fancy escorting me to the folks' house, Neil? I could do with some company.'

'Oh, no, we're, like . . .'

'Great.' Claire nudged him in the ribs. 'Come on.'

'Yeah, come on, Neil. Move it.'

Caught in a pincer movement between Claire and Stevie, Neil relented. 'Er . . . suppose. You do look like you could use some company, sis.'

The three of them ambled back to their parents' house, Neil wheeling his bike, Claire keeping one of her hands on the handlebar. They chatted about Claire's English course, the bad damp summer weather, the trustafarian twit – son of a glass magnate – who'd moved into Neil's squat and painted the bathroom satsuma orange. Neil listened warily, in case his sister incriminated him with an embarrassing anecdote from childhood. Stevie tried to concentrate but was unable to stop thinking about Lara and Sam – what would their child look like? Girl or a boy?

They stopped at the drive of their parents' house. Outside the front door, precariously stacked on the gravel drive, were two suitcases, one with the tip of a navy sock hanging forlornly out the side. Neil and Stevie exchanged glances. It could mean only one thing.

Neil rolled his eyes. 'It's finally happened then. Oh shit.'

Claire looked puzzled. 'I don't get it. What's the matter?'

'Emotional baggage.' Neil nodded to the cases, trying to keep his cool. 'My folks . . . you know I told you they were, like, having problems?'

'I'm sorry.' Claire put an arm around Neil's waist. He flinched at this conclusive display of togetherness.

A cold wet dread settled in Stevie's stomach. So who was leaving this time, mother or father? The sock suggested the latter. 'Not the best meet-the-parents opportunity, Claire. Don't feel you two have to hang around.'

Suddenly, a polished Oxford brogue appeared, wedging the front door open. 'It's not books! I promise it's not stuffed full of books!' her father shouted, emerging into the daylight. Catching sight of his audience, his eyebrows knitted. 'Oh. Hello, folks.'

Stevie and Neil studied the gravel. 'Hi.' Walking in on a heavy parental argument still felt as awkward as if they were to walk in on them having sex.

There was a commotion on the other side of the door. Chris rolled his eyes.

'I will damn well check for those blasted books!' shouted Patti. 'Just you watch me.' Patti flew out the door, as if ejected by a powerful centrifugal force, newly hennaed hair flying around her shoulders. When she saw the assembled group she braked. 'Babies!' she cried. 'My babies!' She smacked Stevie and Neil with kisses. 'What are you doing here? Are you OK, Stevie? You look *very* long faced, darling. You look like you need a big cuddle from Mama.'

Stevie grappled for air inside her mother's arms. 'Easy.'

'But one minute, kids,' said Patti, withdrawing. 'Before I

314

forget, I need to check something.' She picked up one of the battered old suitcases, considered its weight and looked at Chris. 'Hmmm. The jury's out.' Then she put her hands on her large soft hips, threw her hair back and laughed.

Stevie exchanged another glance with Neil. God, they are happier already.

'Are you going to tell them or am I?' said Patti turning to Chris.

Stevie gulped. She wasn't sure how well she was going to cope this time round with another parental separation. It made her sick to the bottom of her stomach.

Chris sighed. 'We . . .'

Neil stepped forward and put a gentle hand on his father's arm. 'It's OK, Dad.'

Claire and Stevie looked down at their feet.

Chris started to speak again, 'We are . . .'

'We are going to *Marrakesh*!' screamed Patti, with a little jump off the ground. 'Marrakesh! Your father is taking me to Marrakesh!'

Their father nodded, a resigned nod. 'It is true. A moment of madness.'

Was this the my-wife-isn't-Rita effect? Stevie smiled at her dad. He winked back.

'This is the best anniversary present ever.' Patti kissed her husband, pushing his glasses up so they collided with his eyebrows. Then they started to snog.

Neil put one hand across his eyes. 'Oh gross, man . . .'

When Patti came up for air she registered Claire, who was staring open-mouthed, edging slightly behind Neil. 'We haven't met,' Patti said, extending her arm of bangles. 'Are you Stevie's friend?'

Claire grinned coyly and, to Neil's evident mortification, slipped her arm back around his waist. 'Neil's.'

Patti's mouth dropped open, speechless. She looked from Neil – who was blushing furiously – to the puppy-eyed Claire and back again.

'His crack addiction?' whispered Stevie to her mother, giving her a sharp nudge in the ribs.

'My God. At last!' Patti, who was near emotional boiling point anyway due to her impending departure for Marrakesh, now spilled over. She lunged forward, thrusting Claire into the crevasse of her bosom while Neil looked on helplessly. 'Welcome to the family.'

'This is so embarrassing. I knew this would happen,' muttered Neil. 'I knew it.'

For Claire's sake, Stevie tried to distract Patti. 'You're off now?'

Patti looked at her watch. 'Your father seems to think so. *I* think we've got a few hours to kill. Who wants to be one of those types who turn up to the airport days before the plane departs?'

Chris rolled his eyes. 'Your mother is a traveller, you see, Stevie, not a tourist. Not for her the bourgeois conventions of check-in times.' He looked at his wife and smiled affectionately. 'I should have just booked a cross-continental donkey.'

Patti gave him a playful pat. 'Ignore the old man. Let's have a quick cup of tea. After all, it's not every day Neil brings a . . . a . . .' Neil appeared to shrink in anticipation of his mother's imminent faux pas, 'a *special* friend home.'

Stevie followed her brother and his new girlfriend into the house. Yes, in life's game of musical chairs, she really was the one left standing.

Forty

Poppy stood on the front step of her Victorian Queen's Park house, in a white broderie anglaise blouse and jeans, a wide-brimmed straw hat shading the tiny bundle in her arms. Piers had one hand around his wife's waist, gazing at the new arrival proudly while Finn and Sophie giggled at their feet. Stevie dumped her work bags on the paved garden path – she'd come straight from the office when she'd heard – and ran up to the swaddled mewing bundle. 'Hello, Tommy.'

'He's my new brother,' piped Sophie.

'And mine,' added Finn. 'I gave him apple.'

'Did you? His first apple? Wow.' Stevie ruffled Finn's ringlets. 'He looks very well on it.'

'Just like a new pet,' pronounced Sophie, before turning on her heel, trailing her feather-boa fairy wand along behind her. 'But smaller than rabbit.'

'Smaller than rabbit,' repeated Finn solemnly, following his sister and pelting indoors.

'Actually, he's now five pounds, which is positively sumo,' grinned Piers, who had lost his jowls since Stevie last saw him, an improvement tempered by a look of ragged exhaustion. 'Nice to see you, Stevie. Hope you're feeling OK, given the circumstances. Chin up, hey?' Piers raked his hair back, harassed. 'Right, er, better get those other two to Alice's party. That's my orders. Children! Heel!' he thundered, disappearing through the house, clattering through the central hall, out into the garden where the children greeted him with teasing whoops.

'May I?' Stevie stuck one finger into the curl of Tommy's tiny damp, soft hand. 'The fingernails! I have larger cuticles.'

'Small but perfectly formed.' Poppy gazed proudly down at her son. 'He's a little trooper.'

Such a scrap of life. A triumph of medical expertise, patience and love. Stevie felt herself welling up. Was it safe to love him now? 'He's got the all clear?'

'Yup.'

Stevie slipped her arm through Poppy's and they walked through the olive-green front door, shutting out the park and North West London's familial bustle of trikes and Bugaboos behind them. 'It must be good to be home,' she said.

'Oh God, heaven.'

Poppy sat down on a chair, unbuttoning her blouse and propping the tiny bundle beneath her bust to suckle. Stevie listened, stunned by the disproportionate loudness of the suck.

'No table manners yet, I'm afraid. He's a ferocious feeder.' Poppy adjusted her nipple. 'Guzzles and guzzles. I lose about a pound a day. He gains it.'

Stevie pulled up a stool next to her sister. 'You're not doing all that Gina Ford scheduling like you did with the other two then?' She had to force herself to ask baby questions. Because these were the questions Lara would surely ask, the debates that she and Sam would engage in, as a line was clearly drawn between their new family life and her new single one, like a new political frontier dividing a previously united state.

'No, not this time. I've relinquished attempts to control any-thing. I'm just so bloody grateful to have Tommy home.' Poppy pointed at the piles of Lego bricks and garish coloured toys car-peting the floorboards. 'Life's completely chaotic, as you can see. But I've ceased to care. I'm all for muddling through.'

'That's not like you.'

'Well, you know what they say. All women turn into their mothers eventually.'

Stevie was unable to stop herself imagining Lara saying the same thing as she gaily suckled her first child, a beautiful baby with its daddy's coffee-bean eyes. 'I suppose.'

Poppy laughed. 'Our childhood was bonkers, wasn't it? Do you remember those family camping trips? This morning I was thinking about suggesting to Piers we all went camping to that woodland site in Sussex, you know the one that everyone bangs on about. But then I remembered the hell of camping in the late seventies. Midges, lukewarm tea, damp sleeping bags. Do you remember how Mum used to wash Neil's pooey Terry nappies out in mountain streams and then tie them to the roofrack of that dreadful old Volvo and Dad would drive at break-neck speed down the Welsh lanes to dry them?'

'Our parents were so embarrassing.' Is this what Lara and Sam's grown-up progeny would be doing one day, filtering their childhood, trying to make sense of it all. Stevie frowned, looked at the ground.

Poppy chuckled quietly to herself. Then the chuckle died down to a sigh, then silence. Neither of them spoke. Poppy studied her sister's face solemnly. 'Stevie, I've never seen you look thinner.'

'Thank you.'

'Or quite so miserable.'

Stevie eyes watered instantly. She gripped the seat of the stool. 'Oh, I'm OK.'

'Do you miss Jez terribly?'

'No.' Stevie smiled. 'I don't, not really. It's weird without him. I'm used to him being around but I don't miss him.'

Poppy frowned. 'Is Sam related to your emotional state in any way?'

'Lara's pregnant, Pops.'

'Pregnant?' Poppy's mouth dropped open. Her nipple – vast, burgundy – popped out of Tommy's mouth. Tommy wailed. 'Oh my god! You are joking?'

Stevie stroked Tommy's velvety head. 'Not.'

'But . . . but . . .' Poppy looked outraged. 'But you and Sam are *meant* for each other.'

'Don't.'

'Lara doesn't want kids.'

'No law against changing your mind.'

'Oh, Stevie.' Poppy crushed her hands to her mouth. 'Oh, I am sorry.'

Stevie dismissed her concern with a wave of her hand. 'Forget it.'

'But . . .'

'*Please*. It wasn't meant to be, Poppy.'

Poppy snapped back her feeding bra and offered Tommy. 'You want a cuddle?'

Stevie smiled, knowing that Poppy meant well but less sure that she wanted to hold a baby at this moment in time. But she had little choice. Her sister deposited Tommy in her lap where he promptly gurgled a backwash of curdled milk on the sleeve of her cloud-grey Agnès b cardigan.

'You need a stiff drink,' said Poppy, buttoning her top and striding off into the reaches of her open-plan designer kitchen. 'I'm going to fix you a Pimms.'

'I'm fine, really.'

'No, Stevie,' Poppy said bossily. 'You really are not.'

320

Forty-one

Stevie didn't go in to work on Tuesday. For the second time in her life, she phoned in sick on Monday night, left a message when she knew no one would be there to answer the phone. The prospect of continuing life – dusting herself down, pretending everything was normal, clocking in, clocking off – left her rattlingly empty. What was the point? What was the point in another working week, month, year? Leading to what, exactly? A holiday, a new pair of shoes, a mortgage on a two-bedroom flat somewhere in zone two? It all seemed horribly meaningless. Being in Lara's flat – a recipient of her generosity – didn't help. Not at all. It made her feel guilty. She still hadn't been able to face calling Lara back in response to the pregnancy news, which undoubtedly made her a wretched, unworthy human being and a poor friend. She would lose both Lara and Sam. Nothing less than she deserved.

Stevie leaned against the duck-egg blue wall, feeling its cool plaster on each vertebra of her newly skinny back, and observed Lara's things, bits of Lara, reminders of a simpler friendship: the battered old leather sofa they used to watch old Hepburn movies on; an inherited Tiffany lamp with a long seam crack, a legacy of one particularly debauched New Year party two years ago that Lara regretted throwing; an armchair restored in candy pink velvet Lara would curl up on the mornings after, wearing vintage-silk camisoles and frilly knickers. Lara's old fashionable boho life. Was it redundant now? Where would she and Sam live? Would they bring up the baby here? Or New York? She hoped they'd stay in New York. It would be less painful.

As she'd walked across the railway bridge two days ago, out of the sunny green haven of Port Meadow into some place darker, the reality of her situation had slapped her face like a dousing of dirty canal water: she'd compromised her life by marrying Jez – by *settling*, how she hated that word – and it had resulted in her present loveless, childless, futureless circumstances. While Lara, who had lived life to the full, taking each opportunity as it came, never apologising to anyone for putting sex and career first, had ended up with the nice guy – the guy she wanted – *and* the baby. It was more than ironic. It was horrible. Yes, she was jealous. She was unbearably jealous of Lara right now, which filled her with more self-loathing.

'Fuck,' Stevie muttered, flumping heavily on the sofa and pressing all the buttons on the remote control at once in the hope that one might switch on the telly. 'Fuck, fuck, fuck.' Fifteen minutes later – as indicated by Lara's over-size vintage wall clock – Stevie realised that she hadn't listened to a word of the programme, a documentary about the mating rituals of dolphins. Instead her attention was rooted to her mobile phone, which lay blinking malevolently on Lara's cluttered sideboard. What kind of friend was she? Pull yourself together, girl. Do the right thing. Feeling shaky and faint, she pushed herself up, one hand on the dry cracked leather of the sofa arm for support, and grabbed for the phone. What would she say? How could she pretend? Surely Lara would know. Wiping a tear from her nose, she selected Lara's name from the contacts book. Do the right thing, she told herself. Just do the right thing.

Ding dong!

Stevie jumped. Who the hell was that at the door? She wasn't in the mood for visitors.

Ding dong!

She wouldn't answer it. She couldn't face seeing anyone. Go away.

Ding dong!

'I know you're in there, Stevie Jonson. Open the god-damn door!'

Stevie didn't recognise the voice, although it sounded familiar. Checking her reflection in the hall mirror – ravaged – she slumped, one foot in front of the other, towards the door, pulling up her sloppy velour tracksuit bottoms as she went. Nothing could make her feel much worse than she already did. She pressed the intercom buzzer. 'Who is it?'

'Who do you think?' The voice didn't sound happy. 'It's Katy. Katy Norris. Open up.'

Katy Norris? Christ. Did she need this? Probably not. But she also felt a strange compulsion to face the woman who'd stolen Jez, or relieved her of Jez, depending on which way one looked at it. She buzzed Katy back into her life.

Katy stood on the doorstep, wild-eyed beneath a plume of blonde hair. 'I hope you're satisfied now.'

'You've got some fucking cheek.'

Katy barged past her. 'Revenge is it? Revenge for stealing Sam from under your nose all those years ago? I thought you might be the type to hold grudges.'

Stevie followed, finding the powerful wake of her perfume hard to stomach. 'What the fuck are you talking about? *You* of all people.' She spat the words out, her sense of righteous victimhood aroused.

Katy turned on the ball of her leopard-print ballet pump. 'Things aren't good with Jez?' She glanced about the sitting room. 'I'm sorry—'

'You're sorry?' Stevie trembled with rage and disbelief. '*Sorry?*'

'But it's no excuse. You, who had so much, who . . . who . . . fucked it up for me.'

To Stevie's astonishment, Katy collapsed on to the sofa and burst into tears, which cut through her flawless beige foundation like tidal streams in sand.

'I'm not with you.' Stevie's voice was hard, unmoved. 'You ruin my marriage and come round here and accuse *me* of ruining your relationship? I dare say you managed to cock up your relationship perfectly well without my help.'

It was Katy's turn to look bewildered. She wiped the tears from her cheeks furiously. 'Ruin *your* marriage?'

Stevie pulled up her tracksuit bottoms, feeling a little like an extra from the *Royle Family* and wishing that Katy wasn't quite so glamorous, in her skinny jeans and lipstick-red silk top. She hated the idea of Katy looking at her and thinking, 'No wonder he's not interested'. Clothes were armour and she was only protected by velour. 'Oh come on, Katy. Jez has told me *everything*.' Stevie blew the air crossly out of her mouth, lifting the scrawl of frizzy curls that had begun to masquerade as a fringe as her wedding cut grew out. 'I should chuck you out of here right now.'

'Everything?' Katy's voice was quieter now, her perfect eyebrows descending to a puzzled botox-defying V. 'I don't know—'

'Oh *please*.' Stevie wondered whether she'd come to gloat. '*Ne comprends pas . . .*'

Stevie's fists clenched. 'Don't *ne comprehends* me. Jez is . . .' She stopped, the words catching in her throat. 'He's in love with you.'

'*What?*' Katy bent forward, slipped her head into her hands, a gleaming wing of blonde hair falling over her face.

'I suppose you did nothing to encourage him.' Stevie snorted sardonically.

Katy shook her head from side to side. 'I didn't . . . I *swear*. I haven't done anything.'

'Oh, say what you like.' Stevie affected her bored do-I-look-like-I-give-a-fuck voice. 'Jez has declared his love for you, our marriage a mistake, hence . . . me living here. Romeo over there.' She stared at Katy, realising that she felt almost comforted by Katy's perfumed blonde perfection. They were so different. You either loved one type of woman or the other. And yes, she thought, Katy and Jez were better suited. She could swallow that. Because she couldn't go back to him now, not ever, Katy or no Katy.

'He never told me, Stevie. I'm sorry . . . I didn't mean . . .'

'Well, now you know.'

'Oh, goodness.' Katy's voice lost its accusatory brittle edge. She sank further into her hands. 'Goodness.'

'Don't tell me it's not mutual?' Stevie let out a hollow laugh like the pluck of an out-of-tune violin string. What a fine mess! Both she and Jez splitting up for lovers who didn't reciprocate. Hopeless in both marriage and divorce.

'Well . . . I . . . I . . .'

'Oh, don't go there. I wouldn't expect you to tell me the truth anyway.' Stevie sat down on the sofa next to Katy. Her voice softened. 'And I'm not about to give you my blessing. But I suppose it's only fair to tell you that, with or without you, Jez and I are seriously over. He's a free agent now.'

Katy flinched back warily, as if anticipating a punch. 'That's very grown up of you.'

'Yeah, well,' Stevie growled. 'Whatever. So what were you shrieking about before? What have I ruined? Or have I taken the wind from your sails now? Bring it on.'

'Seb.' Katy's face clouded over again. 'It's Seb.'

'Run off with an Upper East Side princess, has he?' Stevie knew it was cruel. But her own pride dictated that Katy suffer. 'Now *there's* a surprise.'

'No. You put them in touch.' Katy pulled at her cheeks, as if trying to figure out something incomprehensible. 'Funny, it doesn't seem so important . . .'

'What? *What* Katy? Hurry up and drop your bombshell.'

'It's your friend Lara. He's been shagging Lara.'

'Lara? No, not possible.' Stevie laughed. 'Honestly, he may be shagging half of Manhattan but he hasn't shagged Lara. Lara's going out with Sam. She's . . .' She was about to say, having Sam's baby, but didn't want to voice it.

'She is, or *was*, shagging Seb.' Katy stood up, brushed herself down in readiness to leave. She spoke very quietly. 'I've seen the proof.'

'What? Like a 34C Victoria Secrets bra down the back of the sofa? Come on.'

Katy stood up straight and looked sternly, unflinchingly, into Stevie's eyes. 'I've seen the pregnancy test.'

'What?'

'He's got her up the duff, Stevie. He's gone and got some slapper up the duff.'

After Katy had gone, Stevie slid down a wall like she'd been shot. The events of the past few days were too much to take in and had left her disorientated and spinning, as if she'd popped down a Wonderland rabbit hole to a place where life's rules – all the things she'd accepted as certainties – had inverted. Not only had her safe little marital box been exposed as a sham – Jez had brought neither stability nor predictability – she had been exposed as someone capable of lying to others, but mostly someone capable of lying to herself. That she'd come so close to kissing her best friend's boyfriend horrified her. That she'd come so close to spending a lifetime with a man she didn't love horrified her even more. And now, like a strange, messed-up angel in leopard-print pumps, Katy Norris had come to give as she had once taken away. She'd saved her from Jez. She'd delivered her the news about Lara.

Which meant? There was nowhere to hide. There was now no impeding relationship between her and Sam, just complications. Her life was unmapped: she had to charter it. She bent her head between her knees, relieved, spent. Then an awful thought hit her. What if Katy had got it *wrong*?

The telephone started to ring. Stevie ignored it. After six rings, Lara's clear cheerful voice boomed through the answer-machine. She was at JFK. She'd be back in the morning.

Forty-two

'I thought you'd died or something,' said Lara, pulling her key from the front door.

Stevie hugged her tightly, silently. Lara extricated herself from the hug and stood back and struck a pose, left hip tilting forward, smile lusciously wide. 'Do I look different?'

Stevie nodded. Lara did look different. Plumper, with a Jayne Mansfield décolletage. She was still wearing jeans but teamed with flat thongs, as opposed to her usual heels.

'I do, don't I? Check out these tits!'

'Pornographic.'

The flat looked complete with Lara back in it, thought Stevie, pulling her dressing gown tight around her waist and sitting down on a wicker-backed chair in the kitchen. She was a little unsure of how the conversation should begin, aware that there was A Conversation to have. 'Well,' she said awkwardly, recalling her and Sam's revelations on Port Meadow, feeling terrible about them now that she was confronted with the fleshed-out abstraction of her best friend. 'You must be tired.'

Lara waved her hands dismissively, as if a small hop over the Atlantic was nothing more than a city-to-suburb commute. 'I feel great, actually. A bit sick at times, in the evening, but otherwise great. I needed to come over to see the folks.' She patted her tummy. 'A bit of explaining to do.'

'Sure.' She'd never seen Lara like this, so fleshy, ripe and breezy. It was unsettling. She didn't know how to celebrate, if celebration was appropriate at all. 'It's quite a lot to take in, Lara.'

'I know, I know.' Lara passed her a steaming cup of Earl Grey and sat down. 'The condom slipped off,' she said matter-of-factly. 'I began to feel a bit odd a few days later – light headed, dizzy, crap really – so I got myself checked out, you know, at a clap clinic, thinking I might have caught a nasty. And I found out then.'

'What a shock.'

'Jesus. It was like being told that the world is flat.' Lara cradled her head in her hand and cocked it to one side contentedly, eyes wider and bluer than ever, her cheeks milk-maid-rosy as if pregnancy had lent a kind of pastoral innocence to her features. 'But you know the weirdest thing? Pretty soon after – and I know this sounds strange – I felt like, oh, *of course*. That it was *meant to be* somehow. Now it feels like the most natural thing in the world. It doesn't make sense, does it?'

'You always knew you'd keep it?'

'Absolutely. From the moment . . .' Lara's voice choked up. 'Sorry, it's the hormones. I didn't want babies before, not at all. You know that. But now . . .' She blew out a mouthful of air. 'I crave it, this thing, growing inside. I think, perhaps, the pregnancy hormones have made me broody. And if I hadn't have got pregnant I would never have wanted a baby. It's a weird one.'

The significance of what had happened to Lara finally hit. Stevie felt a bubble of joy rise up her own chest, crack her throat. 'I'm happy for you,' she said and meant it.

'But Sam . . .' stuttered Lara, drawing invisible doodles on the glass table top with a finger. 'Sam . . .'

Stevie froze, her fingers clamping tight around her mug. 'Yes?'

'Sam doesn't know,' said Lara, quietly. 'He's over for the weekend. I'm here to see him too. But I can't face it.'

'It'll be OK,' she said uncertainly.

'It's . . .' Lara looked solemn. 'It's not Sam's baby.'

Stevie's fingers lost their claw-grip on the mug. She realised she'd been holding her breath.

'I've been a bad girl, Stevie.'

'How bad?'

'Do you remember you put Seb in touch with me?'

'I do.' Stevie smiled.

'We met up and, well, one thing led to another. He told me he'd split with Katy.'

'I should tell you now,' Stevie interrupted. 'Katy came round yesterday, said she'd found a pregnancy test. Yours. I wasn't sure whether to believe her.'

Lara's beautiful face crumpled. 'You are joking? Oh fuck. Fuck. *Fuck*. That's bad. That's really bad.' She put her head in her hands, hair falling forward. 'I left it at Seb's office. He wanted evidence you see.'

'Nice.'

'Well, it was unfortunate,' winced Lara. 'It was just sex, to be fair. You know, I think he actually wanted to get back with Katy. Then I got pregnant.' She shook her head. 'It's a bit of a mess.'

A terrible black thought clouded Stevie's relief. 'But . . . if you don't mind me asking . . . how do you know it is *not* Sam's?'

'Oh, Sam and I never slept together,' Lara announced breezily, sipping her tea.

'*What?*' Stevie slammed her mug down on the table.

'It just never happened, I'm afraid. He never seemed that into it. And . . . well . . . I didn't push things. It was kind of sweet, courtly. I thought if I held out – all that dating stuff from *The Rules* – that it would have a better chance of not turning into the usual crash and burn. And . . . I suppose . . .'

'Go on.'

'I wanted it to work. I liked the *idea* of a functional relationship. I wanted to prove – to you, my mother and everyone else – that I could have a proper relationship with a nice presentable guy, not just unsuitable love rats. But the chemistry wasn't there.'

Stevie huffed back in her chair. 'I had no idea.'

Lara raised an eyebrow archly. 'I think he's hung up on you anyhow.'

'Me?' Stevie laughed uneasily, swiftly changed the subject.

Lara grinned. 'You've gone scarlet!'

Stevie shifted uncomfortably, not ready to start exchanging notes. 'But what are you going to do, Lara? On a practical level, I mean.'

Lara smiled knowingly, letting her friend off the hook. 'Stay in New York. Casey is over the moon. We're going to bring the baby up—'

'You and Casey?'

'Why not? She's happy for me to stay on at the apartment. She will be Aunt Casey and New York godmother.' Lara sounded strong, empowered. 'You'll be the London one, I hope.'

'I'd be honoured.'

Lara grinned. 'All I need now is a white-picket fence.'

'What about Seb?'

'Well, I don't think we'll be together, that's pretty clear. But he'll be involved. He's taken it on the chin.'

331

Stevie looked at her beaming, radiant friend and laughed. 'Gosh, you do look happy.'

'I am.' Lara took a sip of tea. 'I tell you, this is weird shit. But I really am happy.'

Stevie looked out of the window and saw a streak of mackerel-marked red clouds, like a stack of arrows pointing west.

Forty-three

Katy put the phone down on Seb, the receiver making a satisfyingly final click. Had she just rejected him? Was that her voice saying, 'No, too late,' when he'd asked her to forgive and marry him? A shiver of triumph goose-bumped her forearms. She tugged on a tattered denim mini-skirt, a nude vintage-silk blouse and woven leather flip-flops, her feet immediately luxuriating in the flat soles. After years of Seb-pleasing corn-rubbing heels, she felt the flats to be symbolic of a new kind of freedom. In her bathroom, Katy patted in her moisturiser and reached for her make-up. She took the lid off the Touche Éclat, clicked it to press out the thick pink paste and brought it to the snooker-hole dip of her eye socket. But something stopped her drawing it on in the usual crescent. She didn't look too bad. Not so bad for thirty-six years old. She put the wand down. No, today she wouldn't do it. She'd declare a make-up amnesty. For some reason, it mattered that Jez see her without war paint. The battle was over.

She checked her watch. OK, it was time. With a courageous inhalation, she picked up her fertility test and stared at the plastic white stick, a kind of parody of a pregnancy test. She sat down on the toilet and pulled the stick from beneath her. Thirty minutes she had to wait. It was the longest thirty minutes of her life. She paced around the flat, drank Diet Coke and tapped her fingers furiously on the kitchen table, wondering if her life was about to dissect into a clear binary: the prelude; the sequel. Perhaps nothing would ever be the same again. And then thirty minutes was up.

She knew the score: one line in the reference box meant she was OK; two lines, the second lighter than the first, was also a reprieve; two lines, the second the same or darker than the first would be disastrous and should come with a button hot-lining the nearest IVF clinic. She took a deep breath and picked up the stick from the mantelpiece, looking but not seeing. The plastic felt warm in her fingers, as if brewing a secret. Focusing with one eye only, she crumpled on to the sofa, anxiety hissing out of her like air from a balloon. Then she punched the air.

It was still hot when she left the flat, the sun, fake-tan orange, slipping west beneath the top of the elms and oaks of Hyde Park. As she walked up one of the gravelled paths that looped across the park like ribbons, she could just see Jez, hunched over, waiting as she'd asked in the patch of long yellow-tipped grass facing the river. She loved the way his strawberry-blond hair – what remained of it – fuzzed majestically around his face. Like a lion's. Goodness, he was magnificent.

Sensing Katy before he heard her, Jez turned and watched her picking her way across the long grass, like a woman from a fancy shampoo ad.

'I'm here,' she announced solemnly, her face rouged with exhilaration.

'You're here.' Jez squeezed her hand.

Katy kicked off her shoes and unfolded her legs, stretching them taut and brown into the clumps of dry summer grass. Jez stroked their waxed moisturised lengths tentatively from ankle to knee, hardly able to comprehend that they were his for the touching. 'You're so fucking beautiful, Katy.' He looked at her face again. 'I prefer you without make-up. Your face suits you.'

Katy beamed with pleasure. 'I don't look a hundred years old?'

'Twenty-seven, tops.'

To her horror, Katy burst into tears. But rather than finding this saline explosion a repellent signal of a needy woman, Jez cradled her in his arms. In those warm pale freckled slabs of flesh, she felt safe, a little girl again. She sucked in Jez's fruity, just-sweated smell, the smell of a man, she thought. 'I'm not over yet,' she said suddenly, unable to stop herself.

'What?' Jez looked puzzled.

Katy realised he'd have no idea what she was talking about. 'Oh, shit, I mean . . .' He'd seen her without concealer and mascara, the man could probably take it. She swallowed. 'I know this sounds a bit sad . . .'

'What, sweetheart?'

'I did a fertility test, one of those home kits that tell you if your ovaries have puckered like old fruit.'

Jez looked stricken. 'It doesn't matter, Katy. Don't cry, baby. I honestly don't mind. I just want you. That's all, just you. Twenty-seven or sixty-seven, it doesn't matter.'

Katy smiled gratefully through her tears, a rainbow of happiness arching over her body. It occurred to her that perhaps *this* was all she had striven for. Not babies. Not marriage. But a man she loved, loving her wholly, committing to her wholly. An equal partnership. A stop to the search. 'I don't know why I'm crying. The test was fine. I'm OK. It doesn't matter. I don't know why I . . .'

'So we can have babies?' Jez grinned wolfishly. 'I want you to have my babies.'

'What?' After years of Seb's run-to-the-hills expression if she ever mentioned children, Katy basked in Jez's words, wanting him to repeat them again and again.

Jez shook his head, grinning. 'Fuck me, I feel like I'm in a cross between a wet dream and *Casablanca*.'

'OK.' Katy giggled and dug her bare toes into the tickling grass, summoning courage. 'But there's something I should tell you.' She planted a kiss on Jez's stubbly pink cheek, her heart pounding. 'Please forgive me. I can hardly bear to tell you. But no secrets?'

Jez shook his head. 'No secrets.'

'Do you promise you'll still want me afterwards?'

'Fuck yes.'

Katy shifted uncomfortably on the grass. 'I've never told anyone this . . . Christ.' She pushed a hand against her mouth. 'This is hard.'

'Take your time, babe. Is it to do with me being married?'

'Er . . .'

'Because we'll divorce. It'll be a simple quicky. Stevie has made that quite clear . . .'

'No, no.'

'Is it Mum? Please don't worry about her. She left the flat this morning, said she was finally ready to go home, face the house.' He smiled, scratched his tummy. '*And* she laughed yesterday for the first time since Dad died. My jokes aren't too bad, you see.'

'No, Jez. It's to do with,' she gulped, 'genes.'

Jez's brow furrowed.

'*If* we have kids—'

'You've got some freaking genetic disorder?' Jez looked sad, then broadened with resolve. 'It's OK, we'll deal with it.'

Katy shook her head. 'No. It's just that I don't want to mislead you.' She cleared her throat. 'It's my nose, Jez.'

'Your nose? What about your nose?'

'My kids won't get *this* nose.' She closed her eyes, unable to face his reaction, still unsure how much her assumed-to-be-natural looks were part of the romantic transaction, wanting, for the first time in her life, to put all her cards on the table. 'My real nose is a shark fin.' She swallowed. 'I've had a nose job.'

There was a terrible pause. Katy kept her eyes squeezed shut, anticipating rejection. Then Jez leaned forward and sucked the whole of her tiny surgically enhanced nose into his mouth with a slurp.

Forty-four

Stevie checked her watch. She was running late. Twenty-five minutes late. Poppy hated lateness, didn't understand it, having forgotten what it was like to rely on badly ventilated trains in tunnels metres below the ground. Stevie ran out of Queen's Park Tube down the Salusbury Road. There was Poppy sitting on a wooden bench outside the local deli café in her favourite empire-line blue sundress, Tommy nuzzling her neck. She waved. She didn't look pissed off.

'Sorry, sorry I'm late,' huffed Stevie sitting down, feeling like a sweaty mess next to her pristine yummy mummy sister. 'Friday. Eleventh-hour changes by editor. Chaos.'

Poppy shrugged and stirred the thick froth on her cappuccino. 'Oh, don't worry.'

'Now what was so important? What wouldn't you tell me over the phone?'

Poppy smiled infuriatingly coyly and licked milk froth off the back of her teaspoon.

'I hate it when you do that secretive look.' Stevie stroked the warm curve of Tommy's back.

'Lara emailed me.' Poppy cocked her head to one side and laughed. 'Very interesting indeed. Don't look at me like that! We have conferred.'

'Oh no. Really?' Stevie put her hand to her mouth.

'Don't worry, she's totally cool about *it*.'

'And what's *it*?' But she could guess. Her heart started to pump.

'You and Flowers.' Poppy sipped her coffee. 'I have something to tell you, Stevie. I hope you're not going to be horribly cross. You probably have every right to be.'

'Sounds ominous.' Stevie kicked her legs out, unspearing her feet from their hot-pink Havaiana flip-flops and tilting her head into the late-afternoon sunshine.

'You've got two hours to go home, pack and get to Heathrow.'

'*What?*' Stevie sat up. 'What on earth are you talking about, Poppy?'

'Your flight to JFK leaves at ten p.m.' Beaming triumphantly, she handed her a chewed up Post-It note. 'Your e-ticket reference numbers. Don't lose.'

Stunned, Stevie stared at the note of paper, pressed her hands to her mouth. 'Oh my god, I can't . . . I can't just turn up. I haven't spoken to Sam or anything. You don't understand. I've totally screwed it all up.'

Poppy held up Tommy, whose head lolled back milk-drunk, and pressed him to her lips. 'You'll screw up worse if you don't go.'

'I said some vicious things. And he hasn't phoned me since he heard about Lara and Seb. If he wanted me he'd have phoned me.'

'Duh. That's not how men work!' Poppy rolled her eyes. 'He feels rejected.'

'But . . . but . . .'

339

'Stop being scared, Stevie.'

'Scared?'

'Scared of following your instincts.' Poppy stroked Tommy's fuzz of hair gently. 'I always used to think I was the more conservative one. Come on, that was my role in the family, wasn't it? We all had roles. But actually I think *you* are the conservative one.'

'Maybe.' Stevie shrugged. 'Maybe I wanted to be like you.'

'You thought I was boring.'

'Only a little bit.' She laughed. 'Until you grew out of your pony fiction. That was very boring.'

'You know what I think?' Poppy leaned back against the café window, her delicate features converging in thought. 'I think you chose someone you didn't really love. So they couldn't hurt you. So it wouldn't hurt if they left.'

Stevie winced with recognition.

'And you did a Dad. You put your head in the sand and hoped everything would resolve itself.'

'OK, OK. I'm not paying you a therapist fee.' Stevie looked up, eyes gold in the sun. 'How do you suddenly know this stuff, clever clogs?'

'I've had a bit of time to think. New-born babies are less fascinating than you might imagine.'

Stevie dropped her head into her hands. 'So I can't really blame Jez, can I?'

'Not really.' Poppy kissed the top of Tommy's head.'

So this was Brooklyn. Carroll Gardens. OK. Nice. She liked it. It reminded her of home, or an idea of home, with its small shops and diners and its breathtaking view of the East River. Stevie admired the trap of the sky caught in the sludgy mass of river, the tesselated skyline. It was one of those grand, imperfect New York skies: a ceiling of low grey clouds, giving the city a sense of enclosure, interspersed with optimistic windows of Disney blue.

Drawing on the city's energy, she bounced along the street in her red summer dress, feeling as though the concrete was elasticated beneath her flip-flops: a youthful woman in her thirties, a mere seedling, life stretching out deliciously before her, years and years of it. She dug out her small black address book from her bag. Its thin pages fluttering in the wind, she flicked through to F, where she'd written Sam's details all those months ago in careful handwriting. Her phone vibrated. A beep. A text message. She flipped it open.

Job interview at my mag Mnday aftrnoon.
P.S. ticket is one way. L x

What? Stevie crushed a hand to her mouth and walked along Hicks Street, grinning stupidly, checking building numbers. This was it. Deep breath. She stood outside for a few minutes, finger hovering above the bell, frozen on the doorstep, immobilised by an overwhelming sense of vulnerability and exposure. Coming to New York unannounced suddenly felt like a girlishly impetuous and risky thing to do. She leaned against the door, eyes shut, as if trying to extract strength from it. Then it opened. Stevie fell forward into the outstretch reflex of Sam's arms.

'Stevie!' He looked down, astonished at his catch. 'What the hell . . .'

'Hi.' She righted herself, blushed. 'Um, just passing.'

Sam stared at her, speechless for a few seconds. 'Come in.'

The apartment was on the first floor, small, sunny and sparsely decorated, a few bits of modern furniture, some serious pieces of sound system and stacks of vinyl records piled up in the corner. Black-and-white photographs – including a

341

print of the defiant dandelion picture Sam had given her last time she was in New York – lined the walls. A tabby cat, presumably the homosexual one, basked haughtily on the fire escape. 'It's very nice,' she managed, walking towards the window, unable to take her eyes from Sam even for a moment.

'I love it.' Sam tried to look casual in a rigid approximation of a slouch. His bare bronze feet tensed.

Stevie parked her small wheelie case. A warm breeze, ruffling in through a large open window, filled her throat with the feeling of summer. There was a pause, the surrealness of jet lag adding to the magic of the moment, as if time had indeed reversed and, here in New York, she actually had the chance to reclaim lost hours and replay part of her life again. 'That day at Port Meadow? When the phone rang, it was Lara telling me she was pregnant,' she blurted.

'Oh.' Sam's face seemed to clear, breaking into a cautious smile. 'OK.'

'That's why I said what I said.' She lowered her head, breaking the intensity of the eye contact by glancing at the stripped pale-wood floor. 'I thought it was your baby.'

'It's not.'

Stevie looked up. 'I . . . I've made a lot of mistakes.'

Sam stepped forward, one step, two, three. Then, there he was, the whole solid muscular reality of him, his dark eyes ablaze. 'This isn't one of them.'

'I know,' she whispered, her voice beginning to fail.

'Come here.' Sam lifted one hand and cupped his palm against her cheek, just as he had on Port Meadow, as if he wanted to finish what they'd started. 'You're not scared, are you?'

'Not any more.' She was surprised at how easy it was to lift her face, open her mouth. He pulled her towards him, his breath hot and hydraulic against her neck. She reached for the soft skin beneath his T-shirt. They fell on to the floor, kissing hungrily, peeling off each other's clothes slowly, stopping to admire each newly exposed plane of panting flesh, until they were naked, laughing. Sam pressed her fingers to his mouth. 'Look up there, Stevie,' he said quietly, nodding at the open window. 'Blue skies.'